It was well past midnight. N such an hour. No one but him. Yet now there was no denying that the pale, slender shape in the flickering water was real, not merely a wraith of his imaginings. More than real—Fionna.

He would simply turn around, go back to his chamber, and come back when she was bound to be gone.

Turn around. . . .

His body would not obey his mind. His instant, raw response did not surprise him. He'd experienced it before, merely thinking about her. The sight of her naked, a few scant yards away, took his self-control to the very edge.

But now Fionna turned over and swam a few yards. Her back was long and smooth, her buttocks rounded, her thighs—

Turn around. . . .

The fire in his blood was banishing all reason. . . .

VEIL OF PASSION

MAURA SEGER

A TOPAZ BOOK

TOPAZ

Published by the Penguin Group
Penguin Books USA Inc., 375 Hudson Street,
New York, New York 10014, U.S.A.
Penguin Books Ltd, 27 Wrights Lane,
London W8 5TZ, England
Penguin Books Australia Ltd,
Ringwood, Victoria, Australia
Penguin Books Canada Ltd, 10 Alcorn Avenue,
Toronto, Ontario, Canada M4V 3B2
Penguin Books (N.Z.) Ltd, 182–190 Wairau Road,
Auckland 10, New Zealand

Penguin Books Ltd, Registered Offices:
Harmondsworth, Middlesex, England

First published by Topaz, an imprint of Dutton Signet,
a division of Penguin Books USA Inc.

First Printing, December, 1996
10 9 8 7 6 5 4 3 2

 REGISTERED TRADEMARK—MARCA REGISTRADA

Printed in Canada

For Katie and Matt with love

Veil of
Passion

CHAPTER ONE

England, March 1215

Wind keened around the dark towers lashed by a cold rain tasting of salt. Within broad walls, behind iron-bound doors, fire leaped. Smoke drifted past rafters. In the rushes, a sleek gray hound raised its head, listening. Voices murmured beneath the strum of the lute. A boy sang softly, eyes tender, conjuring memories of bright days and fair women, far from this lancet of rock thrusting into the troubled sea.

Hugh of Castlerock—Bold Hugh, men called him when they dared to speak of him at all—waved away the servant about to refill his cup. He wanted no more ale, or meat, or talk, or much of anything, for that matter. Slumped in his great, high-backed chair of carved oak, he looked out over the hall where his men sat at supper, fifty of them comfortably settled around four trestle tables laden with wooden platters now picked over and almost bare. They looked well satis-fied, in good cheer, yet ready to pick up their swords and fight at a moment's notice. Exactly as he expected them to be.

Would that he could share their contentment.

Two of his men were playing draughts. He glanced at the game but his interest did not stir. Two others were comparing blades; he knew by long experience they were debating the relative merits of Spanish and Moorish steel. At another time he might have joined in, but not now.

Boredom plucked at him. He had spent too many nights like this of late, safe in hall, nothing threatening, nothing happening, suspended. Waiting.

Bored.

It took little to bore him. He acknowledged that. Long ago, a young priest sent to tutor him had spoken of this particular quirk of his nature and urged the cultivation of patience. But patience was a thing for the battlefield and the counsel hall. There the biding of time was a useful tool that more often than not brought good results. Here, it merely dripped like water falling one drop at a time, maddeningly endless.

A sharp sigh escaped him. Instantly, his men reacted. Every conversation, every diversion, ceased. As one, they watched him.

He rose and his officers stood, too. With a smile he did not feel, Hugh waved them down again. "Be at ease. I merely wish to gauge the weather."

They settled, but cautiously, still mindful of him. One, older than the rest, big and burly, bearing a long white scar down the left side of his face, hesitated. "Do you wish company, lord?" Sir Peyton asked.

Hugh shook his head. Peyton was his second-in-command and as close to a friend as he had. They had guarded each other's backs in more battles than Hugh cared to remember. But in his present mood—the mood that had plagued him for a solid fortnight now—company was the last thing he wanted.

"Stay. There is no sense in both of us getting soaked."

Peyton nodded. He would know that for what it was, a command made no less so for the consideration that cloaked it. "As you say, lord," he murmured, and withdrew back to his seat.

Hugh left the hall. He passed through the heavy wooden door that gave way to a small winding staircase and paused. Behind him, he could hear the sounds of his men's voices picking up again, a shade easier perhaps for his absence. Slowly, he climbed the stone steps to the tower roof. As he opened the second door at the top, he felt the blast of chill air and welcomed it. Putting his shoulder to the door, he shoved it open and stepped out onto the battlements.

A sentry would normally have been posted there, but Hugh had ordered the watch to stand down when the storm began. They were under no threat, the mere rumor of his own presence in the area being enough to secure the peace. But beyond that, not even the most determined enemy would be able to advance on such a night.

Alone then, he began to walk, circling the battlements, his great cloak wind-whipped, head bare, black hair gleaming silver in the rain. His fingers curled in familiar caress around the sword that did not leave his side.

The night suited him. Keening wind and stinging rain served to mute the fury raging within, the sharp spur of impatience, the treacherous voice that whispered: Go. To London and the court, to the center of the great struggle that was threatening to tear England apart. To his honored father's side. Go.

But his father's last message to him was a reminder of the importance of Castlerock, this place hard by the wild west coast of Britain. Hugh knew that full well. He would fight to the death to hold it, if an enemy would just be kind enough to present himself.

He smiled at the thought. Battle would be a welcome antidote to the grinding boredom of the past few weeks. He had hunted until the poorest peasant in the village chewed fresh meat, pausing just long enough to bless his name. He had drilled his men to a fine, deadly edge, honing the skills of the war band that was already the kingdom's fiercest fighting force. He had pressed himself to the limit and beyond in a futile search for the peace of exhaustion. Without relief.

His men felt the weight of his unease. To spare them—and to mute the voice within—he sought the storm. But he couldn't remain outside forever. In a little while, he would have to go in again, to join those in hall briefly, then retire—once more alone—to the small private chamber high up in the tower.

There, by the light of braziers set on tripods of iron, he would listen to the wind batter against the shutters and pursue his most cherished indulgence—his books. In time, if he was fortunate, he would sleep. To wake at first light and begin the whole sorry business over again.

Or would he? From the corner of his eye, barely seen through the swirling darkness, he thought he glimpsed—something. What was that, far out in the inky darkness of the Bristol Channel—a light—? Surely, it could not be. Hours before, when the storm sent its first faint signs over the horizon, every ship that could ran for shelter. Hugh himself had counted a dozen streaming up the channel to the haven of Bristol harbor. Any vessel hapless enough to still be out would have scant chance of survival.

He stiffened, staring into the darkness, half convinced he was mistaken. And yet, there it was again, a light cast about by the maddened sea.

He drew in a quick, hard breath. The light vanished but Hugh did not move. He waited, biding time, and suddenly as though to reward his patience, the light was back, tossed high out of the great valley between waves. Higher and closer. Most definitely closer.

Farewell boredom.

He took the steps two at a time and emerged into the hall, carrying the storm-caught night with him. Head back, hands on his lean hips, smiling as he had not done in too long, he let his voice ring to the blackened rafters.

"To me!"

His men did not so much get to their feet as suddenly appear there. Benches upturned, their clatter punctuated by the sudden yapping of the dogs and the startled cries of servants.

Hugh turned and vanished into the darkness. He did not so much as glance back. There was no need. The war band followed, the only sound the tromp of booted feet against stone and the jangle of their swords.

He led them to the rocky shore below the castle. Peyton ran alongside him. "Intruders, lord?"

"No," Hugh said, and halted just at the water's edge. He pointed. "See, there?"

The light was clearer now, for all that it was tossed by the furious sea. It could be only one thing—the mast light of a ship coming ever closer to the rocks. Ever closer to death.

Pulled high up on the rocky shore was a ship that had brought Hugh and his men to Castlerock. Low and sleek, with the curved dragon's prow in the old Viking style, the craft was designed for war. It could meet no more formidable enemy than the sea itself.

"Launch!" Peyton shouted. As one, the men heaved the ropes. Hugh had ordered the construction of a slipway between the ship and the water. Rain slicked the wooden tracks. Within minutes, the proud vessel was afloat.

"To the oars!" Hugh commanded, and took the rudder himself. This was not the sort of battle to which he and his men were best accustomed, but they would make do. A broad smile split his hard-boned features. Amid the surging sea and howling storm, struggling with all his strength to keep the rudder steady, ever mindful of the vessel about to plunge into the rocks that could claim his own if he was not extremely wary—and lucky—he felt a surge of purest pleasure.

After weeks of being tame as a soft-palmed priest, he could well and truly say that he was no longer bored.

Terror gripped Fionna. All around her, she could hear the screams and shouts of the crew. The captain, a hard-edged Breton, was bellowing orders no one seemed to hear. Two days before, on the dock in Don

Laoghaire, he had impressed her as a calm, reasoned man, very sure of his abilities, but now he appeared consumed with fear.

She could hardly blame him. The night howled. Sky and sea seemed to have become a single devouring entity with no beginning and no end. The wind tore at her tunic and cloak. Her hair whipped around her face. They had left Ireland to a fair breeze and a few stray clouds, and now this—

The deck was alive, a heaving, plunging thing in conspiracy with the wild sea. Sweet mother, she could not keep her footing—Frantically, she grasped for something, anything to hold onto, but her hand fell short and she lost her balance, plunging across the sloping planks almost—so close—to the edge of eternity. Before her horrified eyes, one of the sailors hurtled past her and into the sea. For just a moment, she saw his face, white against the roiling darkness, and his arm thrust up, grasping desperately for life. Then he was gone. Fionna screamed. She heard her own terror as though from a distance, borne on the savage wind.

This could not be happening, not to her. She had always loved the sea, delighted in it, and now—now it was about to kill her. Her fingers grasped a slice of wood, nails digging in. She heard a roar, turned over her shoulder, and saw—a wall where there should be no wall. A dark, writhing thing about to slam down and consume her. She dragged a last, desperate breath into her lungs, filling them to the limit, and then—

The sea took her. Her final coherent thought was that

the priests were wrong, hell was not a place of fire. It was cold. So terribly, terribly cold.

But not, it seemed, quite ready to receive her. For she was thrown up again suddenly, hurtled into the air still clinging to the wood plank. She saw the rocks, looming directly ahead, and would have screamed again but no sound escaped. Not death by drowning, then, but a crushing death, her body broken against remorseless stone.

In the deepest, quietest sanctuary of her soul, a prayer began—

"Sacred mother, receive me, your child—"

A hand lashed out, seemingly from nowhere. With steely strength, she was hauled from the water and into the shelter of—what? Scarcely breathing, chilled to the bone, heart pounding, Fionna lifted her head. The bright curtain of her hair blinded her briefly. She brushed it aside and—

A gasp escaped her, all but lost to the roar of wind and water. Only the man crouched beside her heard it. A big man, hard muscled, dressed in black, the burnished skin of his face drawn taut over remorseless features. A man with eyes of palest blue, dark hair, square jaw. Absurdly, for the moment, she thought: He needs to shave.

His eyes touched hers. For an instant, she felt again the fury of the storm. And then he smiled.

"She's fainted."

From a great distance, Fionna heard the words. She wanted to protest; she'd never fainted in her life and wasn't about to start now. But somehow she couldn't muster the strength to reply.

"Heave to," another voice said, deeper, a voice accustomed to command.

The surface she lay on swung about wildly. With that came a rush of returning fear. The storm . . . the sea . . . she was dying. Gasping, she struggled upward only to encounter resistance.

A hand, rock hard, pressed against her shoulder. "Easy, you're going to be all right. Just stay where you are."

Fionna obeyed. That alone was enough to tell her how very odd this situation was. Obedience was not her strong point. She was far more given to finding her own way. But not here, not in the midst of the wild night where the only steady constant seemed to be the man in black.

She remained still, stunned by her own docility, as slowly the fact that she was alive seeped back into her consciousness. Alive, but for how long? For hard on the heels of relief came the realization that the man had spoken in English.

Who spoke English? The warlords who had ruled the land since William the Conqueror spoke Norman French. The priests—at least those with any claim to learning—spoke Latin. She herself spoke several dialects of Gaelic, French, Latin, English, and a decent smattering of Norse.

Her mother had insisted on the English, even though it was the despised language of a conquered peasant class. She had claimed it would have uses.

English. Perhaps that wasn't so bad after all. If she was being rescued by honest peasant folk, she should be able to manage well enough. But the way the man spoke, as though he had been born giving orders—that suggested a far more ominous possibility.

The western coast of England seethed with smugglers, pirates, and ne'er-do-wells of every sort. And who would be more likely to go out after a ship about to plunge into the rocks, a ship that might be scavanged for rich booty? If that was the nature of her "rescuers"—

"I said to stay down," the man repeated, irritated now, and shoved her hard against the planking. But not before Fionna caught a glimpse of the shore rapidly approaching. They would be there in minutes. In the confusion of beaching the boat, she would have one chance to act.

The brief look she'd had was also enough to tell her that this was no modest curragh. It was a full-fledged war vessel complete with dragon's prow. Now, more than ever, she was convinced that fate had thrown her into the hands of brigands. She took a deep breath, struggling for calm, and braced herself. The water was shallower, they were scraping bottom—Any moment—

"Up oar," the man said. His voice was deep and steady. Despite the raging storm, he seemed perfectly in control. Under other circumstances, she might have admired that. Now she dreaded it.

Despite his order, she got up as far as her knees. Her guess was right. He was too busy now, along with the other men, to notice what she was doing. Gathering her skirts in one hand, Fionna braced the other against the railing. The dark man was very close. His back was to her, but she was nonetheless vividly aware of his size and strength. His shoulders were massive, his torso tapered. She caught a glimpse of a scabbard at his side and redoubled her resolve.

With an easy motion, he lowered himself over the side and joined the others in the water. Together, they hauled on the ropes that brought the ship up onto the shore.

Fionna didn't wait. She stole a moment to gather her courage and then jumped over the side. The water was icy, but her body was still so frozen that she barely felt it. As quickly as she could, weighed down as she was by her sodden clothes, she struggled to the beach.

Her hope was that the bulk of the brigand craft would hide her long enough to reach shore, and that once there she would be able to find shelter in the darkness. Beyond that, she really hadn't thought what she would do. Nothing mattered except to escape.

As desperate as she was, she might have made it. She got as far as the rocky shore, where slipping and sliding over the rain-slicked pebbles, she was almost within reach of friendly shadows cast by the boulders that lay alongside the bottom of the cliff. Another few yards and she would disappear into those shadows, just another—

"Hold!"

The command cut sharp as a knife's blade through moan of wind and cry of water. Cut right through Fionna's courage, as well. Still, she did not stop. The mere thought of doing so never even occurred to her. On the contrary, summoning strength she didn't know she had, she ran.

The beach was treacherous. She half fell, righted herself, and kept going. Her breath was labored, her heart pounding, but every instinct she possessed told her she had to get away. And so she might have were the dark man not fleet as a stag.

She heard him coming, turned, and looked over her shoulder even as she had at the wall of water that destroyed the Breton's ship. This time it was not nature unleashed but merely a man, a very angry and very determined man, who came at her. She gasped and redoubled her efforts, to no avail. The ground flew out from under her, she fell forward and landed hard. Splinters of light whirled before her eyes. Before they were gone, she was dragged upright, face-to-face with the dark man.

"What the hell are you doing?" he demanded.

In French. In pure, unmistakable Norman French. As though he realized that, too, he caught himself and asked it again in English. Very impure English. When that still got no response—mainly because she had no breath with which to speak—he hesitated, then asked yet again in Latin.

Fionna blinked. Was she mistaken? Who was this man who looked like a warrior, rode the fury of the storm, and spoke his choice of languages?

"Escaping," she said in Gaelic.

He stared, his hand hard on her arm lest she try to slip away again. Slowly, he said, "Escaping . . . ?"

Sweet Lord, he had the Irish, too. At least he could understand it to some degree. She stared up into a face that looked carved from granite, lit by sapphire eyes, and surrounded by a tangle of midnight dark hair. Distantly, she acknowledged that he was the most compelling man she had ever seen, but that seemed of little account compared to the possibility that he might—just might—be intelligent.

"Yes," she said, clearing now and in English, "escaping."

"And why would you do that?" He appeared genuinely puzzled, as though the thought that he could somehow be a danger to her had never so much as flitted through his mind.

"Because I don't know who you are." It sounded lame even to her own ears, but she didn't have the stamina or the desire for a longer explanation.

He lessened his hold on her arm ever so slightly but did not release her.

"I am Sir Hugh of Castlerock." For just an instant, she thought he was about to add more, but he did not.

Sir. A noble, then, and a warrior. Not a brigand. At least, not officially.

Feeling the slightest bit embarrassed, Fionna said, "I see . . . and this"—she gestured to the beach and the cliffs—"this would be Castlerock."

He smiled, that same devastating smile she had seen in the boat. "No," he said, and pointed above the cliffs. "That is."

Fionna looked in the direction he indicated. She pressed her lips tightly together to avoid making any sound. A vast mass of stone complete with turrets and battlements dominated the sky. Sir Hugh was master of a mighty fortress built to both demonstrate and assert power. No brigand this, but a ruler and an unabashed one at that.

Satisfied that she understood, he nodded. "Now, come." He dropped his hold and strode off down the beach.

Fionna briefly debated the merits of continued refusal. If she stayed where she was, or tried to flee again, she would accomplish nothing except to make a fool of herself. Hugh of Castlerock would have his way. Not for a moment did she doubt that.

Gathering up the shreds of her dignity, she followed him.

CHAPTER TWO

Hugh turned his back on the Irish creature to keep her from seeing his amusement. It did not do to show any sort of pleasure in the face of disobedience. But amused he was all the same, and therefore tempted to indulge her. Not that he would. She would have to learn the same as everyone else that he was to be obeyed—instantly, utterly, and without question. On such niceties rested the order of the known world.

Damn but he felt good. The brief jaunt into storm and sea had done him well. By the looks of it, his men felt the same. They were laughing among themselves as they finished securing the warship above the tide line. He moved among them, slapping several on the back, receiving their nods, until he came to Peyton.

The older man glanced over Hugh's shoulder. He frowned. "What about her, then?"

Resisting the impulse to follow his gaze, Hugh said, "I imagine she'd like to get dried off, same as the rest of us."

Standing close to his lord, so that his words would not carry, the knight murmured, "Have you actually looked at her, lord? There's women at Castlerock, all right, but none like that one."

An image of fire-bright hair, an oval face with damask smooth skin, and eyes an even lighter blue than his own rose before Hugh. So, too, did the memory of a perfectly formed female body held, however briefly, hard against his own.

"What are you suggesting?"

"I'm *suggesting* if she goes into the scullery or wherever, there's going to be trouble. Unless, of course, that's what she's looking for."

"I have no idea what she is or isn't looking for," Hugh said. As though it might offer some clue, he added, "She's Irish."

Peyton groaned. "God save us."

"Don't count on it."

They continued up the beach. So did the men. And so, too, did Fionna, bringing up the rear, making her reluctance more than clear.

By the time they reached the great hall, Hugh had mulled over Peyton's point and accepted it. He sat down in his great chair and looked out over the stone-arched chamber hung with war banners, pikes, and swords crossed beneath them, the whole redolent of power and will. Glanced, too, at his men, who were making no effort to hide their interest in the woman plucked from the sea.

In his arms, she had felt strong for a woman. But standing there at the far end of the hall, her sodden cloak wrapped around her as though it might offer some scant protection, with her hair trailing down her back, she was unmistakably alone and vulnerable.

Hugh raised his hand, summoning her. She came, but, oh, so slowly. Still, despite all she had endured, she was defiant. His men noted it and grinned. He sensed their growing excitement.

They were good men; he tolerated no other sort. They were well paid and were expected to pay, in turn, for anything they chose to enjoy, be it wine or women. And yet . . . there was no mistaking what he saw stirring among them. There was a certain irony to the situation. He would protect her under any circumstances, exactly as he would anyone who came onto his lands. But if she was a commoner, she would have choices in her behavior. If she was a lady, she would have none.

"What is your name?" he asked.

She held her head proudly. Her voice was steady and melodic. "Fionna."

He waited, in case she wanted to add anything. When she did not, he said, "Of where?"

Her hesitation was so slight that he could have missed it were he a less observant man. "I am of Ireland."

"That much is obvious. I meant what is your clan, your family?" He could have added "your rank," but saw no need. Everyone understood this sort of thing—from the simplest peasant in the field to King John himself. Everyone had a place to which they were born and in which they remained. That place determined everything, including what could be expected in the way of treatment from everyone else.

He thought she was about to say something, but

caught herself and instead shook her head. "Just Fionna."

Slowly, Hugh stood. He walked toward her. She did not flinch nor did she look away. He stopped directly in front of her. She was very pale, but there was no mistaking the light of defiance in her quite remarkable eyes.

Without warning, he reached out and seized both her hands. She resisted, but to no avail. Trying harder would have been futile and would have merely damaged her dignity. He took note of her self-control. Turning her palms up, he looked at them. They were smooth and soft, without blemish, except for a tiny ridge of calluses at the very tips of her fingers. Her cloak, damaged though it was by seawater, showed the unmistakable signs of gold embroidery around the collar. Embroidery done in the ancient, intricate designs still so favored in the misty isle. When the cloak parted slightly, he caught a glimpse of a similarly ornamented tunic beneath.

"You are highborn, the daughter of a chieftain, at least, and"—he smiled, enjoying himself—"you play the harp."

Her eyes narrowed. She glared at him. "You are guessing. I could have stolen these clothes, and the calluses could be from needlework, such as many serving women do."

"The harp leaves its mark on the fingertips, the needle on the side of the second finger. As for the rest, your bearing betrays you far more than clothing ever could." He stepped back slightly, regarding her. She was about twenty, he judged, tall for a woman and slender. The more he looked at her, the more he realized that she might well be the most beautiful woman he had ever seen. The thought was obscurely displeasing. He did not want to be drawn to a woman just now, particularly not one so obviously defiant.

"I ask you again," he said, "who are you? To whom shall we send word that you live?"

"Don't you mean to whom shall you send your demand for ransom?"

He was shocked, plain and simple. He had saved her from the sea, she was under his roof, and she had just insulted him as casually as if he was the lowest villain. The great hall fell deadly quiet, the only sound the swiftly indrawn breath of his men. Even Peyton looked worried.

"You are not a knight," Hugh said very softly, "and you were not captured in battle. Not to belabor the point, but you were rescued from the sea by myself and my men. It might not be amiss for you to thank us."

He saw the uncertainty flit behind her eyes. The emotion appeared foreign to her, and she was unaccustomed to dealing with it. Finally, she said, "I do thank you, and I am sorry to appear ungracious."

He waited, but once again she fell silent. A woman who knew how to use silence to her own ends. He knew only one other like that, and she was the most formidable person he had ever encountered aside from the mighty lord who was his father. It was his honor to call her mother.

"All right . . ." Hugh said slowly. "There are few women here, and none of your rank, but we will endeavor to make you comfortable." He signaled Peyton. "Tell the serving women to make up the tower

room. There should also be some clothing that will fit
our guest."

He ignored Peyton's obvious surprise. More than
ever, he was convinced that this Fionna "of Ireland"
was highborn. He could hardly offer her the garb of a
serving wench.

"That isn't necessary—" Fionna began.

"Suit yourself, but if you remain as you are, you will
be ill by morning and we have no healer here."

Again, he had the fleeting impression that she was
about to say something. Instead, she merely inclined
her head once—her sole acknowledgement of his
authority—and followed Peyton from the hall.

Sweet heaven, she was shaking inside. The storm
outside seemed to have taken up residence within her.
How had she ever found the nerve to face down the
dark Lord of Castlerock? To refuse even to tell him
who she was?

It was done and no sense worrying about it. Done
and done well, for what other choice had she? She
could hardly explain who she actually was and why she
had come to England. The mere thought of doing so
wrung a wry smile from her. What a great to-do that
would cause.

Besides, the truth of the matter was that she was
exhausted. Something about being shipwrecked and
almost drowned had left her wearier than she could
ever remember being. Above all, she needed rest.

"Wait here," the man she had heard called Peyton
told her. He was a big, gruff sort, obviously devoted to
his proud lord. And just as obviously disapproving of
her. She wasn't surprised. It was well-known that this

blighted kingdom's rulers were too weak and ignorant to tolerate strong women. Instead, they followed the teachings of their church and sought to oppress what they could not understand. She knew this and was prepared to deal with it, but just now she felt so very tired—

It didn't help that she was also so very cold. The air held the dank chill of wet stone. Her clothes, sodden as they were, offered no protection. Indeed, they worsened the problem. She pressed her lips together, fighting for control, but could not prevent the trembling that seized her.

The knight returned, followed by a gray-haired woman of ample girth and a kindly, if startled, expression.

"This is Ada," Peyton said. "She is in charge of the kitchen. I leave you in her care. She knows what to do."

With that he departed, obviously glad to be shed of his charge.

"This way, milady," Ada said. She took her arm and led her to a flight of stone steps at the end of the passage. They climbed, Ada puffing as she kept up a running commentary. "What a terrible thing, and such a dreadful night, but don't fret, we'll have you warm in no time. We haven't had a proper lady here since his lordship's mother visited last year, but that doesn't mean we've forgotten how things are done. You're from Ireland, I'm told. My grandmother was from there. She came from Dublin itself, she did. Do you know it?"

"I've visited Dublin," Fionna said.

"Always wanted to see it myself, but I haven't been more than five miles from this place. That's the way of it, isn't it, and no point regretting. But what a thing, to come so far. In here now."

She opened a high wooden door at the top of the stairs and stood aside for Fionna to enter. Beyond lay a large chamber, circular as the tower itself, and so startlingly luxurious that Fionna's breath caught. Whoever Hugh of Castlerock was, he clearly was not one of the many nobles with land and title but no ready wealth. On the contrary. The chamber spoke of both gold and something even rarer, taste.

Tapestries shielded the stone walls. Copper braziers waited to be lit, but they would not be needed for warmth, for along the far wall, obviously added after construction of the castle itself, was the utmost symbol of wealth and modernity—a fireplace. And not just any fireplace, for this one boasted an elaborately carved stone mantel, such as could have graced a palace.

The floor was covered with woven rush mats, instead of the loose rushes Fionna detested. A large wooden table held a basin for water. Beside it was a rack with cloth for drying. A chest stood at the foot of the bed, but Fionna barely noticed that. The bed itself was by far the largest she had ever seen—she was reminded of Lord Hugh of Castlerock's considerable height. It was hung with embroidered curtains and covered with a fur throw.

"We'll pick you out some nice, dry clothes," Ada said, "then I'll show you where to bathe. You're in for a treat there, let me tell you."

Still looking around, feeling rather dazed, Fionna murmured, "I am?"

"Indeed. His lordship says that before this castle was built, there was some other sort of building here.

Traces of it were found when the castle foundations were dug. And that's also when they found—" She broke off, grinning. "Better to show you. You'll have nothing like it in Ireland, I'll wager that. But first—" She opened the chest at the foot of the bed and stood back. "You look, milady. His lordship said you were to have anything you need."

Fionna knelt down in front of the chest. She was startled to find it filled with women's clothing. Beautiful, exquisitely made clothing obviously intended for a woman of very high rank—or a woman indulged by a very powerful man.

"How come these here?" she asked, fingering a finely spun wool tunic embroidered with tiny wild roses.

"His lordship's mother left them the last time she visited."

Fionna's eyebrows rose. "His mother?"

Ada laughed. "He has one, you know, for all that he looks sprung from a thunderclap. Aye, his mother and a lovely lady she is."

"Wouldn't she object to my using her things?"

"Not a bit of it. Besides, his lordship wouldn't have offered them if he thought she'd be offended. No, she isn't that sort, at all. You go on and pick whatever you like."

Fionna was sorely tempted. Her life had offered little opportunity for female frippery. Besides, her own clothes were soaked in seawater and probably ruined. She had to wear something.

"This," she said, gently lifting a chemise of fine linen and the woolen tunic.

"Best take that cloak, as well," Ada advised. "It gets fearsome cold in these parts, even in spring."

Doing as she suggested, Fionna stood up. Pain stabbed through her body. She winced and just barely managed not to groan. All the same, Ada nodded sympathetically.

"You'll be battered and bruised, poor thing. Here, let me take those."

Relieved of her burdens, slight as they were, Fionna followed the kindly woman back down the tower stairs. At the bottom, they turned in a direction she had not been and descended another flight of stone steps. Fionna stopped for a moment. Surely, her ears were playing tricks? She could have sworn she heard the echo of splashing water.

"Here we are," Ada said. She stood aside with the air of a magician at a fair, about to reveal a great wonder.

And so she did. For the subterranean chamber they entered was quite beyond anything Fionna had ever seen. It was larger than the tower room, a spacious chamber in its own right, with a ceiling as high as that of the great hall, crossed by stone arches held up by columns. In the center of the room was a vast stone-lined pool filled with water gurgling up from somewhere far beneath. Flecks of fine white foam told what kind of water it was.

"A mineral spring," Fionna said. She bent down and trailed her hand through the water. It was hot, but not unpleasantly so, and made her skin tingle slightly.

"His lordship says the Romans were here," Ada informed her. "They were great ones for bathing, and built here to take advantage of the spring. This chamber was theirs, but don't worry, his lordship had the stone masons check the columns and the roof to make sure they were still strong, and they are. Isn't that a marvel, after all these years?"

"The Romans built for eternity," Fionna said absently, for her attention was riveted on the chamber. She knew of the Romans, had heard the tales about them, but never had she expected to stand where they had stood, far less to bath as they had.

"They never came to Ireland, did they?" Ada asked.

"Not in force. Scouts were sent, but they reported the land too hard and the people too wild."

"I thought Ireland a fair place?"

"It is. The Romans were . . . misled." And that was all she would say on that score. "Do others use this place?"

"Aye, we do, milady. His lordship uses it, of course, but he encourages all of us to do the same. He says cleanliness keeps away illness."

Fionna turned and looked at her sharply. "He says that?"

"Aye, and I know there are those who think that strange, but I tell you, we have far less illness here than in many another place. His lordship won't tolerate a bit of manure left in the yard or a scrape of food on the floor. And he's forever making sure the villagers keep their cottages clean, even to providing fresh hay for bedding and whitewash for the walls."

"Remarkable."

"Oh, he's that, all right," Ada said with a smile. "Come now, let's get you out of those terrible wet things."

Fionna complied. This time, when she sank into the water, she could not restrain a groan. Her whole body ached. There were bruises on her arms and legs, and she suspected there were more on her back. Her bottom, in particular, felt pummeled. But the water . . . ah, the water. With a blissful sigh, she closed her eyes and let herself float.

Ada examined her discarded clothes, clucked over their condition, and discreetly absented herself. Fionna took a long, slow breath—the first genuinely easy breath she had known in hours—and opened her eyes. Light reflected off the high, arched ceiling. It whispered around the ancient stones of the bath. Watching, listening, she let her mind drift to the countless, unknown people who had shared this place over time. What had they been like? What thoughts, fears, hopes had they carried with them?

She would never know, but floating there, bathed in the healing water of the ancient spring, she floated, too, on time. Eternity whispered around old stone, murmuring of infinite reaches far beyond human ken. She had tasted of this sensation before in her life, but only after days of fasting and meditation. Never before had it come to her so readily. Perhaps this was the gift of her spirit's brush with death.

That she would have died she had no doubt. Proud Hugh of Castlerock had snatched her from eternity's door. For that, she had answered him shabbily. Embarrassment twinged at her. She would have to apologize again before she left.

There was a discreet cough behind her. Fionna turned. Ada stood at the side of the pool, holding out a long length of cloth for drying. "I think you'd best come out now, milady. You look about to fall asleep."

Docile as a weary child, Fionna complied. "It must

be very late," she murmured as Ada squeezed the water from her hair.

"It is that." She dropped the chemise over Fionna's head. "And the storm still raging. I've had a bit to eat and drink brought up to your room, but then I'm thinking you'll want to rest."

"No one else has been found—?"

"I'm afraid not, but the men will search again come morning. Off with you, now." Gently, Ada urged her back up the stairs. In the tower room, as promised, good soup and fresh bread awaited her. But Fionna only managed to swallow a few mouthfuls. Ada helped her off with the tunic. Clad in the chemise, her hair neatly braided, she crept into the huge bed. Beyond the shuttered windows, rain lashed and wind howled. But Fionna scarcely heard. She burrowed deeper under the fur covers, gave a small sigh, and closed her eyes.

Hugh paused at the foot of the tower steps. He glanced upward, thinking of the woman there. There was something about her. A smile came and went. Of course there was. She was beautiful and spirited, and he had been far too long without a woman. Not that there weren't remedies enough for that. He had only to shake off the odd darkness that followed him of late and divert himself as other men did.

Only. He, who had come of age with a sword in his hand and the will to victory in his heart, did not know how to fight this particular battle. He did not even care to think of the enemy that had no name but lurked in every corner of his life.

Enough. He would sleep however long he could manage and with morning, he would determine what to do about the woman. No doubt when she, too, was rested, she would be thinking a good deal more clearly. Once he knew her identity, he could make arrangements to return her to her people. He glanced again up the tower steps, caught himself, and turned away. The sooner the better. He had far too much else on his mind to worry over a fey Irish witch plucked from the sea.

The thought of which reminded him that his clothes were drying on him stiff with salt. He left his men rolling out their pallets on the floor of the great hall and made his way to the bath. Although all were welcome—indeed encouraged—to use it, his privacy was unfailingly respected.

Stripped, he dove into the pool and swam for several minutes. The heat of the water made him realize how chill he'd been. He rarely noticed such things and thought little of them, except to notice that it was hardship that made ease enjoyable. In the absence of toil and struggle, men rotted long before the grave could claim them.

His philosophical thought for the day. He laughed, the sound bouncing off the shadowed walls. Floating, he stared up at the arches, thinking about what it had taken to precisely balance blocks of stone. The knowledge had been lost for centuries, at least to men of his race, but it was returning now, sometimes slowly and painfully, but returning all the same. The only good result, so far as he knew, of the blood-soaked Crusades.

Yet the Romans had possessed such skill centuries before. They'd had it from an older race yet, the Greeks, and they in turn—How far back then did the march of mankind go? How much had been gained and lost—only to be gained again? How much was there still to rediscover, relearn, restore? A lifetime would be but the blink of an eye when held up against such vast expanses of time and struggle.

Rome had been destroyed, his father said. Savage tribes from the north, including their own ancestors, had swept down out of the vast forests and pillaged an empire. When it was gone, a great darkness descended from which they were still trying to emerge.

And making scant progress, if recent events were anything to judge by. England was at peace, or what passed for it in an imperfect world, but it was the peace of a breath held, inevitably to be let go.

Hence his presence in the turbulent west country, guarding his father's interests and his own. Guarding, too, he hoped, whatever chance yet remained that the path to war might not be chosen. Not this time. Not in this place. Not for these people.

He sighed and wondered if he would ever find a way to still the turbulent passage of his thoughts. Judging by his life to date, he doubted it.

A glint of light on the stone floor caught his eye, momentarily distracting him. He glanced absently, then looked again. His feet touched bottom. He reached out and took hold of a small object, lying forgotten near the water's edge.

Turning it over in his hand, he frowned. It appeared to be a talisman of some sort, no more than a few inches across with a hole at the top through which a chain or leather thong could be threaded. Circular in shape, it was etched with what appeared to be three women dancing in long, flowing robes beneath a full moon.

Something stirred far back in his memory. He had seen a similar object somewhere, at some time. But the recollection was too fleeting. It vanished before he could be sure it was even real.

However, the object he held was real enough. Moreover, staring at it, he realized it was made of gold.

It was unlikely in the extreme that any of his men possessed such a thing. Their taste did not run to such delicate ornaments. As for the servants—that possibility was even more remote.

Which left—

His fingers closed around the mysterious object. Again, he felt the faint, deeply buried stirring of knowledge he could not repossess. Fey Fionna—the name pleased him—would miss her talisman. He would return it to her, of course, but not before she explained it—and herself.

Water sluiced off his broad, powerfully muscled torso, down his lean hips and thighs hardened by years in the saddle. It darkened the hair that arched in a fine line down his chest and abdomen to the nest of curls at his groin. Absently, he plucked a length of drying cloth from a nearby basket and knotted it around his waist. Still studying the talisman, he mounted the stairs.

Hidden in the shadows of a column, Fionna took a deep breath and let it out slowly. She had been on the very edge of sleep when she realized the talisman was missing. Saying a swift prayer that it hadn't been lost at sea, she'd made her way back down to the pool to search. Too late, she realized she was not alone.

She had seen naked men before. Her work required

it. Long ago, she had come to the conclusion that all men were fundamentally the same.

She still thought so. Nothing had changed. The fact that her heart was racing and she felt flushed from head to toe was owed to extreme weariness, or fear of being discovered, or—

She closed her eyes, but that didn't help. The image of proud Hugh of Castlerock lingered too indelibly. Mother of all, he was magnificent. She had never seen such strength and grace, such pure male beauty, as though every inch of him had known the attention of a master sculptor.

Tired . . . she was very, very tired. Her wits were addled. Tomorrow would come too soon. She had to think, to plan—The talisman would have to be recovered, but there was so much more as well. In another moment, she would be asleep on her feet.

Wearily, she trudged up the stairs. Around her, the castle was silent. She heard only the distant barking of a dog in the bailey yard, but that stopped almost at once. Without being seen, she regained the tower room and slipped back into bed. Her last thought before sleep claimed her was of Hugh, water flowing down the length of his lean, hard body, rising from the pool and beckoning to her.

CHAPTER THREE

"They've gone back down to the shore, milady," Ada said. "His lordship said you were to stay here."

Fionna set down the slice of sweet white bread she'd been eating. The shutters to the tower room stood open. Bright sunlight and warm air streamed through. In the aftermath of the storm, the day looked swept clean.

"Surely, there is no reason for me to stay inside on such a glorious morning."

"Oh, no, not inside, milady. His lordship only meant you weren't to go to the shore."

"They've found bodies, haven't they?" She already knew there were no other survivors, that being the first question she asked when she awoke an hour before.

Ada nodded. "Two, I think, and there may be more. They'll be brought to the chapel and given good Christian burial. After they're laid out, his lordship did say you might want to see them . . . at least those known to you could be identified."

"I knew none of them," Fionna replied softly,

"except the captain, and he was known to me only by name and general reputation."

"He was not kin to you, none of them were? Or servant, either?"

"I'm afraid not. I was traveling alone."

Ada could not suppress her shock, although good serving woman that she was, she did try. "Alone—"

That was all she allowed herself. Her mouth came as close to shutting with a snap as Fionna had ever heard.

Appreciative of her courtesy—and not a little admiring of her self-control—Fionna said, "With all respect, you seem very tired. I hope you weren't kept up late because of me."

One surprise Ada could take. A second undid her. She blinked hard and for a moment looked about to cry.

"Oh, no, milady, it was not because of you. My little son—Geoffrey is his name—is ailing. Not that it's anything serious. A mere fever of childhood, the kind we've all had. I'm sure he'll be right in a day or two."

"How sick is he?" Fionna asked. Ada's claims notwithstanding, the serving woman had a fine, sharp edge of tension about her that Fionna had seen too often, especially among women with children in the springtime. Or the winter. Or summer or . . . Anytime a child became ill, a mother tended to have the look Ada had about her now.

"I don't know," she admitted. "I thought he was improving, but he's very weak today. He can barely keep down water and . . ." She broke off, recovering herself. "I'm sorry, milady. It's not for me to bother you with this sort of thing."

"I would like to see him," Fionna said. Better to cut

to the heart of it right away. Gently, she added, "At home in Ireland, I saw the sick."

Ada stared at her for several moments. She looked directly into Fionna's eyes not as servant to superior but as woman to woman. Whatever she saw there must have given her hope, at least, if not confidence.

"We have no healer here," she said quietly. "His lordship's mother is trying to find someone to send, but so far—"

"I understand." Healers—true healers, not leech mongers and barber surgeons—were increasingly scarce. The church had seen to that.

"If you really think—"

"Let me see him," Fionna said. She had no equipment, nothing, it was all lost in the storm. But she had her eyes and her hands and her mind. That would have to be enough.

The child lay on a pallet in a small room off the kitchens. He was about nine, brown-haired like Ada, with wide blue eyes and a smile that when he was healthy must have been something to see.

But he was not healthy now. He had the pallor of a wasting illness. Ada caught her breath as she entered the room. She ran to his side.

"Oh, my sweetling, I didn't mean to leave you for so long." Cuddling the child, she said to Fionna, "He had better color an hour ago, and he slept some in the night. I hoped—"

"Has he eaten anything unusual in the last few days?" Fionna asked as she knelt down beside him. Sometimes in the early spring, when fresh food had been scarce for months, people could be driven to eat all sorts of things. Children were especially vulnerable.

"No, I don't think so. He knows better."

"Is anyone else here sick?"

"Not that I've heard, and I would."

"Has he vomited?"

Swiftly, Fionna went through the usual questions. As she did so, she gently examined the boy. His abdomen was rigid, and he was very hot.

"You have the runs?" she asked him.

Miserably, he nodded.

"Tell me true, you ate nothing you should not have? Your mother will not be angry. Just answer honestly."

"I swear I did not," the child replied.

"Water, then. Did you drink anywhere unusual?"

He hesitated.

"His lordship says we are only to drink from the wells," Ada said. "You didn't drink from a stream, did you?"

"It tasted good," Geoffrey whispered. "I was out playing in the fields and—"

"Why does his lordship say to drink only from the wells?" Fionna asked.

Ada looked doubtful. "I don't know, and none of us asks, but I think it has something to do with all the cattle around here." She paused, then said in a rush, "I know it sounds very odd, but his lordship says the water near where cattle are set to pasture is not healthy because they void into it or the stables are cleaned into it. He forbids us to drink it."

Keeping her attention on the boy, lest her eyes betray too much, Fionna asked, "How does he know these things?"

"I have no idea nor does anyone else, but we have all found it best to do as he says."

It was a coincidence. Somewhere in his life he had happened upon circumstances that convinced him cleanliness supported good health. Perhaps it meant he was merely intelligent enough to see what should have been before the face of anyone. Perhaps he had been influenced by someone met in travels. It did not matter. He had merely hit on truths without necessarily understanding anything about them.

Hadn't he?

"I believe the water is what ails your son," Fionna said. "If I can find the right ingredients, I could mix a tea that would help him heal more quickly."

"There are herbs and such in the stillroom."

"Herbs for cooking?"

"No, not just that. Sometimes . . ."

"Yes, go on."

"Sometimes his lordship uses herbs to help those who are ill."

"He said you had no healer here."

"That is true, but he is not without skill himself. We could wait until he returns and ask him—"

"No, he may be all day, and Geoffrey needs help now. Show me what there is."

Ada was clearly reluctant, but her love for her son won out. She gave the child a reassuring smile and rose. "This way, milady."

The stillroom was a small chamber fragrant with the smell of drying herbs. It was filled with wooden barrels and chests, all neatly arranged. Although the room had a door, there was no sign of any lock.

"His lordship has no concern that anyone may come in here?" Fionna asked.

"The cooks come but only to take those things they need. They disturb nothing else."

Either Hugh of Castlerock so struck fear into those he ruled that no one would even think of stealing from him, or he had earned the respect of his people who followed him willingly. Fear was the common currency of power, trust the rarest coin. Fionna thought of the dark, powerful man who had plucked her from the sea, the man she had spied at the pool. He was a warrior incarnate, bred to battle in bone and sinew. Fear would be his natural helpmate. And yet—

"Where does all this come from?" she asked, gesturing at the neat rows of supplies.

"Some we grow right here, some are purchased, some his lordship's mother sent."

Fionna listened but with only half an ear. Her attention was caught. Looking more closely, she saw that many of the small wooden chests bore neatly scripted labels. The names were well familiar to her—fennel, cicely, bryony, tansy, willow bark, henbane . . .

Henbane? That chest at least was locked, and a fortunate thing, too. Henbane had its uses but in the wrong—or merely ignorant—hands, it was deadly poison. Yet his lordship left it in plain sight, the lock more protection against carelessness than deceit.

But then to recognize the use to which the chest's contents could be put, a person would have to be able to read the label and understand its meaning. Hugh of Castlerock, for instance. He could read. Even as she set that bit of information aside for later thought, Fionna had to admire his cleverness. By merely leaving these things about, making no particular fuss over them, he could guarantee they would be undisturbed.

Turning away from the locked chest, she said, "I've found what I need."

"You will explain to his lordship, milady—"

"I will tell him exactly what I took and why. If he truly understands the use of these things, he will not object."

She wished she felt as confident as she sounded. The thought of facing Castlerock's master again set up an odd fluttering inside her. The image of him by the pool rose in her mind.

She pushed it aside resolutely and turned her attention to preparing the medicine. She had to select just the right amount of herbs and roots, taking into account Geoffrey's size and age. Then the ingredients had to be ground precisely, neither too finely nor too coarsely. Water must be boiled and the whole left to steep for just the correct amount of time, no longer. All her concentration was needed, but she welcomed that. It kept her from thinking of other things.

When the tea was ready, she held the cup for Geoffrey to drink. He made a face but did not demure, his willingness telling her how very ill he felt. When he had finished, he gave a long sigh and laid back down again.

"I know that didn't taste very good," Fionna said as she smoothed his hair. "But you will feel better soon, I promise."

He nodded, keeping a firm hold of his mother's hand.

"You should stay with him," Fionna told the older woman. "If there are tasks you would be seeing to, I will be glad to do them for you."

Ada blinked back tears. "You are so kind, milady,

but I couldn't ask you to do my work. Besides, there are plenty of servants here about. I was set to wait on you, though, and a poor job I've done of it this morning—"

"Nonsense. I am well accustomed to waiting on myself. However, if you could just tell me, do you have any idea what became of the clothes I was wearing yesterday?"

"Indeed, I do. I saw to them last night. After a soak in clear water and milk to draw out the salt, and with a bit of mending, they're good as new."

Fionna shook her head in amazement. "I would have thought them reduced to rags. Thank you."

Ada insisted no thanks were necessary, but Fionna felt differently. The saving of her clothes avoided a problem she had not particularly wanted to face. She was already indebted to Lord Hugh for saving her life. She did not care to owe him anything more.

She left Ada caring for her son and returned to the tower room. A servant had left her clothes there. She donned them quickly, then folded the borrowed garments, and laid them carefully back in the chest.

Dressed in her own garb, she felt better fortified to face whatever might come next. Nonetheless, the next few hours dragged painfully. She returned to check on Geoffrey, finding him cooler and more cheerful. Ada insisted she eat a bowl of soup, which she did while seated on a bench in the kitchen where she could better keep an eye on her patient. Several serving girls put their heads together over that, but a stern look from Ada sent them scurrying.

It was afternoon before sounds from the bailey alerted them that the men were returning. Fionna waited. She judged—correctly, as it turned out—that the proud Lord of Castlerock would send for her before too long.

He did. She found him seated in the great hall, his men about him. The burly one who had seen her to Ada the night before stood closest. They were speaking together, but broke off when Fionna entered.

"We have found five bodies," Hugh said without preamble. "They will be in the chapel. I realize it will be difficult, but if you can identify them—"

"I will give any help that I can, of course, but only the captain was known to me."

Hugh did not show any of the surprise that Ada had, but Fionna did not doubt that he found that statement every bit as peculiar. He looked at her long and hard. "He was kin of yours?"

"No, I knew of him by reputation. He was Breton. I think most of the crew were, too."

The conclusion was inescapable. "You were traveling alone?"

"I realize that is unusual—"

"Unusual? It is unheard of. No one travels alone. I would hesitate to do it myself."

Fionna did not doubt him. England was on the verge of civil war, Ireland itself had problems with competing clans. In both, there was a breakdown of established order. Brigands flourished everywhere, hence her own fear the night before.

All the same, she was telling the truth. Merely repeating it would not make it any more believable. Therefore, she remained silent.

He waited. She waited. They stared at one another. He frowned. She did not react. He stopped frowning. A very faint smile quirked at the corners of his mouth. He suppressed it, but not before she caught a glimpse of him she had not known before. Intelligent and with a sense of humor. Hugh of Castlerock seemed more dangerous by the moment.

"I gather," he said at last, "that you do not intend to enlighten me?"

"There is nothing more I can say."

"What conclusion am I forced to, then? That you are mad?"

"If you like."

"Are you?"

"I don't think so."

"Neither do I." The way he said that did not make her feel relieved in the least. "The only other possibility," he continued, pleasantly enough, "would seem to be that you are lying. You do not wish to tell me who these men were or why they were coming to England."

"They were Breton sailors, nothing more."

He stood and came toward her, his stride long and lithe. Fionna stiffened. The memory of him by the pool was still too fresh. She did not want him to touch her.

Or, more honestly, she wanted it too much.

Hands clasped behind his back, he surveyed her. "They took you on board out of the goodness of their hearts?"

She felt her cheeks warm and despised herself for it. Why did this man have the ability to move her so effortlessly? "I paid for my passage."

"How?"

Damn him. "With gold."

"And how did you come by that?"

She did not answer. There was nothing she could say that would not simply prompt another question, or reveal far more than she had any intention of telling him.

The silence drew out. She was keenly aware of him standing so close to her, of his great height and strength. He smelled of wool and salt, reminding her that he had been in the sea again, doing a sad task. So, too, had his men. Although she did not turn her head, she knew they were watching, lazing on the benches, amused by their lord's dealing with her and perhaps also curious about who she might be.

"Come with me," Hugh said. He turned and walked out of the great hall.

Taken by surprise, Fionna hesitated but only for a moment. There was no point in refusing, when she could so easily be forced to obey.

The door he passed through led to a small chapel. Or at least it appeared to have seen such use at some time in the past. The altar was bare, and the air smelled of cold stone, not incense.

Following the direction of her gaze, Hugh said, "We have no priest."

"There is none in the village?" The poorest hamlet in Ireland was tended to by Holy Mother Church. She had thought England was the same.

"A monk comes to say mass, baptize, and the like." The casualness of the arrangement did not seem to bother him. He leaned up against the wall and looked at her. "These are difficult times in England. Peace has always been precarious, but rarely more so than at this moment."

So much she knew, but it did not seem wise to say that.

"You are a very silent woman. Did you grow up in a nunnery?"

Fionna's eyes widened. She could think of few places where she would be more misplaced, and yet he was not completely off the mark.

"No, I didn't," she replied. "I just don't see the point in talking for the sake of it."

"And besides, it's so easy to say something you'd rather not. Assuming, of course, that there are things you shouldn't say." He put a hand into the leather pouch hanging from his belt and withdrew a small object. "Is this yours?"

In the shadowed light of the chapel, the talisman gleamed darkly. Fionna resisted the impulse to reach for it. "Yes, it is. I must have dropped it by the pool."

"You did." Hugh turned it over in his hand, looking at it. "A pretty thing. What is it?"

"Nothing in particular, just a piece of jewelry."

"A bauble?"

"If you like. My mother gave it to me. It has some sentimental value."

"It is also gold, and by the look of it, carved by a skilled artisan. I suppose you want it back."

Her hands curled closed at her sides. Fionna shrugged. "You may keep it, if you like. After all, I owe you a debt."

"You owe me your life." He glanced at the talisman again, then abruptly held it out to her. "Take it. I have no use for such things."

Eyes on him, no more willing to look away than she would be with a dangerous predator, Fionna reached for the talisman. As calmly as she could manage, she said, "Thank you."

"Not at all, milady. After all, I, too, owe you a debt."

"I don't understand—"

"Geoffrey, Ada's little son. He's feeling much improved."

"I was about to tell you. I—"

"Took herbs from the stillroom. I know. One of the stable hands saw you. I was informed as soon as I reached the bailey." He smiled with just a touch of embarrassment. "The people here are very loyal."

"So I gather. Ada also would have told you."

He made a gesture of dismissal. "The herbs don't matter, not so long as they were used properly, and apparently they were. So you are a healer."

"I have some small skill," Fionna said carefully. "Ada says you have the same knowledge. Did you gain it traveling, in the Holy Land, perhaps?"

"I have never been to the Holy Land. Did your mother teach you?"

"As I said, I have only some small skill."

He laughed, the sound sudden and deep in the small chamber. "Another question you will not answer. Is there any end to them?"

"I don't mean to be uncooperative . . ."

"But you are anyway."

She could hardly deny it. He had the measure of her, or at least part of it. There was a great deal she simply would not say no matter how cleverly he might pose the question or how determinedly he might persist.

"I think," she said, "that it is just as well I am leaving."

His face went blank. Already, she knew he did that

when he did not wish to reveal even the smallest part of his thoughts.

"Leaving?" he repeated.

"I thank you more than I can say for saving my life and giving me shelter here. But I have a journey to complete."

"To where?"

"It does not matter. It is not your concern any more than I am your responsibility. The weather promises to be fair for several days. I must go."

"Alone, without escort? Perhaps you are mad after all. I would no more allow a woman to leave this place alone than I would—" He paused, momentarily at a loss for words. There seemed to be no example he could cite that was extreme enough. "Let's just say I wouldn't do it. Now, if you care to tell me where you are going, perhaps I can help you get there, but—"

"I am not sworn to you, Hugh of Castlerock. I am not of your family, and I am not bonded to your land. By what right then would you keep me here?"

From his substantially greater height, he glared down at her. "Right? By simple common sense, woman. You go traipsing alone beyond these walls, and you won't last a day. Didn't you taste death well enough in the sea? Must you seek it on land as well?"

"I say again, I am not your responsibility."

"I cannot accept that. We all have some duty to one another. Would I allow a child to fall from a parapet when I could reach out and grab him? Would I let a horse go overloaded into a river and drown? Would I—"

"I am not a child or a horse," Fionna said. She desperately wanted to control her temper, but it threatened to get the better of her. He was so insufferably

sure of himself, this oversize, overly confident ...
Englishman.

"No, you're not. They both have more sense than
you. We will say no more of this. You will stay here
until you care to tell me who your kin are that I may
either send for them or send you to them."

"You cannot force me—"

Halfway out the door, Hugh turned and looked at
her. Very quietly, he said, "Of course I can, Fionna,
and we both know it."

And with that he was gone, leaving her to swallow
her indignation as best she could.

CHAPTER FOUR

She had to be mad. No other possibility made sense, at least none that he cared to consider. Taken by themselves, the circumstances of Fionna's arrival sowed deep suspicion in him. But that was as nothing compared to her astonishing behavior just now. *Thank you for saving my life. Good-bye.* Only a moon-touched madwoman would say such a thing.

Striding out to the bailey, Hugh considered what he knew of his reluctant guest. She was not stupid. He was convinced of that. She had to know the disorder of the land, the danger of any movement beyond fortified strongholds such as Castlerock. Yet she somehow assumed that she could travel safely on her own.

Safely, that was the catch. Either she cared nothing for safety, and was mad, or she had some hidden reason for believing that she could safely do what the most hardened warrior—namely himself—would hesitate to attempt.

Which led him back to the golden talisman.

Standing in the late afternoon sun, feeling the warmth on his face, he let his thoughts turn cautiously in the direction of the shadowed chamber of his mind, the place he knew was there but to which he rarely went.

It contained so many snatched images, fragments of memory, hidden even from himself. He was a child, not more than four or five, waking in the night and leaving his bed, wandering down a dark corridor—to where? He could not even say which of his family's residences he had been in at the time. But at the end of the corridor he glimpsed a light. Inching open the door, he saw his mother—his beautiful, gentle, adored mother—gazing intently into a small copper cauldron in which something bubbled softly. Her lips moved, words he could not understand. She lifted her arms, bent at the elbows in a gesture no priest made, praying.

And so much else. As he grew, he roamed over his father's lands at will, but one place he did not go without invitation, his mother's island in the middle of a lake where the small cottage she had lived in before her marriage bore all the signs of her continued care. He knew, although he could not say how, that she still went there by herself sometimes and that his father did not object. On the contrary, Conan sometimes went with her. Hugh himself had been there three times, once shortly after his birth, once when he was a young child, and once after he had come to manhood. He remembered the last two visits fondly, as times when the entire world seemed golden, illuminated by his mother's eternal love.

The mother who had stood trial for witchcraft not

long after she and his father met. A gossiping servant had told him of it and of how she had chosen to prove her innocence through ordeal, swallowing poison all agreed should have been deadly but was not. He had gone at once and asked his father for the truth of it. Conan took him aside, speaking to him quietly but with a haunted look in his eyes that told Hugh a great deal of how this mighty warrior had feared for the life of the woman he so loved.

None of which had anything to do with Fionna, so why would he be thinking of it now? Muttering under his breath, he kicked a clod of dirt until it skittered halfway across the bailey. Several stable boys looked up, saw his expression, and promptly vanished into the hay-scented shadows.

His gaze shifted toward the stone chapel. An exterior door stood open, admitting fresh air. The bodies would have to be buried soon. He would learn the captain's name and send it to friends in Brittany. If the family was known, they would be told. Perhaps they, too, could inform the families of the crew. Assuming, of course, that the men were Breton to begin with.

The ones they had found were all dark-haired men, dark-eyed with swarthy skin. Some Bretons looked like that but so did a great many Gallicians, Moors, Gaels, and the like. Men of all stripes were for hire these days. And men seeking to foment rebellion were hiring them.

"Hold this place," his father had said. Castlerock guarded the western marches. In times of trouble—had there ever been any other?—enemies came from the west like sharks smelling blood in water. Too often, England had been torn apart by such conflicting forces.

The kingdom's most honored baron was determined that would not happen now. So, too, was his son.

The sun was fading. Hugh watched it go with half a mind. His thoughts remained on the woman the sea had delivered into his hands. She was beautiful, defiant, and mysterious. She might, or might not, represent a true danger to the kingdom. She was, in short, exactly what he needed. He grinned, thinking of how he'd wished for a good battle to liven things up. It seemed he'd gotten what he wanted, just not in the form he would have expected. Pleased by the prospect, he turned to go inside. If memory served, there was a harp somewhere about. He had some time yet before supper to find it.

Peering from one of the tower windows, Fionna kept well back in the shadows to avoid the humiliation of being seen. Proud Lord Hugh of Castlerock certainly appeared to be in a good mood. But then why shouldn't he be? He—and all his kind—were used to keeping people captive, ordering them around, issuing commands and the such.

Not that she was entirely incapable of seeing his point of view. The notion of a woman traveling across England by herself was . . . perhaps unusual was the best word for it. But then that was also the best word for her life. The very same life she could not reveal to him.

She pressed her hands against the cool stone walls and stared at the sky, at once captive and free. Where her spirit could roam, her will could follow. It would be dark soon—

The door creaked open behind her. Fionna whirled,

feeling absurdly guilty for the mere direction of her thoughts. Hard on that came relief when she realized her visitor was Ada.

The serving woman entered carrying a tray. She looked at Fionna and frowned. "You never finished your soup, milady, and you've had scarce else since rising. Eat a bit of this, and you'll feel better."

"I feel fine," Fionna insisted, though her gaze strayed to the fresh baked bread, crock of honey, round of cheese, and sliced meats. "How is Geoffrey?"

"Ever so much better, thank you. His color is back, and he's sitting up. His lordship had a look at him and said you did exactly right."

"How good of him," Fionna muttered. She could hardly fault the man for being conscientious about his dependents. If only he would understand that she was not among them.

"He's a fine man," Ada said softly, laying out the dishes on the small table near the fireplace. "When we heard he was coming here, more than a few of us were afraid. His reputation is that fierce. The first day I saw him, riding his great horse, wearing black and looking so stern, I thought we'd fallen into the pit of hell for sure. But then—"

"How so, fierce?" Fionna asked. Much as she hated to admit it, she felt drawn to learn more of the man who presumed to keep her captive.

"He's renowned in battle and in the tournaments. His father was England's mightiest warrior, and now it's said the mantle has passed to the son."

"Oh, yes, glorious slaughter. Taking life brings a man honor and fame. Would that giving life was as valued."

"It would be a different world, then, wouldn't it?"

Ada said. "But to be fair, his lordship has never been one for cruelty, as we've learned to our great relief. When he was fighting in France for the king, he always ordered the women and children be spared, along with any man who had the sense to surrender. If a man under his command stole or raped, he met the business end of a noose."

"He hung his own men for that?"

"One or two, and I don't think he considered them his men. He always said men who wished to follow him had to be in control of themselves before they could hope to control anything else."

"What an extraordinary idea—" And not at all in keeping with her knowledge of Englishmen. Never mind that she had met none before coming to this benighted isle, every sensible person knew that the mingling of Norse, Norman, Angle, and Saxon had bred a savage race, seeped in blood and mad with the lust for power. Not to mention incapable of creating decent poetry.

Slowly, she sat down at the table. The food smelled delicious. For all the brutish camaraderie of the place, Castlerock did not lack for certain comforts.

Ada cleared her throat.

"Yes?" Fionna asked.

"His lordship suggests you might like to join him in hall later. He's found something he wants to show you."

"Another body?"

"Oh, no, nothing of the sort. Something you'd enjoy."

"What is it?"

Ada smiled. There was a disturbing twinkle in her

eyes. "It's not my place to say, milady." She dropped Fionna a curtsy and departed, still smiling.

She wasn't curious, not at all. Whatever Castlerock's arrogant warlord had come up with, she really didn't care. She'd have a little something to eat, rest for a bit, and then—

What could it be? Something she'd enjoy, Ada said. But then Ada thought insufferable Hugh was simply wonderful. No doubt everyone else here did, too. Still, she couldn't fathom why he would even want her in hall, much less offer some diversion.

It was probably some scheme to show off his dominance. Men did things like that, or so she'd heard. She couldn't actually say she'd ever witnessed it except with her father, and then only when dealing with sworn enemies. But her father was the wisest of men, far more intelligent and aware than others of his ilk. Her mother had told her so, but she'd also seen that for herself.

But then there were those medicinals in the still-room . . . the insistence on cleanliness and the apparent affection of his people. She chewed a bit of bread thoughtfully. Perhaps, just perhaps, there was more to insufferable Hugh than she wanted to admit.

Not that it mattered. Come dark she would be gone.

And that being the case, what harm could it do to discover whatever it was he wanted to show her?

"A harp," Fionna said softly. Before the words were out of her mouth, she had hold of the instrument, her hands caressing it reverently. Still looking at it, not at him, she asked, "Where did you get it?"

Hugh sighed. His vanity prickled. He didn't experience that very often and wasn't quite sure what to do about it. In all modesty, women tended to pay him excessive amounts of attention. It was merely part and parcel of being handsome, landed, wealthy, and powerful. He made the best of it.

But this woman . . . this fey Irish creature plucked from the sea appeared completely oblivious to him. He might as well have been carved of stone, set in the wall, and neatly plastered over.

"In a market," he said, "in London, about a year ago."

She did look up then, her pale eyes narrowing. "You know it's Irish?"

"No, I didn't, although I wondered. It is said the best harps are made in Ireland." He thought to flatter her. It didn't work.

Fionna shrugged. "The only harps are made in Ireland. All else is imitation. But this one bears an ancient mark." She turned the instrument over gently, showing him. On the base, an elaborately coiled circle had been incised.

"I've seen this before," she went on, "although I don't believe the maker is known any longer. Still, his instruments survive and are much prized."

She touched the instrument again, clearly fascinated. Hugh had a sudden, piercing wish for her to touch him the same way. He quelled it harshly.

Absently, she asked, "Do you play?"

"No, I don't."

That must have piqued her curiosity. She actually looked at him again. "Then, why did you buy this?"

He hesitated. They were seated side by side in the great hall, close enough to have as much privacy as anyone could hope for under the circumstances. His men were making a great show of being busy with their own occupations. No one glanced their way more than once or twice a minute.

In an undertone, Hugh said, "It looked lonely."

Her head shot up. She stared straight at him. "What did you say?"

His cheeks warmed slightly, astonishing for him who prided himself on iron control. What was happening to that, by the way?

"Lonely," he repeated. "I know it sounds absurd, but I was passing the merchant's stall when the harp caught my eye. I was struck by the sudden sense that the thing was lonely, so I bought it."

"How can a thing be lonely?"

"I have no idea."

She fell silent, but he had the odd sensation that he could feel her thoughts turning over and over. When she looked up again, she smiled. "You've never heard it played?"

He shook his head. "We have a minstrel here, one of the local lads, he's around somewhere. He plays the lute well and sings, but when he tried the harp, he said he didn't think it was for him."

"Wise of him." She did not explain why but began fingering the strings. A clear, liquid note poured through the air. Another followed. Fionna nodded. "Someone loved this harp." A shadow danced behind her eyes. "I wonder how it came to England."

"No good way, of course," Hugh said. "It was probably taken as booty in an attack—by Englishmen no doubt—and the harper himself slain."

"Probably," Fionna agreed.

"Is there no chance he died quietly in his bed at a great age and the harp drifted through unknowing hands until it came to yours?"

"The same chance that peace will come to my land in my own lifetime, and all the pain and blood of the past century be forgotten as though it had never happened."

"All that pain and blood *would* never have happened if you Irish hadn't invited us in to try to gain advantage against each other."

He had the satisfaction of seeing her flush. "That was one mad fool's doing with the rest of us left to keen over it. Besides, you would have found some other excuse."

"Probably," Hugh agreed, deliberately echoing her own speech. "How could anyone resist a fair land whose people could not stop battling each other long enough to notice what was right over their shoulder?"

"You might have thought that the land wasn't yours," she shot back, "but then when has that ever stopped you? Tell me, I'm curious, where exactly will you Saxon-Norman-English pillagers finally stop and decide you have enough?"

Hugh leaned back in his chair and grinned. She argued well. He liked that. "I don't know. How big is the world?"

"The ancient Greeks said it is twenty-five thousand miles around."

His mouth dropped open. Seeing that, Fionna laughed. She was clearly delighted with herself. "Truly, they did say that," she added.

"I know, the question is, how do you?"

"You knew it?"

"I know they said it. The Romans kept the knowledge and passed it to the Moors. Of course, there are others who say they were wrong and the world is much smaller. Some even still claim it is flat, but every sensible man knows that is wrong."

"Every sensible Viking, anyway, since they've sailed over a good part of it."

"Some of my forefathers were Norsemen."

"Why doesn't that surprise me? If you haven't traveled to the Holy Land, how do you know what the Moors learned from the Greeks and Romans?"

"Believe it or not, such knowledge is being carried back even to such benighted places as England. I had tutors."

"You can read?" She sounded as though she already knew the answer.

"In Latin and French. I can manage some in English, but I'm still working on that. It's difficult since there's very little written in it."

She nodded in agreement. "I don't suppose—"

"What?"

"Does that mean you have books?"

There was no mistaking the longing in her eyes. Hugh hid a smile. Some women were drawn to jewels and flattery, others to raw power and the willingness to use it. For fey Fionna, the lure was music and books. He could like her for that—very much. If he was foolish enough to let himself do so.

"I have books," he said softly.

"Here?"

"Twelve here, more elsewhere."

She took a quick breath.

As though it was nothing in particular—certainly not

bait dangled in front of her—he said, "Perhaps you would like to see them?"

His men smirked as he left the great hall with Fionna. Hugh caught them at it but said nothing. They would think what they would.

Not that they'd necessarily be wrong.

CHAPTER FIVE

Hugh's private chamber was at the top of Castlerock's highest tower. It was a large, circular room with a timbered roof, a fireplace, and a separate, small set of stairs to the turret. Privacy was a luxury for a leader who must be heard and seen among his men. Hugh never allowed himself to indulge in it as much as he would have liked, but he needed a certain amount simply to feel himself.

For all that, seeing Fionna standing in his sanctuary did not seem at all strange. On the contrary, she appeared to belong there.

Whether she thought so or not was another matter entirely.

"The books—" she said tentatively, as though already regretting her decision to come.

"Right here." He directed her attention to the chest at the foot of the bed. Beside it stood a wooden stand and a copper brazier positioned close for light. Carefully, he selected a book and set it on the stand.

Fionna looked at it but made no moved to touch the gold-etched leather binding. Hugh opened it for her.

"Virgil," he said. "The Aeneid."

She took a step forward, staring, but kept her hands clasped behind her back. "I have heard of this . . . and heard parts of it recited but I never thought to actually see . . ."

"Can you read this script?"

She peered more closely. "It looks like Irish minuscule. Yes, I can read it. Oh, look—'I sing of arms and men.' It really says that." She gazed up at him, delighted. "How astounding to possess such a thing."

"There are others, a great many of them. The monks of an abbey on our family lands are commissioned to copy any book they can borrow or buy. They've been doing that now for my whole life, and the number is in the hundreds."

"Hundreds of books?" The image so conjured seemed to stun her. "What happens to them?"

"Some are kept in our residences, others are sent to universities. In this way, the knowledge that is being recovered will someday spread throughout many lands. All people, not only the nobility and clergy, will be able to read books for themselves."

"That is a dream," Fionna said softly. "For centuries, monks in Ireland have been copying books in a desperate attempt to keep the darkness of ignorance at bay. Yet their efforts have seemed little better than trying to hold back a flood by ladling water with a spoon."

"They did more than copy books. Monks from Ireland founded schools and universities all over Europe. When I was in Lucerne a few years ago, I heard this spoken of. People there and in many other places still tell of the Irish monks with great fondness and respect."

Her mouth was very full and ripe, he noticed. When she was surprised or nervous, she had a tendency to worry her lower lip.

"So you have traveled," Fionna said. "Just not to the Holy Land. And now you are here in this wild place. Do you regret it?"

The question puzzled Hugh. He was there because duty dictated that he should be. Personal preference did not enter into it. "There is need for me to be here," he said. "But surely not for you?"

In the shadowed light of the high tower room, Fionna's smile was soft and tempting. "You are persistent."

"It's one of my more charming traits."

She laughed and turned away, toward the book, but not before he glimpsed her unease. "I would say you are credited with a great many of those," she said. The thought did not appear to please her.

"On the contrary, I am the most modest of men."

Taken by surprise, she made a choking sound.

It was Hugh's turn to laugh. "You don't believe me?"

"Let us just say I don't think of men like you as modest."

His eyebrows rose. "Like me? Are you such a connoisseur of men, then?"

She flushed, darkly and delightfully. "I didn't mean that—"

He leaned against one of the high wooden posts that supported the canopy of his bed. Despite his best attempts to appear grave, he could not quite conceal his enjoyment of her. In all honesty, he had liked many women. Far too many, if Mother Church was to be believed. But they were such marvelous creatures, givers of life and of pleasure. And truth be told, they could be so much more interesting to talk with than his fellow warriors, most of whom thought more than two grunts in succession constituted conversation.

His mother had spoiled him. He knew that, although neither she nor his father seemed to mind. The Lady Alianor had talked to all her children, and encouraged them to talk back. So, too, had their august father, who despite his high position and great power, was extraordinarily patient and gentle with his sons. Hugh had benefited from the wisdom of both his parents. He had the great good fortune to come of age in a setting where intellect was at least as valued as brute strength and ambition.

Not, he reminded himself, that the brutish arts should not be cultivated right along with the refined. The times demanded that men acquire the skills necessary to protect their women, their children, their people, and their lands. That, more than anything else, he had learned at his father's knee.

And yet he liked women, although it was some time since he'd met one who stirred his interest beyond the most basic level. Fionna did that—and a great deal more.

"I know very little of men," she said, a shade tartly, "and to be frank, I am content with that. However—"

He sensed her relenting just a little and stayed

very still, the silent hunter careful not to startle his prey.

"However, I have to admit you surprise me. You have some skill at healing, you read and have books, and you bought the harp. You are—" she paused, searching for the correct word—"unusual."

From her lips, the word tripped as high praise. He grinned and bowed to her. "Thank you, milady. I shall treasure that always. Might I say that you, too, are unusual?"

She looked at him in mock disbelief. "Me? Not at all. I am a perfectly ordinary woman with nothing in the least interesting about me. Certainly, nothing that should make you want me to stay here."

Hugh's good humor faded somewhat. She was as stubborn as he was himself. In him, that was entirely right and proper. He was, after all, a man and a warrior. She was little more than a girl, seemingly homeless, landless, and without any family she cared to acknowledge. She was also entirely at his mercy. At the very least, she might have been just a bit deferential.

"If you were a matron of forty, round as a barrel, and scarred by the pox, I would not allow you to go on alone."

"Would that be the famed chivalry I've heard about? Troubadours, damsels in distress, knights, and the rest? Everyone adhering to some absurdly elaborate code of behavior while busily ignoring the muck beneath their feet."

"That would be the Irish interpretation, I suppose?"

"Is the reality different? You make a great show of being respectful of women, but I can't see it's made any actual difference. We are still regarded as property, still bought and sold in the mockery called marriage, and still allowed to die in childbed in terrible numbers because 'Mother' Church—of all the absurd names— says we must pay for the sin of Eve. Where is chivalry in all that?"

Hugh straightened up. He regarded her with the same care he would have given to a doe who turned suddenly into a dragon.

"No *ordinary* woman holds such ideas, or if she does, she does not voice them. The church has not hesitated to prosecute those who challenge it."

"Persecute would be the more accurate word. But you speak of the church as though there were only one. You mean Rome, of course, but the church in Ireland has taken a different position and, I think, a wiser one. All the same, it is hard for women everywhere."

Her skin was very fair, allowing for the slight flush clinging to her cheeks. Even as he listened to the words formed by her silken lips, Hugh could not give up staring at her. She was fine-boned and held herself with regal grace. The slender beauty of her body would have stirred any man, but the fire in her eyes spoke of fierce pride and courage. She was a woman worthy of conquest, and yet wouldn't the very act of victory over such a woman risk destroying her?

"It is hard," he acknowledged. "But you make it harder still when you insist on refusing help. I will find out who you are, you know, even if I have to send to Ireland myself. You are not the sort of woman who goes unnoticed. People will remember you; someone will know something. Whatever secret you think to keep will come out eventually."

When she made no attempt to dispute him, Hugh knew he was right. For all her claims otherwise, Fionna was as far from an "ordinary" woman as it was possible to be. But if she was not that, then who—exactly—was she? And what had brought her to a kingdom shadowed by the civil war he and his father were sworn to prevent?

It would do no good to ask. She had already made her refusal to answer clear. If he was to learn the truth, he had to rely on other methods.

His eyes went to the book. He'd always liked Virgil. Perhaps the Roman could help him now.

"You may borrow that, if you'd like." He spoke as easily as he might offer a stable pony for an afternoon's ride, but Fionna's reaction suggested he had just held out handfuls of precious gems and bade her take all she liked.

"B-borrow? You mean take it back to my chamber and read it?"

He smiled. Pleasing her pleased him. Later, he might think about why that was, but for right now he had far more pressing concerns. "Yes, of course. I trust you to care for it properly."

"Oh, I would! You really—" Her eyes were locked on the book, once again. He could feel himself fading back into the wall. With a sigh, he accepted the inevitable.

"If it is too heavy for you to carry—"

"Oh, no, I can manage it." With utmost care, she lifted the book from its stand and clutched it tight against her bosom. Happy book. "I cannot thank you enough," she said. "Truly, I cannot."

"Does it strike you at all odd that you thank me more for the loan of a book than you did for plucking you from the sea?"

She had the grace to look embarrassed. "I was very rude yesterday, and I apologize sincerely. I owe you my life."

"Then you will understand that I do not wish you to throw it away?"

The corners of her mouth turned up most engagingly. "Do you never yield a point, Hugh of Castlerock?"

"Yield? What's that?"

"Never mind, I wouldn't want to shock you." Still holding the book tightly, she looked up at him. Very softly, she said, "Thank you."

He was jealous of a book. Wonderful. There were men all over the kingdom—not to mention on the Continent—who would hurt themselves laughing over that, if only they knew.

"Try not to stay up too late," he said, and gathered what shreds of dignity he could about himself.

She felt guilty. No, she didn't. She had nothing to feel guilty about. Well, not much anyway.

Curled up in the high-canopied bed, a fire glowing nearby and the copper braziers adding their own light and warmth, Fionna struggled to remain focused on the miraculous, marvelous book opened before her.

Instead, all she could think of was Hugh.

Proud Hugh.

Insufferable Hugh.

Hugh who lent a book and a harp, who healed, who laughed, who actually listened to her when she spoke. Hugh, who was everything he should not be.

Could not be.

He was the invader, the conqueror. The scourge of Ireland. The warlord who destroyed anything different from himself with no attempt to understand it.

In the final analysis, the reason she was there in England, in a desperate and possibly futile bid to hold back the flood tide of destruction and preserve something for the distant, unknowable future.

Why should she feel guilty?

She had thanked him for saving her life. What more could she do? She was genuinely grateful for that and his other kindnesses. All right, she would admit it, he was generous and thoughtful. He had intelligence and grace.

Good for him.

It changed nothing. She could not tell him who she was or why she had come. And she could not stay at Castlerock. She had to leave.

And soon, if her glance out the window told her anything. The moon was high, full, and ripe. She took courage from it. This night she would walk the silver path.

But first there was stolen time for the book . . . and for her own, very personal thoughts.

Virgil was every bit as fascinating as she'd always thought he would be, but he couldn't compete with Castlerock's master. She gave up finally, with a sigh of true regret, and left the bed.

It was very quiet. The fortress slept around her, or so it seemed. She assumed there were guards posted in the bailey and on the walls. She had a long and perilous journey ahead of her. They were only the first challenge she would have to best.

With a final glance around, she pushed aside the regret that threatened to choke her and walked quickly to the door. Easing it open, she peered down the steps. No one was there, and she heard no sound.

On silent feet, she descended to the great hall. A few torches still burned dimly. She could make out the shapes of sleeping men on their pallets. Dogs curled up with them, man and beast snoring alike.

As a wraith in a fog-draped dream, Fionna stole among them. A single gray hound raised her head. Fionna met her gaze. The dog lay down again soundlessly.

Outside, the night air was cool and damp, exactly as she liked it. With her cloak wrapped close about her, she slipped across the bailey to the far wall. The vast double gates were closed and secured by a single plank, broad and long as the trunk of the mighty tree it had once been, laid across them. But within those gates was a small door, just large enough to admit a single person. She had noticed it earlier. It, too, was secured by an iron bar. She would have to lift the bar, open the door, and slip outside, all without being noticed.

Barely breathing, she closed her hand around the metal and lifted. It came readily. Relief flooded through her. Castlerock was a superbly maintained fortress. It stood to reason that every piece of metal within it was well oiled. With a thankful smile for Hugh's high standards, she eased the door ajar just enough to fit through the opening.

Outside, the countryside lay soft and welcoming beneath moonlight. Her eyes adjusted rapidly to the darkness, such as it was. She could see almost as well as by full day.

Nothing stirred save for a single owl, hunting against the moon. With a soft thought for the bird who represented ancient female wisdom, she closed the door behind her. Her absence would certainly be realized come morning, but at least no guard would notice anything amiss before then.

Feeling more confident than she had since she saw that wall of water about to come down on her, Fionna stepped lightly across the mossy ground. This had turned out to be easier than she'd thought.

Someone coughed behind her.

The sound was a knife blade through her. She cried out and whirled around. Against the outer wall of the bailey, lounging at his leisure, proud Hugh of Castlerock gazed at her.

"And here I thought you safely occupied with harp and book," he said laconically.

"You!" She blurted the word, unable to stop herself. How could he possibly be right there before her and all as though it was the most ordinary thing in the world?

How could he have known?

He couldn't have. That was absolutely impossible. She would not let herself believe otherwise. This was nothing more than some horrible, twisted coincidence.

He straightened away from the wall and walked toward her, tall, broad, silhouetted against the moon. Implacable. His voice was soft as velvet, dangerous as dark water.

"I am running out of patience."

"You are—" She could hardly speak. Still so stunned—and more afraid than she could admit even to herself—she felt as though she had been tossed back into the ice-cold sea.

"There are limits, you know."

"What possible reason could you have for being here?"

There, she sounded more like herself and with just the right measure of annoyance. The damnable man had to realize that he had no right to order her about.

He looked at her quizzically. "You mean on my lands, in my fortress—the place I rule?"

"Do you commonly wander about at night?"

"If it pleases me. Now would you like to tell me what you are doing here?"

"That's obvious. Thank you again for everything. Good-bye."

She turned. A friendly cloud moved over the moon. The world plunged into darkness. She needed no more than a moment or two to reach the obscurity of the forest . . .

She didn't get it. Hugh's hand lashed out, closed around her arm, and yanked her hard against him. His chest a rock beneath her cheek, he said, "Do you conjure the moon, then, Irish witch? Does it do your bidding when I will not?"

Fionna stiffened. With every ounce of her strength, she tried to break free of him, to no avail.

"Stop it," he ordered. "You will hurt yourself." Gripping her shoulders, he held her a little away so that she was forced to meet his eyes. "You are not leaving. Do you understand that? I will not let you go."

"I do not belong to you!"

"You will," he said, and drew her hard against him. A steely arm wrapped against her waist, a hand clasped the back of her head, fingers tangling in her hair.

"You will," he said again, and took her mouth with his.

CHAPTER SIX

He tasted of mead and mint. His mouth was firm but not cruel. He coaxed, rather than demanded. The touch of his body against hers, the sensation of vast strength held barely in check, the overwhelming awareness of virility vanquished reason. Fionna could not think . . . could not react . . . could not do anything except be well and thoroughly kissed.

There was even a fragile moment when she was on the very verge of kissing back.

She caught herself barely in time.

Rage coursed through her. How dare he? How dare she? How dare the whole stupid situation?

She was not here for pleasure, for dalliance. She had a stern and vital purpose. She could not possibly allow herself to be distracted by a . . . *man.*

"Oomphh."

Hugh let go of her. It would have been hard not to do so considering that he was doubled over, in acute pain, and unable to breathe.

Fionna felt just the smallest twinge of regret. He had, after all, saved her life. But he would recover, and he'd be the wiser for it. Fleet as the white doe glimpsed at season's turning, she fled to the forest.

She was at the very edge of it, one arm already within the safety of its shadows, when Hugh caught her. One moment she was free, within reach of her goal, and the next she was lifted off the ground, tossed over a rock-hard shoulder with all the grace of a grain sack—and with as much say in her fate.

He muttered something under his breath—which had apparently returned. It sounded like "witch" but might not have been exactly that.

"Let me go!" Fionna cried. She did not understand how he could have come after her so quickly. Was the man possessed of superhuman strength?

"Be quiet."

He sounded perfectly calm. He wasn't even breathing hard. Heaven help her.

"I won't! Let me go!" She kicked out, hoping to injure him in any way she could.

His stride never faltered. That was worse than anything. She was utterly, completely helpless. Frustration roiled in her. She could not believe this was happening, not to her. How could everything have gone so terribly wrong?

He passed through the high stone wall and crossed the bailey. Fionna could see little. Her hair tumbled about her face, all but blinding her. But she did catch a glimpse of a grinning guard, more fuel for her fury.

Hugh mounted the tower steps. He climbed smoothly and steadily. The man had the strength of an ox—and the bullish temperament to match. A door was

thrust open. A room swirled around her. Without cere-
mony, she was dumped onto a bed.

The same bed she had risen from not long before.
With a quick stab of relief, she realized that he had not
brought her to his own chamber. Scrambling to regain
as much of her dignity as she could manage, she got
her feet on the floor and glared at him.

"You have no right."

He bent down so that his eyes looked directly into
hers. Slowly and firmly, he said, "I have *all* the rights.
The sooner you recognize that, the happier you
will be."

"You insufferable bastard—"

His hand covered her mouth. In measured tones, he
said, "Decry me all you like, but do not libel my
mother."

Fionna bit him. She tasted the salt tang of his blood
on her tongue.

Hugh sighed. He did not cry out, or complain, or hit
her, or anything a normal man might have done. He
merely sighed.

This was becoming truly frightening.

"I wish you wouldn't do things like that," he said.

Fionna stared at him. "Don't you hurt?"

"Yes, of course, I do. And I most certainly did when
you kneed me out there. The trick is not minding."

"How can you not mind pain?"

"You have to separate yourself from it. So now,
what do we do with you?" With perfect conviviality, he
regarded her. "I will not let you leave here alone. That
is not a matter for discussion. Perhaps now you would
care to tell me who you really are and why you have
come to England?"

"Go to hell." She had never been so crudely ungracious in her life. Hugh of Castlerock definitely brought out the worst in her.

"If Mother Church is to be believed, most of us are destined for there anyway. But in the meantime, we do the best we can and that does not include allowing you to get yourself killed."

"I will not—"

"If your efforts to defend yourself from me are any indication, you wouldn't last five minutes."

That stopped Fionna. She could hardly deny it. Nor could she explain that she had been startled, surprised, caught unawares enough to forget the training of a lifetime—and just perhaps unwilling when it came to this particular man to do as she should have done.

This man. The memory of his taste and touch sent a quiver through her.

No, absolutely not. This was neither the time nor place in her life for any such complication. Besides, he was *English,* for mercy's sake. How could she possibly forget that?

"You cannot keep me here," she said, and despised how desperate she sounded.

"You may leave as soon as you wish. All you have to do is tell me who to send to for you, or where you are going that I may give you escort. The decision is yours."

He waited a moment, giving her a chance to reply. When she did not, he shrugged. A moment later the door clanged closed behind him.

Fionna waited the space of several heartbeats before flying to the door. She yanked on the handle, half expecting to find it locked from the outside, but it opened at once.

Opened to reveal a guard in chain mail and hawk's brow helmet, battle ax gripped firmly in both hands, resolutely looking anywhere but at her.

Never in her life would she allow a bird to be caged, Fionna decided. She knew too well how it felt. On her third day in the tower room, she had to use every trick she had ever learned to keep her mind clear and her emotions in check.

Not that her imprisonment was anything but silken. She had the harp, and Virgil had been joined by several companions. Ada brought food regularly, meals that were clearly intended to tempt her taste. So, too, she brought gossip. Geoffrey was fully recovered. The ewes had lambed. There was a new colt in the stables. His lordship was off hunting. His lordship was back. His lordship was wearing a new tunic. His lordship—

Her hands knotted into fists, Fionna forced herself to take a deep, steadying breath. She would not—could not—give in. Eventually, there would be a mistake. Vigilance would be relaxed if only for a moment, and when it was, she would be gone. But until then—

The day sparkled. Sunlight danced off the water. Seagulls and terns cavorted against banks of fleecy clouds. The air was pure and fresh. Everything in her cried out to be free, running over the hills, unfettered in any way.

And here she was, kept close within cold stone.

Damn the man.

And yet she couldn't quite manage to condemn him, even in her thoughts. He *had* saved her life. He *had* treated her with courtesy and patience. He *had* provided her with all manner of luxuries and comfort.

He just wouldn't let her go.

The urge to tell him something, anything that would win her freedom was becoming almost irresistible. He had said that he would give her escort if she only said where she was going. She could name any place in England, go there, and then escape to make her way to her true destination in secret.

Couldn't she?

But to do that she would have to lie, and the idea of lowering herself to such a craven state made her flinch inside.

On the other hand, that very morning Ada had wondered out loud if she wouldn't like a bit of needlework to do. His lordship had suggested it.

Fionna moaned. She leaned her forehead against the cool stone and shut her eyes. She was still standing like that several minutes later when there was a knock at the door.

There was something about knocking on the door of a prisoner that was at least faintly ridiculous. Hugh put his hand down, resisted the impulse to tuck it behind his back, and waited.

The door opened. Looking every bit as maddeningly beautiful as he recalled—and he had recalled over and over—Fionna stared at him.

"Oh, it's you."

The woman overwhelmed him with her adulation.

"May I come in?" he asked gravely.

"It's your castle." She turned and walked back into the room.

From the corner of his eye, Hugh caught the man on guard bug-eyed with shock.

"You know," Hugh said pleasantly enough, "there are people who wouldn't dream of talking to me like that."

Fionna sighed. She looked perplexed. "I've been ruder in the last few days than I've ever been in the whole rest of my life."

"You really don't have to go to all that trouble for me."

"Believe me, where you're concerned, it's no trouble."

"Do you play chess?"

"On occasion. I like morris better. Do you play that?"

"Once or twice, perhaps . . . when I was a boy. I'm not sure I even remember the rules—"

Fionna smiled. Her hair was braided and hung to her waist. She was wearing one of his mother's gowns, a simple robe of finely spun linen, dyed the color of rare saffron and embroidered in the soft green of spring. It might have been made for her.

"I suppose that means there isn't a board about somewhere?" she said.

"My men might have one. Why? Surely, you wouldn't consider giving me a game?"

"No, but I'd be happy to take one from you."

"There's a board carved onto a bench in the kitchen garden."

"Oh . . ." She was striving hard not to show her disappointment. "Then I suppose we can't . . ."

"I get to go first."

Her eyes lit. He fought down a surge of pleasure.

Why did this woman's happiness matter to him? Why should he care if she laughed or wept? She was rude, stubborn, recalcitrant, and not at all like the compliant females with whom he occasionally amused himself.

However, she also wasn't boring, and for that he had to be grateful.

It was sunny in the garden. Mayflies clustered in small clouds above the daffodils and other early blooming flowers. The air smelled of freshly turned earth and new grass.

"It's beautiful here," Fionna said.

He could have added that she lent the garden beauty it could never have on its own, but he was no poet. Or at least he never had been.

"The board is here," he said, and sat down on a broad stone bench beside an ivy-draped wall. Carved into the bench were three squares of different sizes, one set within the other. Four lines, one from each side of the inner square, reached across the second to the third, joining them all. Where lines intersected or met, circles were chiseled.

In a recess in the wall was a box of polished white and black stones, left there by each set of players as a courtesy for the next. It was a small thing, but the sort of civility Hugh expected of his men.

It was true that he hadn't played in years, but as a child, he'd been fascinated by the seemingly simple game of maneuvering stones to create straight lines and block an opponent from doing the same. He'd played for hours, sometimes through an entire day, until the patterns and subtle rhythms became so real to him that he could "see" them flowing outward, move after move, in some way he'd never been able to explain.

Having not played in years, the moment he touched the first cool, rounded stone, familiarity flowed through him. He might as well have played that morning.

Fionna joined him on the bench. He graciously suggested she go first after all to, as he put it, "Help him refresh his memory."

She accepted the white stones but looked frankly skeptical. "Why do I think you are better at this than you admit?"

"Because you doubt everything and everyone?"

"Not true. It's you I don't trust, not the world."

As she spoke, she laid down her first stone. He followed. Before long, each had nine stones in place. Play began in earnest and proceeded rapidly. Fionna was good. Within minutes, she had him on the defensive.

"Do you Irish do anything else besides play morris?" he asked, just a bit grumpily.

"On the contrary, I hardly ever play. The game is so simple, it lacks challenge."

"Liar."

"Perhaps," she allowed as she deftly captured yet another of his pieces.

He retaliated but not well enough. Before long, he was down to two stones and had therefore lost.

"Would you care for another match?" Fionna asked with commendable calm. She did not allow herself to gloat for a moment, although he was certain she was well pleased.

"A good host indulges his guest."

Her eyes widened. "Host? Guest? Surely, the first requirement of hospitality is that it not be forced on anyone unwillingly."

Hugh began laying out his stones again, pretending

to give them all his attention. "It is not forced on you. All you have to do is tell me—"

Putting her own stones in place, Fionna said quietly, "Has it occurred to you that I might have a genuinely good reason for refusing what you ask?"

"Good in the sense of legal and moral, or good as in compelling?"

She did not answer directly. Instead, she said, "You use words well. What accounts for it?"

He, too, could decline to answer questions. "Are all English suppose to speak in grunts?"

"Not necessarily all—It's just that in Ireland words are a kind of music. Everyone celebrates them, even little children. We weave with them, dance with them, bandy them about with abandon, and delight in crafting them into all manner of amusements. Whereas in most other places they seem to be merely . . . words."

"Flat and dull?"

"Exactly. So I must conclude that there is something different in your background. Were you, for instance, very ill as a child and kept close by your mother past the usual age when boys are sent to become men? Did she talk and sing to you? Did she tell wondrous stories and play music for you? Did she encourage you to explore the world through your own imagination so that you would not be bored or frustrated when you could not do as the others were doing?"

Hugh stared at her. A tremor, whisper fine, prickled down his back. "I met a gypsy once who could do that sort of thing. It was an interesting trick."

Fionna smiled. "How ill were you? Or was it an accident?"

"Surely, you could tell me."

She raised her eyes from the board and looked at him. The air in the garden seemed to go very still. A single bird sang, then fell silent. Time passed . . . or didn't. He couldn't be sure.

She paled. "Oh . . ." He caught a fleeting look of surprise, quickly masked. "I really should concentrate on the game."

"It's said the Irish have the gift of sight," Hugh remarked.

"A great deal is said, most of it foolish."

"I fell from a horse when I was six. It was my father's favorite stallion. I wasn't allowed anywhere near him, but I snuck away to the stables and mounted him, although I can't remember how I managed that."

"Did he kill the horse?"

"No, I cried out, apparently, saying that it wasn't the animal's fault, and my father let him live, although he never rode him again."

She gave up the pretext of interest in the game. "How badly hurt were you?"

"Both my legs were broken. It was feared I would not walk again."

Fionna frowned. "You have no limp."

"I was very fortunate. My mother nursed me back to health. In essence, she taught me to walk all over again. But by the time I could do that, more than a year had passed. The other boys my age had already begun their training with sword and lance, while I had mastered reading and learned to love the troubadours' tales."

"From what I've seen, you made up for the late start."

He smiled. Sitting there in the sun with this woman,

he felt more at ease than he could remember in some time. She stilled the impatience that itched at his mind and mocked the shadow of the black cloud that from time to time drifted too near.

But she was not all serenity, not by any means. There were other itches—

"When I was well again," he went on, "my father took charge of me. We did everything together— riding, hunting, training, swimming. Being with him made me feel I could face any challenge."

"You are fortunate in your parents. Do you have brothers and sisters?"

"Two brothers, no sisters, which I suspect is my mother's one great regret, although she has never spoken of it."

"My mother had only me, but my father didn't seem to mind. Of course, he had sons by other women."

Hugh schooled his face to blankness. "I have heard that customs differ somewhat in Ireland."

"No, they don't. Powerful men everywhere have as many women as they like. The church says they can only marry one, but that doesn't seem to make much difference."

"Except, perhaps, to the women."

She finished laying out her pieces and sat back. "I'm not sure my mother ever wanted to marry. She's very independent."

When he did not reply, she laughed. "You'll hurt yourself if you don't say it."

"Oh, all right. Your mother independent? Amazing. Did she also have the sight?"

"Does, she's very much alive, and it bothers me how you never let anything go but just circle back to it."

Hugh made a move. It wasn't his best. "It bothers me that you won't answer my questions."

"You're not sure you want answers. At least the questions keep you from being bored."

He moved again, better this time, and took one of her pieces. "What makes you think that?"

"I don't know," she admitted, "it's just a feeling I get."

"As you got a feeling that I'd been hurt as a child?" When she hesitated, he said, "You are right to be cautious. We live in difficult times. Fear and superstition breed upon themselves, and banish reason."

"I understand that order is desperately needed," Fionna said quietly, "but it seems to be coming at a terrible cost."

"Including that we should be enemies?"

Sitting in the sun, her face turned to him in profile, she looked still as stone but for the rose hue of her lips and the pulse beating in the slender line of her white throat.

"I wish that it would not," she said quietly, and took another of his pieces.

CHAPTER SEVEN

Fionna paused at the entrance to the subterranean pool. It was very late; she really should have been asleep. But after days of making do with a hip bath, the Roman version was irresistible.

She had given Hugh her word. Even now, hours later, she wasn't sure how it had happened. Had they gambled for it, there in the sun-drenched garden with the bees droning lazily? Or had he twisted it out of her somehow with his clever words? Or had she—and she had to at least admit the possibility—offered it of her own free will?

However it had come about, they had struck an accord. She could use the bath and the garden. When she was availing herself of either, she would not try to escape. The rest of the time was left deliberately obscured—by them both.

So here she was, well after midnight, clutching a reed torch dipped in tallow, a drying cloth, and a square of precious soap scented with lilac and honeysuckle. For all its forbidding appearance, Castlerock concealed many surprises. Not the least of which was its master.

Slipping out of her tunic, she thought of the man she had met that afternoon. Not the forbidding warrior she had seen before. Not the demanding aristocrat. No, this man was entirely different. He was relaxed, good company, patient, and very, very perceptive.

That he also played a decent hand of morris was merely an added attraction.

Attraction? In the act of folding her tunic to set it aside on a bench, Fionna paused. Was she truly *attracted* to Hugh of Castlerock? Proud Hugh? Insufferable Hugh? *English* Hugh?

Well, yes, she was, and there in the silence of the ancient chamber, she could not deny it. Stepping into the warm mineral water, she contemplated the trick fate seemed to have pulled on her. At the very time in her life when she most needed to concentrate on her duties, she had met the man who was the greatest imaginable distraction from them.

It really didn't seem fair.

But then there were those who said that when death came as close as it had to her, life began anew and could frequently take an unexpected course. Hers certainly had. What a shame that she had to wrench it back on its proper way.

She sighed and leaned back, letting herself float. Tension eased from her. The quiet reached into her mind, stilling the clamor of her thoughts. She felt utterly safe, there in the timeless pool, alone and at peace.

* * *

On the threshold of the bathing chamber, Hugh stopped abruptly and stared at the pool. By the flare of the torch he carried, and another set in an iron bracket on the wall, he could make out a form in the water.

No one came there at such an hour. No one, that was, but him. He had never encountered anyone and certainly hadn't expected to now. Yet there was no denying that the pale, slender shape in the flickering water was real, not merely a wraith of his imaginings.

And more than real, identifiable. Fionna.

She had a perfect right to be there. He, himself, had suggested the terms of their truce. If she wanted to bath in the middle of the night, that was entirely her affair.

He would simply turn around, go back to his chamber, and come back when she was bound to be done and gone.

Turn around . . .

His body would not obey his mind. Indeed, it seemed oblivious to the fact that he even had a mind. The instant, raw response did not surprise him. He'd experienced it before, merely thinking about her. The sight of her naked, a few scant yards away, took his self-control to the very edge.

She turned over and swam a few yards. Her back was long and smooth, her buttocks rounded, her thighs—

Turn around . . .

He was master of Castlerock. An argument could be made that she was a prisoner being held on suspicion of something or other. At the very least, she was a woman without visible male protection.

Except, of course, for himself. He'd insisted she stay,

on the grounds that her safety required it. When he did that, he made himself responsible for her well-being.

Turn around . . .

There was a god, all right, one with a ribald sense of humor the priests never seemed to credit.

He was fully, almost painfully erect. There was a fire in his blood that threatened to banish reason. Perhaps it already had.

Her mother had not been married to her father and, according to Fionna, had not minded much, being too independent to put much stock in such things.

Was the daughter like the mother?

Was she necessarily a virgin, this woman who thought she could go off across England on her own and make her own way as she pleased? There had been a moment, in that single kiss days before, when she had responded.

Then she'd kneed him.

He took a step closer to the pool. She stood, her body gleaming above the water from the waist up, and began laving soap into her hair. Her breasts were high and firm, the nipples full. He imagined how they would feel in his hands, beneath his mouth, and bit back a groan.

This was absurd. He was a man and a warrior. He liked women, even subscribed to the heretical notion that they were as fundamentally intelligent and moral as men themselves. But his enjoyment was a casual thing, not concerned with the important business of his life.

Except that there was nothing at all casual about the way Fionna made him feel.

She ducked under again to rinse her hair. This time

when she stood, she was a little closer to the edge of the pool with the consequence that the water barely grazed her hips. He could see the fiery tangle of curls at the apex of her thighs and the slight curve of her abdomen.

Turn around . . .

He took another step closer. The torch he held flared suddenly. Fionna looked up, startled.

"I didn't expect anyone to be here," he said, and stepped out of the shadows.

She did not move. Not by so much as a flinch did she reveal any discomfort at his presence. Nor did she make any attempt to cover herself. She merely looked at him.

"I'm finished," she said after a moment.

What was he to make of this? That she was without shame? That she was available to him? Or that she was merely an intelligent, sensible woman who saw no point in making a scene about something that had happened by accident?

"Don't rush on my account," he said, and set his torch in a bracket near hers. If she could be so casual about this, so could he.

She hesitated. "Would you mind handing me that cloth?"

He was relieved to know that she did not wish to leave the pool and stroll naked in front of him. Relieved and disappointed.

"By all means," he said, ever gentlemanly.

Getting herself wrapped up without also drenching the cloth was a bit of a trick. She managed it, but not well. By the time she emerged, the fabric was wet enough to cling to every inch of her and provide rather less in the way of concealment than she probably supposed.

"If you'll excuse me . . ." she said. He seemed to be standing in her path. Solicitously, he stepped aside. She picked up her tunic and gave him a solemn nod. "Good night."

"Good night . . ." His hand reached out. He truly had not meant it to. His fingers closed around the satiny skin of her upper arm.

"Fionna—"

She did not speak nor did she struggle. She merely waited.

He managed a smile. "Are you going to unman me again?"

"I wouldn't have thought that was possible."

"Finally, a compliment." His attempt at lightness failed. He stared at his own hand, holding her. "I would not ever wish to hurt you." He had never found it necessary to say such a thing to a woman. It disturbed him that he did so now.

"I know . . ." Her words were little more than a whisper. She, too, looked at the hard, muscled curve of his hand, bronzed by the sun, honed to wield a sword or lance. The hand of a warrior, but the same hand that turned the pages of a book, that gave her a harp, and that had drawn her from the sea.

She swayed slightly. He put an arm around her waist, keeping her from falling. Only that. She smelled of lilac and honeysuckle. Her eyes were the color of the sky in high summer.

They were utterly alone in the world, and nothing else mattered.

Her mouth was soft and yielding beneath his. She

made a faint sound, like a sigh, and parted her lips. He gathered her to him. A surge of pleasure so intense it could only be called joy came with her. So, too, did a piercing sense of rightness.

This woman, this moment, both made perfect sense to him in a way nothing else in his life had ever done.

He didn't question it. For once, the restless reason of his mind was stilled. Her body pressed against his. He could feel the heat of her skin through the damp drying cloth. Her arms twined around his neck. She tasted of honeyed mead. He felt her hesitation—and her curiosity—and went very slowly. His mouth took hers with long, slow thoroughness.

When he raised his head, her eyes were wide and questioning. She did not move or speak. His lips touched the curve of her cheek, dipped into the sweet hollow at the base of her throat, slid farther downward to the swell of her breasts.

Around them, torchlight reflected off the deep pool of water drawn from the earth's hidden sources, casting flickering shadows against the ancient stone walls. Save for the raggedness of their own breath and the murmur of the buried stream, there was only silence.

He lifted her high in his arms and carried her to the edge of the pool, then stripped off his tunic. Beneath it, he was naked. Slipping into the water, he reached for Fionna. The drying cloth fell away. Their bodies touched for the first time, unfettered.

She tilted her head back and in her gaze he saw not fear—which he would have dreaded—but merely surprise, as though she had come upon something not necessarily unwelcome to her, just unexpected. Behind the surprise, moving powerfully within her, was desire.

He did not mistake it. This woman did not fear him, although it was possible she feared herself. She desired him even as he did her. They were equal in a way he had never thought to find.

Her hands ran over his chest slowly, exploring. He trembled at her touch, he who had known the caress of women who refined their skills in silken chambers where love was played as a variation of politics.

He waited, holding himself in strict check, giving her whatever time she needed. A slow, wondering smile curved the corners of her mouth.

"So much strength," she said, "and yet you can be very gentle."

His jaw was clenched. Blood pounded in his temples. "Strength has no use without control."

She looked up, her smile deepening. "And you are very controlled, aren't you?"

Usually. Just then he couldn't quite remember what control was. Or why he'd always thought it was so important. Or . . .

Her fingers trailed down the corded muscles of his arms, drifted back up and across the broad span of his shoulders. "Haven't there been women who found such control a challenge?"

"One or two." But none of them had ever come remotely so close to shattering it.

Her eyebrows arched. "Then, you read better than you count. There have been many more."

"I am no monk," he admitted, and did not ask how she knew about the lost nights of his youth, spent seeking something he had never found. She knew far too much, this fey Irishwoman taken from the sea.

"But they pass forgotten, all those women, all those

beds." She bent her head and touched her tongue to the soft, dark whorls of hair that arched like an arrow down his chest.

A groan broke from him, shattering the silence. His hands closed on her hips, drawing her hard against his massive erection.

Fionna looked up. Her eyes met his. "*I* will not be forgotten, Hugh of Castlerock. I have shared this with no man. If I do share it with you, it will mark you to your last breath. In all honor, I must tell you that."

There in the darkly moving pool, by whispering water and dancing firelight, Hugh believed her. This was not womanly pride speaking. It was a warning to be taken seriously. He did not come close to understanding it, but every instinct he possessed told him that this woman—this *Fionna*—could change him forever.

Did he want to be changed?

The question had just surfaced in his mind when the clamor of footsteps on the steps above abruptly interrupted them.

The guard who burst into the chamber was young, not more than twenty, and consumed by the urgency of his message. All the same, he came to a sudden halt when he glimpsed his lord, standing in the pool, hands on his hips, his powerful body shielding the woman behind him.

"My lord . . . your pardon . . ."

"What is it?" Hugh demanded. His tone suggested that the young man had better justify himself at once or the ground would swallow him whole.

"A messenger . . . from your lady mother . . . here . . ."

Hugh stiffened. "Come now?"

"Yes, lord, just now despite the hour. He carries a letter with her ladyship's seal, so the watch admitted him."

"Go. I'll be right there."

The young man fled. Hugh climbed from the pool. He held out a hand for Fionna.

"I must see to this," he said.

"Yes, of course."

They dressed quickly. Hugh took the steps to the great hall two at a time. Fionna followed almost as quickly.

It seemed all the men were awake. Torches had been lit. The ever-vigilant Peyton hovered nearby. An exhausted, bedraggled man held all eyes. He stood before Hugh, holding out a letter.

Hugh took it and stepped a little apart to read. His eyes scanned the single page quickly. He turned back to the man. "You did well, getting this here in only four days."

"Thank you, lord," the man murmured. His voice was barely audible. He looked close to collapsing.

Hugh gestured. Two of his men stepped forward, grasped the third, and led him off. "See to his care. Peyton . . ."

They spoke together quietly, the older man looking grim, nodding. It was done in minutes. Hugh raised his voice again, speaking to all. "A token force will hold Castlerock. The rest of us will be at sea by daybreak. Make haste."

The response was instant. Men rushed to do his bidding. In the midst of the ordered chaos, his eyes met

Fionna's. He crossed the hall to her side. She felt the dark ripplings of concern coming off him like waves.

"What has happened?" she asked.

"My father was attacked outside of London. He lies close to death. My mother bids me come."

Through her mind whirled dark turmoil, the shouts of men, blood . . . and the tears of a woman.

"I am so sorry."

He nodded, curtly. "You will come with me."

"I will only be an encumbrance. Now is the time to let me go."

"Never!" The word reverberated through the hall. Men froze in their tracks, recalled themselves, and went hurriedly about their duties, undoubtedly glad their lord's fury was not directed at themselves.

"You will come with me," Hugh repeated. "If you must be trussed up like a chicken, so be it, but you will come."

"To where?" Fionna demanded. Sympathetic though she was to the pain roiling through him, his high-handedness was hard to endure.

"Glastonbury."

"W-where . . . ?" She was back in the ice-cold sea, floundering for her life.

"Glastonbury. It is our family seat, one of them at any rate and the strongest. My mother sends word she is taking my father there."

Glastonbury. The name turned over and over in her mind . . . haunting, echoing. Mocking. In her pride, she had thought herself so wise, so capable. Never had it so much as occurred to her . . .

Glastonbury.

"Who are your parents?" she asked, hearing the

sudden hoarseness of her own voice as though from a distance.

Hugh frowned. "Baron Conan of Wyndham and Glastonbury, and his wife, the Lady Alianor. Why?"

Why? Why why why why . . .

"No reason." Liar liar liar liar . . .

Glastonbury.

She took a deep breath, praying for calm. His face was grim, eyes ablaze. He was, again, the implacable war leader.

"I will come."

He stared at her, as though directly into her soul. "No more arguments?"

She shook her head. "I am truly sorry for what has happened. You have my word, I will not cause any difficulty. Now I am sure you have much to see to . . ."

"Your word?"

"Yes," she insisted, anything to be done with this. She could not bear his scrutiny, not now. "I will not try to escape, I promise."

He looked about to say something more. Before he could, Fionna said, "I must get ready, too." She hurried from the hall.

CHAPTER EIGHT

The gray light of predawn was just beginning to give way to full day when the horned prow of the war vessel cleaved the water below Castlerock. The men took to the oars with vigor, catching cadence from the steady call of the navigator seated by the rudder. A hundred yards offshore, the sails were hoisted and filled with a fair wind.

Hugh gazed back at the fortress rising from the rock. His eyes were shuddered, his face inscrutable. Worry for his father hung heavy within him. If he died—

No, he would not think of that. His father, the man who had guided his every step to manhood and was also his closest friend, would not die. His mother would not permit it. He smiled faintly as he thought of her. In the face of what was surely terrible grief and fear, the Lady Alianor would nevertheless muster every ounce of knowledge and skill she possessed. She would fight with weapons few could claim, only some of which he knew. It was no exaggeration to say she would go down into the very pit of Hades rather than surrender her husband to death.

Yet she might still lose. And if she did—

If she did, he would be Baron of Wyndham and Glastonbury, heir to the most powerful man in the kingdom after the king himself, and some would have said even before.

And he would use that power to wreak vengeance on whoever had killed his father if it meant he had to cut a swathe of death and ruin from one end of England to the other.

His hand was clutching his sword. He had reached for it without thought. Slowly, he released his grip and stared along the line of the boat.

Despite the wind, his men stayed at the oars. They had stripped off their tunics and rowed bare-chested, their backs gleaming with sweat. Around them lay the Bristol Channel and beyond that, far out past Bull Point, was the sea. They would not be going that far. Just north of the Brue River, they would disembark and take horse inland to Glastonbury. If all went well, they would be there in three days.

Then he would face—what?

In the meantime, he had another and more immediate concern. Why had Fionna agreed so readily to come with him? Despite a certain temptation to believe she had simply been swept up in her attraction to him, he dismissed that completely. She had come after learning that their destination was Glastonbury. Was her destination in the same direction or had she merely seen the usefulness of getting away from Castlerock?

He sighed and let himself look finally toward the

prow of the ship. Fionnà sat there, her cloak gathered around her and her face turned to the sun. Her eyes were closed.

He wondered how she was faring. The last time she'd been at sea, she had almost drowned. It stood to reason that she might be uneasy now.

She was a stubborn woman, infuriating, possibly capricious, and shamelessly—all right, magnificently—bold. She could deal with her fears on her own. He had better things to do. At the very least, he could row.

He stripped off his tunic, took a place on a bench, and got to it. The hard, steady exercise calmed him. With a sense of relief, he gave himself up to the rhythm of the ship.

She wasn't going to look, not even for a second. She would just keep her eyes shut, and enjoy the warm sun and fresh sea air. Her lashes flickered. There he was, just as she'd glimpsed him a moment before, chest bare, muscles flexing, rowing right along with the other men.

What was it she had always been told?—a good leader never asks his men to do anything he won't do himself. Hugh was clearly an example of that. He rowed as superbly as he did everything else.

She shivered slightly, although she wasn't cold, and wrapped her cloak more closely around herself. It was two nights since she had slept properly, and she was very tired. Her body still ached from the pounding it had taken during the storm.

Ached, too, for other reasons.

She could not contemplate the scene in the pool

without a sense of amazement. That she could behave in such a way, with such heedless wantonness, astounded her. She felt as though an entirely different woman had emerged within her and taken over, a woman she hadn't even known existed.

And now Glastonbury—

She would not think of that. Too much was unknowable, even unfathomable. She would simply have to wait.

And find some way to occupy her thoughts ... counting clouds, recalling stanzas of poetry, playing music in her head. No, not in her head. For there stood Peyton, right above her, grim-faced, disapproving over what a bother he undoubtedly thought her. In his hand was a sack, and in the sack—

Fionna lifted the harp out with a sense of wonder. She had not presumed to bring it. But Hugh had.

"His lordship thought you might want this," Peyton said. He scowled again and went away.

Fionna played. The sails filled, the oars rose and fell, dripping diamond bright, and the voice of the harp filled the air. Beneath a sky that seemed endless, at one with the sea, the music soared.

At length, she sang, of great battles and bold chieftains, of knights and bards and maidens, of daring and adventure, of sorrow and joy, laughter and tears. And at the end of the day, a hearth to come home to and the glad sound of a loved one's welcome.

The men listened. They did not look at her directly, except once or twice when a young one could not resist, for she was clearly set aside as forbidden to them. But they smiled at the music and renewed their strength at the oars.

The ridge of green-brown shore on either side flew by. The evening star could just be seen when they turned inland toward the quays of busy Weston-super-Mare.

Hugh had visited the port town more times than he could recall. He had taken ship from there for London and points on the Continent, and returned the same way. So frequent were his arrivals and departures that he had found it useful to build a small fortified manor just east of the harbor. It was guarded by men-at-arms, staffed with servants and always ready for use.

Word was sent of their arrival. Before the last of the baggage was off-loaded, an escort arrived with extra horses. Fionna mounted smoothly enough, but it was quickly obvious to Hugh that she was exhausted. By the time they completed the short ride up to the hill above the town, she was drooping in the saddle.

Servants ran out to greet them. Many curious glances went the way of the fire-haired woman, but it was obvious they had been warned that this time their lord did not come alone. Eyes were quickly averted, although there was no doubt tongues would wag that night.

Resigned to his retainers' curiosity, Hugh lifted Fionna from her horse. She made a small murmur of protest but that was all. Her face was very white. There were violet shadows beneath her eyes. She felt very light in his arms.

He carried her inside, through the hall and up the stairs to the room set aside for his own use. The shutters had been thrown open, a fire laid, and the covers of the bed folded back.

He laid her down carefully. Before her head touched the linen-covered pillow, she was asleep. With a wry grimace, he eased her cloak from her, undid the girdle around her waist, and removed her shoes. That done, he pulled a cover of finely woven lamb's wool over her. He doubted she would appreciate his ministrations as lady's maid, but he did not feel inclined to have anyone else tend her.

In the hall, his men were making a great show of their business. So, too, were the servants. No one so much as glanced his way save for Peyton, who came directly to him.

"Was it wise to bring the Irishwoman?" the old warrior asked bluntly.

"Probably not, but I didn't think she could be left at Castlerock."

"You could have sent her back to Ireland."

It was an obvious solution, one he had so far managed to avoid thinking about. "And do what, drop her off on the nearest Dublin dock and wish her good luck?"

"She made her own way here. Seems like she could manage there well enough."

"I want to know why she came here," Hugh said. Ordinarily, he did not go to great lengths to explain himself. But he respected Peyton, and besides, the man did have a point. "A woman does not travel to a foreign land by herself, as she claims to have done, for no good reason. She especially doesn't do it when that land is threatened with civil war."

"If she was bringing anything—a message, arms, whatever—it's at the bottom of the Bristol Channel."

"True enough—" Hugh fell silent. Presumably, Fionna had set sail with some sort of baggage. There was nothing left of her belongings save the clothes she had been wearing and the golden talisman. Yet she had never expressed a moment's concern over what had been lost.

Of course, a message could have been committed to memory, not parchment. And kept all the safer that way.

Was she carrying a message? Was the talisman a sign of her authenticity? Who would send a woman on such a mission?

A wily Irish chieftain bent on taking advantage of the distractions of England's king and nobles for his own gain. A chieftain like the father she had mentioned.

He had no proof. But the suspicion was what had plagued him for days now, ever since she stood dripping wet in the hall at Castlerock, stared him straight in the eyes, and refused to tell him anything.

He had let his desire for her push out such thoughts, but he could no longer afford to do that. Not while his father lay close to death, and England teetered toward war. If Fionna represented harm to what he was sworn to protect, she would rue the day he took her from the sea.

With such grim thoughts for company, he left his men to their rest and sought the solitude of the battlements. There he walked, gazing out into the darkness, until the castle grew silent around him. At length, he made his way to one of the small guest chambers, unrolled a pallet on a simple bed, and slept.

Morning brought a cold rain, a Spartan breakfast, and grim faces. Fionna felt very much alone there in the swirling mass of men going so purposefully about their business. No one so much as glanced at her. She might as well have been invisible. Yet she was certain that she could not move a finger without it being noticed.

Her horse was brought out. She mounted and waited to join the line of march. The day promised to be long and hard. She had a rough idea of how many miles still lay between them and Glastonbury. Riding had never been her favorite activity. She did not look forward to it now, especially under such circumstances. Despite a decent night's sleep, she still ached. But she sat with her back straight and her head high, unwilling to show any weakness.

There was a bustle by the door to the manor. Hugh appeared. He wore chain mail, gleaming darkly over a black tunic. A cloak, also black embroidered with silver, swirled about him. A scabbard hung at his side, the hilt of his sword ready to his hand. In the crook of his arm, he carried a helmet. As she watched, he put it on. The brow was curved in the shape of a hawk's beak. Standing naked in the Roman bath, he was a formidable man. Armed for war, for there was no mistaking that he was, he cast an aura of pure menace.

The stallion brought for him snorted and pawed the ground. He spoke soothingly to the animal for a moment before rising in a single, seemingly effortless motion into the saddle. The significance of the stallion did not escape Fionna. She and most of the others who were mounted were riding palfreys, geldings whose quieter temperament suited them to travel. But Hugh and the men she had noticed were closest to him all rode stallions, although none of the others was as big or powerful as his. Truly, the animal was magnificent but he was bred for the battlefield. That he was being ridden on a journey suggested there was at least a chance of serious trouble.

Hugh did not so much as glance her way. He raised a hand and let it drop. The march began.

They stopped once toward midday, just long enough to see to personal needs and water the horses. Food was eaten standing or back in the saddle.

The rain continued unrelenting. It was the mud season in England—Ireland, too, for that matter. The horses hooves made sucking noises as they rose and fell. Dirt splattered everything. Fionna pulled her hood farther down over her head and willed her mind to go blank. She let herself drift through fragments of thought and memory in an almost dreamlike state in which the awareness of her growing physical discomfort penetrated only sporadically.

But discomfort there was. She was wearier than she could ever remember being. Her head throbbed from it. The rest of her felt as though she'd been pummeled. Impatient with herself, she straightened up and looked around.

They were passing through a dark stretch of forest. Oaks and maples loomed close on both sides. The road was little more than a narrow track forcing the riders into a single file.

It became very quiet. There was only the creak of the cinches, the jangle of spurs, and the softer but ominous thud of scabbards slapping lightly against men's legs. Fionna found herself holding her breath and let it out slowly. All the same, her apprehension grew. Something . . . felt wrong.

She couldn't explain it, but long experience had taught her to never discount such a feeling. Especially not when it was growing stronger by the moment.

It might have been the fatigue, or her concern over so many things, or her instinctive sympathy for what Hugh must be feeling. Or it might not.

Her throat tightened. She could not draw breath. Panic coursed through her. She fought it down, pushing against it like a mighty stone. Slowly, grudgingly, it yielded.

Fionna put her heels to her horse. Before anyone realized what she was doing, she broke out of the line and galloped toward Hugh.

"My lord!"

He turned, dark browed beneath the hawk's helmet. "What is it?"

"Something is wrong . . . up ahead . . . I know this must sound absurd, a woman's fears, but . . ."

"Stay here."

He shouted an order. Instantly, men surrounded her while others formed up behind him. Through the circle of big, mailed men, Fionna could see little. But she heard the sudden pounding of horses and the shouts of men as the war band surged up the road.

The clash of weapons followed. She heard screams, the high-pitched whinnying of horses with their blood up, and she felt—

It was like the whisper of a bird's wings passing unseen in darkness. She closed her eyes, huddled down inside the cloak. Waiting.

It was over soon. Silence fell again, an eerie silence as though the forest itself had stopped breathing.

The rain lessened. A mist rose over the road.

Out of the mist, a shape emerged, horse and man, both big, dark, implacable. Others followed. Hugh came to where she waited. The guard around her opened, clearing a path for him.

There were smears of blood on his cheeks and on his hands. Other than that, he looked untouched. She was grateful for that, but it concerned her, too. Was killing such a small thing to him?

"We will try to identify them," he said, "but they carried no insignia."

"Knights?"

He nodded. "Renegades, perhaps, but not likely. They were trained fighters." He gestured to where several of his men were holding riderless horses. "Their mounts will be of use."

"They are all—"

She didn't finish. The look he gave her made it clear the question was absurd. All the same, she did say, "Surely, they should be buried."

"The forest folk will see to that after they've stripped them of anything that can be used."

He was referring to the bands of landless men, women, and children who found refuge in the thick wood. With the trouble come upon England, they were growing in number. The authorities, such as there were, found it prudent to ignore them.

She supposed he was right, but his callousness sent

a chill through her. Then she remembered that he must be counting every moment until he reached his father.

The line of march formed up again. As they moved forward along the road, Fionna tried to keep her eyes averted but could not. The bodies had been dragged off to the side but were still clearly visible. She counted twenty in all. Not a small band, and certainly large enough to do great damage if the element of surprise had been with them.

A few minutes after they passed the bodies, the road widened slightly. Hugh turned around in the saddle and gestured to her. Fionna urged her horse forward.

When she drew alongside him, he said, "How did you know?"

She had been expecting the question, of course, but now that it had come, she had no idea of how to answer it. Slowly, she said, "I didn't know. I . . . felt."

"Is that what it's like, a feeling?"

She nodded. "People call it the sight, and I suppose sometimes it is that, but usually it just comes as a wave of powerful feeling, in this case stark terror."

"Does it happen often?"

"No, not at all. In fact, it didn't even happen when I was on the ship. I had no warning of any kind."

He cast her a quick, sharp look. "But you didn't die then, did you?"

"No, but only because . . . because you saved me."

"I'm not fishing for thanks." He smiled at his inadvertent choice of words. "It's just that there was no actual danger to you then. Everything was in place for you to be rescued even though neither one of us had any way of knowing that. However, this time—"

On a murmur of sound, Fionna said, "It wasn't my own death I felt."

"Whose?"

She suspected he knew the answer even before she spoke it. "Yours."

He did not deny it, which struck her as odd, since people in general liked to deny the possibility of death. Either that or they dwelled on it ceaselessly. Hugh merely looked thoughtful.

"It would make sense to kill me before I could reach my father—and carry out his orders."

"Of course, they might well have failed."

He shrugged. "I would be hard to kill, that's true enough, but any man can be slain. Sometimes it just comes down to chance. The fact that someone succeeded in wounding my father so grievously reminds me of that."

"You're very calm about this."

"The first battle is a shock, the second less so. After a while, there is a danger of it becoming routine." He looked over at her again. "This talent you have is useful."

"If it's reliable. I have no way of knowing that. This might just have been a fluke." An echo of the smothering terror she had felt rippled through her. She knew, but did not say, that it was hideously real.

"Your men will wonder. Some of them at least must have heard me warn you."

He nodded. "They will wonder, but they will say nothing."

"Can you be sure of that?"

His eyes revealed amusement. "Yes, quite sure."

And that, it seemed, was that. They continued on through the forest, endless hour after hour. The rain stopped, but the day remained gray and listless. Fionna managed as best she could. But by the time a halt was called at last, close to darkness, she could no longer feel her legs. Still in the saddle, she hesitated.

Hugh saw her and came over. Without a word, he held out his arms. She slid into them. As soon as her feet touched the ground, her legs gave way.

"You haven't done a lot of riding, have you?" he asked as he carried her over to where a fire was being laid.

"Believe it or not, I've always preferred boats."

"You might have said something."

"To what point? You must reach Glastonbury as quickly as possible."

He did not deny that but his hands were gentle as he set her down.

They slept that night beneath the stars. The storm, blown out, left a cloudless sky. A crescent moon shone palely against the silver swathe of the Milky Way. Hugh had offered a small tent to Fionna, but she preferred to sleep in the open. Lying on her pallet, she gazed up at the heavens through the branches of young-leafed trees.

Hugh lay next to her, his men on the far side of the fire. His steady breathing comforted her, but still she could not sleep. She desperately needed rest, for the next day promised to be as difficult as this one had been. If only her mind would quiet, her thoughts still. If only—

Hugh woke some time later, as he usually did during the night. He looked over at Fionna. She was turned on her side, facing him. Her lips were slightly parted, her breath slow and steady. He tucked the cover more securely around her but did not let his hand linger.

CHAPTER NINE

Yet another hill rose up before them. Fionna gazed at it glumly. It was late the following afternoon. They had been riding since early morning, with only one very brief stop. She was half convinced that they had crossed the width of England, although she knew that couldn't be true. It only felt that way, especially to her bottom, which come to think of it, could feel nothing at all.

At least the day was fair. She rode with her hood back, the sun kind on her face. An hour or so before, they had passed by a small clearing where there was a cluster of huts. People had recognized Hugh. Instead of fleeing as any sensible folk would at the approach of armed men, they had run out to the road, waving and calling greetings, which the men returned.

No doubt they recognized the banner that, with the ending of rain, was now displayed—a golden hawk in flight against a field of blue. Beneath the hawk streamed the words *Honoris Causa*. For the sake of honor. That had given Fionna something to contemplate during the long hours.

The people's reactions also gave her some faint hope that there would be an end to this. But first one more hill—

They topped it and she saw there before them a good-size town surrounded by a defensive wall. Daub and wattle houses were laid out in neat rows around a center square. On the far side, on another hill, stood an impressive castle complete with towers and battlements. From the highest tower, a banner flew, identical to the one Hugh carried. Not far away, also rising above the town, was what appeared to be an abbey. It was difficult to tell for sure because construction was still underway.

Off in the distance, just visible to her, was the winding ribbon of the Brue, and where it neared the town, a large lake. In the center of that she could make out an island.

She took a deep breath and straightened her shoulders.

Their entry into Glastonbury was joyful. It seemed as though every man, woman, and child came hurrying to greet them. The welcome was wholehearted and unfeigned. It left no doubt in Fionna's mind that Hugh and his family were well loved. Their power did not steam from wealth and armed might. It had a far deeper and more lasting source.

All the same, the people seemed to realize the grim urgency that had brought Hugh there. They kept the road clear and did not impede their swift progress. By the time they reached the castle, the gates stood open for them. They passed through into the bailey. Hugh dismounted swiftly. A woman stood at the top of the wooden steps that led to the high door of the keep. She was of medium height, slender, simply but elegantly dressed in a dark blue robe. She must have just come running out, for she was still fastening the diaphanous veil that covered her hair, hair much the same shade of Fionna's but lightly touched by silver.

Hugh ran up the steps. He gathered the woman into his arms and hugged her gently. They spoke earnestly for several moments. Fionna could not hear what was said, but she knew all the same. Hugh's shoulders lightened, as though a great dread had been taken from them. His father lived.

As he and his mother continued speaking, Fionna dismounted. She stood a little uncertainly. Around her, horses were being led off to the stables, men were collecting their gear and moving toward a stone building adjacent to the keep that must serve as a barracks, servants were hurrying back and forth.

In the midst of all the ordered hubbub, she realized that Hugh had come back down the steps and was waiting for her. He held out his hand. She took it, and together they climbed the steps to the keep.

The Lady Alianor watched them come. Fionna knew that she had to be almost fifty, but her appearance made that seem impossible. Except for the few strands of silver in her hair and a sprinkling of delicately etched lines near her eyes, she appeared much closer in age to Fionna herself. Only the steady calm of her gaze suggested a wisdom that came with years, and then only to very few.

"I have brought a guest, Mother," Hugh said. His voice sounded wry. Fionna realized he found the situation somewhat uncomfortable. He could hardly be blamed for that. A proper young woman would never have been traveling alone as she had, and certainly would not have had to be taken prisoner by her rescuer simply because she refused to tell him who she was. How to introduce such a problematic creature to his own mother? It presented a certain challenge, yet Hugh seemed willing to take it on.

"Her name is Fionna, and she is from Ireland."

Lady Alianor's eyes met hers. Fionna had a sudden, fleeting sensation of peering into endlessly deep water. She blinked, and it was gone.

"Fionna," her ladyship repeated slowly.

"Of Lough Gealach."

Hugh started. He stared at them both. Speaking to his mother, he said, "You've just gotten more out of her in a moment than I've managed to do in days. She wouldn't tell me where she was from."

"How is his lordship?" Fionna asked, ignoring his remark.

Alianor did the same. "Better, although his condition remains serious. He lost a great deal of blood."

"I must hear everything that has happened," Hugh said, "but first I would see Father."

Alianor nodded. "He knows you have come and is waiting for you. Go ahead. I'll get Fionna settled." The two women exchanged a smile.

Hugh took the steps to the high tower two at a time. His anxiousness to see Conan overwhelmed all else. Yet he could not shake the feeling that something was very odd about the encounter between his mother and Fionna. If he didn't know better, he could almost have sworn that they already knew each other. But that was impossible. Except for a few trips to the Continent with her husband, Alianor had not left England. She certainly had never been in Ireland. Truth be told, she much preferred to remain at Glastonbury, although she was resigned to a certain amount of time having to be spent in London. Where, then, could she possibly have encountered Fionna and if she had, why hadn't either of them said so?

He must be wrong and yet—

He shoved the thought aside as he came to the iron-bound door to his parents' chamber. It stood slightly ajar. Nonetheless, he knocked and waited to be bid before entering.

A low, deep voice—dearly familiar—called out. "Come in."

He stepped inside, looking first to the bed, which was empty and neatly made. His father was seated in a high-backed chair before a table spread with a multitude of parchment. Despite being in his early fifties, the Baron of Wyndham and Glastonbury remained a formidable figure of a man. Like Hugh, he was far taller than the average man, and heavily muscled. His hair was still dark as night except for a sprinkling of silver. His eyes crinkled with pleasure as he beheld his eldest son.

"Hugh!" Quickly, the baron rose to his feet. Just as quickly, he mastered the wince of pain that flitted across his handsome features. But not so fast that Hugh didn't see it. He hurried to his father's side. The two men embraced. Conan stepped back a little and looked at Hugh.

"What's wrong?" the baron demanded.

"Wrong? I learn you have almost been killed, speed to your side, and find you out of bed when Mother says your condition is still serious. That's what's wrong."

"No, I mean besides all that."

Hugh looked at him incredulously. "Besides it? What matters besides it?"

"I don't know," Conan said with feigned patience. "That's why I'm asking. Something is wrong."

Hugh sighed. People whispered about his mother's strange abilities. It didn't do to overlook the fact that his father had one or two of his own.

"I brought a woman with me."

Conan looked at him sharply. Finally, he shrugged. "As I assume she's willing, what's the harm?"

"She isn't willing. In fact, she's the least willing woman I've ever met. To all intents and purposes, she's a prisoner."

Conan sat down again. The corners of his finely chiseled mouth twitched with what looked like amusement. "Why?"

"I pulled her out of the sea when her ship went down during a storm. She was coming from Ireland with a crew she claims she didn't know. She says she was traveling alone. The day after she was rescued, she announced her intention to continue on her way. She wouldn't say who she is or where she intended going. So I kept her."

With these last words, Conan smiled outright. "Do I gather from all this that she is not overly difficult to look upon?"

"That has nothing to do with it. There has to be some explanation for her strange behavior. Until I know it, I will not let her go. Besides, how far would she get with the way things are? I do not want to be responsible for her death."

"A fair point. What is her name?"

"Fionna of Lough Gealach, as I have just learned. She told Mother more than she has told me."

Conan frowned. "There's something familiar in all that. It will come to me. In the meantime, sit. We have much to speak about."

"Where were you attacked?" Hugh asked as he took the chair across from his father.

"Just outside of London. I was on my way to meet with several of the other barons. With so much clamor against the king, I thought some quiet conversation might help clarify matters. Unfortunately, this happened instead." He gestured in the general region of his chest. Beneath his tunic, Hugh could make out the shape of a very large and thick bandage.

"How many were there?"

"Twenty, perhaps slightly more. They came without warning. I recognized none of them, but they knew their business. Two of my men were killed and six more wounded. So far as I can determine, half the force engaged my guard while the rest concentrated on me. To be frank, I think they believed me dead when they withdrew."

"Mother was with you?"

"Yes, and if she hadn't been, I certainly would have died. I have no memory of this as I was unconscious, but somehow she managed to stop the bleeding. I came to in a litter, being carried here." He grimaced at the thought.

"There was nothing to tell you who these men might be?"

Conan shook his head. "Unfortunately not."

"Then I doubt it is coincidence that I experienced a similar attack on the way here." At his father's startled look, Hugh explained what had happened. He ended by saying, "I have no idea how Fionna knew there was an ambush. She says only that she had a "feeling," whatever that means. But if she hadn't acted as she did, there is no doubt that at least some of us would have been killed including, possibly, me."

"I see . . ." Conan said slowly. "I suspected this was more than a random incident, and you have confirmed that. As to the woman . . ." He paused, then said, "I believe I have just remembered why her name sounded familiar."

He rose, despite Hugh's quick protestation. "Give me your arm," Conan said. His smile was wryly male. "It is time we had it out with the ladies."

They found them in Alianor's solar, a large, airy room near the top of the keep. High windows set with glass looked out toward the river. A large fireplace took up most of one wall, the windows dominated another, and the remainder were hung with rich tapestries. Freshly woven rushes covered the floor. Beneath the windows were benches heaped with embroidered pillows. A rack held precious books, one of which lay open on a stand. The women looked up as Hugh and his father entered. Their smiles faded.

"Conan!" Alianor exclaimed as she jumped to her feet. "What are you doing? It's bad enough that you insisted on being out of bed but walking about . . ."

"Be easy, my dear," her husband said. "Thanks to

your good care, I can manage fine." All the same, he took the seat Hugh pulled out for him. As he did, he gave Fionna a long, steady look. "You would be Fionna of Lough Gealach?"

She nodded and dropped a quick curtsy. Hugh could scarcely credit her sudden demureness.

"I am, my lord," she said, "and I thank you for allowing me to come here."

"Not at all," Conan replied. He glanced at his son, gauging his reaction. "Besides, how could I refuse? You come at my wife's invitation."

Hugh prided himself on being master of his own emotions. He did not show his now by so much as a flicker. Instead, he merely sat, apparently at his ease as Fionna looked at him a shade nervously.

"I have come to study with the Lady Alianor, to learn more about the healing arts."

"That's nice," Hugh said. A servant had entered with wine and honey cakes. Hugh accepted a cup and took a long sip before he spoke again. "Is there any particular reason why you could not have told me that instead of making such a mystery of your identity and your reason for coming to England?"

She took a seat but remained very upright, back rigid as though in expectation of attack. "I didn't know who you were. You were simply 'Hugh of Castlerock,' an English noble who had rescued me. Grateful though I was for that, I had no particular reason to believe I could trust you."

"Three days ago you learned who I was, yet you still said nothing. You allowed me to believe that I was forcing you to come to Glastonbury when that was your intended destination all along. Why?"

Fionna hesitated. She exchanged a quick look with Alianor. Finally, she said, "Because it wasn't only for me to say. It also involved your mother. I could not know what she would want me to tell you—or not tell you. So I thought it best to wait."

"Fionna was merely being cautious," Alianor said. "In these times, that's only sensible."

Sensible. Beautiful, infuriating, fey Fionna was sensible. That would take some getting used to.

"We're so grateful for your safe arrival," Alianor went on. She gave her son a loving smile. "And I am so looking forward to showing you everything. But if you would both excuse me now, it is time for the baron to rest."

Conan raised an eyebrow. "Is it?"

"Yes," his wife said firmly. "It is. I know you and Hugh have a great deal to talk about, but it will have to wait."

"The tyranny of women knows no bounds." Conan observed. All the same, he stood and accepted his wife's arm. "One condition, you must rest with me."

The smile she gave him was at once indulgent and appreciative.

"Hugh, dear," Alianor said as she and Conan left the solar, "I thought Fionna would enjoy the west tower room. Do show her where it is. Oh, and my maid will help you with clothes. Don't hesitate to tell her what you'd like."

"Thank you," Fionna murmured, but she suspected Lady Alianor did not hear. Her head was bent close to her husband's. They were laughing softly.

Silence reigned. It was late afternoon, almost evening. The windows, standing open, admitted the faint sounds of the town and the rustle of birds nesting in the ivy just outside. A horse whinnied in the stable yard. A young boy called to a friend.

"Well . . ." Hugh said.

"Here we are," Fionna observed. Her hands were clenched in her lap. She tried a smile, but it wobbled away.

"Gealach." Hugh tried the word on his tongue. "If I remember my Irish—and I don't claim to have much— that means moon. You come from the lake of the moon."

"It is a poetic reference."

"Of course it is, it's Irish. What did you do there?"

"Studied, mostly. My mother also has skill at healing. She taught me all she could, but then it was thought best for me to come to Lady Alianor to learn more."

"I have never known my mother to take on a student before."

"I am most grateful that she has done so now."

"Who is your father?"

She hesitated. He sensed she was seriously considering not telling him. At length, she relented. "His name is Dermot. He holds lands in Connaught."

"He holds Connaught, isn't that what you meant? The name is not unknown to me."

"I always forget what close attention you English give to Ireland."

"We've found it wise to do so. More than one plot has been launched from there."

"Nonsense, the Irish have far better things to do. It was just King Henry's gullibility that made him think we were a danger."

Hugh had been about to take another sip of wine. He put the cup down instead. "The late king was many things but no one ever described him as gullible. On the contrary, he was accounted the shrewdest and wiliest of monarchs ever to walk this earth."

Fionna shrugged. "Perhaps by English standards. At any rate, he did us much harm, so it is no wonder his heirs fear we will do the same to them."

"And will you?" Hugh asked softly. It was all well and good, this business about her coming to study. But her father was one of the most powerful chieftains in Ireland, a man who by any measure could not be taken lightly. Why would he send a daughter alone to a kingdom of enemies?

"What did you father think of your coming here?"

"He was against it, but I have always been my mother's child and he recognizes that. Besides, the final decision was mine."

"A respected chieftain who lets the women of his family make such choices for themselves? I find that hard to envision."

"And I suggest that says more about you than about me or mine. Now, if you have no objection, I would like to retire. It has been a long few days."

She stood. Hugh did the same. Across the graceful little table, they faced each other. "I suppose we're in for a bout of studied politeness," he said.

"As your mother's guest, I hardly see any alternative. Besides, I expect you will be very busy with your father."

She was right, of course, damn her. With the mystery of her identity solved, she was well and truly off-limits. A vision of her in the pool with him stabbed through his brain. He stifled a groan.

"Do let me show you to your quarters," he said, and rose, stained with the blood of battle, black armored, grim-faced—the perfect gentleman.

CHAPTER TEN

Fionna closed her eyes and opened them a moment later to sunshine and the chatter of starlings just outside her windows. No time at all seemed to have passed. Scarcely a breath separated evening tide from bright morning. She sat up and looked around uncertainly.

The room was not dissimilar from the one she had occupied at Castlerock, only larger and even more luxuriously furnished. As with the other, there was a fireplace, still a startlingly new replacement for the braziers and open fires that had always been common. The walls were whitewashed and hung with tapestries, there was glass in the windows, and the bed was hung with curtains of finest linen beautifully stitched with scenes of idyllic gardens. Everything smelled of soap and fragrant herbs.

As she slipped from the bed, the cool morning air made her shiver, but her discomfort did not last long. On a chest within easy reach was a robe of thick, soft wool. She put it on and went to poke up the fire. By the time she had finished, a servant was knocking on the door.

"Begging your pardon, milady," the young girl said when Fionna admitted her, "I just wanted to see if you'd awakened yet. Her ladyship said you were to sleep as late as you liked. I hope I didn't disturb you."

"No, you didn't, I was awake. Can you tell me the hour?"

"It's past matins. You must be hungry. Shall I bring your breakfast?"

Fionna allowed that she would like that. The young girl hurried off, apparently relieved to have something to do. It was evident that Fionna had been put in her care and that she intended to make a good job of it.

She returned swiftly with a tray, the information that her name was Bette, and further word that her ladyship was looking forward to seeing Fionna later in the day. Alianor was with her husband at the moment.

"How is the baron?" Fionna asked.

"Still weak, milady, although he'd never admit it. He insists on being up several hours each day, but it's clear that it tires him. Of course, after the wound he had, it's a wonder he can do anything."

"It was that grave?"

Bette nodded. "We all thought he would die. There wasn't a dry eye here when they came and we saw how bad it was. I can tell you I did more praying in a handful of days than I've done in my whole life, and I wasn't the only one. But praise heaven—and her ladyship—the tide was turned, and he's on the mend."

"Still, it will be awhile before he can get about as he's used to," Fionna said.

Taking clothes from the chest, Bette nodded. "You can be sure of that. If only the times weren't so uncertain—"

"You must forgive me but being from Ireland, I know little of circumstances here." This was something of an exaggeration but not entirely without truth. Besides, politics had never interested her overly much.

Bette seemed willing enough to instruct her. Nor did she hesitate to speak her mind.

"It's the king, milady. He wants to be as his father was, absolute ruler, but times have changed. No one has the confidence in King John that they had in King Henry. The barons are insisting on more rights for themselves—at least some of them are—and they're threatening to make war if the king doesn't give in."

"Civil war . . ."

Bette nodded, her face grim. "That's what his lordship fears may happen and what he was trying to prevent when those damnable cowards attacked him. Weak as he is now, there may be little he can do."

And therefore it would fall to Hugh to act in his father's stead. No wonder he was so suspicious of her and of the situation in general. And no wonder he had been so anxious to reach Glastonbury. The death of a beloved father would have been tragedy enough. But when it could lead to the ruination of a country—

"The baron is greatly respected," Fionna said.

"Oh, yes, milady. He's the one man the other barons might listen to. Without him—"

"Or his son."

"It will be up to young Hugh now." She laughed and put a hand to her mouth. "Oh, dear, I shouldn't have said that. No disrespect is meant. It's just that so many folks hereabouts have known him since he was born, even though he's a grown man and a great warrior now, he's still held in deep affection."

"There are worse things to be said of a man than he has the love of his people."

Bette nodded, wise beyond her years. "We hear stories of what it's like in other places but here we've truly been blessed. The baron has always been a good and kind ruler, and he's raised his sons to be the same."

"There are two more, aren't there?"

"That's right. One is off in the Holy Land—"

"On pilgrimage?"

"Well, no, not exactly. It's said he's gone to learn all manner of things. The other went north to visit a Viking friend of the baron's, and apparently they decided to go voyaging. Nothing's been heard from him in almost a year, but her ladyship doesn't seem worried, so I suppose it's all right."

Fionna did not have to ask why that would be the case. Even in the short time she had spent with Alianor, she had begun to understand why it had been so important to come to Glastonbury.

When she had eaten and was dressed, Fionna ventured downstairs. She had no idea what she should be doing, and no one seemed inclined to give her any direction. The great hall stood empty. A few dogs congregated near the main door, but all the activity seemed to be outside, as benefited such a full-blown spring day.

Near the barracks, men were practicing with lance and sword. They appeared good-natured, enjoying their work even as they went about it purposefully. No doubt each understood that skills kept sharp meant the difference between life and death.

Not far away, a blacksmith was at his forge. Several horses were penned nearby, waiting to be shod. Beneath a thatched overhang, several women had set up a loom and were busy at work, taking advantage of the pleasant day. A young girl hurried by, shooing a gaggle of ducks before her. They passed in front of a large shed where fabric was being boiled in dying vats.

All this was familiar to Fionna. She had seen similar scenes at her father's principle residence in Connaught many times. Although the architecture of the buildings was different, the people themselves had a reassuring familiarity to them. She had slept well the night before, probably because she simply no longer had any choice. All the same, she was vaguely aware of dreams that less than half remembered still made her blush.

Curious to learn all she could about her surroundings—and avoid her own wayward thoughts—she found a staircase leading to the top of one of the walls and climbed it. From there she could see the entire bailey. At a guess, more than a hundred people were at work. Considering all the others who must be below in the town and in the nearby fields, she guessed that Glastonbury might hold as many as a thousand souls. That made it a good-size town by any measure.

It was also a very prosperous one. During the brief ride to the castle, she had noticed that every building was well maintained, the roads were unusually clean, the people well fed and well dressed. England might be teetering toward chaos, but the good folk of Glastonbury did not seem affected. She wondered if they gave any credit for that to the abbey under construction on a nearby hill. From what she could see, it was an impressively large undertaking that looked to be about half finished.

She had just turned back to look at the bailey again when a horse and rider came through the main gate. Hugh. He was simply dressed in a plain tunic, without armor, but even from a distance there was no mistaking him. Her throat tightened, and she made a valiant—but fruitless—effort to look away.

Near the forge, he swung lithely out of the saddle and handed the reins to a boy who ran up. They exchanged a few words. The boy nodded eagerly and took the stallion off to a separate pen. The blacksmith himself, seeing what was about, came to speak with Hugh. After a few minutes, they parted, the smith to the forge, and Hugh in the direction of the castle wall from which Fionna watched.

He came straight to her. She had a choice of retreating—and hoping such ignominious behavior would not be seen—or standing her ground. She stood.

"A fair day," Hugh called, looking up at her. He shaded his eyes with his hand and smiled.

"Beautiful," she replied.

"Come down." When she hesitated, he added, "Please."

"Oh, well, if you put it that way—"

She climbed down, vividly aware of his eyes on her every step of the way. When she got to the bottom, he looked her up and down quite blatantly.

"You finally got a decent night's sleep."

"Is it that obvious?" she asked. Had she truly been so careworn?

"Yes," he replied, ever the diplomat. "My horse

threw a shoe and must be re-shod. In the meantime, I thought you might like to come for a walk."

A walk? Surely, this man upon whom so much depended had something better to do?

"Mother will be with Father for some time yet. He remains in more pain that he will admit, and if she isn't with him, he refuses to rest as he should."

"He sounds very stubborn," Fionna observed.

"That surprises you?"

"Not at all. I appreciate your offer, but you really don't have to entertain me."

"I thought of it as more informative than entertaining. There's an interesting story associated with the abbey."

He knew her too well, this proud, compelling man. Somewhere there was an Irish man or woman who could resist a story, but that person was not Fionna.

"What story?" she asked.

"Come with me and I'll tell it."

She went.

"The year before I was born," Hugh said as they walked down toward the town, "a curious event occurred. The abbey monks announced that they had found the bodies of King Arthur and his queen, Guinevere."

"That sounds like something monks would claim. Aren't they forever finding relics of one sort of another?"

"Possibly, but in this case the bodies were accompanied by an iron cross of very old design. Written on it were the words: *Hic iacent sepultus inclitus rex arturius in insula avalonia.*"

"Here lies buried the renowned King Arthur in the Isle of Avalon."

"Your Latin is excellent."

"Thank you," Fionna murmured. Her mind whirled. Could this possibly be true? If so, why had she not heard of it? "Do you believe it?"

"No," Hugh said promptly, "but the monks certainly did and after their abbot, a certain du Sully, was murdered and another monk killed, things settled down somewhat. Queen Eleanor learned of what had happened and took it upon herself to acknowledge the discovery as genuine. Money was raised for the building of a grand new abbey, an endeavor that is still underway."

"You said another monk was killed—?"

"What? Oh, yes, the monk who murdered du Sully and who had killed several other people earlier. He tried to make it look as though my mother was responsible, which got her accused of witchcraft, that almost led to a rebellion, and so on. Finally, the monk tried to kill Mother, so my father lopped off his head, and that was that. They got married shortly thereafter."

He tacked on the last part as though it somehow made sense of all the rest. Fionna couldn't quite see it that way. Women generally preferred posies to severed heads.

They were following the road that led down from the castle, through the town, and back up to the new abbey. People they passed smiled and nodded. No one appeared surprised to see Hugh walking like this, and certainly no one seemed intimidated in any way by his presence. Fionna remembered what Bette had said about many of Glastonbury's folk knowing him since he was born and holding him in affection. If she had needed proof of that, she had it.

The hill up to the abbey was steep. Hugh took her hand as they climbed it. The warm strength of his fingers wrapped around hers sent a tremor through Fionna. She so wanted to be immune to the feelings he evoked. Instead, they remained rawly powerful within her.

In Fionna's mind, great holiness was associated with the sacred wells of Ireland that had existed long before Padraic brought the news of Christianity. It existed, too, in the stone monoliths that were old beyond time, in mossy dells where horned cattle were still said to graze, and most importantly in the liquid light that bathed the land each day.

Here and there, holy monks had sought hidden places where they could devote themselves to God. But as was perhaps inevitable in so gregarious a country, people tended to congregate near such interesting men and women, simple churches were built, schooling began, and before anyone quite knew what was about, the local "hermit" was hard-pressed to find a stray moment of solitude.

What no one in Ireland seemed to feel a need for was great stone edifices that linked divine faith with earthly power. Therefore, the abbey under construction in Glastonbury was something new to her. It was already overly large to her eyes but by no means finished. Half-completed stone walls were surrounded by scaffolding. Raw stone lay in piles all about, waiting to be dressed. The clank of hammers and chisels all but drowned out the rhythmic chanting of monks at their prayers. Stone dust filled the air. The masons glanced up as they passed, several nodded to Hugh.

"I take it this is your family's benefice?" Fionna asked.

"We help support it but a great deal of the money came from the late Queen Eleanor. It was actually her idea to rebuild the abbey in grand style after the 'royal' bodies were supposedly found."

Hugh opened a high oak door studded with iron and stood aside so that Fionna could enter. After the bright day, the interior of the abbey was deeply shadowed. She had to wait several moments for her eyes to adjust. At the far end, behind the altar, a magnificent stained glass window held pride of place. Light flowing through it made the abbey appear to be set inside a jewel. By comparison, the altar itself was fairly simple, a slightly raised platform holding a stone-carved table. On either side, seated on wooden benches, hooded monks chanted their office. The air smelled of cut stone and incense. Fionna could still hear the clanking from just outside and wondered if the monks weren't perhaps praying for the day when construction would be over.

"Eleanor also commissioned that," Hugh said quietly. He pointed to the stark black marble sepulchre that stood in the center of the nave. "The remains are sealed in it."

"And the cross?"

"Also sealed in the stone beneath the altar."

"Very impressive." They were both whispering so as not to distract the monks. Of necessity given the clamor outside, their heads bent close together.

"If Eleanor believed the bodies were genuine," Fionna said, "why don't you?"

"I suppose because it's always been obvious to me that my parents didn't believe it. They were actually here when the bodies were found, and although they certainly haven't discouraged the veneration of Glastonbury as Arthur's burial place, they show no sign of taking it seriously."

"I wonder why not—" Her voice trailed off. There was one obvious reason why the baron and baroness did not believe that the black marble sepulchre held the bodies of the great Arthur and his queen—they knew that the bodies were actually buried elsewhere. But to have such knowledge would mean—

"Why did you come here?" Hugh asked.

She looked up at him, startled. The breeze outside had ruffled the thick ebony mane of his hair. His eyes, deepest blue, were still and watchful.

"You know why, to study with your mother."

"So you've both said."

"I can understand that you wouldn't believe me, but what prompts you to doubt the Lady Alianor?"

Without replying, he took Fionna's arm and led her back outside. They walked away from the abbey. The clamor of the workmen faded behind them. Looking out over the fertile fields that ran off toward the west, Hugh said, "I haven't spent very much time in Glastonbury in recent years. With my own lands, and also needing to be at court, I've been too busy. But coming here yesterday stirred up old memories."

He turned and looked at her directly. "I don't doubt my mother. For that matter, I don't doubt you when you say you are here to learn. It's more what isn't being said that troubles me."

"What isn't—?"

"I was born here. Even after years away, I know this place better than any on earth. Yet there is one part of it where I have rarely been."

The wind flattened his tunic against the powerful, contoured muscles of his chest. One hand lay in its accustomed place on the hilt of his sword. His voice—low and steady—wrapped round Fionna. The rest of the world seemed very far away. She shivered inwardly.

"Before her marriage, my mother lived on a small island in the midst of the lake not far from here. She still goes there from time to time."

"People live all sorts of places, and it's hardly unusual for them to want to return to somewhere they have thought of as home."

"The people hereabouts call her their Lady of the Lake."

"A pretty phrase."

"There was another Lady of the Lake who armed Arthur and who supposedly took him to the holy place of Avalon when he was dying."

"That's only a legend, although the monks do appear to have confirmed at least part of it. Arthur was buried here therefore in Glastonbury, in fact, this very part must have been Avalon."

Hugh nodded slowly. "So Queen Eleanor thought . . . or at least so she wanted others to believe."

"I don't see what possible benefit there would have been to her to make people believe that, if she herself didn't think it was true."

"Perhaps none," he conceded. "But I've always wondered about it, and something finally occurred to me this morning. If everyone believes a place has been found, that we know where it is, can go and see it for ourselves, then there's no point looking for it anymore or wondering about it, is there? Particularly, when it seems to be in the hands of the proper authorities, it becomes devoid of mystery and therefore no longer quite so interesting."

"I suppose . . ."

"Perhaps that was what Eleanor intended. For that matter, perhaps it's what was intended by whoever buried those bodies here to begin with."

Fionna cleared her throat a shade nervously. How was it that nature had not been content to make him merely handsome, powerful, and wealthy? He had to be intelligent as well?

"It seems as though your mind is seeing around all sorts of corners, including some that may not be there."

"I suppose—Why didn't it surprise you when I said my mother had been tried for witchcraft?"

"You mentioned it so quickly along with the other things, heads lopping off and all."

"I think you already knew."

"A woman who swallows paternoster peas in a trial by ordeal and survives is bound to get herself known," Fionna admitted.

His eyes crinkled around the corners. For a man with so many twisting, turning thoughts, he seemed oddly at ease.

"Even in far-off Ireland?"

"Not far off enough, if you ask me. Did your father

bring her to trial?" He wasn't the only one who could toss out awkward questions.

"Of course not!" The very idea seemed to astound Hugh. "He did everything he could to prevent it. At any rate, it all worked out in the end." His hand reached out, catching a strand of her hair loosened from its braid by the wind. He twined it around his long, lean fingers. "And now here you are . . . in Avalon."

"Avalon, as you call it, is a Christian abbey favored by the royal family and watched over by holy monks."

"Is it?"

His head lowered. Though he did not touch her, Fionna could not move . . . could not breathe . . . could not think.

His mouth brushed hers. She closed her eyes against the wave of sensation that threatened to pull her under. Her lips parted. She swayed toward him.

A raven shrieked. The sound shattered the stillness that had come unnoticed. Fionna stiffened, her eyes flew open. The workmen had laid down their tools and gone off to eat their midday meal. The monks had finished their prayers and gone to do the same.

They were alone, except for the raven turning against the sun.

And the young boy who looked anxiously from one to the other. "Begging your pardon, my lord, the baron is asking for you."

"I will attend him directly." The boy nodded and darted off.

"When all is said and done," Hugh observed, "life is mainly a series of interruptions."

Fionna stifled her disappointment. She would have

preferred to deny it altogether but she couldn't quite manage that. He was too tempting by far. She could not always count on being saved from her own willfulness.

They started down the hill. Fionna glanced back once, but the raven was gone and the abbey, slumbering in the spring sun, did not appear inclined to yield up any secrets.

CHAPTER ELEVEN

"Do you remember Gerard Huteuil?" Conan asked.

He and Hugh were in the baron's private chamber. A servant had left wine, cheese, meats and bread. The men were seated at their ease at the large table still strewn with all manner of messages, maps, and what looked to Hugh suspiciously like legal scribblings, much festooned with beribboned seals.

"One of the king's drinking friends?" he asked. "I've seen him around court."

"You won't anymore. He was killed a fortnight ago."

"Not exactly a loss."

"To you or me, but John was saddened. He's been having a rough time of it lately, and Huteuil getting knifed the way he did seemed to effect him deeply."

"Knifed? Let me guess, a tavern fight."

"No, actually it wasn't. He was on his way back to the Tower—John is in residence there at the moment—

and apparently he was jumped in an alley. The odd thing was that his purse wasn't cut, just his throat."

"I would imagine that a man like Huteuil had his share of enemies."

Conan shrugged. "Undoubtedly, however because of the murder, John canceled a meeting he'd promised to hold with several of the barons. They, in turn, took offense and left London. I went after them, hoping to soothe their ruffled feelings."

"You did?" Hugh was surprised. By virtue of the king's trust and his own power, Conan stood higher than any other noble save the man who sat on the throne itself. Why then would he go chasing after a few recalcitrant barons? "Are things truly so bad?"

"Unfortunately, they are. There is no doubt that John has abused the barons' patience one too many times. On the other hand, they sense weakness from his recent defeats and want to seize the opportunity to increase their own power."

"That was the situation when I left for Castlerock."

Conan nodded. Hugh thought his color looked slightly better than it had the previous day, but there was no avoiding the fact that his father still showed the effects of the wound that had almost killed him. "So it was, but with the king seemingly absorbed in personal matters, the barons are more inclined than ever before to strike for the advantage. Of course, if they do so, John will turn on them in fury. We will have civil war."

"They think he is too weak to fight back, and he isn't paying much attention to what they're about. Both are wrong, and their errors could cost the country much."

"Exactly. My own inability to meet with the barons undoubtedly has worsened the situation further.

They've had time to nurse their grievances and lay their plans."

"Then, it is reasonable to think that the attack on you was brought about by someone who wanted to prevent the possibility that you would mediate a peaceful settlement."

"That is what I think as well," Conan agreed. "I should be in London now."

"No," Hugh said flatly. "The journey alone could kill you, and once you got there, you would be worked to exhaustion and surrounded by plots."

Conan grimaced. "You sound like your mother."

"She is right and we both know it. I must go." Even as he spoke, Hugh felt a shock of awareness. He had never thought of what it would mean to take his father's place. The love between them made it impossible to contemplate such a thing. But now it seemed that he would have no choice.

"I don't presume that I could do as you would," he said quietly.

Conan's smile was the same Hugh remembered as a boy. "There is no reason why you should. You will do as you see best, and I have no doubt that will be all I could ever ask for."

Hugh's throat tightened. He looked away for a moment. "Thank you."

Conan nodded. He pulled forward one of the several stacks of parchment he had been studying earlier.

"Eustace Fitzneale is gathering forces on his lands. William deLongueville appears to be doing the same. The two met in Colchester six days ago. That does not bode well."

"Does the king know this?"

"He should, his information sources have always been at least as good as my own." Conan hesitated. "However, that may no longer be the case. The tide is turning against John at a rate that surprises even me. Men who a month ago would have felt it safer to keep his favor no matter what they thought of him may be deciding that it is no longer in their best interest."

"But if the barons get a free hand, they will apply it promptly to each other's throats."

"Exactly. What is needed is a balance. The king has committed excesses, taxing at will, ruining men who displeased him, ignoring the laws his own father put in place. There must be some means to prevent that. However, we cannot have anarchy."

Hugh took a deep breath. The task before him was beginning to appear truly monumental. Could he really hope to keep the king and his barons from war?

"First thing," Conan said, as though sensing his son's doubts, "is to bring John back to a more ordered state of mind. He is not a stupid man. When he is ruled by his wits instead of his passions, most of his decisions are less than terrible."

Hugh leaned back in his chair. He glanced out the high windows, over Glastonbury and the rolling fields beyond. It seemed like another world to the one he contemplated.

"What a ringing endorsement of our sovereign. Are we absolutely certain he should be salvaged?"

"Do you want a Fitzneale on the throne, a deLongueville, or someone like them?"

"No," Hugh said promptly. He looked at his father. "But they are not the only barons."

Something flitted behind Conan's eyes—emotion,

memory, Hugh couldn't say which. Quietly, he asked, "Do you aspire to the throne?"

"Me? No, of course not, I meant—"

"I know what you meant but I am asking you, if you could make a claim for the throne, would you do so?"

"It would mean civil war."

"All the same—"

Hugh hesitated. His father appeared serious. He truly wanted to know if Hugh could see himself—not Conan, but himself—on the throne of England.

"I have no wish to be king. Frankly, the job seems more trouble than it's worth."

The baron laughed, but his eyes remained watchful. "What about the temptation to do that job better than the way it's being done now? Put the country on a wiser course, that sort of thing?"

"No one gets to be king with that kind of thinking. One is either born to it or so possessed by ambition that nothing else matters. But the desire simply to do good—I don't believe that enters into it."

Conan sighed. "You are a cynic."

"I am a realist, and so are you. John held out against all his brothers, enduring their ridicule, their plots, everything. In the end, he triumphed simply by surviving longest, but what did it cost him? Does he have a single true friend? Does he trust anyone? Has he ever known love? Does he come now in the final years of his life to a place where he is respected and honored, or does he sense the vultures circling and know himself completely alone?"

Conan took a bit of bread but did not eat it. "You do have a way of clarifying a situation. All right, John is alone and besieged, but he is not finished yet. If the barons attack, he will fight and the result will be devastation."

"Therefore, a compromise must be reached."

"And for that—" Conan reached for the largest stack of parchments. He sighed with deep regret. "For that, the lawyers are needed."

Hugh's eyebrows rose. He looked genuinely alarmed. "The lawyers?"

"They have their uses. Several have been looking at various matters for me, searching through the endless records they've been keeping ever since the great King Henry raised them to such prominence, and going even farther back. I wonder if any scribe in this kingdom has ever thrown anything out. At any rate, they have one or two suggestions—"

"On the other hand, a good war can clear out a lot of debris."

"None of that. Read through this when you have the chance. But first, there is a great deal more we need to go over."

And so they did through the afternoon and far into the evening. Alianor came by twice, concerned that Conan was overdoing. But she realized the desperate importance of what was at hand and contented herself that he would rest later.

Finally, long after most of the castle slumbered, father and son concluded their discussion.

"I have told you everything I know," Conan said. "Every event, every personality, every alliance, and every rivalry. If I could possibly avoid putting this on you, I would, but I fear there is truly no alternative."

"You must stay here and recover. If whoever is behind this were to succeed in bringing about your death—" Hugh did not go on. He did not need to. His father understood full well what vengeance would follow his untimely demise.

"Someone must put the well-being of this country ahead of all else," Conan said. "It falls to you to do so." In the silence of the night, his voice rang with conviction. "When I was raised to the barony, a very pompous official in some office or other that the great Henry had created lectured me about the importance of selecting the proper crest. It would endure for generations, he said, *if* I were lucky, and it would stand as the symbol of my line before the world. When he learned that I had already made my choice, he was dismayed. He thought the hawk too simple, and as for the motto—"

"Honoris causo."

"For the sake of honor. I gather he didn't understand that at all."

"But we do," Hugh said.

The two men looked at each other.

"Yes," Conan said softly, "we do."

He lifted the pitcher of wine and refilled both their goblets. "One other thing . . ."

It was very late. Hugh was more than a little tired, but his father's tone brought him to full attention. "What is it?"

"I want you to take Fionna with you to London."

"In God's name, why? The last thing I need is a woman who robs me of even the semblance of reason and—" He broke off. His father was grinning broadly.

"That bad?" Conan asked, man-to-man.

"No," Hugh insisted, "not at all. I merely need to find myself some nice, accommodating woman and—"

"If you wanted that, you'd already have it. In fact, you have had it, over and over." He leaned back in his chair, lines of weariness etched around his mouth, but his humor intact all the same.

"Perhaps I should have insisted that you marry."

Hugh grinned. As he recalled, they'd had that conversation when he was about fifteen. Conan had brought up the subject of political alliances forged at the altar and sought to reassure his son that, having married for love himself, he would not force Hugh to do any different. Hugh, in turn, promised to do everything he possibly could to find the right woman, no matter how many he had to try in the process.

"Have I thanked you recently for not insisting?"

"No thanks are needed. All the same, I meant what I said. Take Fionna along. She saved you from ambush, and she could do so again. She's intelligent, perceptive, and brave. You could do worse than to have someone like that at your side."

"We're talking about the very real possibility of war," Hugh pointed out. "I don't want her involved in that."

"You're going to need help," Conan insisted. "You'd accept it from a man, wouldn't you? If one of your brothers was here, you'd take him along without a second thought. Don't try to wrap Fionna up and stick her away on a shelf somewhere just because you want her to be safe."

"If you were going back to London, would you allow Mother to accompany you?"

Conan sighed. "*Allow* your mother. That's an interesting concept, however, not one I've had much use for over the course of our marriage." He looked just a bit abashed. "I don't seem to have any difficulty ruling over our lands, however ruling over Alianor is another matter entirely."

Hugh nodded. That was exactly as he had always assumed. The church might say that women were subordinate to men and must obey them, and the law might agree, but there were always exceptions.

"All the same, I don't want Fionna to go."

"Yes you do," his father said. He spoke mildly enough but his certainty was unmistakable.

"Perhaps a part of me—" Hugh caught himself just as his father laughed out loud, hard enough to make him wince. "Let me put that differently, I can see that Fionna might be useful in certain ways. However, I will be too distracted by concern for her welfare."

"Very noble, but this is a purely pragmatic decision. I won't insist because it is your mission, after all. However, I strongly urge you not to be blinded by your own feelings."

"What about Mother's? Fionna is her student. I doubt she wants her to go traipsing off to London when she's only just arrived."

"On the contrary, I believe she would tell you exactly what I am."

"It seems the decision is not entirely mine, then."

"Yes it is," Conan insisted. "Just be sure you make the right one."

Hugh took his leave a few minutes later. His mother had come up again and looked at him pointedly. He needed no further encouragement. Rising at once, he begged her pardon, said good night to Conan, and withdrew. As he walked down the stone steps leading from their room, he thought of other nights when as a child sleeping in the chamber nearby, he had awakened sometimes from a nightmare. Their door had always been open to him and to his brothers. He remembered being hugged, tucked under covers, reassured, all the while feeling their love and strength surround him. As a child, he had flourished from such affection but had also thought it a natural part of the world. Only as a man did he realize how fortunate he had been—and still was.

He reached the floor below and hesitated. The room he used now was there. He was tired and needed to sleep, yet a certain restlessness kept him from seeking his bed. Instead, he continued on down two more floors, past the great hall to the lower level of the keep.

His footsteps echoed softly as he passed the iron-barred doors of cellars holding barrels of wine, flour, salt, dried and pickled meats, and precious spices. In a pinch, the castle could shelter—and feed—the entire population of the town for a month or more. Despite the hour, good smells still lingered in the vast, stone-arched kitchens. Hugh glanced in as he went by, seeing the same oak tables where the cooks worked and where, as a boy, he had sometimes sat, enjoying an extra custard or other treat slipped to him by indulgent servants. He also remembered warming himself before the fireplace, big enough to turn two hogs on spits side by side, and even helping to knead bread dough when he was very small in the large wooden troughs used for that purpose.

But most of all, he remembered the garden—

At the back of the keep, he opened a small door and stepped outside. The scent enveloped him immediately. He closed his eyes for a moment and breathed in the

fragrance of freshly turned earth, new-leafed trees, cro-
cuses, wildflowers, and even precious jasmine brought
from the East and replanted outside only a few days
before. Soon his mother's herbs would begin to appear
along the neat rows. She would tend them herself,
hours a day, and pick each at precisely the right time.
But she would also still go out into the glens and other
hidden places to find her tame plants' wild cousins,
whose potency she continued to trust more.

And she would go to her island, where he suspected
she grew those plants that could be deadly but which
could also heal when used by a master hand.

During the year of his convalescence, the small
garden had been Hugh's special place. He remembered
the hours spent there while just beyond the high garden
walls, he could hear the shouts of boys going about
their training. He had longed to be with them, yet there
was solace to be found in sitting under a tree reading to
himself, or listening to his mother's gentle voice as she
taught him the properties of a particular plant, or the
habits of one of the many birds who made the garden
their home.

As he grew in strength, he dared to climb an ancient
apple tree that spread its gnarled branches out to shade
some of the more delicate plants. In those branches, he
found a bluebird's nest and watched, holding himself
absolutely still, as the mother bird fed her hatchlings.
As he recalled the moment now, he believed it was
then that he finally believed what his own mother had
told him for months, he truly would recover.

The peace of the garden, and the memories it held,
soothed his weariness. He sat down on a nearby bench
and gazed up at the sky. The moon was almost full. Its

light dimmed the stars but left the world awash in shades of silver.

Not for the first time, he thought what a shame it was that so many people feared the dark. In a violent world, where any shadow could conceal danger, that was understandable enough. But even safe within Glastonbury Castle, there were few people who could wander about at night, and all of them were members of his own family. Aside from the guard dutifully standing watch on the battlements, no one stirred.

Or so he assumed. But as his gaze wandered absently around the moon-washed garden, he caught a flicker of movement near the apple tree. A moment later, a soft voice called out.

"I don't meant to startle you, but I thought I should mention that I was here."

Fionna. She stepped away from the shadow cast by the old tree and came toward him. In the moonlight, the fire of her hair was dimmed to a starry radiance. She moved, slim and graceful, through the night as though it belonged to her.

"I couldn't sleep," she said, "and the Lady Alianor showed me this place earlier, so I hoped she wouldn't mind if I came and sat awhile."

"I'm sure she wouldn't," Hugh murmured.

"Have you finished your discussion with the baron?"

He nodded, not taking his eyes from her. For just a moment, he understood the primal fear men had of such women who embodied power they could not share. Then the sensation was gone, and he was left to dwell merely on her beauty and his own obvious reaction to it.

He cleared his throat. "Yes, I have. I leave for London at first light."

She came closer to where he stood. He caught the scent of lilac that would not bloom for weeks yet. She was simply dressed in a robe and bliaut, her head uncovered, and the long braid of her hair lying over her shoulder. They were alone in the garden. He had only to reach out and—

"The Lady Alianor told me something of the situation. It sounds very bad."

"So I believe." His mouth twisted slightly. "But then I suppose the thought of civil war here does not bring you too much distress."

Her eyebrows arched. She looked at him with genuine surprise. "Why? Just because I am Irish doesn't mean I want to see English people suffer. Certain English leaders, perhaps, but not the people in general."

"Chief among those leaders would be King John?"

She hesitated. "We have no love of him, that's true, but he has actually tried to rein in those of his nobles who see Ireland as fodder for their ambitions."

"He married his daughter to an Irish chieftain."

"And a benighted marriage that's been but I suppose that if I had to choose John over some of his nobles, I'd have to say that the king is the lesser evil."

"Another ringing endorsement."

"What's that?"

"Nothing, only that my father said earlier that many of the king's decisions had been less than terrible."

Fionna laughed. "Poor John, what an epitaph that would be."

"Better than being known as a king whose reign ended in civil war."

Her smile faded. Gravely, she said, "That is true. Good luck in London. I hope—"

"Yes?"

"I hope you will be very careful."

The knowledge that she had some small concern for his well-being startled Hugh. He sensed that this strong-willed, proud woman did not change her opinion of someone easily, yet she appeared to have come to see him in a gentler light.

Or perhaps that was just because he was going away.

"I intended to speak with you before leaving," he said, "but as we are here now—" He paused, looking at her closely. The more time he spent with this woman, the better he got to know her, the more hotly he desired her. He would need all his skill and wits in London. The distraction she presented—

And yet, his father did have a point. She had been of use already and might well be again.

"It is entirely within your right to refuse," he said, "but I would be pleased if you would accompany me to London."

Had he suggested she fly to the moon, Fionna might have looked less startled. Her lips parted on a soft exclamation. She stared at him.

"For what purpose?"

She was blunt enough, he had to give her that. If he said he wanted her along as a bedmate, what would her reaction be? He decided he would rather not find out.

Besides, it wasn't true. At least not entirely.

"Something happened back on the road," he said, "when you saved us from ambush. I'm not sure what it was, and you don't seem to be, either. But if the situation arose again, I would prefer having such warning to not having it."

"I see—"

"As for matters of a more ... personal nature between us, I assure you that you will receive the same courtesy I would extend to any guest."

He was confident she would understand him. If there were any people on earth who honored the duties of hospitality more than the Irish, he had never heard of them. While he would never willfully harm any woman, the fact that Fionna had been invited to England by his mother—and that he was inviting her to London—laid a powerful obligation on him to guarantee her well-being.

She nodded slowly. A cloud moved over the moon. In the hushed darkness of the garden, Fionna's voice was low and soft.

"I will come with you."

CHAPTER TWELVE

And so to London.

They reached it by ship out of Weston-super-Mare, blessed by calm seas and fair wind. As Fionna watched the scattering of hamlets along the coast grow more frequent in number and finally begin to blur into the outskirts of the capital, she breathed a sigh of relief. The five days of travel had seemed interminable. Even as she was aware that the men were pressing themselves to the utmost, she wished they could somehow go even faster.

Hugh spoke barely a word to her, taking his turns at the oars and otherwise keeping his distance. She had mixed feelings about that—glad not to have to confront her desire for him yet at the same time missing his companionship.

At night, lying in the curtained partition set up for her on deck, she courted sleep every way that she knew. But her rest remained fragmentary, shot through with dreams that faded so quickly upon awakening that she could not catch hold of them even for a moment.

But now, finally, she could put all that aside and deal with the reality of London. She had heard about it, of course, but she had never thought to see the city. Now she stood, hands clasping the deck railing, and strained to miss nothing.

Directly ahead as the ship headed upriver, she could make out a bridge connecting the northern and southern banks. Beyond the bridge, it appeared that the river ran for some distance, then curved out of sight. To the south were marshes, woodlands, and some fairly large settlements. But by far most of the buildings were to the north. They passed a substantial-looking Norman church with a host of dependencies. She wondered if that was the hospital she had heard of dedicated to St. Katherine. Just beyond it Fionna glimpsed the city walls, and rising above them—

An immense fortified tower glinted in the sun. It dominated the river, commanding a clear view of anything approaching in either direction, and it dwarfed the city that appeared almost as an afterthought to it. This must then be the great Tower she had heard of, built first in wood by William the Conqueror to secure his control of the newly vanquished capital and later rebuilt in stone at royal command. In a land that had known few such fortifications, it must have come as both a terrible shock and a grim statement of the future facing Londoners.

She shielded her eyes, looking up at the four towers that rose above each corner. Banners waved from them. The king was in residence.

They did not slow their pace but sped on, passing

under the bridge toward the curve of the river. Just before the city walls ended, another substantial tower rose, not as large as the first but formidable all the same. Then it was gone. Fionna frowned. It seemed as though they had bypassed London. Once again, woodland and green fields appeared on both sides of the river with only a few hamlets to be seen. A smaller river emptied out into the Thames, which turned south. Just as suddenly as they had vanished, buildings reappeared directly to the west.

"Westminster," Hugh said. He had come up behind her so silently that Fionna did not realize it until he spoke. "My family's residence is there."

It seemed that the city lay in two parts with the space between them not yet filled in. What would prompt such a strange arrangement?

Almost as though he had read her thoughts, Hugh said, "A century and a half ago, the king then, Edward the Confessor, decided that he hated London but he still saw the need to be near to it. The marshes of the Westminster proved the perfect solution. He had them drained, built a palace and then an abbey. King John generally prefers to be here, as did his father. Most of the landed nobles have built their own residences in the area."

"But the king is at the Tower now," Fionna observed.

Hugh nodded. "In times of trouble, the Plantagenets have always headed for the higher ground. John will be grumbling at the discomfort, but he won't stray from there while the barons threaten war. Unless," he added softly, "it is to take the field."

"Is he still capable of that?" Fionna asked. "I thought his health diminished."

"Is that what they say in Ireland?"

"Some do," she admitted. At his continued silence, she added, "We can hardly be blamed for taking an interest in English affairs when you have proven so interested in ours."

He shrugged. "I suppose, but to answer your question, yes, I believe John is still fully capable of giving battle. He is the kind of man who would drive himself to his death rather than yield to an enemy."

She glanced up at him, seeing the grim set of his mouth and the carefully shuttered expression in his eyes. Their arrival in London clearly brought him no relief. On the contrary, he gave every sign of anticipating serious trouble.

"It sounds as though you admire the king," she said.

"He has been on the throne almost all my life. By all accounts, he isn't as good a ruler as his father or as bad a one as his brother Richard was before him. Richard may have been lionhearted, but he had whey for brains."

Despite herself, Fionna laughed. "What an awful description. He was unlamented, then?"

"By those who actually knew him save for his mother, Eleanor, who held him in unaccountable affection. Of course, the common people thought he was wonderful. He dazzled them."

"Poor John, to follow two such giants, his brilliant father and his dazzling brother."

"It couldn't have been easy," Hugh admitted. "But John has always had one quality in abundance, stubbornness. Unfortunately, that's exactly what could doom him now and the country with him."

Fionna drew her cloak more tightly around her. It was cool out on the river, almost cold. "Will he see you?"

Hugh looked surprised by the question. "Of course, he will. The challenge will be getting him to listen. Are you all right?"

The sudden change of subject caught her unawares. She hesitated. "I'm fine."

He was unconvinced. "I realize the journey has not been easy, but I thought you were resting enough and—"

"It isn't the journey," Fionna said quickly. "It is concern over what we will face here and whether I will be able to be of any real help to you."

Something moved behind his eyes. He reached out as though to touch her. But he stopped himself and said only, "It is not your responsibility to make this come out all right, it is mine. Don't forget that."

A moment later, the boatswain shouted. They were approaching a stone quay. Beyond it was a line of trees, and beyond them Fionna could make out a large, fortified residence surrounded by a wall and cleared land. People were running down toward them.

"Excuse me," Hugh said, and went to help his men tie up.

Ramps were slid into place, and the horses off-loaded first. Fionna followed, standing a little to one side as she watched the activity swirling all around. At least two dozen people had come from the house, men-at-arms and servants both. They greeted Hugh with what looked very much like relief. Questions flew about his father's well-being. He answered them all patiently. Once again, Fionna was impressed by the close connection between this proud, compelling man and the people who depended on him for their very lives.

And who were perhaps understandably curious about the woman he had brought with him to the stately house on the edge of the great river.

The surreptitious glances that flowed her way strongly suggested that Hugh wasn't in the habit of arriving with a woman in tow. Or if he was, he didn't usually go to the trouble of introducing her.

Drawing her forward, he said, "This is Mistress Fionna of Lough Gealach. I'm sure you will all make her welcome."

Two dozen pairs of eyes turned on her. Fionna held herself perfectly still. Although she found such scrutiny unpleasant, she wasn't about to show any kind of weakness. Instead, she forced herself to smile.

"I've never been to London before. It looks fascinating."

Two dozen smiles returned her own. Several of the older women, in particular, exchanged pleased nods.

"We've had a long journey," Hugh said. "Mistress Fionna needs to rest."

Feeling very much the delicate flower, Fionna allowed herself to be led up the path from the river, through a high stone wall, and into a residence that while smaller in scale than that in Glastonbury, was no less grand. Or any less defensible. As the gate shut behind her, she took a long, careful look around.

Guards stood watch on the walls and on the high towers at each corner of the stone building. They all appeared to be large, sharp-eyed men who took their duty seriously, and not because their lord was suddenly present. The great wheel of fortune was poised to spin. Lives hung in the balance, their own and many others.

"We will rest tonight," Hugh said as they passed into the great hall, "and I will send to the king tomorrow. Then we shall see what can be done." He glanced down at her. "I regret you will not encounter London for the first time under better circumstances. The city has a certain charm."

"If you say so," Fionna murmured. She was suddenly, almost overwhelmingly tired. Though it was barely evening, she could scarcely keep her eyes opened. Too much worry and too little sleep were finally taking their toll on her.

"This way," Hugh said, and guided her up a flight of stone steps that curved around and around until they ended finally at the top of a tower. A door gave way to yet another lovely chamber. Were there no end of them?

"Are there just endless rooms like this?" Fionna asked. "All filled with lovely things, always waiting for someone to come along?"

He gestured to the servant, who hurried in with fresh wood and water. When the man had done and gone, Hugh turned back to her.

"What's that?"

"Nothing, never mind, I'm rambling. What's that smell?" Her nose wrinkled.

"Smell? Oh, the river. It always smells like that. Well, except for when it smells worse."

"I didn't notice it on the ship."

"There was a breeze. You get used to it. London has

an . . . aroma all its own." As he spoke, he took hold of her shoulders and pushed her down gently until she was sitting on the side of the bed. He slipped off one of her shoes and began to remove the other.

Fionna blinked at him. "This is very improper."

"I've done it before."

"When?"

"At Castlerock. Do you have any idea how little rest you've had in the last fortnight?"

"I've never needed all that much sleep—" Her voice trailed off.

He smiled, set her other shoe aside, and stood up. She felt his eyes on her even through the fog of weariness that surrounded her. Eyes that were well shuttered.

"I, on the other hand," he said, "seem endowed with an abundance of energy." He turned and headed for the door. Over his shoulder, he said softly, "Good night, Fionna. Sleep well."

The door shut behind him. She was left alone with her thoughts. And before long with her dreams.

Hugh went downstairs to the great hall hung with his family's war banners. Most of his men knew the London residence well and had gone off to find sleeping places for themselves. They'd be back soon enough for the food the servants were hurrying to prepare.

A few had already wandered in and were seated at the long plank tables, drinking ale and talking quietly among themselves. They straightened up when Hugh entered, but he waved them back to their ease.

Peyton had a mug already filled for him. He handed it to Hugh, who took it gratefully.

"Anything new?" Hugh asked after he had drunk deeply.

"Several messages," the older man said, holding out a sheaf of parchment.

Hugh scanned them quickly. His face was grim. "DeCressey has joined the others. There are reports they are recruiting mercenaries in the lowlands."

Peyton snorted. "As though there weren't enough fighting men right here."

"Where's the money coming from?" Hugh asked, thinking out loud. "DeCressey, deLongueville, Fitzneale, they're all powerful men, but I wonder if they're financing this completely from their own pockets."

Peyton shrugged. No amount of treachery could possibly surprise him. "The French?"

"That's likely and if they're in it—" He shook his head, worried and disgusted at the same time. England would disintegrate in civil war and just as it did, the French would attack. It threatened to be Hastings all over again. The blood of William the Conqueror's invaders ran in Hugh's veins; he didn't much relish the idea of being on the other side this time.

"Stupid bastards," he muttered. "Can't they see what's happening?"

Peyton didn't answer. What was there to say? Every sensible man realized that human folly was the great engine of history.

Hugh called for parchment and pen. He wrote a quick message to his father, glad as always that he didn't have to resort to a scribe, then sent for the captain of the house guard. The man came within moments. He stood at attention, waiting as Hugh melted wax, allowed it to drip onto the folded parchment, then applied his seal ring.

"I want this in Glastonbury with all speed," he said, handing the message over. "Send three men and tell them to be wary. It is possible all our movements are being watched."

The captain nodded. He hurried out of the hall. Hugh heard him shouting orders.

More of his own men continued to come in and take their seats. The steward appeared and caught Hugh's eye. With a nod from him, the man hurried off to tell the servants they could begin serving supper.

The food and drink were, as always, excellent, but Hugh ate little and drank even less. His mind was too busy turning over what he would say to John on the morrow. The Plantagenets were notorious for their tempers, and John was no exception. In a rage, he would do anything conceivable, not matter how destructive or shortsighted. He had never made any secret that he despised most of his barons—Conan being the very large exception—and they in turn were fully aware of his contempt. If ever two sides itched to fight each other, it was these.

Somehow, he had to find a way to prevent that. And he had to do it while his thoughts kept trying to wander in the direction of the tower room and the woman sleeping there.

If she was sleeping.

He rose, summoned a servant, and spoke a few quiet orders. Moments later, the man followed him up the stairs. At the top, Hugh turned and took the tray he had carried, dismissing him.

Alone, he knocked on Fionna's door. There was no

reply. Slowly, he opened it and looked within. A tunic lay draped over the foot of the bed. She lay on her side, facing him, the covers pulled up to her shoulders. The slow rise and fall of her breath indicated she was deeply asleep.

Hugh sat the tray down on a nearby table. If she was hungry or thirsty enough, she would awaken and it would be there for her. A wry smile played around his mouth. The one woman he had genuinely desired for too long—and then to a degree he could never remember experiencing before—lay within his easy reach. Yet he could not touch her. The duties of hospitality extended to protecting her even from himself.

There was a joke in that somewhere, but he couldn't seem to find it.

He left the chamber abruptly. The sounds of laughter and the strum of a lute floated up the stairwell. His men were enjoying themselves, and they were not alone. Some of the castle women had joined them. No one who did not choose to need lie alone that night.

He certainly did not have to, and the knowledge of that did tempt him. It would be nothing short of sensible to find a pleasant woman and cool the heat in his blood. But even as the thought flitted through his mind, he knew it would not become reality. The idea of any woman, save for Fionna, was oddly distasteful to him.

How convenient it would be if a man could detach his conscience now and then, set it aside until he decided he had need of it again. In all likelihood, there were men like that. But he was not one of them.

John, on the other hand—

Hugh sighed. He turned away from the great hall and sought the relative quiet of the stable yard. The sweet scent of hay masked the familiar smell of the river. He found his favorite stallion in his stall, munching on oats and honey. The horse whinnied softly.

Without thought, Hugh plucked a currying brush off a peg on the wall and began grooming the big, graceful animal. He was a descendant of a stallion that had been Conan's favorite before Hugh was born and whose line still flourished. Without exception, they were fierce, courageous, yet calm and highly sensitive to their masters' moods.

The horse flicked his head back, eyeing Hugh. "Easy, Sirocco, good lad."

The horse calmed and went back to his oats. Hugh continued brushing him. It was hard to say who was calmed more by the steady, rhythmic motion—horse or man.

In the quiet of the gathering night, the man upon whose strength and skill the fate of a country might well rest gave his full attention to the grooming of his horse and let himself think of nothing else at all.

CHAPTER THIRTEEN

Fionna tried to breathe only through her mouth. That made the stench a little more bearable. It was all she could do to resist the urge to pull the edge of her cloak over her face and hide as deeply as she could beneath it.

This was London? The city Hugh had described as having a certain charm? How could a man she had come to feel so close to be so utterly and completely wrong?

This was a hellhole, a charnel house, the front door to purgatory. The stench alone was enough to send her reeling, but add to that the throngs of people coming and going in all directions, the earsplitting clamor, the buildings pressed so closely together as to admit little light, the roads clogged with waste, the animals . . . and on and on . . . Add all that together and it was everything she could do not to dig her heels into her horse's sides and break for the clean, open spaces that had to be out there somewhere, beyond this horror.

Charm?

She winced and forced herself to take a careful look around. They had ridden east from Westminister following a broad and actually pleasant road that passed the precincts of several religious orders before crossing the Fleet River. Shortly thereafter, they entered the city walls and everything changed.

From the west came the stink of tanneries that dumped their waste into the river. Ahead lay a warren of narrow streets filled with buildings shoved up one against the other, some leaning so far out over the road as to block almost all sunlight. Where there was any open space, it was filled with meager gardens, grazing animals, or garbage dumps.

From every building and from the streets themselves, smoke rose. It clung like a pall over the entire city, virtually concealing the sky. Although she could try to block out the worst of London's stench, Fionna had no choice but to breathe its air, even as she wondered how anyone endured it.

And then there were the people—men, women, children—all bustling about, pushing and shoving their way along, with every conversation a shouting match.

Her head hurt.

Off in the distance, down the densely packed lanes, she could glimpse the river. Long wharves ran beside it. Dozens of ships seemed to be loading or off-loading. She saw men she knew must be from the far reaches of the world—swarthy Greeks, golden Norse, and even a few with high cheekbones and eyes that slanted at the side who spoke a tongue incomprehensible to her.

Even mounted and surrounded by heavily armed men, Fionna could not help but find the city intimidating.

She was a child of the glen and vale who had come of age listening to the wind whisper between green hills and whose lullaby was the murmur of soft rain. To grow up instead in such a place as this, to consider it somehow normal— She could not comprehend any of that.

But she could grasp well enough what she was seeing. Even as they entered the city walls, she was vividly aware of the reaction of the people around them. There was surprise, then shock, a wave of fear, and hard upon it what could only be described as pleased excitement.

She saw the quick glances and hurried exchanges between passersby, saw how their eyes went to the hawk banner and from it, to Hugh itself. The deeper into London they went, the more distinct the murmur that grew around them.

"Castlerock."

It floated on many tongues, passed from ear to ear, a whisper at first swift and uncertain, but growing rapidly in conviction.

"Castlerock."

They knew him then, these Londoners. Knew him well by the look of it, for here and there, some dared to give him another name.

"Bold Hugh!"

Said with a smile of recognition and relief. Said right out loud, tossed in his direction like a bouquet.

That bouquet. Her eyes widened. Surely, that wasn't—

A daffodil flew by. It landed smack against Hugh's broad chest. He took hold of it and looked up at a window two stories above. A young woman hung out—so far out that Fionna thought she must surely topple to her death at any moment. What a shame that would be.

The woman grinned broadly and waved. "Bold Hugh," she called. "Welcome back!"

Others took up the cry. More flowers followed. Hugh and his men—and even Fionna once or twice, inadvertently—were pelted with posies of every description—dried, fresh, a few with dirt still clinging to them. That Londoners had such things at all astounded her. That they would choose to put them to such a use was bewildering.

That so many young women should have nothing better to do with their time than hang out of windows waving wildly . . . Perhaps it was better not to examine what she thought of that.

"Friendly people, Londoners," Hugh said.

"The female ones certainly are," Fionna said, and gave him a smile chipped from ice.

He drew back ever so slightly, then grinned. "Surely, you realize that this kind of welcome is a political statement."

"Nooo, I didn't know that. What exactly makes it political?"

"Civil wars are bad for business. Most business, at any rate. Therefore, Londoners disapprove of them on principle. They know by now that my father was trying to prevent war and that he was injured. So they're simply glad to see me here to take up his standard. That's all."

"Foolish me. I got the distinct impression that the welcome was more, shall we say, personal."

"Surely, you don't imagine that I could possibly know all these people."

"They certainly seem to know you. Bold Hugh, indeed."

He blushed. Beneath a night's growth of whiskers and shadowed by his war helmet, his cheeks actually reddened.

"It's just a nickname," he muttered.

"Please don't tell me how you got it."

He stared at her for a long moment but said nothing. Slowly, infuriatingly, he smiled.

"I am not jealous," she said.

His eyes widened in mock innocence. "Did I say you were?"

"No, but you thought it awfully loudly."

He chuckled, a deep-throated, wholehearted sound of male amusement. "Sweet Fionna, if you really knew what I was thinking, you wouldn't be jealous."

It was her turn to blush. She turned away quickly, hoping he would not see, but it was too late. He laughed again, in high good humor.

"Aside from this little matter, what do you think of London?"

Grudgingly, she answered, "It's . . . crowded."

"Is that all, nothing else?"

Fionna took a breath and let it out quickly. "It also smells."

"True enough, but there's so much more to the place than its stink. Once you've been here awhile, I'm sure you'll agree."

The thought horrified her. As calmly as she could, she asked, "How long do you think our stay will be?"

"That depends to a large extent on the king. I've

instructed Peyton to show you the markets. He's got a large purse and a general idea of what we could use, although anything you select will be fine. Don't stint. While you're doing that, I'll see what John has to say for himself."

He was sending her shopping. She didn't know whether to be amused or insulted.

"I should warn you that I am shamefully bad at chaffering."

"I don't think you'll be overcharged."

He didn't have to say more. From the grandest merchant to the smallest stall holder, no one would risk the wrath of Hugh of Castlerock by cheating the woman who spent his coin.

The guard divided. Half went with Hugh, the other half stayed. They closed ranks smoothly, completely surrounding Fionna. She could barely see in between them and could not crane her neck high enough to see over their heads at all.

Peyton drew rein beside her. He looked like a man riding to his doom. "His lordship suggested you might want to look at the cloth market first."

She took pity on him, and on herself. "We don't really have to do this, you know. I'd be perfectly content to return to Westminster."

The older man frowned. "His lordship said you would shop."

"I think he just meant it as an entertainment . . ."

Peyton clearly did not. He sat there, grim-faced and implacable, bound and determined to do his duty.

Fionna sighed. The sooner she went along, the sooner she'd be done.

"Then we shop," she said, and gestured for him to lead the way.

They came first to a stretch of road crowded with all manner of drapers. Two-story daub and wattle buildings crisscrossed with beams and whitewashed seemed to overflow with goods. Fionna glimpsed linen of every description, but also rare silks and velvets, ribbons, beads, needles of all sizes, threads of every conceivable hue, wools, embroidery frames, small looms, everything in any way connected with the getting and using of fabric.

Seeing her, merchants held up their choice items, shouting to get her attention.

"Fine silk, mistress, no better to be found!"

"The best linen, twenty thread to the inch, feel it for yourself!"

"Velvets fit for the king, milady . . ."

"From the Indies . . ."

"From the harems of a Moorish sultan . . ."

"Only the most discerning . . ."

"Milady!"

Slowly, Fionna dismounted. The men-at-arms kept everyone well away from her, but she could feel their stares, hear their shouts all pressing in. She moved forward and the guard moved as well, maintaining the cordon.

"Does his lordship really need cloth?" she asked Peyton. Surely, Lady Alianor took care of this sort of thing. Fionna would be willing to bet that the storerooms at Glastonbury held everything offered here and more.

"I think he wants to present something to the queen," the older man said.

That made sense. John had a much younger and reputedly very beautiful queen. Her favor might help sway her husband in the right direction. But how to choose something for a woman she knew almost nothing about and who surely had the first choice of anything she might desire?

Especially, how to do it when she was surrounded by very large, hard-faced men who wouldn't let anyone near her?

"Sir Peyton, would it be possible, do you think, for me to have just a little more room? I can't actually see much of anything."

His dark visage darkened further. Fionna thought he would refuse but with the utmost reluctance, her protector barked an order. The cordon opened, not much, but just enough.

Breathing a little more freely, Fionna stepped up to one of the stalls. She managed a smile for the round-faced woman who held up a length of cloth for her examination.

"Only beauty such as your own could do this justice, mistress. See how fine the weaving? You won't find anything else like it. The light goes right through."

And so it did. The fabric was virtually diaphanous. Fionna had never seen the like of it before, but she had heard of such things. Perhaps this was the woman who had mentioned the sultan and his harem. The cloth looked like something that would be useful in such a place.

"It isn't for . . . ," she said hastily, then stopped herself. A fair price for a gift for the queen might not be the same price it would have been if the purchase was intended for humbler hands.

"It isn't quite what I had in mind," she said instead, "but it is very lovely. How much is it—"

The woman quoted a price. Fionna did not have to pretend to be shocked. She rightly realized that she had no experience purchasing such luxury goods, but the amount the woman was asking would buy a nice piece of farmland in Ireland, several cows, a plow, and various other tools, seed, clothes, a horse, a wagon—

Fionna offered half.

"But, milady," the woman protested, "I cannot make a gift of it to you, much as I'd like to. I have my children to feed, after all." She dropped a tenth.

"Perhaps the sultan should have kept it," Fionna suggested, falling into the spirit of the moment. "It hardly seems worthwhile to send it all this way when it can't possibly be sold." She came up a tenth.

And so it went back and forth while Peyton kept a watchful eye and the guards loomed over all.

At last, they settled on a price that Fionna still thought was breathtakingly high but which didn't seem to please the woman over much.

"I do hope the queen likes it," Fionna said after Peyton had paid and they were walking away from the stall. She was shaken by the very thought of having spent so much money. What if Hugh objected?

"You did well, mistress," the older man said. He sounded surprised. "'Twas a fair price."

"Was it really? Good Lord, things cost the earth here and yet people have the coin to buy them. What manner of place is this?"

He shrugged. "London. The goldsmiths are down that way, if you'd like to go there."

"Surely, the queen should be happy enough with what we've already bought. Is more really necessary?"

Peyton hesitated. He appeared to be thinking things over. Finally, he said, "His lordship thought you might like to visit the scribers."

"Here, in the market?"

"There are some. Most are monks serving only their abbeys, but a few laymen have set up shop."

"I had no idea of that. People buy their wares?"

"Those who can afford it. His lordship has made several purchases."

She remembered Hugh telling her that he had found some books in the London market. How amazing. The only people she had ever known who copied books were monks who saw it as their holy duty and a few others privately employed by her mother.

"I would like very much to see this," she said.

Peyton escorted her back to her horse and saw her safely mounted, then took his place beside her. The guard moved out. Once again, the street cleared before them. She saw the people staring at her intently and realized that everyone must know that she had come with Bold Hugh. If they knew him as well as she suspected, they would realize full well that she was not a woman of his family. Had he married since his last visit to London, word of that assuredly would have spread. That left only one possibility—

Her back stiffened as she realized that in all likelihood people would assume she was Hugh of Castlerock's mistress. For that matter, the men guarding her probably assumed the same. A woman did not travel so freely with a man to whom she was not related unless they had a close, if unsanctioned, relationship.

The awareness of what people must be thinking made her acutely uncomfortable, especially when combined with her own complex feelings for the man to whom she was presumed to already belong. Not for the first time, she wished she could hide herself away.

It was all so different in Ireland, so quiet and predictable. At her mother's residence, the days flowed one into another with serene purpose. Even when she visited her father in Connaught, her position in his household assured that her privacy was always respected.

But here—

Here was only tumult and uncertainty.

She needed all her resolve to sit head erect, eyes forward, hands still on the reins of her mount, as they traversed yet another warren of narrow streets and crowded shops. As they came around a corner, one of the guardsmen's horses shoved aside a young man who had just emerged from a doorway. He was knocked back and cried out in protest.

"Bloody hell, who do you think—"

For a moment, his eyes met Fionna's. She saw a man about her own age, pale with wispy whiskers and red-rimmed eyes. A scribe, no doubt, for all that he was not a member of the clergy. She saw the anger in him, but saw, too, how quickly he assessed the situation. His gaze went to the hawk insignia emblazoned on the armor of the guards, then shifted to her. Abruptly, his expression changed, becoming both knowing and resigned.

He said nothing more, but stood aside, well out of their way.

"We are here," Peyton said. He appeared not to have

noticed the incident at all. Helping Fionna down, he said, "If you see nothing of interest, we can go elsewhere. London is full of markets."

That was exactly what she feared. It came to her that Hugh had given his trusted captain very precise directions. She was to be kept busy, amused, *and* indulged. Peyton had paid the cloth merchant from a pouch heavy with coin. Apparently, she was expected to spend a great deal.

Lowering her head, she ducked under the lintel of a shop door. Inside, an older man sat at a long counter near the windows, laboriously copying a book that sat on a stand before him. He looked up, startled, when she entered.

"Oh, hello," he said. "I'll be with you in just a moment."

Fionna nodded. She was content to wait. For the first time since coming to London, she smelled only good things—parchment, ink, leather, and glue. The aroma reminded her of home and filled her with a sweetly aching longing.

Peyton entered behind her. He snorted when he saw the scribe still working. The man looked up again, frowning at having his concentration broken. He, too, saw the hawk.

"Is Hugh here?" he asked pleasantly.

Peyton's eyebrows rose. "Hugh? You speak of the Lord of Castlerock, I presume."

The man smiled. He set down his pen and rose. "I most definitely do and pardon me if I have spoken poorly." He bowed in Fionna's direction. "Pardon me, dear lady, I did not mean to neglect you. I was just completing a rather difficult passage."

"There is no need to apologize," she assured him. "What book are you copying?"

"It is a story of the early Israelites and their escape from slavery in Egypt."

"Exodus," Fionna said. "I know this story but I thought few did. Are you—"

"A Hebrew? Yes, I am, although I was born right here in London." He bowed again and smiled at her. "My name is Joseph Wolcott and you are—?"

"Fionna. I come from Ireland. This is Sir Peyton—"

"Oh, I know the good knight," Joseph assured her. "He has come before with his lordship." The proper address deepened his smile. He was about to say something more when the door banged open behind them. The young man Fionna had noticed in the street appeared suddenly, the back of his neck held firmly in the grip of one of the men-at-arms.

"He insisted on entering, sir," the man explained to Peyton. Although his captive's face was turning red and his eyes beginning to bulge, the guard appeared unruffled. He was merely doing his job, and doing it easily at that.

"Let him go," Fionna said urgently.

The guard did not so much as glance her way. He waited for Peyton's response, which came with no more than a gesture. As the young man struggled to get his breath, Peyton said, "Who are you?"

"My son," Joseph said quietly. "His name is Samuel."

Fionna was horrified. The young man had every right to be where he was. Her guard had overreacted terribly.

"I'm so sorry," she said. "I believe they were given

rather stern orders to see to my safety, but that is no excuse—"

"On the contrary," Joseph said kindly. "We live in troubled times. I can well understand why they would go to any lengths to assure your well-being."

"Nonetheless, I truly regret—"

"It's all right," Samuel said. His voice was hoarse but otherwise he seemed to be recovering quickly. "My father is correct. They would be fools to take any chances." He managed a faint smile. "If I weren't something of a fool myself, I wouldn't have barged my way in here."

As grateful as she was for their understanding, Fionna was still troubled by what had happened. Turning to Peyton, she said, "Perhaps you would be good enough to wait outside."

He hesitated and for a moment she thought he intended to refuse, but finally he shrugged and left, taking the guard with him. In the silence that followed their departure, Joseph pulled out a stool and offered it to Fionna.

"Your courtesy is much appreciated," he said, "but Samuel really should have been more cautious. Everyone is on tenterhooks these days."

The younger man nodded. He rubbed his neck ruefully. "And will be until this whole stupid business is settled. I assume his lordship is here in London?"

Fionna nodded. "He has gone to see the king."

"And his father?" Joseph asked.

"Still in Glastonbury." She said nothing more, for as much as it was her instinct to like both men, she felt the situation called for discretion. As it turned out, that was unnecessary.

"Cowardly devils, whoever attacked him," Samuel said matter-of-factly. "There's all sorts of speculation about who they were working for. The betting favors deLongueville and his crew."

"Betting. . . ?" Surely, he was using that as a figure of speech.

Samuel nodded. "Didn't you know? Londoners will wager on anything. Ten days ago, the lay was five to one that the baron would die. Now it's even money."

"That's terrible! He risked his life to keep this country from war, and people are actually betting on his death?"

"Not that many people," Samuel said reasonably. "The odds came down as fast as they did because everyone wants to believe he will recover."

Fionna was not mollified but she supposed this was city ways and she would simply have to get used to it.

"You've upset her," Joseph said. He shot his son an reprimanding look and picked up a small bell. Barely had it rung once than a tiny woman peered out from behind a curtain on the back wall.

"What . . . ?"

"Don't pretend you've only just arrived, Miriam. You've been lurking there all along. This is my sister," he explained to Fionna. "She keeps one of the best kitchens in London, if I do say so myself."

Smiling at the praise, Miriam came forward. She looked Fionna up and down, and said, "You've missed too many meals."

"I eat very well," Fionna protested, caught by surprise.

Miriam sniffed, unimpressed. "On the run, catch-as-catch-can and skipped entirely because you've been tired of late."

"How could you possibly know that?"

The woman's smile spread to her bright hazel eyes. "The Irish aren't the only ones with sight, mistress. I've just made a very nice soup and you'd be pleased to have some."

Fionna would not dare refuse. Besides, she had eaten little at breakfast and was suddenly aware of hunger.

"We'll eat together," Joseph said. He held out the curtain and stood aside for Fionna to enter.

CHAPTER FOURTEEN

Hugh paused as the doors to the royal quarters closed behind him. He stood in the corridor and took a deep, calming breath. Around him, the busy life of the Tower went on, but he ignored it. He could think of nothing but his meeting with John.

Stubborn, infuriating, close-minded John.

John, who could think of nothing but his own cares, who just when his leadership was most vitally needed, seemed sunk in self-pity.

Hugh could have throttled him. Of course, that would have led to all sorts of problems, but since there was obviously going to be a civil war anyway, why not make it worth something?

His jaw clenched against a wave of pure disgust. Yes, his father had been right to send him to London to try to make peace. Yes, the goal of compromise between the king and his barons was important and honorable. But how in the name of all that was holy was he supposed to have any effect on a man who could not see beyond the end of his own royal nose?

Striding down the steps of the great keep, Hugh scarcely noticed the sharp, assessing glances that came his way. The Tower was very full. Those nobles still professing loyalty to John—for whatever that might be worth—were making it their business to be close to the center of things. They wanted to be able to jump at a moment's notice if the situation changed.

Proud, wily men, all tested many times in battle, never hesitant to protect what was theirs with unrestrained savagery, yet seeing the dark-visaged lord of Castlerock, they were careful to step out of his way. So black was his mood that he gave off waves of anger as he passed. In his wake, speculation began at once.

Had he split with the king? Was Castlerock going over to the rebels? Did he speak for his father as well? Would the great Baron of Glastonbury and Wyndham make a try for the throne? Would his son?

All this and more, Hugh heard in the tide of whispers washing behind him. He ignored it and went on, out into the stable yard, where he summoned a nervous, wide-eyed boy to find his mount.

"And be quick," he said, then tossed him a coin to soften the order.

The boy grabbed it on the fly, dared a grin, and ran off. He was back in moments with Sirocco.

"He kicked a groom, lord," the boy said pleasantly.

"Fool shouldn't have gotten in his way." He mounted, nodded to the lad, and rode out. The Tower gates still stood open, although they were heavily guarded. Hugh wondered how much longer guards would be enough. John might be determined to ignore his enemies, but he could hardly count on them to ignore him.

He rode with his guard back to Westminster. The people in the streets called out and waved as they had before, but his grim face told them what they did not want to know. As he passed, worldly, pragmatic Londoners looked at each other. Without words, they exchanged agreement on the situation. Shop owners chose the moment to begin examining the strength of shutters and doors. Several women snatched up small children and held them close. A pall spread over the city that had nothing whatsoever to do with the smoky fires.

Beyond the walls, the troupe of armed men moved at the gallop. They reached Westminster and went directly to the great house on the river.

Dismounting, Hugh said, "Double the guard on the walls and close the gates."

The captain paled slightly. He did not have to be told that the closing of the gates before dark was a certain sign that the Lord of Castlerock expected trouble. He might as well have issued a proclamation to that effect.

As the man ran to do his bidding, Peyton joined Hugh. He took one look at his young lord's face and did not ask how things had gone.

"Mistress Fionna does not particularly like to shop," he said instead.

"She doesn't?" It was a relief to concentrate on something other than the king.

"She bought some fabric after I did as you said and told her it was for the queen. Is it?"

"No, of course not. I'd have to be mad to encourage Isabelle. What else did she buy?"

"A book."

Hugh's eyes lightened. "From Joseph Wolcott?"

"He and his irascible son."

"I'm glad she met the Wolcotts, they're good sorts even if Samuel has an aversion to being told what to do. I wonder what book she bought."

He didn't expect Peyton to know and was merely grateful that Fionna had found some diversion in the city. Perhaps she would think better of London now. The urge to see her was sudden and sharp, but he delayed.

"I need to bathe . . . and to think. Ask Mistress Fionna to join me in an hour in the solar."

If Peyton thought it at all unseemly for the Lord of Castlerock to request a woman to attend him, rather than simply order her, he said nothing. Hugh took the steps to the keep two at a time. He had scarcely reached his chamber when servants staggered in with buckets of the water that was kept constantly hot for washing. He waited as they filled the oversize tub that he found vastly more comfortable than the cramped hip baths others used. When they had done and gone, he stripped off his clothes and with a sigh of relief stepped into the water.

Much as he would have liked to, he did not linger but spared a single thought for the old Roman bath at Castlerock before soaping himself vigorously. Half an hour later, washed and shaved, he used a silver-backed brush to put the thick ebony mane of his hair in as much order as it could stand. Plucking clothes from the chest at the foot of his bed, he began to dress.

Isabelle had teased him about his rejection of fashion. He frowned as he thought of that. Ornate velvets and silks were the fashion for the nobility. Men vied with each other in the elaborateness of their garb. Perhaps he had inherited his father's taste, for Hugh would have nothing to do with such frippery. He dressed plainly and favored darker colors. His shirt was of finely woven bleached flax, his tunic of lamb's wool dyed black and embroidered at the hem in intricate patterns of silver. Around his lean waist he buckled a leather belt that held his sword and scabbard, both far more serviceable than elaborate. His boots were also leather and so well made that he doubted he would see any reason to replace them for many years. Lastly, he fastened a short cloak held at the shoulders by the only real insignia of his rank—brooches set with bloodred rubies.

All this he did without thought. His appearance counted for nothing with him. He was simply glad to be clean again and to have put John out of his thoughts for at least a little time.

The solar was much like the one at Glastonbury, a large, cheerful room with high windows and many of the small touches that bespoke domesticity. Fionna was seated on a bench next to one of the windows. She was looking out at the river but turned quickly when she heard him come in.

She, too, had bathed and changed. Her fire-graced hair hung loosely down her back. She wore a simple tunic of pure white wool with an embroidered girdle around her waist.

"I hope your mother won't mind that I keep borrowing her clothes," she said.

"Not at all, but you shouldn't hesitate to have anything you'd like made for you. Peyton said you didn't buy much in the markets. The merchants will be happy to bring their wares here if you prefer."

When she hesitated, he suddenly realized the problem. "Fionna ... you're not reluctant about this because of the money, are you?"

She looked a little startled at his perceptiveness but nodded. "Well, yes, as a matter of fact, I am. I did bring money with me from Ireland, as well as plenty of clothes, but all that is gone. I can certainly send for more, but it will be some time before anything gets here."

"You really should not feel this way. As a guest . . ."

"But not a member of your family," she said with quiet firmness. "As much as I truly appreciate all the kindness I have received, I am well satisfied to borrow clothing rather than have more made. Besides," she added, "I can't get over what things cost here. I hope the queen appreciates her gift."

Hugh decided this was not the time to tell her that it was intended for Fionna herself. He'd wait until her stubborn pride softened a little.

"About the book . . ."

Her face lit up. She reached for a wrapped parcel on the bench. "I hope you will like it. Not being sure of your taste, I was concerned, but Master Wolcott says that if you don't want it, it can be returned."

Hugh put aside the cloth and looked down at the leather binding. He read the words embossed in gold. "*The Voyage of Bran,* being a tale of the ancient Irish.

"This is wonderful," he said with unfeigned enthusiasm. "How did Master Wolcott come by it?"

"He copied it from an original lent by an Irish monk who stopped in London late last year on his way back from the Continent. He lodged with Master Wolcott for several months, during which time the monk copied one of Master Wolcott's books while he copied his. The arrangement suited them both."

"I would imagine. Good for Joseph. He's always had an eye for what would interest me."

"But if it doesn't . . ."

"It does," he assured her gently. "I will enjoy reading it, and you are welcome to as well, of course, although I assume you already know the story."

She nodded. "It's a wonderful adventure. There are some who think it true."

He sat down on the bench beside her and put the book carefully aside. That she had bought a book about Ireland encouraged him. Perhaps she didn't think he was a totally unredeemable English oaf, after all.

"Did Joseph have anything else to say?"

"Only that he hopes you are successful. He believes John has done things that were wrong, but he doesn't trust the barons at all, saving you and your father. He fears that unless the tension can be eased quickly, ordinary people will suffer terribly."

Hugh nodded. "He's right, unfortunately."

"What did the king say to you?"

The anger he had managed to hold at bay welled up in him again. His disgust was palpable as he said, "He did not want to discuss his problems with deLongueville and the rest. There were more important matters on his mind."

"More important? How could that possibly be?"

"I would have to be John to explain that, and praise God, I am not. It seems there's been another murder."

Fionna shook her head, confused. "Another . . . ?"

Hugh leaned back against the cushions. It was very pleasant in the solar, quiet and private. It occurred to him that he liked sitting there with her, talking over the matters that troubled him. Of course, there were also other things he would have liked to do—

"I'm sorry," he said before his thoughts could march too firmly in that direction, "I should have remembered that you did not know. Before my father left London, a friend of the king's, one Gerard Huteuil, was knifed to death. John took it hard. Now it seems another friend of the king's has met an untimely end. His name was Bertrand Foucault. He fell into the Thames last night. They found his body this morning."

"That's terrible, but people do have accidents—"

"He fell in because someone plunged a knife into his back. John insists that it isn't coincidence. He says someone is killing his friends in order to hurt him."

"I would say more to hurt them."

"So would I but our king tends to see everything strictly from his own perspective. As he dwells on all this, the political situation does not concern him."

She lifted a pitcher set on a small table and poured a goblet of cider, offering it to him. He took it gratefully.

"Does the king have any idea who the killer could be?" she asked as she returned the pitcher to its place.

Hugh shrugged. "He flings accusations about—the barons, the French, Rome, various and sundry enemies he's made over the years, and so on and so forth. If he is to be believed, there is no shortage of suspects."

"But there is no actual evidence against any particular person?"

"None whatsoever nor is there likely to be. Huteuil

was buried, of course, and Foucault goes to his grave tomorrow. Neither man is going to tell us anything."

"It's a pity . . ." Fionna began.

"What is?"

"That no one thought to compare the knives that killed both men. That might have been a starting point to discover—"

"Who wielded them. Yes, I see what you mean. Knives are as common as cowpats, but I've never seen two that were completely alike . . . and most carry a maker's mark. I wonder . . ." He took another swallow of the cider. "It might still be possible to get hold of the knives."

"John would have to know, and then he might have expectations—"

"That I would find the murderer. Yes, I suppose he would but—"

"It might be best if you actually could. At least then he'd—"

"Be able to put his attention where it's really needed."

Fionna nodded.

They stared at one another. Uppermost in Hugh's mind was the realization of how easily their thoughts flowed together. This woman who was a fire in his blood was also a cool balm of reason in his mind.

"Would you have any actual experience in solving murders?" he asked.

She smiled ruefully. "I'm afraid not. You?"

"Not directly, but I've heard stories . . ."

"From the baron and Lady Alianor?" At his quizzical look, she explained, "You said a monk was killing people and then tried to kill her ladyship?"

"Yes, but my father discovered who was behind the murders just in time to stop him."

"I suppose it's a matter of intelligence and perseverance," Fionna said.

"And luck. Let's not forget that." He set down the goblet and stood, holding out his hand to her. "I'm starved. Will you dine with me?"

"In hall?"

"Under the circumstances, I think it would be best if the men saw me this evening."

She hesitated. He waited, giving her time. His fey Irish beauty was a woman of great reserve, almost shy. But she also had steely courage and a willingness to confront new challenges, even to relish them.

"All right," she said at last. "I would be very pleased to do so."

He smiled, suddenly carefree as a boy. John and all the rest of them be damned. He would seize a few hours for himself . . . and her.

But it was not to be. They reached the hall to news that a messenger from the king had arrived. The man approached in haste, dropped to one knee, and recited:

"His Majesty bids you join him for supper." His eyes strayed to Fionna and were instantly snatched back. "And he extends the invitation to your . . . guest."

CHAPTER FIFTEEN

Fionna stood on the water steps directly below the Tower and looked up. Seen by moonlight, the fortress that rose high above its surrounding walls was not inherently ugly. There was even a sort of grace to the four corner towers topped by pointed slate roofs and the arched windows gazing in her direction. Had the place not symbolized all she had been raised to hate and fear, she might even have found some good in it.

Behind her, Hugh gave instructions to the boatman to wait. He spoke quietly with the head of the guard accompanying them, then turned to take her arm.

"You can still change your mind," he said gently.

She managed a wan smile. "And when else will I have the chance to meet a king, even one as annoying as John?"

"It's an experience you could do without," Hugh replied. His face was grim. She knew how very close he had come to refusing the royal "invitation." Only the quiet touch of her hand on his arm and the silent message of her look had stopped him.

They both knew this was what she had come to London for, to be of help to him. She could hardly do that nestled safely away in his keep.

"I still don't like this," he said as they walked up the steps and across the quay.

"Perhaps the king has realized that he should have behaved better this afternoon."

Hugh snorted. "John has never found fault in his own actions. There were too many people in his family to do that for him. Now that they're gone, I think it's too late for him to acquire the habit of reflection."

"Then, he needs a conscience, even if it isn't his own."

He paused just outside the water side wicket gate, set small and almost unnoticeable in the vast walls, and looked at her. "Are you suggesting he borrow mine?"

"It seems to be in working order."

"Wait now, I believe that's the second compliment you've paid me."

Warmth curled through her. She could feel her cheeks darkening and was glad kind moonlight would conceal it. "Oh, well then, I'd better stop."

The gate opened. They stepped through, their guards following. One of the king's own lieutenants awaited them. He scowled at the heavily armed men.

"Weapons are forbidden in the king's presence."

Hugh's face remained impassive. "Since when? I was here scant hours ago, and that rule didn't seem to be in effect."

"Not for you, milord," the man said hurriedly. He

had some instinct for self-preservation. "For your guard. They must leave their arms with me."

Hugh laughed. He stood there in the bailey made bright by the moon and did not conceal his amusement. "I like a man with a sense of humor."

The lieutenant's discomfort mounted. "It is no joke."

"No," Hugh said, suddenly serious. To Fionna, his voice sounded like the drumbeat of doom. "It is no joke in these times to try to strip men of their weapons. Stand aside and be glad I do not take the attempt as an attack."

Behind him, his guard shifted closer. There was an avidness in their eyes that made Fionna's stomach plummet. These men would relish a fight.

It was their very eagerness that turned the tide. The guardsman hesitated, thought better of it, and spun on his heel. Hugh cocked an eyebrow. "I gather we are supposed to find our own way."

His men made low, grumbling noises of pleasure. Surrounded by them, virtually engulfed, Fionna reminded herself that these were indeed dangerous times. Only a fool went unprotected even to sup with the king. But walking across the bailey within a cordon of armed and armored men who towered over her, she couldn't help but wonder how it had come to this.

Ireland seemed very far away.

Men-at-arms on duty before the entrance to the keep made no attempt to stop them. Had they been so inclined, one look at the Lord of Castlerock and his companions was enough to dissuade them.

Barely had they stepped into the great hall than a steward rushed up. "My lord . . ." He glanced at Fionna enveloped in her cloak and frowned slightly.

"Mistress . . . His Majesty is expecting you. Please follow me."

"My men will wait nearby," Hugh directed.

"Yes, of course."

"And you will kindly feed them."

His men chuckled.

"Well," Hugh added.

The steward looked from him to the cordon. He swallowed quickly. "Yes, certainly, only the best. Now, if you would . . ."

Fionna smothered a sigh. She felt sorry for the poor fellow. It couldn't be easy never knowing who would be coming to supper or what their mood might be.

They were led down one corridor, along another, and up a flight of steps. At the top, the steward paused. "His Majesty preferred to dine privately tonight." He knocked on an ornately carved door.

A voice bade them enter. Fionna's first impression was surprise. She wasn't sure what she had expected, but it wasn't this. The room was small and furnished with pleasant simplicity. Several quite good but not new tapestries covered the walls. There was no fireplace but copper braziers filled with charcoal provided warmth against the spring night and tall candelabras holding white tapers cast a soft light. A large table was set for three.

The steward bowed low. A man turned from the window. He was of medium height with a narrow face and dark, somewhat lank hair. His eyes were large and well-set, and filled with frank curiosity. They swept over Fionna.

"So this is the lady who has London on its ear." He

smiled and came to her, holding out a hand. "Welcome, my dear. It's very kind of you to come."

Fionna darted a quick glance at Hugh. Surely, this couldn't be John? This courteous, even pleasant man?

"And you, Castlerock," he continued, "scowling again . . . or is it still? Welcome. Do sit. They're having venison in hall tonight, but I seem to recall the Irish have a fondness for salmon. I hope that's right." He looked at Fionna.

"Perfectly, sire," she said, and smiled.

John beamed at her. He took her elbow very properly and guided her over to the table. With a conspiratorial nod, he said, "We must do what we can to improve poor Hugh's mood, don't you think?"

"I believe he's merely worried, sire."

"Poor" Hugh made a sound deep in his throat, but he took his seat. Servants hastened to pour wine, but when the food was brought out, John waved them away.

"I do believe we can deal with a deceased fish. Off with you."

There was a quick rustle, the soft thud of the door closing, and they were alone with the king. John pushed the sleeves of his saffron-hued tunic back and eyed the salmon.

"I loved fishing when I was a boy, couldn't get enough of it. You've splendid fishing in Ireland, don't you?"

Before Fionna could reply, Hugh stepped in. "Might I ask how you know Mistress Fionna is Irish, sire?"

John began serving the salmon quite deftly. "Nice sauce with this, made with peppercorns, I believe. You mean aside from that lovely Irish lilt? Because I heard all about her, man. The chief business of London is gossip. Surely, you've realized that?"

He handed Fionna her plate with a kindly look. "You've certainly livened things up, my dear, and don't think I fail to appreciate it. It's been far too grim around here lately. Londoners love a story almost as much as you Irish, and you're a good one. The extraordinary beauty possessed of a loveliness to eclipse mere mortals, guarded jealously by the great Lord of Castlerock himself."

"That's terribly exaggerated, sire," Fionna ventured.

"No," Hugh said, interrupted yet again. "It isn't, especially the jealous part." He eyed John with a directness that might not have been thought entirely appropriate between sovereign and subject.

The king laughed. "Bold Hugh is reminding me of my checkered reputation. I am said to have a dreadful weakness for beautiful women. There is some truth to that, however, were I to pursue every female I am accused of lusting after, I would never have time to rule."

He finished with the salmon and sat down. Looking directly at Hugh, he said, "And make no mistake, fond though I am of the ladies, they are no substitute for a throne."

"Then it might be wise," Hugh said, "to consider what it will take to safeguard that throne."

John sighed. He took a bite of the salmon, swallowed and nodded. "Excellent as always. You are as blunt as your father, although time has tempered him somewhat. Are you also as clever?"

"There's only one way to find out, isn't there?"

"Set you to negotiate with the barons and risk a

kingdom in the process?" John shook his head. "No, I don't think so, at least not yet." He set down his knife. "Two men who were my friends have died by violence in a fortnight, both within the shadow of this very Tower. I realize you give that no particular importance, but I do."

Hugh began to speak, but John waved him to silence. "If there is one thing I have learned over the turbulent years, it is to trust my instincts. Right now they are telling me that there is something to these murders. I want to know what it is."

"They may yet be no more than coincidence," Hugh said.

"I know, but if they aren't—" John did not complete the thought. It was clear enough. If a murderer was striking at the friends of the king, how long would it be before he would be tempted to raise his sights?

"I would need full cooperation from everyone, including those at court," Hugh said.

If John was startled by Hugh's apparent willingness to consider a matter he had dismissed earlier, the king didn't show it. "You shall have my warrant to do as you see best, within the confines of the investigation, of course."

"Of course."

Fionna looked from one man to the other over the rim of her wine goblet. She still had difficulty believing that she was privy to such a discussion, but she was there and she needed to do her best to understand it.

John was more intelligent than she had expected, and vastly more clever. She suspected the numbers of people who had underestimated this shrewd, patient man were legion. Even now, in what might well be the gravest crisis of his reign, he was insisting that Hugh prove himself before he would trust him.

Solve the murders and the king might—just might—allow Hugh to represent him with the barons. Fail to solve them and . . .

"Enough of such sorry matters," the king said. "Let us speak of more pleasant things. Ireland, for instance. Is it as lovely as everyone claims?"

"Oh, no," Fionna said promptly. "It is a poor land, very rocky, with no good rivers or harbors. The people are a surly lot, uncooperative in the extreme. The weather is dreadful. Really, the place has nothing whatsoever to recommend it."

John looked at her with unalloyed delight. "A quick wit and the courage to use it. Excellent." As though there were only the two of them in the room, he added, "You know he's had trouble finding a woman who could hold his interest more than a month or two. I expect he's damned glad you came along."

Hugh coughed. More precisely, he seemed to be choking. John reached over and patted him on the back solicitously. The king's humor seemed to be improving by the moment.

Fionna sighed. Did everyone in London assume she was Hugh's mistress? But then, why shouldn't they when the Lord of Castlerock himself did nothing to discourage the idea? He brought her to London, surrounded her with guards, sent her off to the markets to spend his gold, and gave every indication of considering her very much his own.

A part of her resented all that tremendously, but seated there in the tower chamber, watching this proud, compelling man try to bring his king to accept what must be, she could no longer deny the overwhelming yearning she felt for Hugh of Castlerock. She could barely remember that she had seen him as an enemy, or even merely as a warrior. He was a person to her now—a leader and protector of his people, a loyal and loving son, and a companion with whom she had talked, laughed, and shared comfortable silences.

And with whom she would also share danger.

Life offered no promises. The times were dire, and there were no assurances that both of them—or either, for that matter—would survive. Even if they did, the tide of events might well take them from each other.

"Wouldn't you agree, my dear?" John asked.

Fionna looked up, startled. She had lost the train of the conversation. "I'm sorry . . ."

He smiled indulgently. "I was just saying that the queen would welcome a new face. She dislikes the Tower with its few amusements. Perhaps, you would like to visit with her tomorrow."

Fionna looked to Hugh, but before he could speak, John said, "Now, now, none of that. It doesn't do to let him control your every action. Next thing, he'll be taking you for granted. Besides, you want to come, don't you? You're curious."

Hugh shrugged. He left it in Fionna's hands.

John was right, she was curious. Indeed, curiosity all but consumed her. The only court she had ever known was her father's, and by comparison to this, it seemed simple in the extreme. Here she sensed wheels within wheels, stratagems hooked to deceptions, a great knot of ruses, artifices, and schemes twining one upon the other endlessly.

"I'd love to come," she said, and took another hasty sip of wine.

The candles burned down to pools of transparent wax and sputtering wicks. Off in the great hall, the musicians drooped their heads, songs stilled. The servants crept to their rest. Peace, such as it could ever be, sank over the Tower.

Hugh and Fionna took their leave. The king saw them off with the pleased smile of a good host. "Come in the morning for the warrant," he said to Hugh. To Fionna, he added, "And to visit the queen."

Their guards seemed the only people left awake in the hall. But once outside, Fionna saw the ranks of men-at-arms watching on the Tower walls. John might not wish to talk about his troubles with the barons—not just yet, at any rate—but he nonetheless appeared fully aware of them.

The boatman jerked to alertness as they came down the water steps. Hugh handed Fionna into the skiff and took his place beside her. At this hour, there was no traffic on the river. They reached Westminster without incident.

The night air was soft on Fionna's face as they disembarked. Only the guards standing watch just as others were at the Tower disturbed what was otherwise a peaceful scene.

"It must be my imagination," she said as she and Hugh crossed the bailey. Torches burned brightly, dispelling the shadows that would otherwise have lurked in every corner. No chances were being taken.

"What is?" he asked.

"The worst of the smell seems to be gone."

He smiled down at her. "I hate to tell you this, but you're getting used to it."

"I couldn't be."

"London is a very seductive city. She beckons you in, challenges you to love her, then doesn't let you go."

Fionna wrinkled her nose. "Sounds more like some of the spiders I used to watch in my mother's house. The big ones are all female, you know, and the poor males—"

"I don't think I want to hear this. You did very well, you know."

His praise warmed her. She tried not to think about it too much. "The king was not at all what I expected."

"He was on his best behavior," Hugh admitted.

"I wonder why?"

"I wondered about that myself. Either he simply had a chance to think things over or . . ."

"Or what?"

"Or he genuinely wanted to meet you. Remember, he is Eleanor's son. He grew up with the example of a woman who always seemed to know exactly what to do and the moment to do it. Even Isabella, for all her posturing, has intelligence and cunning. When the crunch comes, he may find it easier to rely on a woman."

"But he doesn't even know me," Fionna protested. "And besides, I'm Irish."

"Now, how could John possibly overlook that?"

She knew he was teasing her and wasn't sure what to make of it. It was late; she should have felt tired, but a strange, bright energy flowed through her. She thought again of what had occurred to her earlier—how very precarious it all was. How easily life could round a corner and be gone.

They walked up the stone steps to her room together. At the door, both stopped. Fionna looked at him uncertainly.

"I am glad I was able to go with you," she said.

His voice was low and slightly roughened. "So am I." He reached out a hand and gently stroked the curve of her cheek. "Fionna . . . ?"

That was all, just her name said in the shadowed dark by this man who had plucked her from the sea and hurtled her into a maelstrom of emotions.

And there, quite suddenly, in the hushed quiet of the great stronghold, it was all so very simple.

Her hand caught his. She rose, graceful and lithe, and touched her mouth to his.

CHAPTER SIXTEEN

Firelight glinted off the tapestry-hung walls, shone dully along the high wooden posts of the great bed, vanished within the folds of the ornately embroidered canopy and curtains.

Firelight caressed bare skin revealed as clothes were cast aside, tumbling in a heap onto the stone floor, falling softly amid low murmurs.

Firelight . . .

Fionna shivered, not with cold but with intense pleasure. Hugh's hands, the palms callused by long years of holding rein and sword, cupped her breasts, his thumbs rubbing leisurely over her nipples. The sensation was almost painfully exquisite. She took a long, deep breath and wondered how much longer her knees would hold.

Never had the gulf between knowledge and experience seemed so wide. She had known, in a distant sort of way, that she was capable of such sensations. But never had she realized what they would actually mean.

She reached out, her fingertips stroking the broad, powerfully muscled width of his chest. Was there no softness at all to this man? He seemed carved from granite, hard, unyielding, so utterly different from herself.

So fascinatingly different . . .

His hands slid down her back, pushing her robe to her hips and below. His lips found the pulse beating in her throat and lingered there.

Fionna moaned. She clung to him as the world threatened to dissolve. He made a harsh sound and lifted her. A few quick strides took them to the bed.

For a moment, he stood over her, naked and unrestrained, and raked her with his eyes. She resisted the impulse to cover herself but looked at him instead, savoring every perfectly formed sinew and contour of his magnificent body.

Hugh smiled. He came down on top of her, his weight held on steely arms. His thigh, honed rock hard by years in the saddle, slipped between her own.

"You are," he murmured as his mouth trailed fire from the cleft between her breasts down to the softly rounded curve of her abdomen, "perfection."

Her hands tangled in his hair, urging him back to her. Their lips clung, devouring, one breath, one soul. She twisted beneath him, unable to get enough of him. He caught her hands in one of his.

"Easy . . . we have all night . . ."

She could not bear this all night, or even much longer. She would die from it before long. Her eyes narrowed to glowing slits, her breath soft and fast. "Please . . ."

His tongue circled a nipple, coaxing it to taut

firmness before taking it into his mouth and suckling her. Wet, hot pleasure tore through her. She gasped and tried to break free of his hold, but he would not let her.

"Wait . . ." he said, a deep growl of sound that enveloped her, and stroked the satiny flesh of her inner thighs, coming ever higher . . .

At his touch, Fionna cried out. Every muscle in her body tightened. She bit down hard on her lower lip and tasted a tiny droplet of blood. Hugh released her. He grasped her legs, spread them wide and entered her.

His first thrust was slow and long. She was aware of only the smallest instant of discomfort and then it was gone, replaced by an exquisitely voluptuous sensation that grew and grew with each farther stroke.

He withdrew almost entirely, and she was bereft. Her hips rose, drawing his back. They moved as one, locked in a dark, deep passion, joined by firelight and night wind as time hung suspended and the world faded to nothing.

An owl, returning from the hunt to nest in the eaves outside the tower windows, paused a moment. The soft, ecstatic cry of a woman, followed by the deep, primal groan of a man faded away out over the river. There was only silence.

Hugh woke to the gray light of predawn and a vague sense of disorientation. Accustomed to being fully alert at a moment's notice, he lay on his back, looking up at the canopy, and struggled to order his thoughts.

It did not take long. Memory crystallized with stunning clarity. Instantly, his body hardened. He stifled a groan, part rueful, part resigned, and gazed at the woman curled next to him.

Fionna slept deeply. Her hair, unbraided the night before, curled around his arm. There was a tiny frown between her brows.

Without thought, he touched his lips just there. She stirred slightly. A soft smile lifted the corners of her mouth, but she did not wake.

It was just as well. He had no idea exactly what he would say to her, or she to him, for that matter. In all truth, he didn't think either of them could claim that what had happened was a surprise. But that still gave him no assurances about how she would feel by morning's light.

He left the bed, wrapped a fur throw loosely around himself, and poked up the coals still simmering in the braziers. It was then that his eyes fell on the book she had bought from Joseph Wolcott. At Hugh's insistence, she'd been reading it first. But now he felt stirred to take a look for himself.

It was either that or find some excuse to wake her. The temptation was immense, but he reminded himself of how badly she needed rest. To the best of his knowledge, no man had ever died from exercising a little self-control. Or perhaps the cases were just hushed up.

With a sigh for the wanderings of his own thoughts, he settled in a chair and drew the book to him. He meant only to take a look at it, then wash and break fast with his men in hall, if Fionna had not awakened by then . . .

But the story proved more enthralling than he'd expected. He slipped into it easily, reading of the woman who came to the hero, Bran, in a vision and described to him the wonders of her world beyond the sea.

And so the hero set sail, along with his boon companions, and had many adventures along the way until they came to the Island of Women. There they were met with gracious hospitality, their every desire fulfilled in a magical kingdom of contentment.

But all the while . . .

There was a sound behind him. With the instinct of a warrior, he turned. Fionna was sitting up in the bed, looking at him. Her eyes were wide and thoughtful.

"Good morning," she said.

To his great relief, she sounded perfectly calm. Had she appeared remorseful, he was not sure how he would have reacted.

"Good morning," he replied, and stood, coming over to the bed. Full day was upon them now. Light flowing through the high windows revealed her lips slightly swollen, a reddening of the delicate skin near the curve of her breasts, just above the covers she clutched, and the glorious tangle of her hair like fire broke wild from the hearth.

He slid his fingers through the silken strands. She made no effort to draw back but sat very still, as though contemplating his touch. After a few moments, she looked up and smiled.

"Forgive me, but I have absolutely no idea of the etiquette in these situations. Is it horribly rude to mention that I'm famished?"

These situations. There was a vaguely casual note to that, as though this was all somehow normal.

"Not at all," he said coolly, and sat down on the edge of the bed. Slipping a hand around her waist, he drew her close. The covers fell away. Her naked breasts moved against his chest. He wrapped the fur throw around them both and buried his head in her throat.

She moaned, a sharp, almost plaintive sound that jerked him upright.

"Are you hurt?" The very thought stabbed through him.

She took his meaning and flushed. "Oh, no . . . I'm not . . . it's just that—"

"What then?"

"Just feeling a bit overwhelmed, I'm afraid. But please don't be concerned. I'm sure I'll be fine."

He sat back and took a long look at her. She was undoubtedly pale, and she seemed to be having some difficulty meeting his eyes. A surge of protectiveness tore through him, and with it came honesty.

"I've never lain with a virgin before," he said. "I tried to be careful but . . ."

She put a finger to his mouth, stilling him. "You were, truly. And more . . ." Her smile was slow and pure, infinitely female. "I'm not hurt, I swear it. But this is all so new, and I didn't quite realize how . . ." The smile deepened. "How impressed I'd be."

"Impressed?"

"Oh, yes, most definitely impressed."

Hugh cleared his throat. The feeling that he was ten feet tall and could move mountains would pass, no doubt, but it was undeniably pleasant all the same.

He set her back carefully in the bed and tucked the covers up around her. "I'd better see about something to eat . . ." He could feel her gaze on him as he walked to the door. That, too, was pleasant.

He was just beginning to wonder how late they could arrive at the Tower without annoying John unduly when footsteps rang just outside the room. In a single, fluid movement, Hugh dropped the fur throw and unsheathed the sword left near the bed. He did it without the flicker of a thought, a lifetime's training surging to the fore.

Behind him, Fionna gasped softly. There was a quick, sharp knock. Hugh flung open the door and stood back.

Peyton froze. He looked from one to the other. With admirable aplomb, he said, "Your pardon, my lord. I tried everywhere else I thought you might be. There is a message from the king. He summons you at all speed."

Hugh lowered the sword. "That had better be because the barons are coming over the Tower walls," he grumbled.

"If they are, they're finding a queer way to do it. There's been another murder."

Hugh and Fionna exchanged a look. "Who this time?" he asked.

"One Robert Pearse. I gather he was something of a scholar. He and the king played chess together."

Hugh went very still. He slid his sword back into the scabbard but did not set it down. "I know Robert Pearse. He is . . . was a good man. How did he die?"

"He was knifed."

"Like the others," Fionna murmured.

"Tell the messenger we will be down directly," Hugh said. "And tell the cook to send something up quickly."

There was no time left . . . not for dalliance, or passion, or even dreams of what might be. Nothing remained save a dark, keening wind deep in his soul.

* * *

John saw them in the same private chamber where they had supped scant hours before. He was pale and unshaven, his manner distracted.

"Why poor Robert?" he asked, plucking at the sleeve of his tunic. "A decent soul, no vices save for chess, and surely that doesn't count."

Hugh stood by the windows. He gazed unseeingly at the river. "Pearse was a friend?"

The king nodded. He gave a harsh laugh. "As close a one as I have had. He never asked for anything, save a good game. I offered him lands years ago, but he said no; he preferred to stay as he was."

Then the dead man had been a true rarity, Hugh thought. Intelligent but without ambition, content with what he had and wanting nothing more. How did such a man manage to get a knife in his back?

"I suppose there is still a chance this is all coincidence," Hugh said, but even to his own ears, he sounded skeptical.

"Do you know how many people have been murdered in London in the last fortnight?" the king asked. Before either could reply, he went on, "I didn't, either, and it wasn't easy to find out, but as best I can gather, the number is five. Five murders: one of a woman killed by her drunken husband, one man killed over a gambling debt, and three others all well-known to me. It is not a coincidence."

"Why would anyone want to kill your friends?" Fionna asked. "What would the point be?"

The king looked at her as though perhaps she wasn't as intelligent as he'd thought. "To hurt me, of course."

"But if you're the real target, why not just kill you

and be done with it? I realize you have many guards, but any man can be gotten to if the killer wants it badly enough."

Hugh inhaled sharply. John sighed. "That's the Irish for you. Not happy with a king? Do him in. It's that kind of thinking that's caused you people so much trouble."

"With all respect, Your Majesty, it's actually you English who have—"

"Never mind about that," Hugh said hastily. "We will need to determine if these three men had anything else in common besides their friendship with Your Majesty. Did they, for instance, share any business dealings? Is there any possibility that they were attracted to the same woman? Could they have somehow offended the same person sufficiently to make him—whoever he might be—want to kill them?"

"I don't see how," John said. "Gerard and Bertrand might have had dealings together. They were both good-natured wastrels, but Robert was different."

"Nonetheless," Hugh insisted, "it will bear looking at. You mentioned a warrant . . ."

John picked up a parchment lying on the table. It was already signed and emblazoned with the royal seal. "Here it is. The usual—acting in the name of the king, all subjects charged with full aid and assistance, no hindrance, you know the sort of thing."

As he handed it to Hugh, he added, "I want this ended quickly, Castlerock. It has not escaped my notice—or, I hope, yours—that the killings are come more closely together. It is possible that I may actually have to pay some attention to the barons before too long, and I don't want to be distracted while I'm doing it."

That was progress of a sort, Hugh supposed. Fionna said as much when they had taken their leave from the king and were walking back down toward the great hall.

"At least he seems willing to admit that the barons are a problem," she said.

"The barons are on the verge of all-out war. I would hope the king would at least see that as worthy of his notice."

"Is there any possible link to the murders?"

Hugh stopped. In the light streaming through the high stone windows that fronted on the river, he said, "I've been thinking about that, but it just doesn't fit. DeLongueville and the others are the kind of men who would just as soon charge straight through a wall as try to go around it."

"Not given to subtlety?"

"Lord, no. I can't imagine them bothering with this sort of thing." He was silent for a moment, looking at her. No one else was nearby. They moved together as one, their bodies flowing together, clinging, stealing a moment from the greedy world.

Her mouth was sweet, warm, and welcoming. He kissed her long and deeply, wishing it could go on and on, and knowing that it could not. The pleasure was intense but bittersweet. With great reluctance, he raised his head but did not let go. They held each other as much for comfort as passion.

"The queen will be expecting you," Hugh said at length.

Fionna nodded. "Then, I suppose I must go." She

took a small step back. "Any words to the wise before I meet my first queen?"

"Why do I suddenly fear I am throwing a lamb to the wolves?"

Her eyes crinkled with amusement. "Are Isabella and her ladies that bad? Well, then, let them be. I am no lamb."

"Even so," he said, having deep reservations about letting her anywhere near John's consort, "I don't think—"

"Hush," she said, and softened it with a smile. "Let me see if I can allay your fears. The queen and her ladies are beautiful, pampered, and vain. Their gossip is incessant and frequently malicious. They have a penchant for using weak-minded men, sometimes merely for their own amusement, occasionally for more serious purposes. Is that about it?"

"You learned all this in Connaught?" He was thinking of her father's court and wondering how much time she had spent there.

"No, I learned it at my mother's knee. There is another way to look at all this, you know. These women, whatever the material comforts of their lives, are sold into marriage to virtual strangers who can treat them any way they like, including beating and even killing them. They bear children at appalling risk to their lives. They are told from tenderest childhood that everything done to them is justified because of the sin of Eve, for which they must constantly make amends. And if they dare to try to have any say about decisions that may destroy their own futures and those of their children, they are treated as criminals. Under such circumstances, it isn't surprising that women employ all sorts of wiles and subterfuges to survive."

Hugh listened calmly. When she was done, he said, "All very true, and unfortunate; however, I'll be interested to hear what you say after you've actually met Isabella."

That, at least, gave her pause. While she was thinking it over, he added, "A pleasure you'll have to delay. I'm going to take a look at Robert Pearse's body, and Foucault's as well, if I can. Do you want to come?"

She hesitated. "Let's see, dead bodies or the queen . . . dead bodies or the queen . . ."

"Dead bodies," he said, and steered her down the corridor.

CHAPTER SEVENTEEN

Robert Pearse, or what had been him, was laid out on a stone slab in a small building adjacent to the hospital of St. Katherine. The complex of church, nunnery, and several buildings for the care of the sick and dying lay just outside the city walls, adjacent to the Tower. It was watched over by the Prior Martin de Coureville, who despite his Norman name, looked Saxon born.

His slender face, pale-eyed and topped by a sheaf of wheat-hued hair, was somber as he eyed the dead man.

"One blow, I believe," de Coureville said. "To the back just to the right of the spine. He may have been dead before he hit the ground."

"Where exactly was he found?" Hugh asked.

Beside him, Fionna tugged her cloak a little closer and tried not to shiver. They were in the cellars of the main hospital. The air was cold and damp, and held the unmistakable smell of death.

"Right at the end of Woodruff Lane, within sight of the Tower."

"Was the knife recovered?"

The prior shook his head. "I have not seen it. It is possible someone removed it before he was brought in or—"

"Or the killer did," Hugh finished. "Another man was killed two nights ago. His name was Foucault. Would you know anything about him?"

"Indeed, he is being buried from here today. He, too, was knifed, but again, we have no weapon."

"Were the wounds similar?" Fionna asked.

The prior looked startled, but he recovered quickly. All the same, he addressed his reply to Hugh, not to her.

"Both men were knifed in the back, and both died at once. Apart from that—" He shrugged. "I suppose they could be linked."

Hugh did not comment, but he did say, "Another man died a fortnight ago, Gerard Huteuil. Was he also brought here?"

"Huteuil . . . no, I don't recall that. Generally speaking, we care for the dead who have no kin to claim them. When we were asked to look after Foucault and now Pearse, the request was made in the king's name. I gather neither man attended one of our many churches with any regularity, hence our instructions to bury them from here."

"Then, I can assume Huteuil had relatives in London who saw to his interment whether he attended a particular church or not?"

De Coureville nodded. "I would say so, yes. If you like, I can make inquiries and try to locate the priest who officiated."

"I would appreciate that," Hugh said. "Thank you.

I would also like to see Pearse's and Foucault's belongings."

"Of course, this way—"

As the two men went to leave the cell, Fionna held back. Very softly, she said, "I would like to see the wound."

The prior's face was a mask of shock and outrage. "My lord . . . ?"

"That is a good idea," Hugh said smoothly. "I should have thought of it myself. If you would be so kind as to help me turn him—?"

It was clear that there was nothing de Coureville wanted to do less, but he could not refuse the king's representative. Grimly, he did as Hugh bid. Even so, he did not conceal his extreme distaste when Fionna bent near to get a better look. When she removed the brooch holding her cloak in place and used the pin to delicately probe the wound, the prior went ashen.

"My lord, how can you permit—?"

"That's enough," Hugh said, silencing him. He waited patiently until Fionna was done.

She straightened and nodded. "You might also wish to view the body of Foucault, my lord."

They did so, although there appeared a risk that the prior would not survive it. By the time they were done, veins were bulging on the sides of his forehead. At last, they also examined the victims' clothing and belongings, although there was little enough to see. Both men had worn perfectly ordinary garments. Foucault had a few coins in his pouch, nothing more. Pearse had been carrying an ink box and quill, again unsurprisingly. Everything was consistent with each man's life and the manner of his death.

De Coureville saw them out with palpable relief. He still could not bring himself to look at Fionna.

As they walked back together toward the Tower, Hugh said, "If he'd fainted, would you have been able to revive him?"

"The good prior? Oh, I suppose, but think what a marvelous tale he's been given. He can dine out on it for months."

"Nice for him. Did you see anything interesting? They looked like standard knife wounds to me."

"Forgive me if I don't know what that means. I haven't spent my life learning how to chop people up. The wounds are indeed similar, as the prior said. In fact, I would go further and say they are almost identical. They appear to be of equal depth and width, and at the same angle. There is an excellent chance they were made by the same knife, one about eight inches long and two inches wide. Oh, yes, the killer is left-handed and probably taller than either victim."

Hugh stopped in mid-step. He looked at her in astonishment. "How could you possibly know that?"

"The height because of the downward angle of the blows. In addition, each veers slightly to the right, indicating that it came from the left, therefore from a left hand."

"You said you'd never done this sort of thing before."

She shrugged. "It's merely common sense. I could draw a sketch of the possible weapon, if you would like."

"Please," he said, very courteously, as though she had offered to sing him a song. "Oh, and thank you for not suggesting we dig Huteuil up to take a look at his wound. That really would have finished the prior."

"How on earth did you know I considered it?"

He smiled. "Common sense."

"Two weeks is too long. The body—"

"I know. Do you feel ready for Isabella now?"

"I suppose . . . oh, no!"

Hugh's hand went to his sword hilt. "What's wrong?"

"We forgot to bring the fabric for her."

"The fabric . . ."

"That I bought in the market yesterday. That beautiful, insanely expensive cloth. I completely forgot . . ."

Hugh released the sword. "It's not for her."

"I don't—"

"It's for you. I told Peyton if you hesitated to buy what you liked, to tell you it was for the queen." He smiled and dropped a quick kiss on her upturned lips.

"But I can't possibly . . . it was too . . ."

"Besides, it will look vastly better on you than it ever would on Isabella."

And that, it seemed, was that, although it did not escape Fionna's notice that he referred to the queen with a certain familiarity. A short time later, she had cause to remember that and to wonder just how well Bold Hugh knew his sovereign's wife.

"The Irishwoman," the queen said. "Do come in, my dear. His Majesty told me you would be coming by." She smiled charmingly, revealing the twin dimples on either side of her perfectly formed mouth. Gathered around her like gaily colored butterflies, her ladies also smiled prettily even as their eyes bored into Fionna like so many steel-tipped drill bits.

She took a deep breath, composed herself, and stepped into the royal solar. With a graceful curtsy, she said, "Thank you, Your Majesty. It is very kind of you to receive me."

"Not at all," Isabella said. She patted a stool next to her. "You have come from Glastonbury, I hear. How is the dear baron?"

"Much improved, but still in need of rest and care. Lady Alianor needed all her skill to save him."

Eyes the exact shade of cornflower blue narrowed ever so slightly. Fionna watched with something close to fascination as Isabella pouted sweetly. The queen was in her late twenties, of below medium height, and slender except for the swell of her generous bosom. Her hair was golden, her skin alabaster, her features exquisite, her every gesture the epitome of feminine grace. She looked more like a man's imagining of the perfect woman rather than an actual flesh-and-blood person. Fionna found her quite extraordinary.

"Poor Alianor, this must have been so dreadful for her," Isabella said. "I simply cannot imagine how I would feel if anything like that ever happened to my own dear lord."

Her ladies fluttered soothingly. "Never say . . . dear lady . . . not think . . ."

The queen silenced them with the merest flicker of a finger. She looked again at the stool, pointedly.

Fionna sat. She was beginning to wish that she had suggested digging up Huteuil after all. How bad could that have been compared to this?

"Are you related to the baron and his lady?" Isabella asked.

"No, my lady, I am not."

"But you are traveling with Hu— with Castlerock?"

"Yes, my lady."

The queen exchanged a knowing smile with her ladies. They tittered appreciatively.

"Dear Hugh . . . so bold. You do know that is what he's called, don't you? Bold Hugh."

More tittering.

"Actually, Your Majesty, as I recall that is what they were shouting from a good many windows and rooftops when he marched into London yesterday."

Isabella's smile appeared just the smallest bit strained. "He is popular, isn't he?"

"Extremely so, it appears. I gather his skill in battle is surpassed only by his sense of honor."

"Or by his skill in the bedchamber," one of the ladies said. The others giggled, slanting glances at Fionna.

Sold into marriage. Blamed for the sin of Eve. Suffering in childbed. She really had to try to remember all that.

"Now, now, ladies," Isabella said, "we don't want to shock our visitor. I suppose this is all very different from Ireland, isn't it?"

"In some respects," Fionna said. "Certainly, I have never been anyplace like London. But when all is said and done, I suspect people are much the same everywhere."

"Really?" The queen looked amused. "You actually believe that people raised to rule are anything at all like those born to root about in the mud?"

Fionna waited for the general hilarity to subside.

Patiently, she said, "I have no idea why anyone is born into a particular situation, whatever it may be. But in Ireland, those who lead don't necessarily do so because of their birth. They have to earn the people's trust."

"Thank heavens we're in England!" another of the ladies said, followed by more laughter.

Fionna waited for it to subside. Quietly, she said, "No ruler survives without trust." She looked directly at the queen. "None."

Isabella's smile vanished, as though it had never been. She raised her head imperiously. "Leave us."

For a moment, Fionna thought she was being dismissed. So did the ladies. It took that long for them to realize it was their departure the queen intended.

They went in a flurry of brightly hued garments, wide-eyed amazement, and whispers. When the door had closed behind them, Isabella groaned.

"Thank God, I couldn't have stood that another moment."

She stood up, plucked off the circlet of gold that held the veil over her hair, and dropped it onto a table. "Damn thing's too tight."

"My lady . . ." What had just happened? Something had changed—drastically.

"There's some quite good wine. Will you join me?"

"Yes . . . I suppose . . . thank you."

The queen filled two goblets and handed one to Fionna. She smiled and suddenly looked far younger than her years, almost like the twelve-year-old girl seized from her betrothed and married to a king.

"How is Hugh? This must be awfully difficult for him."

"Fine . . . worried about his father, of course, but . . ."

"He adores Conan, as he should. The man's absolutely extraordinary. I could cheerfully hate Alianor if she weren't so utterly nice. Besides, what would be the point? I truly don't think the baron has noticed another woman since Eleanor sent him off to Glastonbury these many years ago."

"They do seem very devoted but—"

"Like father, like son, it is said. Is he in love with you?"

Fionna put her wine down hastily before she spilled it. "L-love . . ."

"Oh, dear, you are new at this, aren't you? I should have guessed. Look, it's really very simple. Hugh is one of those tender, fierce sort of men who imagine they're invulnerable to all sorts of things. He knows love exists because he's seen it between his parents, but he's convinced himself that was some sort of fluke. Of course, any woman worth her salt knew he was absolutely ripe for the same sort of thing himself. So what I'm asking is: are you it?"

"I just came to help . . . I mean . . ."

Isabella looked incredulous. "You're not saying that you haven't been to bed with him?"

At her heated blush, the queen laughed. "Thank heavens. What a waste that would have been. Did you grow up in a convent?"

"*He* asked me that," Fionna said. From some hidden source, her composure reasserted itself. "No, I did not. But I did grow up in my mother's house, and she taught me that matters between men and women were private."

"Oh, dear, I've had my wrist slapped. Never mind. Enjoy him and, if you don't mind a word of advice, keep him if you can. Men like that don't come by very often. Now, then . . ."

The queen resumed her seat, sipped her wine, and said, "Do you think my husband is going to lose his throne?"

Huteuil. Definitely, she should have opted for Huteuil.

"I don't know," Fionna said. "The situation is very difficult."

"But there is a real possibility?"

It was on the tip of Fionna's tongue to say that the queen really ought to ask Hugh about all this. He was far better informed than herself. Then she considered whether she really wanted the man in whose arms she had lain the night before to be closeted with this beauty who sang his praises so unabashedly.

"The barons are massing troops," she said.

"Including mercenaries from the lowlands," the queen added. "What a mess."

"The king has angered a great many."

"Of course he has; he's the king. That's what they do. But what does anyone seriously believe is the alternative? Give control to the barons and the country will be ripped apart."

"There has to be a compromise."

Isabella's eyes widened. "Compromise? Kings don't compromise. Did the great Henry ever compromise? Did Richard? John won't do what his father and brother never did. How could anyone expect him to?"

"He may not have a choice," Fionna said quietly. "The wars in France . . ."

"Went badly, yes, I know, and the taxes were undoubtedly too high, but none of that makes the barons even the tiniest bit more trustworthy, or more capable of ruling this country. My son . . ."

"Is very young. Were the worst to happen now, do you seriously think he would have any chance of gaining the throne?"

Isabella took a long shuddering breath. Almost to herself, she said, "I have never understood why John felt compelled to try to be like his father and brothers. It would have been quite enough for him to simply be himself."

"They waged great wars and won new lands, so he felt he had to do the same?"

"Yes, but there was more. He said if you didn't show that you were strong enough to be on the top of the heap, you would be pulled back into it and devoured."

"What a horrible idea."

"But perfectly correct. That's exactly what it's like. Furthermore, I don't believe for a moment that it's any different in Ireland. If your father appeared weak before his people, how long would he last."

"What do you know of my father?" Fionna asked.

Isabella's smile returned, if a bit strained. "Did you really think I allowed you to come here today without having any idea of who you really are? For that matter, did you really think John didn't know? He made inquiries as soon as he heard about the beauty who rode into London with Hugh of Castlerock. It didn't take long to find out who you are."

"But I don't see how—"

"Ships put into London from Ireland all the time. There were men who had heard about your coming here and were willing enough to talk about it."

Fionna's sigh was pure chagrin. "It never fails to amaze me what people will speak of."

"A daughter of the clan chieftain of Connaught being sent to England? That's hardly an ordinary matter."

"Did they also say why I had come?"

"That was rather garbled," Isabella admitted.

"In other words, they did not."

"Why have you come?"

"To study with the Lady Alianor. My mother is a great healer, but she felt I could learn even more in Glastonbury."

"I see . . ." the queen said slowly. "I have heard stories about the Lady Alianor from time to time, but I have never known how much to believe them."

When Fionna said nothing, Isabella went on. "She was tried as a witch."

"And acquitted by ordeal."

"Do you think that settled the matter in people's minds?"

"Perhaps not, but I imagine her marriage shortly thereafter to the Baron of Wyndham and Glastonbury ended most of the speculation, if not all."

"True enough. John enjoys a good bit of gossip as much as the next person, but he's always made it clear that where dear Alianor and her husband are concerned, discretion was the watchword."

"Very sensible of him."

The queen reached over and refilled both their goblets. Fionna noticed a slight sheen of perspiration on her forehead. For all her apparent calmness, Isabella radiated tension.

"I am very worried for my son," she said, and raised

her eyes, meeting Fionna's. "There is nothing I would not do—nothing whatsoever—to protect him."

"He is fortunate to have such a mother."

"I have prayed until my knees are swollen, paid for thousands of masses, donated money to every church in London and beyond—"

"All very admirable, Your Majesty."

"Yet I wonder if it is enough. What if I am . . ." She hesitated briefly. "What if I am looking to the wrong quarter for help?"

Fionna frowned slightly. She didn't understand what the queen meant. "If you mean should you be trying to counsel your husband—"

"Good lord, of course not. He can be brought around on certain matters readily enough but not anything of this magnitude. No, I meant if prayers to God don't work—"

A jolt of pure shock stiffened Fionna in every bone and sinew. She had to be mistaken. "Majesty . . ."

"I'm not asking you to tell me anything," the Queen said hastily. "I really wouldn't want to know. But it is possible to conjure the help of—"

Fionna stood. With all the dignity she could muster, she said, "I do not serve the Devil, Majesty. Indeed, I know nothing of him. If you are curious, ask your priests. They invented him."

She was trembling as she left the solar. By the time she reached the hall, she was afraid she would vomit. Bile burned the back of her throat. To be thought capable of—

A man stepped in front of her suddenly. He was tall and strongly built, in his fifties, dark-haired with a

Norman look. His garb, so much as Fionna could notice, marked him as noble.

"Are you ill, mistress?" he asked.

"No, I . . ."

"Sit down." With matter-of-fact firmness, he urged her onto a seat beside one of the windows. "You look about to faint."

Fionna managed a wan smile. "I assure you, I will not. But you were right, I did need to sit, sir . . ."

"I am William, Baron of Lancaster, and you are . . ."

"Fionna."

Not her voice but another. A deep, commanding voice that brooked no dispute. Fionna turned her head. Hugh stood, dark and powerful, holding out his hand to her.

"Thank you, my lord," he said coolly. "I am grateful for your assistance in my absence, but now . . ."

"Of course." The baron stood up. He gave Fionna a pleasant smile. "I trust you will feel better, Mistress Fionna." After a moment, he added, "Private meetings with the queen can take a toll."

She shook her head in bemusement. "Does everyone know everything that happens here?"

William laughed. "Not everyone. There are one or two scullery maids who occasionally miss something." With another smile, he was gone.

"Who is he?" Fionna asked.

Hugh sat down next to her on the bench. He studied her grimly. "A friend of the king's."

"Oh, no! He seems so nice. I'd hate to think he could be next."

"What happened?"

"Where . . . oh, with the queen? Nothing to speak of.

She sent her ladies off, served me wine, and asked me to conjure the Devil for her."

There was a silence so profound the air seemed to shudder. Finally, he said, "You're not joking?"

"I'm afraid not."

The look that passed behind his eyes chilled Fionna to the bone.

He rose, gathered her up in his arms, and carried her out of the Tower.

Every man and woman within sight froze. Even the horses looked stunned. There was not a sound to be heard save for the steady, remorseless steps of the Lord of Castlerock.

"I think you should put me down," Fionna said as they crossed the bailey.

Eyes straight ahead, dark-browed and unyielding, Hugh said, "And I think our king had better *conjure* what it means that a meeting with his wife left you ill."

Behind them, a low, buzzing whisper began and grew rapidly. Several hundred voices spoke at once in fearful speculation.

CHAPTER EIGHTEEN

"This is very silly," Fionna said. "I am not sick."

Hugh tucked the fur throw more securely around her, satisfied himself that she was warm enough, and settled into the chair he had pulled up beside the bed. "You need to rest."

Fionna suppressed a sigh. They had been back at the stronghold for over an hour, and Hugh was still angry. He looked perfectly calm and in control, but she wasn't fooled. Rage simmered in him, waiting only for an outlet.

"I need to remind myself that there are foolish people everywhere and let it go at that. So do you."

"Isabella is worse than foolish, she has the capacity to do a great deal of harm. What do you think the result will be if she begins spreading vicious rumors about you in a city already on the knife-edge of panic? A city where, I might add, a series of mysterious murders are occurring?"

"You're thinking of what happened to your mother,"

Fionna said, suddenly understanding. "But there's no reason to believe anything of the sort would happen now. Besides, there's no hint of 'witchcraft' in these killings. They're just straightforward murder."

"There's nothing straightforward about murder so near the king." He was about to say more when there was a knock at the door. At Hugh's command, Peyton entered, cautiously.

"My lord, there is a message from the Prior of St. Katherine's."

He handed over a rolled parchment. Hugh unsealed it and read quickly. "Good, de Coureville's located the priest who buried Huteuil. It's probably too late to send for him this evening, but tomorrow—"

"There is more, my lord," Peyton said.

"Another message?"

"Of a sort." The knight turned and gestured to a servant hovering by the door. The man entered carrying a heavy basket covered with linen. "His Majesty has sent a gift of oranges and his regrets that Mistress Fionna is indisposed," Peyton said.

"Now, isn't that nice," Fionna said. She looked at Hugh encouragingly.

"He might ask his wife what indisposed you."

"That's neither here nor there. The king is making an effort. Besides, I love oranges."

"Perhaps you'd like to have some soup with them," Peyton suggested.

At both Hugh and Fionna's puzzled looks, he said, "Master Wolcott just delivered a pot of soup that he describes as his sister's best, excellent for curing virtually any ailment. It seems word has spread."

"How many people are there in London?" Fionna asked.

"About fifty thousand," Hugh replied. "Why?"

"I'm trying to understand how one very small event could become known to one of the very few out of all those fifty thousand I've actually met. It seems remarkable."

"That's London," Hugh said. He looked at Peyton. "Has there been any trouble?"

"There was a small gathering outside the Tower an hour or so ago, some angry muttering by the usual assortment of apprentices and students, a few handfuls of mud were thrown, but it ended quickly enough. Traffic on the river seems a bit heavier than usual, but nothing extraordinary."

"All the same, tell the watch captain to change the guard every three hours, not four. I want to be sure the men are alert."

Peyton nodded and took his leave.

"Are you really expecting rebellion to start here in London?" Fionna asked when they were alone again.

"I think it already has started. It's just that no one's made a formal announcement to that effect, so people are still trying to convince themselves it isn't happening. When they finally accept the truth, I fully expect Londoners to side with the barons and against the king."

"Because John is bad for business?"

"Because bad government is bad for business. The problem is that the barons wouldn't do any better. They have no more concern—or interest—in what it takes for ordinary people to live than does John himself."

She reached for an orange and began to peel it. "Then, it would seem there is little hope for compromise."

"There's only one hope. We need to be a nation of laws, not just of men. King Henry understood that but since his death, no one's done much to advance it."

"It is your intent to make laws that the barons and the king alike would have to respect? Is that it?"

"Essentially." He grimaced. "I realize it doesn't sound as noble or glorious as hacking one's enemies into small pieces and razing their cities, but when all is said and done, it has the potential to mean far more."

Fionna couldn't help but smile at the big, hard-muscled man before her. "You would seem to make an unlikely lawyer."

"I'll do whatever I have to," he said.

She sat up, kneeling on the bed, and held out a segment of orange. He allowed her to feed it to him. They shared the orange and another. By the time they were done, Hugh's mood had improved.

"Are you really all right?" he asked.

"The only thing wrong with me is that I need a bath." She sighed. "I keep thinking about the pool at Castlerock—" Her eyes met his.

He stood, crossed the room, and opened the door. "I'll be right back."

He must have instructed the first servant he encountered, for within minutes, a steady stream of them were coming and going from the room, first bringing in an enormous tin tub, then filling it with steaming water.

"Unfortunately," he said when the last of the servants had departed, "it isn't big enough for two."

Warmth curled through her. "That is too bad."

"However"—he drew her to him—"I'd be happy to scrub your back."

Fionna's eyes drooped shut. Her head fell forward. She made a low, almost purring sound deep in her throat.

Heat surrounded her—the heat of the water, steam rising from it—was the smaller part. The heat of his touch, strong and steady, moving over her naked back, reached deep inside her, met by heat of her own.

A distant part of her mind marveled at how utterly right it all felt. She had no self-consciousness with him and seemingly no modesty. She who had always been so private now felt incalculably bold. The sensation was as though she had sprouted wings and discovered they could carry her far from all the ordinary concerns and restrictions of life.

She turned, eyes still closed, and sought out the hard, broad wall of his chest. He had stripped off his tunic, claiming he did not want to get it wet. His skin was warm, smooth, infinitely inviting . . .

His hands, slick with the honey-scented soap, cupped her breasts. She opened her eyes, gazed into his, and smiled.

"I think I'm very clean."

"That's good," he said, his voice low and hard. He stood suddenly, drawing her up with him. Water sluiced off them both.

"We'll soak the bed," she protested.

Hugh grinned. "Very domestic of you." He tossed the fur throw onto the floor. "Very practical, even housewifery."

She made to swat at him. He caught her hand,

laughed, and laid her down. Kneeling over her, he stroked the slender length of her body from the curve of her shoulder to her thighs and back again.

"You have the most exquisite skin, like satin."

"Thank you," she murmured, pleasantly surprised that she could still talk.

"And such good manners . . ."

"You do, too, such very, very good . . . oh . . ."

His tongue circled her nipple, drawing it into his mouth. At the same time, his hands moved between her legs, stroking and caressing her.

Thought fragmented, time fled. She was vaguely aware of her own harsh breathing muted by exquisite, ever mounting pleasure.

He turned suddenly, and Fionna gasped as she suddenly found herself above him, her hips held by his powerful hands.

"The floor's too hard," he said, as though that somehow explained it all.

Such freedom enthralled Fionna. She ran her hands down his chest, over the hard ridges of his ribs to his flat abdomen and beyond. He moaned thickly.

A tantalizing sense of possibilities filled her. She lowered her head, touching him with her lips.

"Fionna . . ."

He fascinated her, this fierce, compelling man who always seemed to be in command of himself and others. To know that she could move him like this, that her touch could—

He lifted her, adjusted her position slightly, and—

Fionna gasped as he filled her. But that was nothing when she discovered that she would move. He was waiting, letting her set the pace . . .

She rose, tentatively, and lowered herself again. The sensation was unlike anything she could have imagined. A soft groan of voluptuous delight escaped her.

"Take all the time you'd like," he said, the consummate gentleman.

If ever she'd heard a challenge, that was it. Fionna smiled. She lifted the heavy curtain of her hair away from her face and braced her hands against his lean hips.

"Really, all the time?"

"Mmmm, absolutely, don't hurry on my account."

The hard glitter of his eyes and the jagged pulse beating in his throat belied the civility of his words. She moved slowly, almost languorously, sheathing him in wet, hot silk.

He groaned.

She moved again, watching him in fascination, gauging his every response until, abruptly, her own overwhelmed her. Her pace quickened. She arched her back, drawing him ever more deeply into her, and let the dark, whirling pool of ecstasy take them both.

Hugh woke to the far-off sound of a dog barking and the same sense of disorientation that was becoming embarrassingly familiar.

He turned his head, finding the bed beside him empty. By the light streaming in through the windows, he judged it to be early evening. There was no sign of Fionna.

Quickly, he rose and pulled on his clothes. Outside in the landing, it was very quiet. Only a few sounds filtered up the stairwell. He went down very quickly and entered the great hall. Servants were setting up the tables for supper. They looked up, startled, as he strode past.

Outside in the bailey, everything appeared normal. The guards were on the walls, men and women were going about their usual tasks or just relaxing. It was the time of day when there was a pause, a gathering in of thoughts, before the conviviality of evening.

A serving girl was passing with a last basket of laundry, neatly folded and ready to be put away in the linen press. Hugh corralled her and asked if she knew Fionna's whereabouts.

The girl's eyes widened at being addressed so directly. She reddened and said quickly, "I believe she is walking down by the river, my lord."

Hugh stiffened. What could Fionna be thinking of? How could she possibly have gone outside the stronghold by herself?

And why hadn't he thought to forbid it?

He went through the riverside wicket gate and down the path that led to the water. Elm and hazel trees were coming into full leave. The evening song of birds filled the tranquil air. It would have been perfectly pleasant but for his overriding concern.

She was right there, near the bottom of the path, seated on a large rock. Her gaze was on the river. She did not hear him until he was directly behind her.

Turning, seeing him, she began to smile. That vanished instantly when he said, "What the hell are you playing at?"

She looked at him in honest bewilderment. "I don't . . ."

"What are you thinking of to go outside the walls by yourself? Don't you realize what could happen?"

"But it's so peaceful here. I was just thinking how remarkable it is that such a lovely place exists so close to such a teeming city. What possible harm—"

"It would need only one person to come along who was bent on mischief." He reached out, took hold of her arm, and drew her upright. "One man drunk on too much ale, one apprentice or student angered by royal authority and willing to lash out at anyone, one crazed wanderer, one would-be rapist . . ."

"Stop! This is absurd. If it was so dangerous for me to take a step outside, to breathe freely for even a moment, why didn't anyone stop me?"

Hugh had been wondering about that himself, but he thought he knew the answer. "Peyton would have had he seen you, but he didn't. As for the rest, I suppose none of them thought they had the authority to tell my . . . guest what to do."

"Your guest?"

"Yes, what else . . . ?"

"Your mistress. Your possession. Yours to decide what I can and cannot do. That's what they really think, isn't it? Moreover, it's what you yourself believe."

"Fionna, be reasonable . . ."

"No, you be reasonable! I came out here for just a few moments to enjoy the peace of the evening. If that was dangerous, then why didn't you tell me I shouldn't do it? Tell me, that's all. Just explain, give me a good reason and trust that I will have the intelligence to behave sensibly."

"I don't want you to be frightened . . ."

"Stop protecting me! I was raised to take care of myself, and believe me, I know how to do it!"

The air shimmered. Hugh was not sure then—or afterward—what exactly he saw or felt. An instant later, everything was as it had been. Except that he was no longer holding Fionna's arm.

"What did you—?" he began, then stopped. He had to consider the serious possibility that he did not want to know.

"Stop protecting me," she said again, more calmly. "I'm here to help you. Remember that? But how can I if you surround me with guards and don't let me take a step on my own?"

"You don't understand the risk."

"Oh, yes, I do. I saw Isabella's fear today. I *felt* it. She is a disagreeable woman, but not a stupid one. I understand full well how close we all are to chaos. Look, this is what I was doing before I came out here."

She drew a parchment from the pocket of her tunic and held it out to Hugh. He unfolded it and looked at it carefully.

"That's a drawing of the knife that could have caused Foucault's and Pearse's wounds. The blade is to the correct measurements, the handle is a guess. I wish I could be more precise but—"

"How sure are you of the blade?"

"I probed the wounds. My assumption is that the blade went completely in."

"There's a curve here at the tip." He pointed at it.

Fionna nodded. "Because that's what I felt in each wound."

"Then, this is a very unusual knife. In fact, I've never seen one like it."

"Why, because of the tip? Surely—"

"No, not just that. The size of the width to the length . . . what's that called . . . ?"

"Ratio? The ratio of the width to the length?"

"Yes, that's it. This is what, eight inches long? I've a knife that long myself, but it's an inch wide, not two inches. The wider blade taken with the curved tip would indicate this knife was not made in England, or anywhere near here for that matter."

"Could it be Saracen?" Fionna asked.

"That's exactly what I'm thinking. Enough weapons have made it back from there over the years. But even so, this wouldn't be common."

"Then, there might actually be a chance of finding it?"

"Some," he acknowledged. He was well aware that she had distracted him from the matter of her behavior. But he also recognized the importance of what she had discovered.

"I will make inquiries. In the meantime . . ." He produced a smile of gracious patience. "Would you be so kind as to return inside with me?"

She slanted him a chiding look, then smiled. "Since you ask so nicely."

"That's me," he said, taking her delicately boned hand in his much larger, sinewy one. "Nice Hugh."

Fionna giggled, a most unlikely sound from her. She tried to contain it and failed. A laugh escaped, followed by another. "I'm sorry," she said, sputtering. "I don't know why that's so funny . . . It's just that . . . Nice Hugh." She broke down, tears streaming down her cheeks, laughing helplessly.

"It's so nice that I can amuse you."

"Oh, please . . . don't . . ."

"Nice, nice, nice, *niii-ccce.*"

"I can't stand it . . ."

"Isn't that what you said a couple of hours ago?"

"Oohhh." She landed a fair-size punch on his upper arm but still couldn't stop laughing. In between all-out guffaws, she said, "You need a new banner . . . forget the hawk . . . something n-nicer . . ."

She was lost, holding her sides. Patiently, he guided her back through the gate and into the bailey. They were met by startled glances quickly averted.

By the time they reached the hall, Fionna had regained some control of herself, if only barely.

"I'm sorry," she said, wiping her eyes. "I don't know why that struck me the way it did, but . . ." She looked up at him. "Nice isn't the first word I'd associate with you."

"I'm much relieved to hear that. Now, I suggest we have supper. If you would prefer upstairs—?"

He waited, giving her the choice. She hesitated, and he could see that it was a struggle for her, this proud and private woman who found herself in a position she could not possibly have imagined. But quickly enough she shook her head.

"I think your men would prefer to see you in hall this evening, don't you?"

Hugh smiled, pleased by her courage and her perceptiveness. He held out his arm. She placed her hand on it lightly. Together, they entered the hall and took their places.

CHAPTER NINETEEN

The juggler tossed his glittering balls high, caught them deftly, and took a bow. From the trestle tables set up around the hall, the men cheered. Hugh and Fionna did as well.

The meal was all but over, only wine and savories remained, but the entertainment continued. An acrobat spun across the cleared space at the center of the hall, flipping head over heels, over and over until he came to a stop directly in front of the high table where Hugh and Fionna sat. He bolted upright, grinned, and signaled for the rest of the troupe to join him.

"Where did they all come from?" Fionna asked as a bevy of young men scrambled to form a tower that reached clear to the corbeled ceiling a good twenty-five feet above.

"They began showing up at the gate this afternoon," Hugh said, "offering to entertain. There's nothing unusual about it; they make their living going from inn to inn, or as here, making the rounds of the manor houses. A small thing like the threat of civil war would not deter them."

Fionna stared in fascination at the whirling men. That human beings could do such extraordinary things—

"In fact," Hugh was saying, "there is nowhere they are not admitted." He fell silent.

Fionna glanced over at him. "What are you thinking?"

"Huteuil and the others were killed at night, probably after curfew. Pearse was merely forgetful, likely to lose track of the time, but the others were probably just accustomed to being out late at their revels. As, indeed, are the jugglers, acrobats, mime singers, and the rest."

"Then, one of them might have noticed something?"

"It's possible."

He stood. In the space of a single breath, silence descended.

"Good people," Hugh said pleasantly. "I thank you all for coming. There is no place like London for a fair night's entertainment."

They smiled appreciatively but waited for what he really meant to say.

"But sometimes," Hugh continued, "there is more to life than amusement. Lately, trouble has come upon us."

A ripple ran through the assembled crowd. Would he really speak of what was happening with the king and the barons? Would he acknowledge the danger hanging over them all, and if he did, what would the result be?

Choosing his words with care, Hugh said, "I refer to the murders of three men in the past fortnight, all killed within the shadow of the Tower, all knifed. I seek information about their deaths, and I will generously reward anyone who provides it."

He waited, giving them a moment to ponder that, then smiled. "Now, let the revels resume and good cheer to you all."

At a signal, the minstrels began again, and after a further moment or two, the acrobats did the same. But here and there, all around the hall, people glanced at one another thoughtfully.

"Will it do any good?" Fionna asked when he had resumed his seat.

Hugh shrugged. "Probably not, but it's worth a chance. At the very least, the murderer will know of my interest."

She paled. "That's right, I didn't think of it. Why would you want him to know?"

"It may make him feel a certain pressure, and that could lead to mistakes."

She sat back in the high, carved chair and tried to give her attention once again to the entertainers. But her efforts faded, and she was glad when, a little while later, Hugh rose and held out his hand to her.

The little church of St. Dunstan in the east was a small, unpretentious building with a foundation of stone topped by wood and a slate roof within spitting distance of the wharves at Billingsgate and only minutes from the Tower. So far as Fionna could see, it was little different from the vast majority of churches that seemed to pop up around every corner of London.

The exception was the great Cathedral of St. Paul with its huge lantern windows and great timber tower still under construction. She and Hugh had passed it that morning after entering the city through Ludgate. Coming over the wooden drawbridge and beneath the iron portcullis, she had seen lepers being turned back, children begging, and heard the now familiar din of clanking carts, raucous peddlers, chiming church bells, and all the rest that announced one was about to enter London.

Beyond Ludgate, into the maze of streets, she felt the same sense of shock that she had before but just a little less keenly. Like it or not, the city was no longer entirely alien to her.

They drew rein before St. Dunstan's. A priest, alerted by the stir in the street, was waiting outside. He was a young man who could not entirely conceal his nervousness when confronted by so august a personage as the Lord of Castlerock.

"Are you Father Francis Pellier?" Hugh asked him.

He swallowed with such difficulty that his Adam's apple bobbed frantically, and nodded. "I am, my lord. Forgive me, had I known you were coming I would have made proper preparations. I thought . . . that is . . ."

"You expected me to summon you. I preferred to come here instead. I trust you don't object?"

The young man paled. He looked from Hugh to Fionna. His gaze lingered just a moment before he yanked it back with a visible effort. "Object? No, of course not, how could I . . . that is, come in, please."

He stood aside to admit them. They stepped into a space perhaps twenty by thirty feet, illuminated only by the light that filtered in through half a dozen smallish windows on either side. At the far end stood the main altar. Two other smaller altars were set against opposite walls along the nave. There were no benches or seats of any kind. The air smelled of old incense and damp stone.

"We are a simple church, my lord," Father Pellier was saying. "But we try our utmost to serve our small parish."

"Who comes here, for the most part?" Hugh asked.

"Fishmongers, carders, fullers, a few others."

"Including Gerard Huteuil?"

"No, I fear not. I gather he was something of a lost soul, but his brother is far more regular in his devotions. When he asked for the funeral to be held from here, I could hardly refuse."

"So you received the body here directly after it was found? It wasn't sent anywhere else first?"

"Not to the best of my knowledge," Pellier said. He was relaxing just a little, becoming more confident about his ability to converse with the great lord who was said to stand so close to the throne itself.

"What condition was it in?" Hugh asked.

"The body? There was nothing unusual. He appeared quite peaceful, as though he must have died instantly."

"From one wound?"

"Yes, in the back."

"Was he buried in the same clothes he was wearing when he died?"

The priest thought for a moment. He shook his head. "No, he wasn't. They had blood on them, you see, and that troubled his brother. So after the body was washed, it was covered in a winding sheet."

"What happened to the clothes? Were they thrown out?"

Pellier hesitated.

"The truth, Father," Hugh said. "If you please."

"There is much poverty hereabouts. I could not bring myself to discard clothing that might be salvaged. I put the garments to soak in cold water in hopes of removing the bloodstains."

"They aren't still there?" Fionna asked. It was the first time she had spoken, and the effect was like a thunderclap. The priest almost jumped, so startled was he.

"Uh . . . no, not still. The stains did come out, but I thought it better to wait a bit before giving them away. Let the memory fade, as it were."

"Let us see them," Hugh directed.

It took some little time to find Huteuil's clothing amid the jumble of other garments, small tools, discarded household items, and the like that the good father appeared to collect. He shrugged apologetically. "Things come along. I try not to get rid of anything that might be of use to someone in the future."

"Very conscientious of you," Hugh murmured. "Now, if we might . . ." He carried the cloak and tunic back out into the main church where there was more light. When he had laid it out on the floor, both he and Fionna knelt down for a closer look.

"There," she said, pointing, "you can see where the weapon entered."

Hugh measured the distance with his fingers. "About two inches."

"The same blade."

He nodded and stood, gathering up the garments. Returning them to the priest, he said, "Did Huteuil's brother have any idea who might have killed him?"

Pellier frowned. "I gathered the deceased was considered a wastrel. He was unmarried and had no steady employment."

"Yet his clothes are not those of a beggar," Fionna pointed out.

"He had money," the priest agreed. "Apparently, he gambled, arranged gaming matches, helped entertainers gain admission to the royal court, that sort of thing. Such men, living on the edge of society, do tend to die early."

"But he had no known enemies?" Hugh asked.

"Not that I have heard of."

"If you hear otherwise, send word to me."

The priest assured him that he would do so. He appeared properly impressed by the magnitude of the encounter. Indeed, by the time they departed, it was hard to say whether he was more alarmed or excited.

"What now?" Fionna asked as they left St. Dunstan's behind them. They were moving slowly through the crowded streets, the guards watchful as ever. It would have been impossible for any man, woman, or child anywhere thereabouts to miss the fact of their presence.

"That is what this is about, isn't it?" she went on before Hugh could reply. A horrible possibility had just occurred to her, and she could not let it rest. "You are showing yourself, driving home the point that you are searching for the murderer. That's why you went to Pellier instead of having him come to you."

"Sometimes you can learn more on another man's territory rather than your own."

"You're making yourself a target." The words were out before she could stop them. And with them came the sickening realization that they were true. Nothing else made sense, not the announcement he'd made to the entertainers that night before and not this.

With mounting horror, she said, "You are being seen as a friend of the king's, trying to help him in this time of trouble. You are trying to draw the murderer to you."

He reached across the space separating their horses and touched her hand gently. "Nothing is going to happen to me, Fionna."

Her stomach heaved. She took a deep, shuddering breath and struggled for calm. If only he had denied it. If only he had claimed to just be in the mood for a ride through London on a spring morning.

How dare he endanger himself so deliberately? With all the peril in the world—and in London, in particular—how could he possible justify such a crazed stunt as this?

"It's the quickest way," he said mildly. "I believe we're running out of time."

This was the man in whose arms she had lain the night before. She had awakened with his body close against her own, the scent of him on her skin, the heat of him still within her. Awakened with the memory of voluptuous pleasure still coursing through her. Awakened to the tenderest of thoughts, the gentlest of feelings . . .

She wanted to throttle him.

"You worry about me taking a walk by the river, and you do *this*?"

"Fionna," he said patiently, "there is a great deal I could say to try to reassure you, but I think it's more important right now to point out that you just aren't a good enough rider to get mad while you're sitting on top of a horse."

Her eyes narrowed to shards of blue tinged with ice.

"I am not mad," she said sweetly, "merely startled. If you want to risk your life on such a harebrained scheme, go right ahead."

To her fury, he smiled. "Do you honestly believe that one man with a knife can kill me?"

She looked at him then, really looked, past the man she had come to know as companion, lover, and even friend. For the merest flicker, she allowed herself to see what she had always understood was there—the warrior honed to battle from tenderest youth, strong, fierce, unyielding and, if need be, remorseless. A man who would kill far more readily than be killed.

Even so, she said, "No one is invulnerable."

"That is true, but I make a damn harder target than Pearse and the like."

And that, it seemed, was that.

Within sight of the river, Hugh halted. He dismounted, tossed the reins to a squire, and helped Fionna down. "I want to show you one of my favorite places in London."

Despite her lingering anger at him—and her fear for his safety—she couldn't quite suppress her curiosity. They were right next to the wharves that ran alongside the river. The lane widened at the water's edge into a large market area. Dozens of stalls were set up there, hawkers shouting the advantages of their wares. Incongruously, in the middle of it all sat a large wooden building with long trestle tables in front and nearby a long metal grill laid over glowing coals.

"You won't find better fish," Hugh said as he led her over toward the tables. His men followed.

"It comes off the boats right there." He pointed toward the wharves. "Gets cleaned and goes straight on to the grill. They also have oysters, if you'd prefer those."

"You eat here?" Fionna asked. They were drawing a great deal of attention but none of it particularly surprising. People were smiling and nodding, as though pleased to see that whatever problems they might all be facing, the Lord of Castlerock wasn't letting them get in the way of enjoying himself.

"Every chance I get," he said, and pulled out one of the benches beside a table. His men sat nearby.

A very large, round man bustled out, saw Hugh, and grinned.

"Took you long enough to get here, my lord," he said. "Been in London what, three days now? What have you been eating in all that time?"

"Oh, this and that, Raymond, nothing I remember. Fionna, this is Raymond Dellacourte. He's lost count of the number of noble families that have tried to lure him into their kitchens, offering the most shameful bribes, I might add. But he prefers to stay here, sharing his talents with the world, or as much of it that has the sense to come to London."

"Master Dellacourte . . ."

He beamed her a smile, bent over her hand, and said with great sincerity, "Dear lady, you do my humble establishment inestimable honor. For you, I have something most special, the finest swordfish brought from the waters of the North Sea, flavored with the purest olive oil, a touch of garlic, a leaf or two of basil, and grilled to perfection. What do you say?"

"It sounds wonderful . . ."

"Ah, yes, it does but there is more to tempt you. Oysters poached in cream and butter, a hint of pepper, and the merest suggestion of saffron. Or, if you prefer, herring in a mustard sauce that I frankly think is one of my finest creations ever."

"Do I get any of this?" Hugh asked. He looked completely relaxed and in good humor. Even his men, watchful as ever, seemed pleased to be there.

Several buxom serving maids hurried out and busied themselves pouring wine. Banter ensued, but it did not escape Fionna's notice that the guardsmen were courteous and respectful.

"Your daughters?" she asked Master Dellacourte.

He rolled his dark eyes. "The Lord has blessed me with eight angels. Now, if I can only find a son-in-law who wants to run an inn . . ." He looked at Hugh. "What about some of your men? Aren't any of them tired of the fighting business?"

Hugh leaned back, hands folded over his chest, eyes squinted against the sun, and smiled. "I suppose that's possible. Besides, for one of your daughters a man would give up much."

Dellacourte nodded solemnly. "That's true enough. Well, keep a look out. If one of them says anything, send him my way."

He bustled off to see to the food.

Fionna turned to Hugh. "He wants you to play matchmaker?" She could not hide her astonishment. That the Lord of Castlerock was held in esteem and affection was one thing. That he was treated virtually as a member of the family was another, especially when the "family" seemed to be London itself.

"I've done it before," he said, and laughed at her expression. "Did you think all I did was fight? That's the smallest part of being a leader. The rest of it's far more interesting stuff—making sure the land is used well, encouraging trade, seeing to the general welfare of the people. The chroniclers don't tell of it, but that's what life is really about."

"Does John see it that way?"

"John . . . sees the throne, as his father and brothers and mother all did. He knows nothing else."

Fionna took a sip of fruity Rhine wine. "Wouldn't it be better if all a king had to do was sit on his throne and look kingly while others tended to the really important matters?"

"Perhaps the barons should get you to negotiate their side of things."

"That bad?"

"Let's just say I wouldn't go mentioning it to John."

One of the angel Dellacourtes appeared with a smile and a basket of freshly baked breads. They ordered, nibbled, and very promptly, the most exquisitely delectable meal Fionna had ever enjoyed appeared before them.

Closing her eyes on a savory bite of swordfish, she said, "Who exactly is Raymond Dellacourte that he can work such magic?"

"Italian by birth," Hugh said, finishing off an oyster. "His mother was cook in the residence of a cardinal, one thing led to another and . . ."

Fionna nodded. Rome was far better at preaching chastity than practicing it. At the next table, the guardsmen were enjoying their own meal. Others—merchants, workmen, sailors—were doing the same nearby. Unlike almost anywhere else she had ever been, there seemed to be very little sense of privilege at Master Dellacourte's establishment.

"Is this why you like London so much?" she asked. "Because you can get out and mix with people, not always be set apart?"

"That's part of it. I like the strength and courage of the people, and I especially like their independence."

"Fickle London, isn't that what William the Conqueror called it?"

Hugh nodded. "He spoke of the populace as vast and fierce, and distrusted Londoners on principle. They returned the compliment, and still do."

"So if it comes to a match between the king and the barons . . . ?"

"London will hold its collective nose and go with the barons. I have no doubt of it."

Fionna was tempted to ask more—if John could keep his throne if he couldn't keep his capital city, whether they were days or weeks away from finding out, and the like. But she restrained herself, considering it far more important that Hugh have a chance to simply relax and put aside the trials of their world for at least a little time.

Too soon, the meal was finished. With many compliments to Master Dellacourte and promises to come again soon, they departed. But not back to Westminster, for Hugh had another stop in mind first.

CHAPTER TWENTY

The sweat-drenched man looked at the parchment in his gnarled hands, scowled, and handed it back to Hugh.

"Never seen it."

Behind him, the fires of his forge glowed red-hot. Apprentices, bare-chested beneath leather aprons, were working the bellows and hammering iron. The air shimmered, so scorching as to almost raise blisters.

"Not an English blade," Hugh suggested.

The smith nodded. "Not Spanish either or anything thereabouts. Closest you're going to get is—"

"Saracen?"

"Most likely. I've seen a few of them from time to time. Nasty things." He said it as a compliment.

"Have you ever sold one?"

The man smiled, his begrimed face lighting with amusement. "Aye, I have but not many. People bring them for trade occasionally."

"Would you know of anyone in particular who might have a preference for them?"

"You mean a collector like?" He thought for a moment, then shook his head. "I suppose that could be but I've never heard of one. Sorry." On an afterthought, he added, "You might try the gypsy."

"I will, but pass the word, if you please. I'll pay well for the information."

Outside in the cool spring air, Fionna inhaled gratefully. They were standing at the edge of a large field beyond the city walls. Stables, forges, and inns surrounded it. Groups of young men were practicing archery, tilting at quintains, wrestling, or were energetically hacking away at each other with sword and buckler.

"Is it always like this?" Fionna asked when Hugh had followed her from the forge.

He looked out over the scene and nodded. "Except in winter, then they make do with the marshes at Moorfield. They tie shinbones to the bottoms of their boots, and hurl themselves along with iron poles until they crash into each other and are sent spinning across the ice."

"I could say something about men having more courage than sense, but I won't."

"You won't?"

She shook her head solemnly. "It might be taken as a comment on your efforts to attract the attentions of a murderer."

"Still on that?"

"I'm afraid so. Where next do you mean to show yourself? You've told the entertainers and the priest and Master Dellacourte and now the smith. Isn't that enough?"

"It should reach most of London," he acknowledged. "However, there's one more place."

"Where?"

"The gypsy, of course. Care to come?"

"As though I could pass that up. Where in London does a gypsy reside?"

"Not in London at all, but nearby."

Beyond Smithfield, along a winding, narrow road, they came to the edge of a wood. Just within it, the day darkened and silence surrounded them.

At a signal from Hugh, the guardsmen fell back. They proceeded alone.

"Where are we going?" Fionna asked. She caught herself whispering, but knew why. There was a hushed tension to the place, as though nature itself was waiting.

"Not far," Hugh replied quietly. He led the way down a trail she could barely make out to a small clearing, where they both dismounted. After they had secured the horses, he took her hand. They continued on foot a short distance.

Fionna smelled the brambly scent of wood smoke. It was coming from a small hut set beside a stream. There was no one to be seen except for a ginger cat who peered from behind a rock.

"We wait," Hugh said.

Minutes passed. Fionna resisted the impulse to ask why they were doing this. She held herself very still, as Hugh was also doing. They were rewarded at last by a soft rustling from the back of the hut. A small, bent shape emerged, leaning heavily on a cane.

From beneath a dark shawl, a face like a winter apple peered out. A slow, hesitant smile formed.

"Castlerock." The voice was high and reedy, weak with age—or illness. "What brings you here?"

"You, of course," he said, and stepped forward. With great gentleness, he took the old woman's hand in his own. "It's good to see you again, Sula."

"And you, but who's this you've brought? A beauty, to be sure."

"My name is Fionna." She spoke softly, not wishing to give alarm.

Sula looked at her closely. The old woman's eyes were large and black, the only part of her that still seemed vividly alive.

"From a far place."

"From Ireland," Fionna said with a smile. "Is that far enough?"

"Not there, another. Where the moon bathes."

Fionna swallowed tightly. It would be so easy to dismiss the old gypsy's words as the mutterings of a frail old woman. Or as coincidence.

Hugh looked from one to the other. He said nothing, waiting. Gathering her breath, Fionna said, "What do you see, old mother?"

Sula tightened her grip on her staff. Lines of pain were so deeply etched into her face that they appeared to have always been there. But beneath them, all but vanished, Fionna caught a glimpse of a far younger woman, straight and proud, laughing in sunlight.

"What do you see, fair one?" Sula countered.

Pain shafted through Fionna. Terrible, gnawing, soul-destroying pain. She needed all her strength to gather her forces and throw it off. Shaken, she said the only thing she could—the truth.

"You."

Sula's sigh was the whisper of wind in the ancient oaks.

"Come and sit," the old woman said. She held out a hand to Fionna and guided her gently to a large rock by the stream. "It's all right now. You won't feel it again."

She patted Fionna's arm with gnarled fingers that were swollen at the knuckles. "Broken," she said as she followed Fionna's gaze. "Like so much." Her smile twisted. "But enough of that. What do I see? The land torn asunder, blood on the moon, a generation cast down unless . . ."

Hugh went down on his haunches next to her. Very quietly, he prompted, "Unless . . . ?"

Sula's eyes were blank. Her lips moved as of their own volition. Fionna tried but could not feel her presence. It was as though she had gone a long way off.

"Find the one with the knife of Kalil."

A long shudder ran through Sula. She inhaled raggedly. "So much death . . ."

"From the knife?" Fionna asked.

The old woman looked up startled, as though she had forgotten they were there. "Yes, a knife. I saw that. Not a large one but very strong. There was already much death in it, and now there is more."

"Who, or what, is Kalil?" Hugh asked.

"I don't know. It means nothing to you?"

He shook his head. Standing, he helped Fionna up, then handed a pouch to Sula. "Take this, old mother."

"I have no need of so much."

"Indulge me. I would know of your comfort."

"You were always a good one, Lord of Castlerock. To you, I tell what I will never tell to others."

"I know that, and if you should ever reconsider the rest . . ."

She shrugged. "The hut suits me. And since you made your concern known, I am left alone. That is all I ask."

"All the same, remember, there is always a place for you beneath my roof."

Sula nodded. "I will remember." She turned to enter the hut. Almost inside, hidden by the shadows, she called, "Blood on the moon. You remember that, my lord."

They left in silence. Neither spoke again until they had remounted and rejoined the guard, waiting for them near the edge of the wood. The men were clearly relieved to see them unharmed.

It was not until they were on the road back to London that Fionna gathered her thoughts enough to speak.

"Who is she?"

"Just what you saw, an old gypsy woman."

"All right, then, who was she?"

"A young gypsy woman, I suppose. One who sometimes was able to see things others couldn't. Years ago, the priests got it into their heads that she was a witch. She was arrested and tortured. Her legs and arms were broken, and a great deal else was done. Richard was king then, and he approved of such things. But he died before she could be given to the flames, and in the tumult of one reign's end and another's beginning, she was released. She's lived here ever since."

Fionna's chest was tight. She felt as though she could hardly breathe.

"That's why you wanted me to come with you."

"I did think she might speak more readily if you were there."

"No, it wasn't that. She said herself that she's told you things she tells no one else, because you've protected her and she trusts you. No, you wanted me to see what can happen to a woman accused of being a witch."

He hesitated, but it was not in him to lie. "You were protected in Ireland. That was good in its way, but it may have left you unprepared to deal with a different sort of situation."

Fionna turned in her saddle so that she could look at him directly. "You are far too concerned with protecting me."

He shook his head. "The further this goes, the more I think it was a mistake to let you come."

His words hurt, but she concealed that. "Why? Because I can't mutter a few curses and produce your killer for you?"

"Of course not!" His annoyance flashed out, but it was gone as quickly as it appeared. More gently, he said, "Where the moon bathes. That was a pretty phrase Sula used."

"You knew what Gealach meant."

"True, but I also thought of it as being in Ireland. Sula said it isn't."

"Then, she is wrong. If you're seriously suggesting I'm not Irish . . ."

He laughed. "Oh, no, you're Irish all right. I think she just meant that sometimes a place isn't necessary where—or even what—it appears to be."

Fionna caught her breath. She reminded herself that he was Alianor's son. At a crucial time in his childhood, he had spent an unusual amount of time with his mother. What had he learned ... or guessed?

"I know another place like that," he said.

"Where?" She realized the answer before he spoke.

"Avalon," he said, and urged his horse on.

Moonlight flowed through the stone-arched windows, across the flooring of woven rush mats, between the bed hangings left open to the cool spring air. The light, crossing over Fionna's shuttered lids, woke her.

She did not move, but lay listening to the sounds of the silvered night and the steady breathing of the man beside her.

They had not made love. In the aftermath of the meeting with Sula, passion seemed as distant to her as the moon itself. She could think only of the older woman's suffering and of what it meant to all those who were not, as Hugh said, protected as she was.

What did he know?

She turned her head slightly, the better to look at him. Long, dark lashes shadowed his cheeks. His mouth was slightly parted, gentler than she knew it to feel when the mood was upon him. He looked younger, as though in dreams the burden of his days was set down.

What did he sense?

He had felt the distance in her and made no objection. But he had also refused to leave her to sleep alone. More than she wanted to admit, his nearness meant the world to her. To be bereft of it now—

She must not think that way. Her purpose there was to help him, and so far she had done precious little of that. He had an idea of the knife because of her, but nothing more.

Kalil. What could it mean? Why had Sula seen it?

And why was the moon of her vision bloodied?

A chill went through her. Instinctively, she moved closer to the strength and warmth of his body. A sigh escaped her. He stirred in his sleep and drew her closer.

Her head rested on his hard, bare chest. His arms were around her waist. Their legs intertwined.

Fionna closed her eyes and willed herself to sleep.

It was very late. Who knew what morning would bring. She had to rest.

Her leg moved very slightly.

Nothing.

Her hand stroked down his chest, feather light.

Too light.

Her lips touched the warm skin stretched like velvet over stone.

To no effect.

Piqued, not a little challenged by his apparent indifference, she shifted against him so that her breasts, covered only by a thin chemise, were pressed against him.

Truly, he must sleep in Morpheus's arms, for he didn't react at all.

How revealing that after two scant nights he could remain so impervious to her nearness. How humbling.

And how intensely annoying.

She propped herself up, wiggled out of the chemise, and dropped it onto the floor. Pushing the covers back, she gazed at him.

He was the most extraordinarily beautiful man—long of limb, every muscle and sinew perfectly articulated, graceful, stirring . . .

Yet asleep.

Kneeling beside him on the bed, she bent over and dropped light, tantalizing kisses across his chest, down the line of downy curls arching to his naval and beyond. Her breath was silken soft, her mouth warm against his skin, her hands—

Her hands were grasped suddenly in his as he opened his eyes and smiled.

"Were you wondering how long I could bear it?"

"I thought you were asleep," she protested.

He laughed and turned without warning, drawing her under him, big and hard over her, dominating. "Then, madame, you do surely underestimate yourself. Never have I been more delightfully awakened."

She thought to say something tart—about his fooling her, about . . . something. But the impulse faded away beneath the hot, searching hunger of his mouth and the fierce skill of his hands.

Her head fell back against the pillows. A wanton languidness seized her. She surrendered to the dark, voluptuous passions he so effortlessly evoked. But not before her eyes opened wide and looked directly at the moon beyond the window.

For the space of a heartbeat, she could have sworn the silver sphere was stained bloodred.

She blinked, and the vision was gone. Passion mounted, eclipsing all else. She moved to draw him to her and thought no more.

CHAPTER TWENTY-ONE

"He's what?" Hugh demanded.

The messenger flinched at his tone but manfully repeated, "His Majesty has decided to hunt this day. He bids you join him."

"Fellow's mad," Peyton muttered. He was standing beside Hugh in the bailey, where together they had been drilling the men. Some pretext of that was continuing but most had stopped to take a look at what was happening.

"Who?" Hugh asked, heedless that the messengers—and others—were hearing every word. He was that angry. "The messenger or our sovereign? He picks a fine time to venture out among a host heavily armed and provided with the convenient confusion of a hunt."

"Reminds me of Rufus," Peyton said.

"That was over a hundred years ago. How do you think of such things?"

"It pays a man to know a bit of history," the knight said placidly. "The Conqueror's son, and king in England after him, rode out to hunt and never came back alive. The arrow of a supposed friend sent him from the saddle straight to the arms of the Almighty. At least, one presumes that's where he went."

Hugh moved a little away. Peyton followed. Indiscretion had its uses, but there were limits. "Are you suggesting John courts the same?"

"Who knows what's in his mind? I'm just glad I'm not the one who has to fathom it."

But Hugh was, and it was becoming more difficult by the day. With an almost visible act of will, he pushed aside all the irritation he felt at the king and focused on what needed to be done.

"Tell His Majesty I will come."

The messenger bowed low and still bowing, backed away. Better that than risk annoying the Lord of Castlerock any further.

Hugh wiped the sweat from his forehead and spared a last, wistful glance for the bailey. He would have liked nothing better than to spend the morning in hard, physical exercise with his men. The clash of steel, the thud of lances, the whisper of the bow, were exactly what he needed.

Of course, there were also other needs, and he had only to glance up at the window of the solar, where Fionna sat, to be reminded of them.

Sweet heaven, the woman was a fire in his blood. He could not get enough of her. Even last night, when they had pleasured each other to exhaustion and beyond, had merely left him wanting more.

"Tell the men to be ready within the hour," he told Peyton. "Full regalia, war banners, all of it. I want the king to be reminded of who he's dealing with."

The older man grinned and hurried off. Hugh climbed the steps to the keep. He needed a bath, clean clothes, and time to think undisturbed. He got the first two but not the last.

Fionna was waiting for him at the top of the tower steps. She got right to the point. "What does the king want now?"

He spared a moment to appreciate the warm sensuousness of her beauty before dragging his mind back to less pleasant matters.

"To hunt." Before she could comment, he went on, "I know, you don't have to say it. If the man wants to get himself killed, he could hardly pick a better way."

"I'll go change," she said.

"Why?"

"Because I'm coming with you, of course."

She was? First he'd heard of it. "Fionna, you have many talents—" A purely masculine smile escaped him. "I can certainly attest to that. However, riding, especially at the hunt . . ."

"Will Isabella and her ladies be there?"

"I expect so."

"Excuse me, I have to get ready."

"Wait just a moment, I haven't agreed to your going. Why do you want to do this?"

She raised her head, with her back very straight, and looked right at him. "Because I thought about what you said yesterday. And I thought about Sula. Is that answer enough?"

It was. Glad though he was that she had taken his point seriously, he still hesitated. "You don't have to prove anything to Isabella."

She looked surprised at the idea. "Of course, I don't.

But it seems I do have to prove something to myself. Now, if you don't mind, we're wasting time."

He let her go but not without a certain sense of pride that he supposed was absurd. He could hardly take credit for her strength and courage. But he could—and did—admire them.

The Tower bailey was a scene of barely controlled chaos. Dozens of lords and ladies on horseback milled around, barely keeping their mounts in check, downing goblets of wine, their conversation ever more clamorous, their color high. Beaters, guardsmen, and hangers-on were out in force, going in every direction, adding to the general confusion. The dogs, brought from the kennels, strained frantically at their leads and filled the air with their yapping.

Only to have it all die away suddenly—save for the stray, solitary barking of a few hounds—when a war party rode into the bailey.

A collective holding of breath rippled through the assembly. For just a moment, a jolt of pure panic made the air vibrate.

Then it was gone, replaced by shocked recognition.

The Lord of Castlerock sat, armored and helmeted, on his warhorse. Behind him, arrayed in battle ranks, were his men, weapons at the ready. To the front, the hawk banner blew proudly.

Far in the back, surrounded by her own cordon of guards, Fionna swept her eyes over the crowd and hid a smile. Even in the throes of anger, Hugh was a master strategist. Nothing could have had more impact than this sudden, almost barbarous appearance in the midst of so much civilized frivolity. He was a living, breathing reminder of the conflict that threatened to consume them all.

In near total silence, they rode into the center of the bailey and stopped directly in front of the king.

John was scowling. Gloriously arrayed in burgundy velvet trimmed with jewels, a golden circlet on his head, and a wine goblet in his hand, he said, "Did you misunderstand me, my lord? I summoned you to a hunt, not a battle."

"No misunderstanding, sire," Hugh replied smoothly. "At least not on my part."

John's dark eyes widened at the unmistakable reprimand, but tellingly, he did not reply. Instead, he affected a tolerant smile. "If you really think all this is necessary, Castlerock, then so be it. I, for one, intend to enjoy myself."

Sensing their cue, the nobles gathered around him laughed. Hugh ignored them. He turned Sirocco in a tight circle and signaled his men. The laughter died away. Not even the most sycophantic courtier could deny a surge of apprehension when confronted by the grim-faced Lord of Castlerock.

They rode out, through the bailey gate and north along the eastern edge of the city toward Aldgate. Criers went ahead of them, clearing the way. Peddlers scrambled to get their carts to safety, parents snatched up their children, everyone scattered. But not so far that they could not observe their sovereign riding out on a day's hunt.

The faces Fionna saw were shuttered, blank but for a current of puzzlement and vague disbelief. Nothing the aristocracy could ever do would really surprise them, but John's behavior on this fine spring day came close.

Once outside the city, they turned north. Before very many miles had passed, the royal preserves appeared. Set aside since the Conqueror's day, their sustenance denied to the ordinary people who in previous generations had depended on them, the mixed wooded and cleared land was ideal hunting ground.

John drew rein and signaled to the falconers. They ran up, carrying the hooded birds on perches. The king selected a favorite, said something, smiling to one of his companions, and released the bird.

Beaters, moving through the scrub grass, had raised a flock of grouse. The birds fled into the sky, their wings beating frantically. The hawk climbed above them effortlessly, circled, took aim, and fell straight as a stone. It snared its prey, knocking it from the sky.

Bells rang, summoning the hawk as retrievers ran out to collect the grouse. Cheers were raised for the king's first kill.

Fionna turned away in disgust. Her father and his men hunted, but not like this. They did the work of killing themselves, and brought home meat for high and low alike. This business of hunting with birds, or dogs, was effete. She despised it.

Something must have shown in her face, for just then her eyes caught the queen's. Perched on her gelding, riding sidesaddle with enviable ease, Isabella smiled coldly and whispered something to one of her ladies. The two women laughed.

Fionna's spine felt as though it was about to crack in two and she could not feel her bottom at all. Whoever had invented the notion of a woman riding with her entire body twisted to one side so that she did not commit the unpardonable sin of parting her legs truly hated her sex.

Hugh had made it clear that he didn't care how she rode. There were tunics and robes cut to protect a woman's modesty while she sat a horse with a modicum of comfort. But Fionna refused to give in. If Isabella and her ladies could do it, she damn well could, too.

She smiled sweetly at the queen and inclined her head. Isabella frowned and looked away.

The hunt proceeded. More falcons and hawks were brought up, more unleashed into the sky, more helpless grouses fell before them until Fionna lost all count. It was all a strange mélange of boredom and cruelty mingling together, leaving her to feel as though she had no place in being there.

Just as she was wondering how long the whole business would go on, her guards suddenly closed ranks around her. Fionna's first thought was that Hugh's fear had proven justified, they were under attack. But she quickly realized that was not the case.

"Can you actually breath in there?" an amused voice inquired, "or are they smothering you?"

Fionna peered in between her guards. The same dark-haired man who had come to her aid in the Tower was sitting astride a chestnut mount. Finely garbed in velvet only a little less regal than the king's, his lean face burnished by the sun, William, Baron of Lancaster, looked much amused.

"I'm sorry," she said quickly, and gestured to the guards to let him approach. They did so, but only after a moment's hesitation and even then, they kept close watch.

"I can't remember when I've seen a lady so devotedly protected," Lancaster said when their horses were side by side. "Our queen herself is not as well guarded. Does Castlerock expect trouble or is he hoping for it?"

At her startled look, Lancaster laughed. "Forgive me. I know you've had little time at court, and I shouldn't expect you to engage in the usual repartee."

"The sort where people pose as friends to trap each other?" She might have little experience with John's court, but she had a great deal at her father's, and they were not entirely different. Although she saw no reason to say so.

"Exactly," Lancaster agreed. "Instead, let's do something totally outrageous and be direct with one another. What do you say?"

"I say you go first, my lord.".

His smile warmed a face that was otherwise austere. "Bravo, mistress. I'm glad to see your encounter with our queen did not dampen your spirits. All right, here you are. I came over to speak with you because you look as utterly bored as I feel. Are you?"

"I seem to have little taste for hunting," Fionna said carefully.

"This sort of hunting, at any rate?"

"All sorts really, I simply don't enjoy it. But this . . . I suppose I just don't get the point. Does it have to do with how well trained the birds are, that they'll leave their kill and return on command?"

"Yes, that's it exactly. They demonstrate the superiority of man over beast."

Fionna cast him a seeking glance. "Do you really believe that?"

"I would say it depends on the man . . . and the beast. Did you enjoy your tour of London yesterday?"

Fionna did not so much as flick an eyelash in surprise. She had already accepted that Londoners gossiped at least as readily as they breathed. "Was that what it was, a tour?"

"It certainly sounded like one, judging by how it was mulled over at court. First to St. Dunstan's, then down to the wharves—tell me, how *was* the swordfish? I tried to hire Dellacourte, one of many who have dreamed of him in their kitchens, but no luck."

"It was excellent, thank you." She, too, could play the sophisticate even as she tried to imagine what her mother would have made of such loose tongues.

"Then Smithfield. Surely, Castlerock knows the difference between an iron smith and a goldsmith, or do you have to enlighten him?"

"And surely you know by this time exactly why he went there. Would you like to see a drawing of the knife?"

"Not really. I've heard it described now at least a dozen times. The spectacle of a noble of the realm running all over London trying to identify a mysterious blade has everyone thoroughly distracted."

"It's killed three men," Fionna said. "All friends of the king. Are you his friend?"

"Yes," Lancaster said quietly, "from tenderest boyhood. We have hunted, jousted, marched, fought, drank, and counseled together these many years. Indeed, I have been called his shadow."

At her startled look, he added, "Before the king created me Baron of Lancaster, I was known as William of Troyes. I spent my youth at Queen Eleanor's court in Aquitaine. It was there that John and I became friends."

"I have heard of you . . ." Fionna said slowly. Even in Ireland—or perhaps especially there—the doings of British nobility were well mulled over. "John Lackland's shadow. Yes, that is what you were called."

"About the Lackland . . ."

"Forgive me, I meant no disrespect, but he was long referred to that way."

"Indeed, but it is well to remember that the name no longer fits. It hasn't since he succeeded to all his patiently awaited honors."

"I'm sorry about your son," Fionna said gently.

William's head jerked. For just a moment, his reserve dropped. "How do you know of that?"

"His death in France last year was a tragedy. I don't remember all the details, but it was a skirmish of some sort, wasn't it?"

Slowly, William nodded. "A particularly pointless one in what turned out to be a very pointless war. Still, Philip was a fine young man. I have no doubt God received him well."

"In such matters, faith must be a great comfort."

"It can be. Ah, look, we seem about to move on. Do you like venison? I suspect it will be on the royal table tonight."

The handlers brought the dogs up. The smell of the dead grouses all but drove the animals mad. A chase ensued. Most of the participants seemed widely enthusiastic about it—ladies and lords alike whooping and hollering as they sped over fields, through woods, up and down hillocks, and through streams.

Fionna made no effort to keep up. She knew the king would be somewhere at the front and that Hugh would be near him. With her own guards surrounding her, she did her best to find some pleasure in the day. The royal preserve was really very beautiful. Under other circumstances, she would have enjoyed strolling among the oak and hazel, finding the wildflowers that were blooming, and sitting quietly to watch the woodland animals.

But it was not to be. At the edge of a copse of birch trees, she caught up with the hunt. Men, women, and horses alike were all mulling around in confusion.

"Lost the scent . . ."

"Damn dogs . . ."

"What's happened?"

"The king . . ."

"It seems to be a blind," William said as he rejoined Fionna. "Now, why would that happen?"

Fionna shook her head. "I don't understand."

"A blind is a false scent, laid down deliberately to confuse the dogs and draw the hunt in a particular direction. The locals have been known to do it on occasion when they don't want us stomping all over their crops or some such. But the penalties are harsh, and besides, this is royal land. No one else has any business being here."

"Except to lure a king . . ."

A cold wind blew suddenly. She and Lancaster looked at each other. He paled.

"John . . ."

Without hesitation, Lancaster plunged into the wood. Fionna followed. She could hear her guards right behind her but gave them no thought. Nothing mattered except that she find Hugh. If John was in danger, if he had been lured into a trap, then in all likelihood Hugh was in it as well.

Her heart hammered against her ribs. With every passing moment, she feared to hear the clash of weapons and the screams of dying men.

But instead she found only silence. A small clearing lay up ahead. William had already drawn rein beside the king, who sat, gazing up at an ancient oak.

Nearby, Hugh's horse pawed the ground as his master's sword flashed.

Fionna put a hand to her mouth. She, too, looked at the tree.

Something hung from it, man-shaped, dangling from the neck . . . dear heaven . . .

"A straw man," Hugh said, and with a single swipe of his sword, cut the thing down. It fell with a soft thud to lie unmoving.

Hugh dismounted and sheathed his sword, although his men kept theirs at the ready. He walked over to the straw man and turned it over.

It had been made with some care, Fionna noted dully, even down to the stub of a male member, all that was left after the rest had been hacked off. The chest and limbs were streaked with blood. A distorted visage, complete with protruding tongue, stared at them unseeingly. On the head, a circlet of painted gold glinted darkly.

"Not a very flattering likeness," John said. They had left the clearing and were proceeding back along the road to London. The king rode surrounded by Hugh and his men. William was also with them and Fionna as well.

The hunt was over. Word of what had been found in the clearing had spread rapidly. They rode in almost total silence, the company grim-faced and wary-eyed.

CHAPTER TWENTY-TWO

They feasted at the Tower that evening. John insisted on it. Barely had they returned then he instructed the servants to prepare every manner of delicacy, summoned minstrels and the like, and insisted that everyone join him in the great hall.

"We're making far too much of this," he said as Hugh met with him shortly before going into supper. "It's just the sort of trick Londoners would pull. I should have expected it."

"I'm glad it didn't disturb Your Majesty," Hugh said dryly. He had seen John's face at the instant the straw man was discovered and knew very well how terrified the monarch had been. "However, I still think it should be considered a serious warning."

The king sighed, sat back in his chair, and looked from Hugh to Fionna. He had drawn her along into his private chamber, with William of Lancaster, as well. Isabella had tried to join them, but her royal husband had sent her off with some excuse or other. The queen was not pleased.

"What do you think, my dear?" John asked. "Should I be lying awake in my bed at night terrified of merchants, peddlers, and the like?"

"Not by themselves," she said frankly, "but in combination with the disaffected barons? Then, yes, I'd say you have something to worry about."

John shook his head. He looked amused. "What is it about your family, Castlerock? I don't understand this penchant for plainspoken women. Although I suppose when they're this beautiful . . ."

"She is right, my lord," William interrupted. The king's "shadow" looked so finely drawn that Fionna feared for him. "We all saw the straw man. How can you possibly dismiss that? When subjects reach the point of commiting such an atrocity, even in proxy, they must be taught a harsh lesson."

John lifted his wine goblet but did not drink from it. He twirled the stem between his fingers. "What would you have me do, William? Hang a few worthy aldermen? Lay waste to a few city blocks? Or perhaps just burn the whole thing? That would solve the problem, wouldn't it?"

He jumped up suddenly, startling them all. His cloak flapping around him, he strode over to the windows. "That's the answer. Raze rebel London to the ground, set the army to loot and pillage, invite the barons in for a share. When it's done, I can build myself a new city more to my liking and who will miss London, after all? The rest of the country despises it, and rightly so. Send for the scribes. I'll dictate the orders right now. We can have the place in ashes by morning."

"Majesty . . ." William began.

John sighed again. The strange, frantic energy seemed to go out of him as quickly as it had appeared. "But what's the use?" he said, more to himself than to them. "It won't solve anything. When the barons have finished gorging themselves on the spoils, they'll turn on me."

Abruptly, he faced Hugh. "What is it that they want, Castlerock? What is it *you* want, for don't try to fool me, you and your father are as close to deLongueville and the rest as you've ever been to me."

"That is not true, Your Majesty," Hugh said quietly. "If it were, I would not be here."

John laughed, a harsh sound that rang sharply in the small room. He slumped in his chair again and reached for the wine. William stepped in, filling the goblet and handing it to him.

Looking at Lancaster, the king said, "He means it, you know. He really does. He didn't have to come. He had a choice."

A thin smile played around his mouth. "You didn't know I knew that, did you, Castlerock?"

Hugh frowned. "I'm not sure I understand, sire."

"Surely, you and your father had a *chat* before you departed for London?"

"Of course we did, but . . ."

"And he asked if you had any desire to be king."

Fionna shot a surprised look at Hugh. His face had gone completely blank.

"He didn't want it for himself, you see," John went on. "Conan decided that a very long time ago. But he had to know how you felt."

"If Your Majesty has ever had any reason to question the loyalty of my family . . ." Hugh began.

"Not at all," John said. He waved away the suggestion. "Not a bit of it. Mother told me, you see, just before she died. Explained it all."

"All . . . ?" The word was out before Fionna could stop herself.

John focused his gaze on her. He smiled. "Well, no, perhaps not. I have the oddest feeling you may be a better judge of that than I ever could be. But what she did explain was why I should trust the estimable Baron of Glastonbury. Oh, yes, Wyndham, too, although I daresay Glastonbury comes first in his heart. Wouldn't you agree, Hugh?"

"I believe my father has always done his utmost to care for all our lands and the people on them."

"Absolutely," John agreed. "And just look at the results." He turned to William, as though informing him. "You won't find more prosperous yeoman anywhere in our kingdom. They have the most fertile fields, the fattest cattle, the most buxom wives, the healthiest children. It's a marvel, truly."

"I'm not familiar with . . ." William began.

"You really should visit Glastonbury," John urged. "It looks almost ordinary . . . town, abbey, castle, the usual. But when you look a little more closely . . ." He broke off, turned to Hugh, and said, "How is your dear mother these days? Still visiting that island of hers?"

Fionna sucked in her breath. She had dared look at Hugh. When she did, it was to see that his eyes had narrowed to shards of ice.

"I wouldn't know, Highness," he said.

"She does, count on it. Did you know Eleanor was there a time or two?"

"I wasn't aware . . ."

"Of course not, why would you have been? But you have visited the island, haven't you?"

"I don't see where this is . . ."

"Neither do I," William said forcefully. He appeared genuinely perplexed. "There are serious matters to decide, Majesty. This serves nothing."

"No," John said slowly. "I suppose not." He spared a last long look at Fionna. On a note of genuine regret, he murmured, "I apologize for my wife, my dear. I hope it didn't concern you over much."

Shocked by his frankness—and his understanding—Fionna said, "It is forgotten, Majesty."

"If we could consider more immediate matters . . ." William urged.

The king looked suddenly tired, but he made an effort to rally his attention. "All right, we won't burn down London."

"That's good," Hugh muttered.

"What happened to the straw man?" the king asked.

"Two of my men stayed behind to destroy it," Hugh said.

John smiled. "Always thinking. Good, then we shall put it about that it was a pagan symbol, nothing at all to do with me. Rally the priests to preach the usual sermons. Maybe find someone to make an example of . . ."

"No," Hugh said. His voice rang hard. "That you will not do."

John looked surprised. "No? Why not?"

"Because innocents would suffer."

Fionna let her breath out slowly. She had been thinking of Sula, wondering how to get word to the old woman—and get her to safety.

"Oh . . . I suppose that's so. Very well, then, no examples, just good rousing sermons, hellfire, damnation, the sort of thing they've hurled at me so well in the past. Time they gave a little back." He smiled. "Get everyone stirred up over the straw man. Distract them from other things."

"I'm not sure that will work," William ventured. "These are Londoners we're dealing with, after all."

"Of course it won't actually work," John said, as though explaining a simple point to a child. "But they'll know I don't expect it to, and they'll take it for the entertainment it's meant to be. In the meantime . . ."

The king stood slowly. To Fionna's eyes, he appeared stiff and ailing, as though the weight of the world bore down on him.

"Find the killer," he said to Hugh. "Bring him to justice. DeLongueville and the others are no more nor less than I expect them to be. But this man, whoever he is, is too close. Find him."

"He is only one man," Hugh said quietly. "The barons are raising an army."

"One thing at a time," John replied. "And now I must show myself in hall." He gestured to William. "Let us put off care and muster good cheer, old friend. Can you manage that?"

"I can try, Majesty," William said, and went with him.

"I'm not sure I can," Fionna said when the king and his shadow had gone. She felt unutterably weary and deeply confused. What exactly did John know?

"Today, when I saw you in the clearing with your sword drawn, I thought you might mean to kill him."

Hugh came to her. He took her into his arms, drawing her against his warm, hard, and now familiar body. His hand stroked her hair.

"Hush. You're very tired."

"I am," she agreed. "So very tired. It all presses in too much sometimes. Did you think of killing him?"

"Not then. I just meant to cut the thing down before too many saw it."

"When?"

He did not misunderstand her. With a sigh he said, "When I heard what Isabella said to you, I thought why not be rid of them all?"

"That's impossible. There will always be more. Superstition and prejudice know no bounds."

He nodded against her hair. They stood like that for several minutes while the growing sounds of revelry filtered up the stair. Whatever worries the lords and ladies had brought back from the hunt, they seemed willing enough to put them aside, if only for a few hours.

"Let's go," Hugh said suddenly.

"Shouldn't you . . . ?" She was thinking that this night above all, it was surely important for the king's most powerful ally to show himself at his monarch's side.

"Yes I should, but I'm not going to. John is playing too many games. He doesn't seem to know any other way, but I've had enough of it. Besides," he added as his fingers curled under her chin. "I can think of far better ways to spend the time."

* * *

It was very quiet out on the river. Along the wharves, a few dim lights flickered from the odd fire, but otherwise there was no illumination save for the stars flitting between clouds and the moon, waning now.

By the time they reached the water steps at Westminster, Fionna was almost nodding off. She was grateful for Hugh's strong arm to lean against. But when he lifted her, she felt duty bound to protest.

"You're always doing that, carrying me about as though I can't manage on my own."

"That's not why I do it," he said softly. A guard on the wall called the challenge. Hugh replied. The wicket gate opened for them. "I do it because I like it," he went on, carrying her through. "You feel good in my arms. Besides," he added, smiling down on her, "at least this way I know exactly where you are, if only for a few minutes."

"Does it matter so much, where I am?"

"Yes, but you knew that, didn't you?"

"I wasn't sure," she admitted. A smile tugged at the corners of her mouth. "There's a great deal to be said for ancient wisdom, but it doesn't necessarily cover every specific situation."

He laughed and mounted the stairs to the keep. She was not a particularly small woman, yet he carried her effortlessly. The reminder of the vast strength he possessed, strength of will as well as body, sent a small tremor through her.

"John will have missed us by now," she said.

"To hell with John," Hugh replied, and lengthened his stride.

"It's not fair," Fionna complained when they reached the tower chamber.

"What isn't?"

"That you're not even breathing hard. How many steps was that?"

"I've never counted them. However, if you'd like to wear me out, I can make a few suggestions."

She rolled her eyes and laughed. He dropped her on the bed and began unfastening his sword belt. She lay there and watched unabashedly. He was such a magnificent man, the epitome of virility and strength. Yet he was capable of such gentleness. He made her feel more excited and at risk than she ever had in her life, even as he wrapped her in a cocoon of protection and security.

He laid the sword beside the bed, within easy reach.

"Is it ever farther than that from your hand?" she asked.

"No," he replied, and stripped off his tunic. His body shone in the moonlight, lean and hard, without softness, the thin white lines of scars visible here and there.

Fionna raised herself and ran a finger along one such mark that crossed his chest just above his flat abdomen. "How did you get this?" she asked. The heat of his body surrounded her. She inhaled the unique scent of him—a combination of leather, soap, wool, and pure man—and felt her senses whirl.

"Fighting in France with John," he answered, and lifted her higher. Their kiss was long and heated, tongues playing, mouths clinging. When they broke apart at last, she joined him in making swift work of her clothes. Naked, they fell across the welcoming bed.

His mouth and hands cherished her, but when she would have returned his caresses, he stopped her.

"Wait," he said hoarsely and turned her, lifting her hips, covering her as the stallion does the mare.

Fionna gasped as he entered her. His penetration touched to the very core of her being. His hands cupped her breasts, circling her nipples, as he moved with slow, deep thrusts that brought her rapidly to the edge of madness.

She cried out, her voice muffled, moving with him, unable to get enough of the exquisitely erotic sensations he unleashed. Just when she thought she could not possibly bear it a moment longer, his rhythm quickened and she was gone, hurtling over the edge into oblivion. In the next instant, he followed, spilling his seed deep within her.

Starlings were arguing outside the window. Fionna opened her eyes to their chatter. She lay for a few moments before the echoes of her dreams faded away. Slowly, she sat up.

She was alone. It was full daylight. From the bailey below came the usual sounds of the men drilling.

Winding a sheet around herself, she left the bed. Funny what she thought of as usual now. Listening to the preparations for war. Waking in the bed of an English lord. Being quite calm about the wild twists and turns her life had taken ever since stepping off the wharf in Dublin.

Perhaps not entirely calm. A glance in the bronzed mirror on the table showed her a woman with wide, somewhat dazed eyes, swollen lips, and very mussed hair.

That wouldn't do at all. Clean, still-warm water sat in an ewer on the table. She filled a basin, washed quickly, and brushed her hair until her eyes stung. There were fresh clothes in the chest at the bottom of the bed. Selecting a simple saffron-hued tunic and light blue bliaut, she dressed, then left the chamber.

The day was bright, the air soft. Incredibly, the air actually smelled good. She stood at the top of the wooden steps leading down to the bailey and looked around. The scene, now so familiar, was filled with purposeful activity. Not one but two forges were at work, smiths straining at their work.

Groomers were tending to the horses, currying, checking shoes and tack, mixing the oat and honey mixture the animals had to make do with while in stable. Before too long, they would need the good grass that grew on the limestone plains, for every sensible person knew it was from there that the strength of their bones came.

Several women were taking advantage of the day to set up their loom outside. Nearby, several more were spinning. Savory smells issued from the bakers' ovens, placed a little apart from the wooden structures along the walls.

Fionna shielded her eyes, looking at the guards keeping watch. They stood upright, no lounging, and did not speak with one another. All their attention was focused outward, to the river and the London road. As it had been for several days, the portcullis was down, but people were coming and going through the small wicket gate.

Her eyes widened slightly as she recognized one of

them. Coming down the steps, she went to greet Samuel Wolcott.

"Good morning," she said.

He looked startled but pleased to encounter her. "Mistress Fionna, how are you feeling?"

"Much improved, thank you. Your aunt's soup proved the perfect cure."

He laughed, his young face more relaxed than she had seen it before. In the moment before he replied, she noted that he was very well if discreetly dressed. His garments were plain but of the finest fabric. There was an air of confidence and determination about him.

"I'll tell her you said so. She'll be pleased. Is his lordship about?"

"I believe he's drilling with his men. Shall we see?"

He nodded, and they walked along together across the bailey. Before they reached the far side, in the yard set apart by an inner wall, the clash of arms could be heard clearly.

Fionna and Samuel paused at a safe distance. Anyone coming unawares upon the scene could have been forgiven for thinking a small battle had broken out. The men were paired off, fighting in apparent earnest, swords flashing in the morning sun. They wore full chain mail, no concession made either to the mounting temperature or their exertions.

In their center, Hugh shouted a word of encouragement here, a direction there, all the while keeping not one but two knights at bay. Taller than the average man, endowed with greater strength and agility, he was a natural—and fierce—leader. It seemed utterly impossible that this savage figure was the same man who held her so gently in the soft hours of night.

Fionna's throat clenched. One slip, one misjudgment, and——

"Bit more than the usual drill," Samuel observed. "I would say his lordship is readying for war, and that he expects it soon."

"I suspect you're right," Fionna murmured. "At any rate, I don't think we should interrupt him."

"I wouldn't dream of it," Samuel assured her. "Perhaps you can help. I understand his lordship is trying to identify a certain knife?"

"Yes, that's right. I have a sketch of it, the blade part at least." She drew it from her tunic and showed him.

Samuel looked at it long and carefully before handing it back to her. "May I ask where this came from?"

"I drew it."

"How? Since you don't have the knife, how could you determine what it looks like?"

Fionna hesitated. She liked the Wolcotts instinctively but she also knew little of them. Cautiously, she said, "There are ways to determine such things."

Samuel's dark eyes were very penetrating. Slowly, the expression in them changed. He looked at her with new respect. "You examined the wounds. That's the only way you could have gotten this."

"I believe it is accurate," Fionna replied quietly. "One of the bodies was no longer available, but the width of the blade at least is consistent with the cut on his garments where he was struck."

"Very thorough." He studied the drawing again. "It isn't English."

"No, his lordship thinks it's Saracen, and a smith he

took it to, who seemed very knowledgeable, said the same."

"I'd have to agree," Samuel said. "I've traveled in the Holy Land, and blades shaped like this are not uncommon."

"Apparently, some were brought back by returning Crusaders."

"That would make sense. I suppose the owner of this could have purchased it here, but generally such things have been kept by those who first acquired them."

"So we're looking for someone who's been on Crusade."

Samuel shrugged. "Unfortunately, that includes thousands of people. It doesn't do much good."

"No, it doesn't but . . ." Fionna hesitated. She took Samuel's arm and guided him a little way of where they could speak with greater privacy. "Does the name Kalil mean anything to you?"

"Kalil? What has that to do with this?"

"Perhaps nothing, but it is possible that the knife may have a name. Kalil."

He looked at her for a long moment. She feared he was about to ask how she could have learned that, but instead he said, "Kalil is Arabic for good friend."

"Good friend? That's all, it doesn't mean anything else?"

"I'm afraid not. It's a common enough name in the Moslem world."

"Whoever owns this knife called it *good friend*? That's . . ."

"Men develop all sorts of feelings for the weapons that keep them alive. Surely, you realize that?"

"I suppose, but *good friend*? That sounds like

something a man would call his—" She stopped. There were some things she really shouldn't say, especially not to a man she barely knew. Things men liked to believe women didn't know.

Samuel started. His cheeks reddened slightly. "Yes, well . . ." He cleared his throat and tried again. "There is that, I suppose."

He sounded doubtful, and Fionna thought she knew why. To Samuel Wolcott, men who made their way in life through force of arms probably seemed all cut from the same cloth—dangerous yet uninteresting. She might have thought the same were it not for her experience at her father's court and more recently among Hugh and his men.

"Look there," she said, drawing Samuel's attention back to the practice yard. "Do you see that older man, fighting with the redheaded fellow?"

"What about him?"

"His name is Sir Peyton. He's his lordship's trusted lieutenant. He doesn't say much, at least not when I'm nearby, but I have the feeling he misses very little. Now, can you imagine him going around with a knife he calls *good friend*?"

"I suppose not—"

"He'd think it was ridiculous. It's the sort of thing he'd scoff at. But he's an older man. Who knows what he was like in his youth? He's lived long enough to mature, gain some perspective, that sort of thing. Whoever named this knife hasn't."

"A young man, then?"

Fionna nodded. "Who has been on Crusade."

"And who knows the king's friends."

They look at each other excitedly. But Fionna felt

compelled to introduce a note of caution. "It's all speculation, unfortunately."

"Do you have anything better?"

She acknowledged that she did not. "I'll speak to his lordship about this as soon as he's free. Perhaps something will occur to him."

Samuel looked at the melee underway in the practice yard. His face was grim. "I hope so. This is going to get very bad very fast, and when it does, people will die."

CHAPTER TWENTY-THREE

"Good friend?" Hugh repeated. He had returned to the tower room to strip off his sweat-soaked tunic and bathe. Stretched out in the tub, he stared at Fionna. "What the hell kind of name is that?"

Perched on a stool nearby, she twined a strand of red-gold hair around one finger and shrugged. "Samuel and I were wondering the same. We thought it might indicate a certain immaturity on the part of the owner."

"Immaturity? It's a joke. If you're going to give a blade a name, you give it a decent one—Blood-Drinker, Widow-Maker, Foe-Cleaver, something like that."

"Those are all ghastly."

"They're supposed to be, that's the whole point. The only blade I ever heard of that didn't have a name like that was Excaliber, and it was named by a woman."

"The Lady of the Lake?"

"Exactly."

Their eyes met. Neither of them particularly wanted to pursue that topic just then.

"You may be right about it being a young man," Hugh said. "And a damn foolish one at that."

"But no one in particular comes to mind?"

"I'm afraid not. There are so many foolish young men around John. Why would one of them do this?"·

"To avenge some wrong, imagined or otherwise?"

Hugh soaped his broad chest absently. Fionna considered offering to do it for him but thought better of that. They really did need to talk.

"It wouldn't have to be imagined where John is concerned. He's wronged more people than anyone could count."

"Surely, there aren't that many who would feel compelled to go about killing his friends?"

"No," Hugh acknowledged. "Most of them would just go off and join the barons."

"Why wouldn't this person do that, whoever he is?"

"I don't know," he said slowly. Abruptly, he rose. Water poured down his tall, hard body. "It makes no sense," he continued as he reached for a cloth and began drying himself. "There's a civil war brewing. Unless John's luck changes, there's a very real chance he could lose his throne and be killed in the process. Why isn't that enough for this fellow?"

"Maybe we've been wrong all along," Fionna suggested. She stood up and took another cloth, helping to dry his back. The simple, almost wifey task helped steady the turbulence of her thoughts. "Perhaps, Huteuil and the others really were the intended victims, and this has nothing at all to do with the king."

"We still have to find the killer, if only to prove to John that he wasn't the target."

"But you still think he was . . . is?"

Hugh nodded. He slipped an arm around her waist.

She laughed, protesting. "You're going to get me wet."

"I'm going to do a good deal more than that," he said, and drew her hard against him.

It was mid-afternoon when they returned to the Tower. There were more guards than before on the walls, and the bailey was unusually quiet. On the way through London, Fionna had noted the many shops that were now shuttered, and the fewer people in the streets.

"People are leaving, aren't they?" she asked as Hugh helped her from her mount.

He nodded. "They're remembering they promised to visit their aged uncle in the countryside or recalling that they really do need to pay more attention to their estates. Traffic at the wharves is down to less than half what it was as recently as a few days ago. Even the ship captains are going elsewhere."

"Do you think John knows?"

"He must. But if I mention it to him, he'll just tell me to find the killer first. Sometimes I think the barons could be at the gates, and he'd still be yapping about the damn killer."

"It may be easier for him to deal with the idea of one man against him rather than the entire breakdown of what passes for social order."

"Easier and a good deal more dangerous, but that's John. He's taken insane risks all his life, and he's still doing it."

No one challenged them as they climbed the steps to the royal keep. Inside, servants were scurrying around as usual, but they looked as tense and grim as people everywhere else.

Hugh stopped one man. "Where is the king?"

"In his privy chamber, I believe, my lord. He has not shown himself today."

"Is he ill?" Hugh demanded.

"Not that I've heard, my lord."

"All right, go on." The servant slipped away quickly as others eyed them nervously.

"Is it like John to stay shut up?" Fionna asked.

"Only when he's brooding. The straw man upset him more than he wanted to admit. I warrant he slept little."

They found the king slumped in the same chair he'd occupied the previous evening. He was alone, even to the extent of being unguarded. His hair was disheveled, he was unshaven, and he appeared to be wearing the same clothes they had last seen him in.

"My lord . . ." Hugh began uncertainly. This was more than mild malaise. Something was very wrong.

"Ah, Castlerock and the lovely Fionna. Come in. I was just thinking about you."

As they approached, Hugh stepped in front of Fionna, instinctively shielding her. A knife lay on the table before the king. He was toying with it.

"What has happened?" Hugh asked.

John blinked, set the knife down, and looked at him. "Happened? Oh, happened. There's been another killing, that's all. Nothing unusual, certainly not around here."

Fionna inhaled sharply. This couldn't possibly be true. "We would have heard—"

The king's eyes, sharp and red-rimmed, bored into her. "You'd think so, wouldn't you? Except I sealed the door when I found him this morning. No one's been allowed in."

"Found who?" Hugh asked quietly. He was moving closer to the table—and the knife.

"Francis Desmond, Father Desmond he was, only damn priest I could ever stand. Did you know him?"

"We met once or twice. How did he die?"

"How do you think? He was stabbed, like the others." The king's face went blank, his gaze unfocused. "Blood all over, he was soaked in it . . ."

Hugh's hand reached across the table. He lifted the knife. "Was he killed with this?"

John looked up, momentarily confused. "No, of course not. That's mine. Put it back."

When Hugh did not obey, the king laughed, a hollow sound Fionna thought was close to a cry. "Put it back, man. What did you think, that I intended to use it? Well, I do, but only if the same bloody bastard comes at me. He's going to eventually, you know. That's what this is all about."

Slowly, Hugh released the knife but he left it well outside the king's reach. "Where is Father Desmond?"

John jerked his head toward a door set in the wall to his left. "Right through there. He came late last night, arrived from the lowlands. He knew there was trouble brewing here and thought I might need some company. Good soul, always understood what I was feeling. We're so crowded here—or at least we were—I gave him my own chamber." He reached into the pouch hanging from his belt and removed a large, iron key.

"See for yourself."

Hugh opened the small door. The smell that emerged made Fionna gag.

"Stay here," he directed, and stepped inside.

The priests had come and gone, taking the remains of Father Desmond with them. His body would lie in the Tower chapel until arrangements for his burial could be made.

The death chamber had been given over to the servants, who were hard at work cleaning it.

John remained slumped in his chair. The knife still lay on the table, but now a pitcher of wine had joined it.

"I knew him before he took his vows," the king said. "When he said he wanted to become a priest, I thought it a fine joke."

"You were very close?" Hugh asked quietly.

"Years ago, yes. Then not close at all. But again recently . . . I found him very calming." He shrugged as though it was all a matter of puzzlement to him. "We talked a great deal, not about politics, he had no interest in that. But about life, faith . . . what happens after death."

A twisted smile spread across the king's features. "I suppose he knows all about that now."

The door to the king's chamber opened. William entered hurriedly. He looked flushed and anxious.

"Sire, I just heard—"

"Ah, a friend, and one still able to walk about. Come in. Give us your opinion on this. Can you think of any particular reason, aside from his acquaintance with me, that Francis would get himself killed?"

Lancaster hesitated. He cast a quick look at Hugh

and Fionna, then went over to stand beside the king. Almost gently, he said, "This one is different, my lord. You must realize that."

"How different?" John inquired. "He was knifed, same as the others. When our dear Fionna has finished, we will undoubtedly hear that the same blade was used. I see no difference."

"What do you say, Castlerock?" William asked. "Do you imagine this is just as the rest?"

"Not entirely." At John's frown, he explained. "Sire, Baron Lancaster has raised an important point. Father Desmond died in the chamber you yourself would have been occupying. We must recognize the possibility that whoever did this mistook him for you." He paused a moment, then said, "May I ask where you were sleeping last night, sire?"

John reached for the wine. He poured himself a generous measure and downed it in a single swallow. Entirely unabashed, he said, "In the stable."

Hugh's brows rose. "Sire?"

"Oh, don't worry, I wasn't alone. A very buxom milkmaid was with me. I have no doubt that had it come to it, she could have protected me more than adequately."

Despite herself, Fionna felt the beginnings of a smile. She didn't particularly like John. He could have been a far better king if he'd simply made the effort, and all the angels knew he was no friend of Ireland's. On the other hand, neither was he a coward. She was a true child of the moon's lake, yet her father's world was also her own. She knew the way of the warrior, and she did not despise it.

"I have amused Mistress Fionna," John said. "Did you imagine I was past the milkmaid stage, madame?"

"No, sire, as a matter of fact, I did not. Indeed, given the choice between your sleeping within these stone walls or joining a warm woman in the hay, who could deny that you made a very sensible decision?"

John laughed. His shoulders shook with the force of it. The exertion seemed to dispel the aura of despair that had been gathering around him.

"Plucked her from the sea, did you, Castlerock? I'd say that's the best catch you'll ever make." He laughed again. Even William, confronted by his sovereign's good humor, managed a tentative smile.

John hoisted the wine. "Let's drink to poor Francis, wherever he is now. And let's drink to all the rest of them, all the merry dead, legions of them here, in France, everywhere. They're a damn sight better off than we are."

"Amen to that," William murmured. He accepted a goblet from the king and drank deeply of it.

"The same blade," Fionna said quietly. She straightened up from her examination of Father Desmond. "A single blow. Our killer is quite expert."

Beside her, Hugh said, "This place teems with men who know how to kill. It's the one thing almost all of us can do."

"But this is a young man, left-handed, taller than average, who has been on Crusade and who is very well acquainted with the Tower, able to go even into the king's private chambers. There can't possibly be many like that."

"No, there can't," Hugh agreed. He took her arm and

led her away. Behind them, the priests who had been watching with simmering disapproval, moved in to reclaim their own.

"I don't understand why no one saw anything," Hugh continued as they left the chapel. "This is the single most heavily guarded place in all of England right now. How could anyone walk straight into the royal bedchamber, commit murder, and walk away with no one even catching a glimpse of him?"

"He would have to know a great deal . . . the guard schedule, the servants' routine, all of it."

"But not that the king preferred the company of a milkmaid."

"I'm not sure of that," Fionna said slowly. "We're presuming John was the intended target this time, but what if he wasn't? What if this is just one more killing intended to torment him?"

"Ratcheting up the tension?"

"Yes, and doing it just when John most desperately needs to clear his mind and deal with the barons. People are deserting him, we've seen that for ourselves. He's running out of time."

Hugh's face was grim. "We all are."

They returned to Westminster. There seemed nothing else to do after the king absolutely refused to allow Hugh to keep watch on him.

What John had actually said to the suggestion was, "For God's sake, you can't possibly want to spend the night with me rather than Mistress Fionna. That's carrying loyalty a damn sight too far."

"You are my liege lord, sire," Hugh said patiently. "And someone may very well be trying to kill you."

"Finally convinced of that, are you?"

"Yes, sire, completely convinced. Now, as to guarding you——"

"There are no fewer than three hundred men-at-arms within the Tower right now, and several thousand more within easy reach. If they can't keep me safe, what makes you think you could?"

He paused, surveyed the proud Lord of Castlerock, mailed and armed for battle, and shrugged. "Well, perhaps you could, but never fear. I intend to sleep well surrounded tonight, if I sleep at all. That milkmaid is still about somewhere——"

The king smiled. "That's the way to go, you know. If you can't die in battle, do it in the arms of a willing woman. Anything else, you might as well be a mewing monk."

"I'll keep that in mind, sire, but I still think——"

"Go," John ordered.

They went. At Westminster, a message awaited them.

"From Father," Hugh said, opening the sealed parchment in the bailey where a servant had handed it to him. He read by the light of torches set in iron brackets along the walls, their smoke rising to the darkening sky. Clouds were moving in. It looked as though a storm was approaching.

"Is he——?" Fionna asked.

"Much improved but Mother still insists on coddling him. He has more word of the barons . . ." He read on.

When he was done, he rolled up the parchment, tucked it into his tunic, and led Fionna into the keep. She did not ask what more there was, and he did not tell her, until they were alone in the tower chamber.

"Father has been in contact with deLongueville and

the others. He is urging them to formulate their demands, actually put them in writing to provide a basis for negotiation."

"Will they do so?" Fionna asked. She moved about the chamber, lighting the braziers and turning down the covers of the bed. The servants would have done all that, but it soothed her to have such ordinary tasks.

"Only if they believe there is some purpose to it. If John will listen—"

She eased her shoes off and set them to one side. On the table nearby was a heap of parchment, letters, and such like that Hugh had been reading. Nearby was a chest of books.

He read, as did his father. They were men of letters as well as the sword. But the barons . . .

"Perhaps I am being too Irish," she began.

Hugh stripped off his tunic, dropped it on a bench, and grinned. "You? Never."

She shot him a chiding look that faded as she became somewhat distracted by the magnificence of his body. With an effort, she dragged her thoughts back.

"It's just that I have a hard time imagining such men as those sitting down and calmly writing a list of their demands. To begin with, can they write at all?"

"I've no idea," Hugh admitted. "But they have scribes."

"All the same, they have to be able to think it out first. I thought you said they were the sort to go through a wall rather than around it. That hardly rings of reasoned discourse."

Naked, he hefted his sword, set it by the bed, and laid down. Stretched out to his full length, he patted the mattress beside him.

"No, but it definitely rings of my father. Now, if you wouldn't mind, perhaps we could postpone the rest of this discussion until morning."

With just a touch of self-consciousness, Fionna finished removing her clothes. The feel of his eyes on her warmed her all the way through. Her nipples hardened reflexively, and she felt a tightening at the core of her womanhood. Slowly, she approached the bed.

"I do apologize," she said sweetly. "You're bound to be tired."

"You think so?"

"Well, we were up rather late last night."

"Speaking of up . . ."

She followed the path of his eyes and blushed, yet she could not draw her gaze away. He was utterly compelling in his untrammeled masculinity.

He reached out, caught her hand, and drew her to him. Hardly aware of what was happening, she found herself lying above him, their bodies touching all along their length.

Go slowly, a part of her mind whispered, *savor every moment of this. Who knows what lies ahead . . .*

But hot, sweet yearning coiled through her, banishing thought. Passion flared. They moved together as one, tasting, tempting, pleasing.

Firelight fell over their naked bodies. The silence of the stone chamber yielded to the soft cries of a woman and the heated groans of a man. Their joining was fevered, swift, almost savage in its boundless need. Outside, storm clouds massed. Thunder reverberated off the fortress walls, lightning cleaved the sky, but neither Fionna nor Hugh noticed. They were lost in a storm of their own making.

They fell unmoving for some little time, but quickly enough the nearness each to the other stirred desires that could never truly be sated. Again they came together, more slowly, lingering with the attention of connoisseurs while rain slashed against the windows and the air filled with the rich, fecund scent of waking earth.

Sleep claimed them at last, but not before Hugh pulled the covers over them both and settled Fionna close in his arms. His muscled thigh lay between her own, his massive chest was beneath her cheek. The sound of his heartbeat echoed in her dreams.

CHAPTER TWENTY-FOUR

Fionna woke suddenly. Even before her eyes were open, she saw the intense flash of light that turned the tower room bright as day. An eerie ghost reflection of it lingered for several moments before soft darkness returned, but only briefly. The sky groaned and rumbled, several more bolts of lightning coursed between heaven and earth.

She shivered and instinctively burrowed deeper beneath the covers, grateful for the warmth and nearness of Hugh's powerful form.

He slept on.

She lifted her head a fraction and stared, part resentfully, part in amazement. How could anyone possibly sleep through such a tempest? Yet sleep he did—deeply, utterly, obliviously.

Amazing.

She shielded her eyes from another flash of lightning and wished the storm would end. Instead, it seemed to be settling in. The tumult abated, but sheets of rain followed, drumming hard against the earth.

Fionna settled back down, closed her eyes again, and courted sleep. It would not come. She tried again. The more she pressed, the more elusive it became. Before long, she was acutely awake.

With a sigh, she sat up, pulled the covers higher, and glanced once more at Hugh. Perhaps he would also awaken and then . . .

Barely had her thoughts swerved in so unseemly a direction than she yanked them back sharply. Surely, she was not so far gone in lust as to deny a man much needed rest?

Rest, moreover, that he'd amply earned.

Resigned to the need to have just a wee bit of consideration, she lay listening to the rain fall and let her thoughts wander.

So much had happened . . . so much turmoil and danger . . . so much unknown . . .

Moonlight glinted on honed steel. The plaint of a lute echoed softly. Amid the shadows cast by torches down the long stone halls of the royal keep, a murderer stalked, this time his target a king.

Fionna's eyes flew open. What was this? Had she slept after all, and dreamed? Or had she experienced a strange waking vision such as were sometimes known to come in times of peril?

The room was dark. Far above the clouds that shrouded London, the moon rode in all her glory, but not a hint of her light reached the city through the storm.

No vision then, or at least not one unfolding in the

world at the same moment, for she had seen the scene etched in silver light. A little time must be left.

But for what? They had clues aplenty, dead bodies heaping up, and no direction in which to turn.

Something teased at her mind, a random thought, a fragment of memory. She knew better than to chase it but lay very still, waiting, coaxing the whisper to come to her.

France.

France?

What did that mean? The blade was Saracen, from the Holy Land. It had nothing to do with France.

Who had mentioned France recently? Oh, yes, John, in that toast of his.

. . . All the merry dead, legions of them here, in France . . .

John had been fighting in France the previous year, trying to regain what he regarded as his possessions there. The attempt was followed with interest in Ireland, never loath to see the English take a beating. And they had, being routed by the French when all of John's attempts at strategy went amiss. That's where Hugh had gotten the wound that, had it been a few inches lower, would have killed him.

Amen to that.

What? Amen . . . ? Oh, yes, William, lifting the wine goblet the king handed to him and drinking deeply.

William's son had died in France. How many other parents had suffered similar losses? Far too many, no doubt, and most of them ordinary folk whose mourning would never be anything but private.

She turned, looking at the man beside her, and

thought again of the precariousness of life. How very precious every moment was.

Hugh murmured in his sleep. She bent closer, loving the touch and scent of him, the strength and gentleness, all that made this one extraordinary man so unique in her experience . . . and in her heart.

Loving . . .

His eyes opened. He saw her and smiled. "Sweetling . . ."

His hands were reaching for her, his body moving to hers, when he stopped abruptly.

Fionna eased herself up and looked at him. "What's wrong?"

He grimaced. "I fear we're not alone."

"What?" She glanced around, horrified that anyone might observe them at their lovemaking.

"Not that," he said quickly. "I keep thinking of John. He is too much in my mind. I shouldn't have left the Tower."

"He ordered you to go. Besides, he's got his milk-maid and you've got . . ."

Hugh groaned. He caught her questing hand in one of his and kissed her palm. "Don't, my resolve is weak enough now as it is."

"Odd, it doesn't seem weak to me." She smiled mischievously.

He swatted her bottom, swung his legs off the side of the bed, and stood up.

"Where are you going?" she asked, her stomach plummeting, for she already knew.

"Stay here. You need to rest. Besides, I doubt the streets of London will be safe much longer. Peyton will guard you."

"What about you?"

"I'll take men with me." He reached for his tunic and began to dress.

Fionna watched him with apprehension that was very close to despair. She did not want him to plunge back into the cauldron that was the royal court. She wanted him safe with her, perched high on the sea at Castlerock or at Glastonbury close by the misty isle. Anywhere but here, in the midst of treacherous currents threatening to unleash a flood tide of destruction.

Yet what could she do? Plead with him to turn aside from duty, cower in the silken bower of a woman, forget everything he was and was pledged to protect?

She lifted her head and dry-eyed, said only, "Be careful, my lord."

His going left her bereft. She lay for a little time, thinking sleep might come, but it did not. Giving up finally, she rose, wound a blanket around her, and poked up the coals simmering in the braziers. By their light she saw Joseph Wolcott's book, lying open on the table where Hugh had left it.

Fionna sat down, drew a candle near, lit it, and began to read. She knew the story so well that she could have recited it, but still she found herself caught up in the cadence of the words as though she was encountering them for the first time.

After a time in the fabled land where all desires were fulfilled, Bran and his men decided to return home to Ireland. The vision woman warned that they must not touch foot to their native soil, but her words were dismissed.

Coming within sight of the self-same place from

which they had departed, one of Bran's men was overcome by excitement, and leaping into the water, made his way to shore. The instant he did so, he fell dead, his body turned to ashes.

What had been a year on the fabled isle, had been centuries in the world outside. Bran's kinsmen had lamented his loss, never forgetting him, yet never believing he would return.

Nor could he, for no man can cross the barrier between one world and another. He sat in his curragh for all the day, telling those who gathered on the shore about his many adventures. And when he was done, he bade them farewell and sailed away, never to be seen again.

They were left only with the memory of him to keep alive as best they could.

Fionna sighed deeply. It was such an intrinsically Irish tale, and Joseph Wolcott had captured it so well. On many of his pages were small, charming drawings. To her mind, the most evocative of them came at the very end. She studied the multitude of faces of those left behind, watching as the curragh disappeared into the mists again, each face replete with sorrow and loss.

For a little time, she had been able to cast off her worried thoughts, but now they were back again. She stood up and went to gaze out the window. The storm had ended. Clouds scudded across the sky. Without warning, the moon emerged and bathed the world in molten silver.

Far off, born on the wind, she thought she heard the plaint of a lute.

Ridiculous. No one was playing the lute at this hour. She was merely overtired and worried about Hugh. It would be light in a few more hours, and when it was, she would find some good, distracting occupation for herself. He would send word, no doubt, that he was safe. She would be consoled by that, and she would not let the dark edges of fear creep their way into her soul.

Amen to that.

He took the goblet from the king and drank deeply.

Took it with his left hand.

She was back, for an instant, in the royal privy chamber, watching the scene unfold as though from a distance. It was all happening again before her eyes. There was John, pouring the wine, leaning forward with a goblet . . .

And William . . . taking it.

William of Lancaster was left-handed.

What of it? Uncounted people were the same. The ignorant and superstitious ascribed some special meaning to it, but she most certainly did not. It was only one of the multitude of natural differences that occurred among all men and women.

He was taller than the average.

Again, so were others. Hugh, for instance, was far taller than most other men. She herself topped most women by several inches.

His son had died in France. Died because John's plans went so amiss.

Still . . .

She turned suddenly, dropped the blanket, and began to dress. Scant minutes later, she left the tower chamber and seizing a torch to light her way, hurried down the stone steps.

Sir Peyton slept in a small chamber off the great hall. Fionna sought him there but found the chamber empty. She was not surprised. Hugh would have wakened him before he left, charging the trusted knight with her protection.

Perhaps he had gone outside to reflect on that. Or perhaps he just liked the night air after a storm. At any rate, she found him at last seated on the topmost step leading down to the bailey.

He started when she whispered her name, and leaped to his feet.

"Mistress . . ."

"I am sorry to disturb you," Fionna said quickly. "But I could not sleep. I have been thinking . . ." She hesitated. Now that she was actually there, facing him, it seemed absurd. And yet . . .

"Were you in France with my lord?"

"Yes, of course."

"Did you know Philip, William of Lancaster's son?"

"I knew of him. My lady, it is very late, and I believe his lordship would prefer for you to be—"

"What was he like?" She clasped her hands so tightly together that the nails dug into her flesh. "Please, I know this sounds very strange, but if you would just—"

"Like most of them," Peyton said, and for just an instant she saw a look of pure contempt flash across his grizzled face. "Arrogant, overbearing, pompous, and brutal. Is that enough for you, my lady?"

"Almost. Was he ever in the Holy Land?"

"Who, Philip?" Peyton scowled. Moonlight bathed his scarred and weathered face. "I don't know . . . Probably not . . . Wait, I think. Yes, I did hear he'd been in Acre for a while. His father sent him there. Something about a drunken brawl, a tavern boy killed. Rich men's sons do not stand before the bar of justice. Surely, you know that."

"I know we all stand before it eventually," Fionna said quietly. "And in the end, Philip was no exception." She took a deep breath, lifted her eyes to the radiance of the moon, and breathed a silent prayer.

"I must go to the Tower at once," she said, and girded herself for Peyton's reaction.

He did not disappoint her.

His face darkened. He took a deep, long breath, struggling manfully for control. In a voice taut as a bowstring, he said, "I do not believe his lordship would want you to do that."

"His lordship doesn't realize—"

Peyton held up a hand. "You are not going to persuade me. I would clap you in irons myself before I allowed you to. The best I can do is send a messenger." He looked straight at her. "But you will not take one step beyond these walls. His lordship would have my head if you did, and rightly so."

Fionna opened her mouth to argue further but thought better of it. Time was speeding by. There was none to waste. She turned and went back inside.

Striding through the great hall, she debated silently what to do. If she wrote a message, what could she say? How to explain her reasoning to Hugh? How to convince him of the danger?

How to even be sure he would ever see the message?

She would be sitting here, safe within the walls of his stronghold, not knowing whether she had succeeded in warning him or not. That was not to be borne.

She liked Peyton. Beneath his grizzled exterior, he

was a brave and honorable man. But right now he was also her captor, and she had no moral obligation to obey him.

In the tower room, she paused only long enough to pluck her cloak from a peg on the wall. Shrouded in it, the hood pulled well up over her head, she slipped back down the stairs.

When she was a very small child, Fionna's mother taught her how to swim. Somewhat later, as she grew, she also learned how to handle a small boat. Visiting her father's home, she discovered that they shared a love of the sea. Soon the proud Lord of Connaught and his beguiling daughter could be seen plying their fast, agile vessels all along the western coast.

The memory of that was keen in Fionna's mind as she descended the water steps beyond Hugh's fortress. A small skiff was tied up there, next to the far larger boats Hugh used to move himself and his men back and forth to the Tower. One of these was missing.

She got into the skiff, released the bowline, and with great caution, took up the oars. There were guards posted all along the stronghold walls. Very alert guards. If one of them noticed her before she was well out onto the river—

A cloud moved across the moon.

Fionna breathed a quick sigh of relief, took up the oars, and drew away from shore. The current of the great river as it moved toward the sea caught her. Within minutes, the skiff was skimming along.

By the time the cloud had moved away, she was out of sight of Hugh's stronghold.

Well aware that she did not know this river, Fionna kept a close watch. There were always eddies and minor currents, shoals and even fallen trees that could present problems to the unwary boater. But her luck held and before very long the walls of London appeared alongside her.

And now she faced a problem. Common sense told her it would be the height of idiocy to draw up at the Tower water steps and simply expect to be admitted. With the tension so high, it was likely she would have an arrow through her breast before she set both feet on ground.

Like Bran's companion, she would perish before she could ever tell her story. Yet unlike the hero Bran himself, she could hardly expect to be heard if she remained safe.

There had to be a middle way. Passing Billingsgate, not far from the Tower, she saw it. With the merchant traffic in and out of London so greatly diminished these last few days, the wharves held far fewer ships than usual. She was able to maneuver in between those that were present and find a place to tie up without too great difficulty.

Even so, she went very cautiously as she stepped up onto the dock constructed of great wooden pilings and stretching well out into the river. The few ships in port rode at anchor, bobbing on the wash. Only a scattering of lights could be seen on them, and their only sounds were the creaking of wood as their crews slumbered. Off to her right, she could make out the battlements of the Tower. Closer in, the buildings she had passed in daylight huddled dark and silent.

She took a quick breath, gathered her courage, and started up the nearest lane. Before too long, she realized that she was passing Master Dellacourte's establishment. The table where she and Hugh had sat was there. But the building was shuttered on the first floor, although windows stood open above to catch the breeze.

The innkeeper, his daughters, and his servants would all be there, asleep. She could go to them, ask for help, and they would surely give it. Knowing that, she still did not so much as hesitate as she passed the inn. There was danger abroad in London this night; she would not place anyone else at risk.

But that still left her with the problem of how to enter the Tower. Anything she said or did to call attention to herself might bring an instant—and deadly—reaction.

A rat skittered out between barrels stacked along the lane. Fionna stiffened and jumped back. Another rat followed. She held her breath, fearing there would be a whole stream of them, but no others emerged. After a moment, she dared to move on, but the sight had set her nerves to strumming. There were never rats at her mother's house or for that matter, in her father's stronghold. An army of much valued cats saw to it.

Nor had she seen any of the vermin at Castlerock or Glastonbury, although she did recall spotting a high tossed tail from time to time, a flash of whisker, and a pleased meow.

But here in London—

If war came, if the order of everyday living broke down in any way, plague would follow. People seemed to regard all that as inevitable. Their passivity angered Fionna. Adversity was to be fought with every weapon that came to hand, not meekly accepted.

Beyond the Tower walls was a broad open area in which no buildings were permitted. There was a purely military reason for that, to provide the castle guards with a clear line of fire. But it meant that the moment Fionna moved from the obscurity of the crowded lanes, she would be on what amounted to a killing field.

All the same, she saw no alternative. Gazing up at the moon, she said a silent prayer and waited. If only a stray cloud would happen by . . .

None did. They could not be commanded, it seemed. She would have no choice but to cross the open space in the full flare of moonlight. Either that or wait hours until the moon had set.

Hours too late.

She girded herself, summoning the courage instilled in her over a lifetime. All that had gone before, all that she was, had a purpose. She had never truly doubted that, but she knew it now with a stone-cold clarity that stilled the tremor within her and quieted the fearful murmurs of her soul.

Fionna stepped from the shadows of the lane. On impulse, she dropped her cloak. If the guards at least saw that she was a woman, they might . . .

Her mouth twisted. What a foolish thought. Men, women, children, all would die with impartiality if what she foresaw came to pass.

So be it.

A last breath, deeply drawn, for she would need to run so very, very fast . . .

And so she was about to, poised to make that life-or-death dash across the killing field, when from the deeper shadows behind her a soft voice called.

"Wait!"

CHAPTER TWENTY-FIVE

Fionna's blood surged through her veins. For a sickening moment, she thought she might actually faint. With the greatest effort of will, she forced herself to turn and peer into the darkness.

"Who . . ."

A shape resolved itself from the shadows. She saw a man, medium in height, slender, darkly dressed to obscure himself, his face pale and . . . smiling . . .

"Are you mad," Samuel Wolcott asked pleasantly, "or is this some strange Irish tradition with which I am unfamiliar?"

Fionna stared at him wide-eyed. Whatever she had expected in shuttered, rat-skittering, ominous London, it was not the book smith.

"What are you doing here?" she asked, and was pleased that her voice almost held steady.

He leaned back up against a wall and regarded her steadily. "The same as you, watching the Tower."

"I'm not watching it. I'm trying to figure out how to get into it."

He frowned slightly. "Why do you want to do that?"

"Because I have news for his lordship that is most urgent. You haven't answered me, why are you watching?"

Samuel hesitated. He cast her a quick, sidelong glance, then asked quietly, "Are there any Jews in Ireland?"

Fionna had to think about that for a moment. "A few, I believe, mostly merchants in Dublin."

"But you never met any of them, did you? Never gave them any thought?"

"I had no opportunity," she said softly. "My life has been in the west country. It is beautiful land but very rugged. There are few enough of us Irish there, much less anyone else."

Samuel accepted that explanation, but she could still sense the caution in him. "John has protected us, for the taxes we pay him, of course, but still, it has been a good deal better than it was under Richard. When the so-called Lionhearted was crowned, massacres of Jews happened all over England. Almost two hundred of us died in one rampage in York alone, and there were many more elsewhere."

"You think that will come again." It was a statement, not a question. She understood all, all at once—the reason for Samuel's simmering anger, for him watching the Tower on this night, for the feeling she had from him that he was never truly at ease or off guard. He might not like John, but at least this particular king had refrained from murdering Samuel's people. If the barons gained the upper hand, that could all change and change quickly.

"I am sorry," she said quietly.

He shrugged and looked away, as though he did not want her to see the emotion in his eyes. "That's how it is, it isn't your fault. So I keep watch here—" He gestured to the nearby shadows. "As do others, that this time at least, we may have some warning."

Her throat was thick. She wished there was something she could say to him, some comfort or reassurance, but there was none. Samuel was doing the only thing he could, preparing for the worst.

If only it could be avoided—

"I have to get into the Tower," she said.

His eyebrows rose. "Forgive me, but surely you've noticed they don't want anyone coming in?"

"Castlerock is there. I must speak with him."

The young man surveyed her steadily. She met his gaze with calm determination of her own. "It will be morning in a few hours," Samuel said. "You can—"

"And the king will be dead. I must go now. If you cannot help me . . ."

"Wait, what do you mean, John will be dead?" His face was taut with urgency, every muscle of his body vibrating.

"There is no time, every moment counts. I must find a way—"

"I know how."

He said it quickly, in a rush as though getting the words out before he could think better of them. In a rush, he continued, "There's a way in but few know of it. If we are caught . . ."

"Just show me. I will go alone."

He was shaking his head before she was done. "Never." A smile lifted the corners of his young mouth. "I may wield a pen rather than a sword, my lady, but I am not about to let you go alone into that den of wolves. Come, as you said, there is no time."

They went. He led her around a corner and down a back alley to a small, stone church, one of the many that dotted London. The door was closed but not locked. They stepped inside. Samuel walked quickly toward the altar. At her hesitation, he turned and smiled, "It's all right. We won't be struck dead, at least not here."

"How do you know of this place?" she whispered as they entered the sanctuary. The smell of incense was heavy on the air. Despite herself, she could not restrain a spurt of fear.

"I've made it my business to learn a good deal about London," he said as he drew aside a curtain on the far wall. "You'd be amazed at the old charts and maps that are still to be found."

Behind the curtain was an opening. They entered it and proceeded down a narrow corridor. Fionna could feel the air growing colder and the floor beneath her feet slanting downward.

At length, they reached another door. It, too, yielded to Samuel's touch.

"We need a torch," he said, and took one from an iron bracket beside the door. The torch was cold, giving evidence of not having been lit in a long time. "Wait here."

He disappeared back down the corridor they had just

traversed but returned moments later, his presence heralded by the flickering light of the now smoldering torch.

Fionna did not ask how he had lit it; she knew. The only fire anywhere nearby was the one always left burning in the sanctuary. Their purpose was a good one. She saw no sacrilege in aiding it.

"Stay close to me," Samuel said, and plunged into the darkness beyond the door.

They were in a tunnel, Fionna realized. A narrow, low-ceilinged one, but a tunnel all the same. By the look of the stone walls flecked with moisture seeping from the nearby river, it was not new.

"Who built this?" she whispered, just loudly enough for Samuel to hear her.

"William Rufus, I think. He's the one who tore down the Conqueror's wooden tower and replaced it with stone. It's likely this was done at the same time. Although, it's possible the Conqueror himself saw the need for some such escape hatch. He hated London and never trusted its inhabitants."

"Surely, it remains a closely guarded secret?"

He smiled at her over his shoulder. "There are very few secrets in this city, my lady. Surely, you've realized that."

She took the gentle reprimand in good humor. They were moving quickly through the tunnel. By her estimate, they must be at or even under the Tower walls. At the thought of what it would have meant to her to try to cross them in any other way, a shiver ran down her spine.

"Almost there," Samuel murmured.

The tunnel was rising slightly. A little distance

ahead, Fionna saw a crack of light. Samuel turned and put a finger to his lips, cautioning her to silence. He put the torch out by rolling it over the stone floor and extinguishing the last few sparks with his foot.

Together, they moved toward the door.

Hugh prowled the great hall of the Tower, a dark, menacing figure of coiled anger. His men kept a respectful distance away and did not let down their guard for a moment.

At this hour, there would normally have been dozens of servants and men-at-arms asleep on pallets on the floor. But few were in the mood for sleep this night, and waking suddenly to find the Lord of Castlerock among them, they had scurried off to find their rest elsewhere.

He had the hall to himself and his men, and a damn good thing it was. If he had to speak to one more of John's simpering lackeys, endure their supercilious, insufferable idiocy . . .

His hand gripped the hilt of his sword, almost drawing it from the scabbard. He itched to hit out at someone, to find some venting for the swirling morass of anger and worry that threatened to pull him down.

The king could not be disturbed.

He had left clear instructions.

The captain of the Tower was very clear about that. He had admitted Hugh, but grudgingly and only because the alternative was obviously a pitched battle. But once inside the bailey, his mood was implacable.

The king had foreseen this eventuality. He had wagered that the Lord of Castlerock would not be able to follow his orders and remain in Westminster. He had anticipated Hugh's return and said he would see him in the morning.

In the meantime, John had retired not with the milk-maid, as he had claimed, but to the quarters of Isabella herself.

Hugh cursed under his breath. He could do many things—indeed, would do them without a flicker of hesitation—but not even he could go barging into the private chambers of the queen in the middle of the night. The best he could do was inspect the guard stationed outside, console himself that they were sharp, well-trained men who took their duty seriously, add a few more of his own to the lot for good measure, and return to the great hall.

He was beginning to feel foolish for having come, yet he could not shake the feeling that every passing moment brought danger nearer. The Tower was a vast labyrinth of passages and rooms, much added on to over the years, divided and redivided so that in many ways it was little other than a warren. The kind of place a killer could move with ease, unseen and unsuspected until it was far too late.

At least Fionna was safe. He could find comfort in that. His dark mood lightened somewhat as he thought of her. Had anyone told him scant weeks before that a fey Irish beauty would be delivered to him out of the throes of a storm, and that he would find with her more joy than he had ever known, he would have dismissed it all as the ravings of a lunatic.

Yet such were the vagaries of fate that he could no

longer imagine his life without her. She was passion, warmth, intelligence, humor, pride, and dignity, all wrapped up in a tempting, enthralling woman who at once challenged and delighted him.

For years, he had presumed that the special bond his parents shared was unique to them. Nothing in his experience of the world had disabused him of that. Never had he expected to find any such thing for himself. He had intended to marry someday—in the fullness of time—solely for the purpose of siring an heir. Now he found himself thinking of it for far different reasons.

Abruptly, he shook his head as though to clear it. This was not the time to be mooning like a lovesick boy. He needed to keep his mind focused on the business at hand.

The business of keeping a king alive.

With another muttered curse, he wished John pleasure in his wife this night. For himself, there would be none until the whole sorry business was at an end.

Fionna and Samuel emerged from the tunnel into a small chapel she had not seen before. They stood, unmoving, both straining for any sign of guards nearby. When they heard nothing, they continued on, but with the greatest care.

"Do you know where we are?" Samuel whispered.

Fionna shook her head. "I've seen little of the Tower and definitely not this part. But I believe we must not be any higher than the main floor."

"Where the great hall is?"

"Yes, but so is a good deal else. I'm not even sure which side we're on."

Samuel admitted that he wasn't, either. The tunnel had curved just enough to disorient them. He looked around with concern.

Fionna placed a hand on his arm gently. "Don't worry. It's your turn to follow me now. If we are seen, it's important that we appear to belong here."

"Can we pass for servants?"

"We can try." She gave him a quick, encouraging smile, and stepped out into the corridor.

"Where is Castlerock likely to be?" Samuel asked as they made their way.

"With the king, wherever that is." She hesitated. "We may have to find the stables."

The young man's eyes widened. "Why?"

"I think it would be better if I didn't explain."

"All right, then, perhaps you'd just like to tell me what it is that Castlerock needs to know so urgently?"

"Who I think has been killing the king's friends." She went on quickly, before he could ask. "But I may be completely wrong. It seems so unbelievable."

She broke off suddenly. A door opened, and a man stepped into the corridor. Fionna stiffened. She made a quick gesture to Samuel to get out of sight. He moved swiftly behind a stone pillar and did his best to fade into the shadows.

The man turned. A frown marred his aristocratic features, but it was replaced quickly with a smile.

"Mistress Fionna," William of Lancaster said. "Forgive me, I did not recognize you at first. I thought you had returned to Westminster."

"We did," Fionna replied with forced calm. "But my

lord could not rest easy and decided he preferred to be here."

William was very still, watching her. "I see . . . but surely he could have left you to your rest?"

She lifted the corners of her mouth and said lightly, "I daresay you have noticed, sir, that I am not the most biddable of women."

He laughed, but his eyes never faltered from her. Without warning, he said, "Is something wrong?"

"Wrong? No, of course not. I merely . . . had a call of a private nature. If you will excuse me, I will return to my lord."

"Where is he?" William asked. He stepped closer, his tall, hard body, still powerful despite his years, blocking her path.

"W-with the king."

He was still smiling, but there was nothing of humor in it now, only a twisted malice. "No, I don't think so. Our sovereign is honoring his marriage bed."

"But I thought . . . the milkmaid . . ."

"Milkmaids, queens, they're all the same to John." He took another step forward and reached out suddenly, grasping her jaw. Instinctively, Fionna struggled. Pain shot up through her head.

"That's the one thing he is actually wise about," William continued, as though they were having the most ordinary conversation. "You are all the same . . . weak, conniving, and treacherous."

His grip tightened. Icy, paralyzing fear coiled through her. She fought it with every ounce of her strength, driving it down deep, knowing that if she yielded to it for even an instant, all would be lost. Even so, despite her best resolve, a moan escaped her.

From behind her, there was an angry expletive, a rush of motion, and Samuel hurled himself at her attacker.

"Damn you! Let her go!"

"*Nooo . . .*" The scream was Fionna's, her fear for him rather than herself. The pen, not the sword, he had said, and it was all too terribly true. Samuel was a brave man, all the more so for knowing how badly mismatched he would be. Yet against a warrior of William's training and experience, he stood scant chance.

Especially when that warrior was armed with a black hilted, curving blade.

It flashed in the faint light of the corridor. Fionna gasped, recognizing it at once. She made to seize William's arm, only to be flung off. She landed with brutal force against the wall. For precious moments, her senses threatened to leave her. As though through a fog, she saw William lash out at Samuel.

Saw the Saracen blade strike him in the side.

He stood stock still, then slowly crumbled.

Dazed and sickened, Fionna crawled to her knees and desperately tried to stand upright. She had to reach Samuel, had to help him.

But before she could take a step, William was upon her. He coiled an arm around her waist, held the blade before her eyes, and said, "I strongly advise you not to fight me, mistress. The more Kalil drinks, the more it seems to thirst."

With a last, horrified glimpse of Samuel, she was thrust down the corridor.

CHAPTER TWENTY-SIX

How much longer could he wait like this? The water clock showed four hours yet to dawn. He would be mad before then.

Stomping back across the great hall, Hugh's glance fell on a hapless servant, a man skittering out of a corner.

"What ails you, fellow?" he demanded. "We haven't lopped anyone's head off yet, we're not likely to start now."

The man gulped, straightened up slightly, but did not look at Hugh directly. "I only thought, lord . . . that is . . . your men . . ."

"What about them? Stop that gibbering and speak plain."

"If they wished refreshment . . . if you did . . ."

So that was it. They had been in the great hall for over an hour, the tension growing more palpable by the moment. Trust it to an experienced servant to try to soothe their temperament with drink.

"Water only," Hugh said, "or sweet cider, nothing hard."

The man nodded and ran off. He was back within minutes, shepherding several other servants who looked as though they most devotedly wished to be anywhere else.

"We have brought breads, meats, and cheeses as well, lord," the man said. "It is early yet for breakfast . . ."

"That's fine," Hugh said, waving him away. "Stoke up the fire and be off."

He was obeyed with such alacrity one might have suspected the servants' feet had grown wings. When they had the hall to themselves again, Hugh signaled his men to eat. For himself, he wanted nothing. Except, of course, for an end to the whole sorry affair.

Fionna would be asleep back at the stronghold, her body like warm silk, so soft and pliant, so strong and passionate. So near to his hand if he'd had the sense to be there with her. He felt the instant hardening of his groin and stifled a groan.

He was considering the irony of his position—attempting to safeguard a king safe in his own wife's bed while the woman Hugh himself desired more than any other slept alone—when there was a sudden disturbance near the great doors.

In the space of a breath, he was on his feet.

"Who goes?" he demanded.

The captain of the Tower appeared out of the gloom. His face was twisted in an ugly sneer. "Your man demands entry, lord. He appears to have brought a war band with him." He stared hard at Hugh. "Is that your intention, to attack from within?"

"Be silent, fool," Hugh snarled. He shoved the man

out of his way and walked out into the bailey. At his shouted command, the gates were open and the portcullis raised. No one was so foolish this night to challenge the Lord of Castlerock.

Peyton came across the moat with a great clatter of horses. Hugh's startled glance swept over at least eighty men arrayed behind him.

"What is this?" he asked quietly as the knight flung himself from the saddle and approached him at the run.

"Mistress Fionna," Peyton said. His face was pale. For the first time in their long years together, Hugh saw that he was afraid.

And seeing that, was afraid himself.

"You will never get away with this," Fionna said. William had thrust her into a small room, one of the very many she had never noticed before. But this one struck her as especially odd. It had no windows, only four blank stone walls punctuated by a single door.

"What is this place?" she asked. Even in her fear, her curiosity would not be contained.

William turned from securing the door. He looked amused by her interest. "It was one of the king's strong rooms. He has sent much of his treasure elsewhere, anticipating the fall of London to the barons."

"Why have we come here?" Her hands were very cold. She concealed them within the long, wide sleeves of her bliaut and wished she had thought to hide a knife the same way.

"To talk, of course." His smile was wolfish. "And to wait. You were at Westminster, weren't you?"

"You know we were. The king ordered—"

"No, I mean by yourself. Castlerock came back here

without you. He would never have brought you at such an hour, especially if he was anticipating trouble. You followed him for some reason. Why?"

"I don't know what you mean, and I don't understand why you attacked that poor man in the corridor, or mishandled me, for that matter. I realize this has been a great strain on all of us, but even so you did not seem the sort to behave in such a way."

He stared at her for a long moment, then shook his head. Almost kindly, he said, "It won't work, Fionna. I know perfectly well you recognized my son's blade. Moreover, I saw your knowledge in your eyes even before then."

It was no good; she could not pretend ignorance, keep him talking and pray someone would come. He was too clever for that.

"All right," Fionna said. "No lies then. I could not sleep after Hugh left. I lay awake, thinking about all that has happened. It came to me that no one is closer to the king than you. You come and go even in his privy chamber as you please. But you are left-handed and tall, as I knew the murderer to be. And I remembered about your son."

"Philip . . ." For just a moment, such terrible pain flitted across his features that Fionna was almost moved to pity.

Then it was gone and in its place was the closed, shuttered look she realized—belatedly—was William's accustomed expression. He had kept so much of himself hidden for so long that it had become second nature. But now that facade was crumbling. The festering wounds on his soul would no longer be denied.

His mouth twitched. He drew the blade out again and studied it, still stained with Samuel's blood.

"He died near Montmarcy," William said, as though to himself. "He and half a dozen others were sent out on a reconnoitering mission by John. They were so eager to show their mettle, to win honor and glory in the way of young men, they did not realize that John knew the French forces lay in wait for them."

Fionna stared at him. Surely, he must be wrong. "I don't understand. Why would the king knowingly send his own men into a trap?"

"Because he had no idea of how many of the French there were. He wanted to flush them out, learn their positions, and the like. Besides, he'd been drinking and wenching all night when he gave the orders. I doubt he thought much about them at all."

"My God . . ."

William looked at her sharply. "God? What has He to do with it? And especially not your God, mistress."

At her startled response, he gave a hollow laugh. "Do you think I didn't know what you are? Coming from Ireland as you did, that cursed place, and traveling with Castlerock, sharing his bed, being brought by him even into the presence of the king as though you were a personage in your own right. Do you imagine I didn't know you were his sorceress? You serve him as his mother serves his father, to the same unclean ends."

"That is not true!" she protested, horrified by the idea. It was Isabella all over again, a sick and twisted perversion of the truth.

"I am trained in the old ways of healing, but there is no evil in that. Indeed, I have never understood why the Church wishes to deny such hope and mercy to the faithful. Why they should suffer so unnecessarily."

"The better to serve Almighty God," William intoned. "The purpose of this life is to suffer, to be tested in the fires of temptation and tribulation that we may rise pure and free to sit at the feet of all that is holy."

Fionna had heard that there were some who believed that was the sum total of the glorious world, but she had never met one of them before.

"Did you feel this way before Philip died?" she asked.

"Before . . . I cannot remember before. I began the moment I looked down at his disemboweled body and saw all my hopes in ruins."

"Other sons have died." She should not have said it, but she was thinking of the tavern boy Philip was said to have killed, for whose death he had escaped punishment.

William dismissed that. "They were not mine. My *only* son."

He looked at the knife again, musingly. "He was so young and with so much yet to learn. But he never had the chance because of John."

"Then, why kill the others?" Fionna asked. She was all but choking on her horror of this man, of what he was and what he had done, what he would still do unless some way was found to stop him quickly.

"Because they helped to make John what he is. They encouraged the worst in him. Huteuil and Foucault were ever ready to drink and wench, but they were only the beginning. Pearse, that pompous ass, encouraged

John to believe he had the wit to make policy for himself instead of being guided by those far more able."

"Yourself?"

"Of course me. *I* wouldn't have sent foolish young men to their deaths because I wasn't paying any attention. And there was a time when he listened to me, but then Desmond came back, filling John's head with talk of God! As though he knew anything of Him. Sweet heaven, I remember Desmond before he stumbled over sanctity. He whored with the best of them. Then suddenly he was a priest and daring to comfort John, telling him his sins could be forgiven."

"Isn't that exactly what the Church teaches?"

"No! Not for men like John. They are beyond forgiveness."

Fionna had her quarrels with priests, but even she knew this was not true. Only in a twisted mind such as William of Lancaster's were there sins that could not be redeemed.

"So you killed them first," Fionna said. As she spoke, she moved back against the wall, if only to put a little more distance between herself and the man she was now convinced was mad. "And you sent men to attack Conan and later Hugh, so that they could not help the King. But what of John himself?"

"I saved him for last," William said. His eyes glittered. "I wanted him to be afraid, to think of nothing but what it would mean to die so ignominiously, in his bed." He laughed. "Do you know that has always been our king's greatest fear?"

"No . . . I didn't." She moved a little more, the wall scraping against her back.

"It's because he was great Henry's whelp, and

golden Richard's brother. They were such glorious heroes, and here comes poor John. Lackland, they called him, and a good many other things, not the least of which was coward. He went to France because of that. He was going to show everyone, eclipse all who had gone before him, and claim his place in history at last."

"Instead, he was beaten."

"Aye, but not quickly enough. Not before Philip died." William sighed deeply, a man looking at a task that must be done, no doubt about it. "He will be just one more victim, no glory, no fame, no honor. Just death."

"You will never escape."

He looked at her as though she was the one who was mad. "Of course, I won't. Do you seriously believe I would want to? No, John and I were friends once. The last service I can do him is to assure that he won't enter hell alone."

He meant to kill himself. William of Lancaster meant to slay his king, plunge his country into civil war, and finish by taking his own life. He would not see the havoc he wreaked, nor would he find any earthly justice. He would escape, and the rest of them would be left to deal with what he left behind.

No, not all the rest of them. Not herself and in all likelihood, not Hugh.

"Why do we wait?" she asked.

"For the one man who could still stop me to come, that I may deal with him first."

The tightness in her breast was almost unbearable. She willed herself to calm. She would need all her resources, all her control. Yet fear gnawed at her. If she

faced death this night, so be it. But not Hugh. By all
that was merciful, not him.

"He will not come. He has no idea that I am here."

William laughed. He seemed to find her genuinely
entertaining. "Do you truly believe you could leave his
stronghold, and your absence could go unnoticed? All
of London is talking of how jealously he guards you.
His lust disarms his reason. He will come."

Peyton. A sickening sensation twisted through her.
Peyton would have wondered when she did not return
with a message for Hugh. He would have searched and
found her missing. Without doubt, he would waste no
time bringing word to his lordship.

And he would remember their conversation on the
bailey steps. He would recount her questions, and
Hugh would realize what they meant.

He would come.

She closed her eyes, seeking the deep pool of
strength and courage to which she turned in direst
times of need. William could easily defeat even a brave
man like Samuel, who had no training. But Hugh was a
seasoned warrior, the mightiest in England. He was
taller, stronger, younger, and more able. Why didn't
Lancaster fear that?

He was watching her carefully. "Do you understand
now?"

Bile rose in the back of her throat. Slowly, she
nodded.

He would tear the Tower down stone by stone. He
would lay waste to it. When he was done, men would
not be sure anything had ever stood on this cursed
place hard by the Thames.

"Lord . . . ?" Peyton was waiting for instructions. So were Hugh's men, drawn up throughout the great hall, mailed and helmeted, weapons at the ready. The captain of the Tower was there as well, having reluctantly placed himself under Hugh's command when he realized what was happening. Even a few of the bolder servants hugged the shadowed corners, watching wide-eyed as the legendary warrior strode back and forth, a caged lion dark of mien and savage of heart, cursing the fate that had brought him to this.

"Find her," he said. And then, in a roar that reached to the high-arched ceiling and beyond, he repeated it.

"Find her!"

Torches flared. The silence of night gave way to shouted commands and the tramp of booted feet. Doors slammed, women cried out. Within minutes, the Tower seethed with activity of a deadly purpose.

In the strong room, William heard the sounds at the same moment that Fionna did. She hugged the wall, shivering, her hands pressed against the stones. He smiled.

"Come here, my lady."

"No."

"So brave? Or is that how you enticed Castlerock, by refusing his every command?"

Before she could reply, he snarled and reached out, seizing her brutally and jerking her against him. The blade flashed, coming to rest against her slim white throat.

Fionna willed herself not to move. Anything she could do would only make the situation worse, at least just then. She had to wait, regardless of the panic that ate at her and the fear that threatened to consume her reason.

He would kill Hugh.

She could think of nothing else. He would trap him in this room, forcing him to disarm in order to save her, and then he would—

A fist pounded against the door. A voice called, "Open up!"

"Only to Castlerock," William shouted back. "Get him."

There was silence, but only for a moment. Fionna heard the rush of running feet, muffled commands, and then that which most filled her with terror.

"Fionna?"

"Answer," William ordered, and laid the knife's edge just a little closer against her skin.

"I am here," she called. "Do not enter! He seeks to—"

"Be silent, bitch!" William screamed. The hand holding Kalil shook. She felt a razor pain against her throat and knew she had begun to bleed.

A mighty force was hurled against the wooden door. So powerful was the blow that the stout oak planks bowed inward. But they did not break. Again, they were struck, and again. Fragments of white wood began to show.

Fionna held her breath, biding strength, waiting . . .

The door shattered. Powerful hands yanked away the fragments. Through the opening, she saw Hugh. It was he, the same man in whose arms she had lain night after night, who haunted her dreams waking and sleeping, and filled her with greater happiness than she had ever known.

Yet it was not. She had always known there was

another side to him, the man glimpsed so briefly on the road the day they were ambushed, the man spoken of as a legend. That was the man she faced now, merciless, savage, a warrior to the very core of his being.

"Order your men back," William said. His voice shook slightly. Even for him, such a sight was quelling.

Hugh did not hesitate. He barked a command. At once, they were alone.

"Let her go," Hugh said.

"In due time," William replied. "Drop your sword."

The blade fell from Hugh's hand as though it was of no account whatsoever.

"The helmet and mail as well," William directed.

Fionna closed her eyes. It was all happening as she had known it would. He would have Hugh at a disadvantage, and he would make the most of it.

"Now, enter," William said. He seemed to like giving orders. It amused him.

Hugh stepped into the room. He looked at Fionna. His eyes grazed her throat where the thin line of blood glowed darkly against her skin. The hard lines of his face drew tauter still. "Are you all right?" he asked.

She nodded just a fraction, for the knife still bit against her.

"You want her very much, don't you?" William said. "Then, come and get her."

Hugh studied him, appraisingly.

"Why do you hesitate? All you have to do is take her from me. Surely, so great a warrior as yourself can manage that?"

"You cannot escape," Hugh told him quietly. "And you cannot hope to reach the king. End this now."

"End it for me," William goaded him. "Come and get her."

"Don't," Fionna gasped. She caught Hugh's gaze and frantically jerked her own toward the wall against which she had stood. Again, she motioned, praying he would understand.

Hugh moved but not toward her. Instead, he began to circle around William toward the wall.

"Not there!" Lancaster said. To emphasize his words, he yanked Fionna's head back farther and pressed the point of the knife against the soft underside of her chin.

"How quickly do you think she will die, Castlerock? I was merciful with the others, but I am running out of patience. Come!"

The room went very still. To Fionna, it seemed as though time itself stopped. Nothing happened. Nothing . . .

The air bent, giving way before a primal force of nature that hurtled through it, straight for William.

The madman had believed himself ready. He had thought it all out so carefully. He was so much more clever than the rest of them, and so right in his cause. But he had not counted on two things: the fury of Hugh's will and Fionna herself.

Even as he moved to throw her against Hugh, knocking him off balance long enough to drive the knife into his heart, she was not there. His hands were empty.

A scream of rage tore from him. He thrust with the knife but missed. Hugh slammed his joined fists into Lancaster's head, knocking him to the ground. The knife clattered onto the stones. They grappled for it.

For a sickening moment, it appeared that William would reach it first. But the floor was slanted— perhaps. Old floors so often were. The knife slipped a precious inch or two, coming within Hugh's grasp. He took hold of it, raised his arm . . . and had no chance to do anything else. With a snarl that seemed torn from the very pits of hell, William dove straight for the blade and impaled himself on it.

Far in the distance, a woman moaned. Fionna was surprised to recognize the voice as her own in the instant before her strength gave way, and she crumbled to the floor.

CHAPTER TWENTY-SEVEN

"I have never fainted in my life," Fionna said. "The very idea is preposterous."

"That's the second time it's happened since we met," Hugh insisted. He was sitting beside Fionna on the bed in the tower room of his stronghold. One of her slender, fine-boned hands was clasped in both of his.

He needed the physical contact to reassure himself that she was really there, alive and whole. At the moment, hand-holding was the best he could do.

A grim smile played across his mouth. "I shall have to take better care of you, my lady."

"I should hope so," John said. He shifted more comfortably in his chair, refilled his wine goblet, and looked chidingly at them both. "Going through London on her own, in the dead of night. What kind of thing is that to do? Really, Castlerock, I'd think you'd have more control over her, or at least some."

The king had come calling an hour ago. He'd brought more oranges, a book of French poetry, and his thanks. That was all well and good. The problem was that he was still there.

Hugh sighed. He was trying so very hard to be patient with his liege lord when he wished the man would have the courtesy to drop through a hole in the ground.

"If she hadn't gone, you would be dead, my lord," he said. "She delayed Lancaster long enough for him to be stopped."

John looked just the smallest bit abashed. "I realize that and don't think for a moment that I fail to appreciate it." A bleak look crept into his eyes. "When I think what good friends we were . . ."

"I actually warned him," Fionna said softly. "I was concerned that he might become a victim."

Hugh's hands tightened on hers. "So he did." They shared a glance, remembering the scene in the strong room where William of Lancaster had died.

But Samuel had not. Hugh's men had found him wounded, yet clinging to consciousness. It was he who pointed them in the direction William had taken with Fionna. Samuel was recovering now in the capable care of his Aunt Miriam.

"The Wolcotts deserve your thanks as well, sire," Hugh said. "Had it not been for Samuel Wolcott's great courage—" He left the statement unfinished. The king needed only so many reminders of how close he had come to death.

"Interesting that he knew about the tunnel," John said. "That's been one of my family's most closely guarded secrets."

"And William knew about the other," Fionna said. "The one from the strong room to the queen's chambers." The tunnel she herself realized had to exist almost as soon as William thrust her into the windowless room. There was no other explanation of his confidence that he could kill Hugh—and her—and still reach the king.

"Actually, I'd almost forgotten about that one myself," John said. "My dear wife occupies quarters that in time gone by were more commonly taken by the sovereign himself. I suppose it made sense to have a secret way of reaching the strong room."

He mused a moment, then went on. "I think I should have a talk with young Wolcott. There ought to be a better way to safeguard such information. Perhaps he can come up with something." He looked up sharply. "He's not a lawyer, is he?"

Fionna frowned in puzzlement. "He is a book smith, sire, as is his father."

John relaxed. "That's all right, then." His dark eyes narrowed in some private amusement. "I should have realized he wasn't a lawyer. London seems to have been stripped of them."

Hugh hesitated. He wasn't sure he wanted to know, but finally, he could not resist. "Why would that be, Majesty?"

"Oh, didn't you hear? Your father has summoned them to Glastonbury. He appears to be massing a veritable army of lawyers, clerks, and the like. I imagine them rising every morning, sharpening their quills, pursing their lips, and seeing what new horrors they can invent. I don't know who's supposed to be more frightened by all this, the barons or myself."

"Lawyers?" Hugh repeated. "At Glastonbury?"

"Legions of them. If I were you, when I left here, I'd

take this fair lady back to Castlerock instead. You'd have some chance of safety from them there." He sighed deeply. "Or perhaps not. I think we'll wake one day to find them ruling over all."

He downed the rest of his wine and stood. "Dear lady, I have tried your patience long enough. I'll take my leave."

Hugh rose as well, in courtesy to his king. Quietly, he said, "Majesty . . . ?"

John hesitated at the door. Emotions played across his drawn face. To Fionna's eyes he looked ill and tired. William's betrayal had cost him more than perhaps he even knew.

"All right," the king said abruptly. "You and your father handle the barons. Come to an agreement with them. Let me know when it is done."

Fionna stifled a gasp. Such simple words, so matter-of-factly uttered. Did John truly understand their significance? With them, he placed the greatest power possible in the hands of Hugh and Conan, the power to shape England's future.

Hugh inclined his head gravely. "It shall be as you say, sire."

John shot him a quick, hard glance. For a moment, his terrible weariness seemed to fall away, and Fionna saw him as he must have been, a powerful, striving, clever man determined to prove his own worth.

"No," John said. "It will not be, but I am resigned to that. Good day."

He was gone. For a moment, Hugh did not move or speak. He appeared almost dazed.

Fionna pushed the covers back and sat up, kneeling on the bed. Reaching out a hand, she drew him to her.

"It is over, my lord."

He came to her, hard and warm and strong. She rejoiced in the feel of him. A vast wave of relief and delight poured through her, submerging the memories of the last few hours of pain and fear.

Hugh joined her on the bed. He nestled her close against him, his big hand stroking her hair with infinite gentleness. There was a light in his eyes she had never seen before.

His mouth brushed hers, thistle soft. "It has only begun, my lady."

She did not know whether to be reassured or concerned, but it did not matter. For his hands and lips were moving over her, drawing off her clothes, playing her as only he could. He left her for just a moment to bar the door and discard his own clothing. Fionna lay on her side, watching him with unabashed pleasure. When he caught her gaze and returned it boldly, her nipples hardened and she shivered with anticipation.

He came to her then, covering her, his passion hot and driving, lifting them both to realms of ecstasy where neither had ever journeyed before. He drove her mad with pleasure, coddled and indulged her, gave her free rein with his own body, and claimed the same with hers. Until, at last, just when she thought she could not possibly bear more, he drove within her, hard and wild, and brought them both to shattering release.

They journeyed, not to Castlerock as John had suggested, but home to Glastonbury.

"You're just anxious to join the lawyers," Fionna teased as they stood side by side, looking out beyond the railing of the fast bark carrying them away from

London. "I can see you now, quill in hand, pursing and parsing with the best of them."

"God forbid," he said with such fervency that she could not help but laugh. He heard her, glowered in pretended anger, and lifted her clear off the deck. "You mock me, madame. There is a penalty for that."

Fionna squealed, a most extraordinary sound for her, and pressed her hands against his massive chest, all to no avail, as she had known. And as she wished.

He carried her to the tented enclosure set up at the far end of the deck, ignoring the amused glances of his men. Inside, he set her down with greatest care, then proceeded to kiss her the same way.

She was so infinitely precious to him, so rare and lovely, all he had unknowingly dreamed of all his life. And he had come so very close to losing her.

His hard, callused finger traced the thin line of red still visible where her throat was healing. A pulse beat in his cheek.

"There are times when I would like to be able to kill William again . . . and again."

"Don't," she whispered, and caught his hand, drawing it to her lips. "He is dead. Don't let him touch us anymore."

He acknowledged the right of what she said and beneath her own touch found the beginning of the healing he, too, needed. So the days at sea passed quickly, and the nights even more swiftly, until at length they came within sight of the quays of Weston-super-Mare.

They did not tarry at the manor there but took horse at once for Glastonbury. One more starry night Hugh and Fionna shared along the way. They made their bed a little distance from his men, who had become most adept at giving them the privacy they required. And there beneath the gentle moon, they plighted their love once again.

Day brought the final stage of their journey and before midafternoon, their first sight of Glastonbury. Fionna gasped to see how very crowded the town had become in their absence. Every road and lane was thronged with people. Rude structures appeared to have been thrown up wherever there was a little free space. Tents had sprouted on the common. There were even simple plank tables set up outside to catch the light, with men gathered urgently around them.

"Lawyers," Hugh muttered.

"They can't all be," Fionna insisted, looking around her in wonder. "There aren't that many lawyers in all of Christendom."

"Great Henry encouraged them, and they've been breeding ever since."

"Sweet heaven . . ."

The crowd thickened as they made their way toward the castle. Word of their coming spread, and men and women dropped their tasks to line the streets in welcome. Fionna was put in mind of Hugh's entry into London and took note of the difference. There the cheers had been for his might and power. Here they were simply for the man.

Riding beside him, she felt an immense surge of pride. He was such a magnificent man—bold and fierce, yet capable of such tenderness. He stirred her in ways she would never have believed possible and made her dream dreams that filled her with incandescent longing.

Yet he did not destroy her reason altogether, at least
not all the time. Her pride in him was misplaced. He
was in no way her own. They were two very separate
people, and even now, riding beside him to the cheers
of the joyful throngs, she assumed nothing. So much
remained to be done—by him and by her. Life might
well draw them in very different directions.

All this she knew, but even more tormented her,
fears she had kept buried ever since first awakening to
her feelings for him.

Hugh did not know who she was. Undoubtedly, he
thought he did. Indeed, the very notion of otherwise
would strike him as absurd. But he did not.

For whatever reasons—and she thought she could
guess at them—his parents had kept certain things
from him. That would have to change now, and when it
did . . .

She straightened in the saddle and stared ahead.
Above the castle battlements, waving boldly in the
breeze, the hawk banner flew.

Alianor was first down the steps. She flew, lithe as a
girl, into her beloved son's arms. He gathered her up,
laughing, and spun her around. His eyes were tender
when he set her down.

"Are you well, Mother?"

"I am now," she said with a radiant smile that was
shared with Fionna. "Oh, my dearest, I am so glad to
behold you both. There were times . . ." Alianor
stopped. She would not allow any shadow of her fears
to darken this day.

"Come," she said, and slipped her arm through
Fionna's. "We have so much to talk about."

"Indeed, we do," a deep, amused voice said. Conan, Baron of Wyndham and Glastonbury, stood right behind his wife. His dark hair glistened in the sunlight, his burnished skin held the glow of health, and he walked with the easy agility of a man who did not know pain.

"Father," Hugh murmured, almost choking in his gratitude.

The two men embraced. They were of a size, both large and heavily muscled, fierce warriors who could smote any foe with terror. But they held each other with such tenderness that tears formed in Fionna's eyes. Alianor saw them and smiled gently.

"I think we'd best give them a moment," she said, and led Fionna into the hall. The men followed, talking quietly between themselves.

Inside, there was little less activity than in the town itself. The great hall appeared to have been transformed into some sort of . . . office. The war banners and shields hanging on the walls looked oddly misplaced, even superfluous. The trestle tables were covered with books, scrolls, and half-completed parchments. Knots of men stood about in intense discussion. They barely glanced up when the family entered.

"I suggest we retreat upstairs," Conan said.

Hugh looked around him in amazement. "As we appear to have been invaded, I agree." As they mounted the steps, he said, "They aren't really all lawyers, are they?"

Conan laughed at his concern, but he looked as though he shared it just a little. "Not quite. In fact, a goodly number of them are knights, merchants, freemen, deacons, and such. However, they all have opinions."

"About what?" Hugh asked.

His father paused. Quietly, he said, "About this document we seem to be writing. The barons have agreed to state their demands in ink rather than in blood. What I don't think they realize quite yet is that a fair many others want a say in it." Conan sighed. "For whatever good it may do. If John still refuses—"

"He does not," Hugh said, and began to relate all that had happened in London.

Much later, after they had all dined together, the dishes were removed and only the wine left behind, Hugh leaned back in his chair, looked at both his parents, and said, "There is one thing that still puzzles me."

"What is that?" Conan asked. He was seated beside his wife, his hand holding hers. The easy affection between them touched Fionna deeply. She saw in it the richness of years spent in true love and respect. Alianor and Conan were already very dear to her. Above all, she did not wish to envy them, and yet a tiny part of her could not help but do so.

"John knew that you had asked me if I wanted to be king."

The older couple exchanged a glance that swift though it was contained volumes.

"Did he say how he knew?" Conan asked.

"Something about Eleanor having explained everything to him before she died. Although then he allowed as to how it had perhaps not been quite everything."

When neither spoke, Hugh went on. "He also said

that you, Father, had decided long ago that you did not want the throne. Now I realize we live in times of uncertain loyalties, but it struck me as very odd that John should think both of us would be presented with such a decision."

In the quiet that followed, no one moved. Finally, Alianor spoke quietly. "There is a reason for that."

Hugh's face was gentle, but there was a determination in his eyes Fionna recognized too well. He had come to the end of all his wondering. He wanted to know—and know all.

"What would it be, Mother?"

Conan met her eyes and nodded. Alianor took a deep breath. Fionna sensed her great relief that this moment had finally come. But she could also feel her concern . . . feel and share it.

"In the first year after her marriage to the great King Henry," Alianor said, "Queen Eleanor gave birth to a son. Amid all the rejoicing, only a very few knew that the boy had a twin, a girl named Gwyneth, who was smuggled away. She was brought here to Glastonbury in fulfillment of a vow Eleanor had made, and put in fosterage with the woman who lived then on the island at the center of the lake, Matilda. In time, Gwyneth grew to womanhood but she never truly came to belong here. Matilda knew this and did not blame her for it. She was preparing to tell Eleanor that some other arrangement would have to be made, when a young man came to the island."

Here Alianor paused. She was very pale but her resolve did not weaken. After a moment, she continued.

"He was the son of Eustace du Blois, then heir to the throne of England. Before this young man departed on pilgrimage to the Holy Land, Gwyneth was with child."

A slight, sad smile curved over her mouth. "The man who sired me never returned. He died a few months later. In the fullness of time, I was born, but by then Gwyneth's mind had become disordered. When I was scarce a fortnight old, she walked into the lake and drowned."

"Merciful God," Hugh muttered.

"I remained on the island with Matilda," Alianor went on. "In time I, too, grew to womanhood but unlike my mother, I belonged here. Eleanor knew of my existence, and she kept a careful if distant eye on my welfare. When trouble came to Glastonbury and I was threatened by it, she sent Conan to protect me."

Her husband smiled. He lifted her hand to his lips and kissed it gently. "Personally, I always thought there was more to it than that. Eleanor was an inveterate matchmaker. Certainly, she showed no surprise when we announced we wished to marry."

"Yet surely," Hugh said slowly, "she understood what that could mean." He gazed at his parents with new understanding. "Eustace du Blois and Henry Plantagenet were the two great contenders for the throne of England. Mother is heir to them both. She would have stood higher in the line of succession than any of Eleanor and Henry's children, and as her husband—" His gaze shifted to Conan. "You could have chosen to enforce her claims."

"I could have," the baron agreed. "But I did not." He released his wife's hand and stood. A soft breeze entering through the open windows caused the candles to flicker. The high shadows of their flames danced against the stone walls.

"We are not the rulers of this land," Conan said. "We are its protectors."

CHAPTER TWENTY-EIGHT

Hugh and Fionna rode out alone together, turning west toward where the sun had set hours before. Behind them, the lake lay mist-draped and moon-filled. Fog rose to cling in wispy tendrils around the upper branches of the trees.

Several miles along the road, they emerged from woods. Directly before them, a large hill rose. Fionna drew rein at its base and dismounted. Hugh followed. They left the horses tethered and began to climb.

The hill was higher and steeper than any closer to the town. Its sides were more symmetrical than it seemed nature would have intended. They flowed smoothly upward to meet at a flat top high enough to provide a view for miles around.

Fionna walked out across the top and stood, arms wrapped around herself, looking in the direction of the lake. Hugh did the same. He could see the water glinting silver beneath a cloudless sky.

So bright was the moon that it drowned the stars. Yet

it could not conceal other lights that slowly, one by one, began to flicker, not in the sky but on the land itself.

Fires.

As full night descended, fires were being lit. A large one burned in Glastonbury itself but there were others, smaller, appearing here and there in scattered clearings, along the shore of the lake and all along the Brue River.

Bonfires burning on this warm spring night when the moon rode high and the owl called.

"It is Beltane," he said softly, and marveled that he had not known. In all the confusion at court, with all the danger, he had lost sight of the great festival of spring celebrated by high and low alike.

"The merry month of May," Fionna said with a smile. "They will be doing the same in Ireland."

He drew closer to her, breathing in the scent of lilac, honeysuckle, and woman. His arms went around her waist. He eased her back against the hard length of his body.

"At Gealach?" he asked. "At the lake of the moon?"

She nodded. "There and everywhere. They will celebrate in the old ways, so old no one really knows when they began. Most will have little idea what they do or why, but all the same, they will reconfirm their connection to the land, to the great wheel of time, to all that creates and sustains life regardless of what name we may wish to give to it."

His hands slid up her gown, cupping her breasts. His breath moved along her throat.

"Why have you come here?"

He did not mean the hill, and she did not mistake

that he did. Quietly, she said, "You are your father's true heir, Hugh. In you courses all the strength and courage that are his legacy. I have no doubt your brothers are the same."

"But—"

"The Lady Alianor has no daughter."

Far below, another fire caught and flared brightly against the darkness.

He understood, without words, knowing in the blood that flowed through his veins, in the touch of the woman he loved, in the air that moved over the land.

"She, too, must have an heir," Hugh said.

In an age when male children counted for all, he had never truly thought of that. But now he saw it, flowing like the river, endless and eternal. There were different ways to protect a land and all that lay within it. For him and for his father, that meant the feint and parry of court politics, always backed by the force of arms, the visible struggle of the world as they knew it. But there was another world, not so easily seen or understood, yet ultimately all the greater.

His mother and Fionna—and who knew how many others—were the link to it. Only they could forge the chain reaching back into the mists of time, to preserve the ancient wisdom of the earth and carry it into the future.

Fionna nodded. She turned in his arms and touched his face with wonder. A smile played over her lips. "I did not want to come. I had never thought to leave Ireland but to come here, to England . . ." She laughed and shook her head. "How little I understood."

Her hands slid beneath his tunic, stroking the hard

muscles of his chest. "And now I cannot imagine how I could belong anywhere else."

The soft, fragrant ground received them gently. Their cloaks laid over moss made a bed more welcoming than any they had known. There in moonlight, close to the ancient earth, they came together in love and in joy. The whispers of their love words and the urgent cries of fulfillment rose as though on wings to the gently enfolding sky.

In time, Hugh slept with Fionna close in his arms, and dreamed:

Dawn had come. He stood on the edge of the hill looking down toward the wood below. A horn sounded, puncturing the morning stillness.

Hugh smiled when he saw the huntsmen emerge suddenly from around the base of the hill. Their cloaks billowed out behind them. He caught the glint of their helmets and breastplates. Lean hounds raced before them, barking their excitement. He heard the men call out to each other, unable to catch the words but recognizing their pleasure in the day and in themselves. They were well mounted, their horses spirited. In moments, they were disappearing down the track that led through the forest.

If he could have gone with them, he would have.

One, riding at the front, glanced back at him. The leader's hand rose in acknowledgment, lingered a moment, and was gone.

Hugh turned and found Fionna watching him.

He blinked to clear his eyes and spoke calmly. "My father told me a story once, when I was a child. He recounted how some believe that on Beltane, Arthur and his huntsmen still ride over this land they fought so valiantly to protect. It is given to very few to see them, and never to me before."

She rose from the bed they had shared upon the earth. Straight and slender in the morning light, she offered her hand to him. Hugh took it. Together, they walked down the hill.

The church bells were still ringing. Their clamor filled the twilight air, drowned the irate chatter of the birds, and muted even the joyful shouts of the people intent on celebration.

As he lit the candles beside the bed, Hugh spared a moment to give thanks that he and Fionna had been able to sneak away. It was his father who had suggested they come to the island, with Alianor quickly seconding him.

The revelries in honor of the marriage of the Lord of Castlerock and Fionna of Gealach would continue until morning, if not beyond. Even at this distance from the town, there was no mistaking the delight felt by the people of Glastonbury. They rejoiced with abandonment to witness the continuing of all they held most dear.

At the castle, the tumult was even worse. Almost all of England's barons were there, quaffing ale, talking endlessly, arguing, disputing, debating, and managing to have a high old good time doing it.

But as for him . . . He had a far more private celebration in mind.

A soft sound alerted him. Hugh turned. The sight that met his eyes robbed him of breath. Fionna stood before him, her glorious hair tumbling free down her back, garbed only in a gown made of the diaphanous cloth she had purchased in the market in London.

Sweet, hot lust bolted through him as his eyes raked over the high swell of her breasts, the rosy aureoles clearly visible, along the narrow curve of her waist to the swelling chalice of her hips and the downy shadow of curls between her tapered thighs. He wanted to plunge himself into her to the very hilt, to stay sheathed within her hot silk forever.

But running right alongside all that was his deep and abiding love for this woman, love that would endure a lifetime and beyond. He came toward her, only to stop when he saw the sudden look of shyness she gave him.

"This is all so strange," she said. "I never really thought to be a wife, and certainly not to a lord so great."

Hugh smiled. "I can see how you might find it intimidating."

She frowned. "I wouldn't say that, exactly."

"But you are young, biddable . . . you will learn."

Her eyes glinted. "Biddable?"

He dared a step closer. "Certainly, now that you are a wife. I'm sure you realize the virtue of doing precisely what I tell you, fulfilling my every whim, that sort of thing."

Without warning, his arms lashed out. She yelped and tried to resist him, but he would have none of it. Gently but implacably he lifted her and carried her to their marriage bed.

"Most importantly," he said as he lowered her beneath him, "you will not go roaming around places like London, confronting murderers, and causing my poor heart to falter."

Suddenly serious, he gazed down at her with all of his great love stamped clearly on his proud features. Nothing between them remained to be concealed or withheld. "Indulge me that much at least, wife."

Fionna met his eyes. Slowly, she smiled. Her struggles ceased. Her arms twined around the muscled column of his neck. "I shall try, my lord," she said, most meekly and drew him to her.

Author's Note

For John—exhausted, disheartened, in failing health—there was a final rendezvous with history on a field called Runnymede, where the wisdom of better men resulted in the signing of the document known as *Magna Carta*.

The following year, John died, but not before making a last attempt to repudiate the agreement with his barons. His death freed them to turn aside a French invasion and give their backing to his son, Henry III, who became known for his great piety.

The building of the abbey at Glastonbury continued. It became a favorite site of pilgrims who came to see the black marble sarcophagus, wherein the bodies of King Arthur and his queen were said to lie.

In 1274, an earthquake destroyed the abbey. Several years later, Edward I ordered the re-interment of the bodies in a new tomb, where they remained until the dissolution of the abbeys during the reign of Henry VIII. Today, their whereabouts are unknown.

As for the Isle of Avalon, it remains as perhaps it always should, a mystery.

WE NEED YOUR HELP

To continue to bring you quality romance
that meets your personal expectations,
we at TOPAZ books want to hear from you.
Help us by filling out this questionnaire, and in exchange
we will give you a **free gift** as a token of our gratitude.

- Is this the first TOPAZ book you've purchased? (circle one)

    YES   NO

    The title and author of this book is: _____

- If this was not the first TOPAZ book you've purchased, how many have
  you bought in the past year?

    a: 0 - 5   b 6 - 10   c: more than 10   d: more than 20

- How many romances in total did you buy in the past year?

    a: 0 - 5   b: 6 - 10   c: more than 10   d: more than 20 ____

- How would you rate your overall satisfaction with this book?

    a: Excellent b: Good c: Fair d: Poor

- What was the main reason you bought this book?

    a: It is a TOPAZ novel, and I know that TOPAZ stands
       for quality romance fiction
    b: I liked the cover
    c: The story-line intrigued me
    d: I love this author
    e: I really liked the setting
    f: I love the cover models
    g: Other: _____

- Where did you buy this TOPAZ novel?

    a: Bookstore b: Airport c: Warehouse Club
    d: Department Store e: Supermarket f: Drugstore
    g: Other: _____

- Did you pay the full cover price for this TOPAZ novel? (circle one)

    YES   NO

    If you did not, what price did you pay? _____

- Who are your favorite TOPAZ authors? (Please list)

- How did you first hear about TOPAZ books?

    a: I saw the books in a bookstore
    b: I saw the TOPAZ Man on TV or at a signing
    c: A friend told me about TOPAZ
    d: I saw an advertisement in_____magazine
    e: Other: _____

- What type of romance do you generally prefer?

    a: Historical   b: Contemporary
    c: Romantic Suspense d: Paranormal (time travel,
       futuristic, vampires, ghosts, warlocks, etc.)
    d: Regency   e: Other: _____

- What historical settings do you prefer?

    a: England   b: Regency England   c: Scotland
    e: Ireland   f: America   g: Western Americana
    h: American Indian   i: Other: _____

- What type of story do you prefer?

  a: Very sexy   b: Sweet, less explicit
  c: Light and humorous   d: More emotionally intense
  e: Dealing with darker issues   f: Other

- What kind of covers do you prefer?

  a: Illustrating both hero and heroine   b: Hero alone
  c: No people (art only)   d: Other_____

- What other genres do you like to read (circle all that apply)

Mystery	Medical Thrillers	Science Fiction
Suspense	Fantasy	Self-help
Classics	General Fiction	Legal Thrillers
Historical Fiction		

- Who is your favorite author, and why?_____

  _____

- What magazines do you like to read? (circle all that apply)

  a: *People*   b: *Time/Newsweek*
  c: *Entertainment Weekly*   d: *Romantic Times*
  e: *Star*   f: *National Enquirer*
  g: *Cosmopolitan*   h: *Woman's Day*
  i: *Ladies' Home Journal* j: *Redbook*
  k: Other:_____

- In which region of the United States do you reside?

  a: Northeast   b: Midatlantic   c: South
  d: Midwest   e: Mountain   f: Southwest
  g: Pacific Coast

- What is your age group/sex?   a: Female b: Male

  a: under 18   b: 19-25   c: 26-30   d: 31-35   e: 36-40
  f: 41-45   g: 46-50   h: 51-55   i: 56-60   j: Over 60

- What is your marital status?

  a: Married   b: Single   c: No longer married

- What is your current level of education?

  a: High school   b: College Degree
  c: Graduate Degree d: Other: _____

- Do you receive the TOPAZ *Romantic Liaisons* newsletter, a quarterly newsletter with the latest information on Topaz books and authors?

  YES   NO

  If not, would you like to?   YES   NO

  Fill in the address where you would like your free gift to be sent:

  Name: _____

  Address: _____

  City:_____Zip Code: _____

  You should receive your free gift in 6 to 8 weeks.
  Please send the completed survey to:

Penguin USA•Mass Market
Dept. TS
375 Hudson St.
New York, NY 10014